TALES FROM THE PRINCE OF STORYTELLERS

ROBERT LOUIS STEVENSON

TALES FROM THE PRINCE OF STORYTELLERS

EDITED AND WITH AN INTRODUCTION BY
BARRY MENIKOFF

NORTHWESTERN UNIVERSITY PRESS EVANSTON, ILLINOIS

Northwestern University Press
Evanston, Illinois 60208-4210

ISBN   CLOTH   0-8101-1059-8
PAPER   0-8101-1084-9

The paper used in this publication meets the minimum requirements of the
American National Standard for Information Sciences—Permanence of Paper
for Printed Library Materials, ANSI Z39.48-1984.

For Karen, with love

Contents

Preface

On 14 October 1877 the *New York Times* published a short story, "A Lodging for the Night," with no signature other than the name of the English magazine that had printed it a month earlier. The editor clearly had an eye for good copy, for three more stories were lifted from their English magazines over the next few years. Thus the *New York Times* has the distinction of being the first publisher of Stevenson's fiction in America. Some years later, just after Stevenson died, a *Times* reviewer recalled that first experience, raining plaudits on the newspaper for its perspicacity and shrewdness of judgment. Of course that was many years ago, when the retrospectives and encomiums were still fresh, and when every literate person shared a common conviction that Robert Louis Stevenson, whom the gods loved, was already a classic of English literature. That judgment could not survive the First World War, when all things Victorian were either innocent and antique or directly responsible for the recent carnage. Still, the collected editions of Stevenson's work continued unabated—the Pentland, the Vailima, the South Seas, the Tusitala, to mention only the grandest and most lavish of them. Nothing could more graphically illustrate the distance between readers and savants than the steady publication of Stevenson's writings and their indifferent reception by modernist critics.

Stevenson today is quite possibly the most anomalous figure in literary and cultural studies. There is not a single writer in England and America whose name is more universally recognized and who is at the same time so little read or understood. Everyone, so the saying goes, remembers reading *Treasure Island* and *Kidnapped* and *A Child's Garden of Verses* and (of course) *Jekyll and Hyde*. Even if this were the case, how many know "The Merry Men" or *The Silverado Squatters* or *Familiar Studies of Men and Books*? Or *The Ebb-Tide*? *Travels with a Donkey? Underwoods?* In truth, Stevenson's versatility and productivity astonish anyone who happens upon the volumes of essays, travels, novels, plays, poetry, criticism, and correspondence that constitute one of the most extraordinary bodies of work in nineteenth-century English letters. But the variety and complexity of that work were nothing more than a mirror of the man. Stevenson was intellectual (he submitted his name for a chair in constitutional law and history at Edinburgh University), bohemian (the sobriquet "velvet-coat" attached to him during his salad days), and consummately romantic (he crossed the Atlantic in steerage and the United States in a train in order to follow to California a married woman whom he had fallen in love with in France). It is unreasonable to think he would not transmute the intensity of that personality into his work. Walter de la Mare said it best: "We actually see him in every line he ever wrote—that long face, those dark dwelling eyes, that straight hair, those tapering fingers." If sophisticated critics today *know* that Stevenson's work could have no interest for an adult audience, we might turn back to George Meredith and Viola Paget and Henry James and Andrew Lang, adults who knew differently.

Virtually all of Stevenson's contemporaries recognized that his claim on immortality—fame was not even the question—was made in his fiction, and particularly in the short story, a genre he defined both in theory and in practice. From George Saintsbury and Henry Seidel Canby at the turn of the century to V. S. Pritchett and Sean O'Faolain more recently, Stevenson was synonymous with this new form. In 1914 Frank Swinnerton called him "among the best English writers of short stories." Five years later *TLS* reassessed the body of his work: "In the short story his art found a province narrow enough to dominate." Edith Wharton in 1925 considered him one of a modern English triumvirate, along with Henry James and Joseph Conrad. And John Buchan, at the end of the decade, affirmed all these judgments: "Stevenson was one of the best story-tellers that ever lived. He was a kind of bard who spoke in prose rather than verse, with all the bard's swiftness of narration and sudden bursts of lyric beauty. He was a great short-story writer." Stevenson's influence on the short story was pervasive. He became part of the consciousness of the modernist sensibility, and the poles of his short-story art can be seen in two later masters of the form—Jorge Luis Borges and Graham Greene.

Stevenson's centenary will be celebrated in 1994. *Tales from the Prince of Storytellers* is a contribution to that celebration. It is for a new generation of readers, still open to experience and enthusiastic about the possibilities of magical art. In "Providence and the Guitar," Stevenson's brilliant riff on the theme of art and life, Léon Berthelini is a second-rate performer with an inflated sense of self-importance and a dated style. Nonetheless he is a genuine artist: he delights and instructs a younger couple who are having a marital conflict over the artistic life but are struggling resolutely to hold on to each other. Léon's wife advises the younger woman that a good man may be hard to find, and it is worth keeping the father of your child, even if he is not a very good painter. Painting, after all, is not everything. Léon, with his guitar, performs the noblest service of art—the affirmation of life. And Stevenson, the supreme performance artist, silently nodding in the direction of the reader, confirms both the reality and importance of the entire enterprise.

Two of the stories in this collection are reproduced for the first time directly from Stevenson's autograph manuscripts: "Markheim" is published by permission of the Houghton Library, Harvard University (MS Eng 269.3), and "The Isle of Voices" by permission of the Rosenbach Museum and Library. I thank Mrs. Teddy Osbourne Schieferle, Executor of the Stevenson Estate, for permission to edit and publish the holographs. And I thank Martin Ridge, former Director of Research at the Huntington Library, for his long-standing support of my work on Stevenson.

Introduction: Fable, Fiction, and Modernism

Barry Menikoff

I

Few developments in contemporary fiction in the past quarter century match the extraordinary rise in the status of the short story. In both output and quality the achievement has been nothing short of astonishing. Many of the most acclaimed (and popular) writers in England, Ireland, Canada, and the United States are primarily short story writers: William Trevor and Edna O'Brien in Ireland; Angela Carter and Fay Weldon in England; Raymond Carver, Mary Robison, and John Edgar Wideman in America; and Alice Munro and Bharati Mukherjee in Canada. The belated recognition by critics of the historical and formal importance of the genre, considered alongside the annuals of the "best" short fiction and the prizes awarded to individual volumes of stories, provides ample evidence that the short story has finally come into its own.

But it would be a mistake to imply that the short story suddenly emerged from nowhere, or that nobody had ever paid it much attention before. On the contrary, it has an extensive and impressive history. We need only recover the origins of the form in the last quarter of the nineteenth century to recognize that the impulse that gave rise to its development was not fundamentally different from that which makes it such a viable form today. The short story evolved in tandem with the modern novel. They had in common a single objective: to reduce the size of the book and concentrate the art of the fiction. There is no question that a certain fatigue had set in with the reading public, as well as with the writers themselves. It is hardly coincidental that the two most successful fiction writers of the last two decades of the nineteenth century were Robert Louis Stevenson and Rudyard Kipling. The latter declared an end to the triple-decker novel, and the former considered it a feat of strength to complete one. For the Victorians, of course, at least the High Victorians, the triple-decker represented an achievement emblematic of high seriousness and moral integrity. To fill up three complete volumes with complicated stories that reflected the variety and multiplicity of ordinary lives was almost a vocation. Although it is a commonplace that the Victorian serial anticipated the contemporary soap opera in its kaleidoscope of characters, involuted plot, melodrama, and sentiment, it is equally true that the major Victorians were serious writers whose subjects were not conditioned solely by the marketplace. They were also driven by their compulsion to dramatize their profound if not obsessive themes.

What was the situation of the novel in the last quarter of the nineteenth century? Dickens and Thackeray were dead. Eliot had completed her important work. Trollope was writing his last novels. The only major novelist who was still productive was George Meredith, and Meredith, as everybody knows, was caviar for the general, a writer whom other writers could admire but whose work was destined to fail a larger audience. This was the situation when Robert Louis Stevenson began his career. If Harold Bloom's idea of generational rebellion is viable, then any serious writer coming of age with Stevenson might exhibit an antagonism to those monuments of powerful and daunting intellect, monuments of assurance if not indeed arrogance that were sold in three thick volumes to an elite audience for thirty shillings. In any event, nobody growing up in the 1860s and 1870s could fail to be awed by them. Certainly Stevenson was awed, perhaps even intimidated, although it is equally clear that he recognized exactly what they represented: a vision of the world that could only be contained within a formal text akin to the Victorian epic. It is hardly surprising that he considered Victor Hugo's *Les misérables* the consummation of fiction on this scale, or in this manner. But it was not the avenue that he pursued, nor was it the avenue that was pursued after him. Stevenson realized that the Victorian novel had finally exhausted itself, that it was of a time, and a place, that had long passed. He had the remarkable ability to recognize both the achievement of the novel and its limitations. Just as he admired Walter Scott, as a fellow countryman and a writer whose subject touched him personally, he also knew that Scott's fiction had played itself out, or at least that Scott's method was defunct. In brief, the age demanded an image of its accelerated pace; the age demanded the short story.

What was the status of the English short story when Robert Louis Stevenson first signed the initials R.L.S. at the end of "A Lodging for the Night" in the October 1877 issue of *Temple Bar*? For the most part it was moribund. The form was clearly not one that the English novelists had been able to master. Serial publication of fiction placed a premium on elaborate plots, and the continued dominance of the three-volume novel inhibited the development of techniques that would highlight the strengths of the short narrative. If one wanted models for shorter fiction there were only two: the Americans and the French. Stevenson was naturally attracted to both. For the Americans, Hawthorne and Poe were the dominating presences. That Poe had provided the theoretical underpinnings for the short story, or had elaborated a formal process that rationalized his own practice, was apparent to anyone. Stevenson read Poe avidly, and used him with impunity. The fascination with "doubles" (symbolized by *Jekyll and Hyde*) that runs as a motif through Stevenson's fiction is well known. In a letter to Andrew Lang, for example, he readily acknowledged his familiarity with one of Poe's masterpieces in the genre ("Yes, I knew William Wilson" [undated letter to Andrew Lang, Huntington Library, HM 2490]). The earliest reviews of Stevenson's short fiction are rife with references to Poe, who appeared to critics as the model and inspiration for Stevenson's tales of horror, and for that morbidity which was recognized early as a prominent strain in his fiction. Stevenson's affinity with the American theorist must be taken as a fundamental.

But it was Hawthorne that Stevenson was most intensely drawn to. The New Englander's stories of religious obsession and guilt, framed by the hard doctrines of Calvinism, held a special appeal for the writer whose own country was haunted by a staunch and unyielding Presbyterianism. Even tales of superstition and the super-natural found their echo in the terrifying stories of witchcraft told him by his childhood nurse, and which were among his earliest memories. Hawthorne also displayed a powerful moral strand that was absent from Poe but that struck a deeply sympathetic chord in Stevenson, who could never quite shake free of the strict faith of the orthodox. It is not surprising that from the beginning critics have commented on, and not always favorably, an abiding moral element as one of the salient characteristics of Stevenson's fiction.

Stevenson knew Cooper and Twain too, of course, and he chided Melville for his failure to transcribe accurately the Marquesans' speech in *Typee*. But the question is not how many of the American writers he knew. He read voraciously, omnivorously, and there is little he was unaware of. That Hawthorne was his intellectual model is as undeniable as that Walt Whitman was his most profound emotional inspiration. Stevenson found in the outspoken poet a zest for freedom that was the antithesis of the crimped and dour Scots mentality. In Whitman, as in Thoreau, he found an idea, perhaps even an ideal, that was associated with America, an idea as persuasive as it was seductive to a young man growing up beneath the overhang of Edinburgh Castle, in the damp and darkness of a northern city.

If there is any single thing Stevenson might have learned from Hawthorne, it is unquestionably the use of light, a visual image that dominates Stevenson's fiction from his first published story through the final brilliance of *The Beach of Falesá*. But America did not represent "light" in fiction as opposed to the "dark" of Scotland. Rather, Whitman and Thoreau represented the elevation, indeed the exaltation, of the individual, and the idea of freedom that was so strong an element in Stevenson's personality. Yet the antithesis to that idea of freedom was just as deeply rooted in a man who read the stern Scottish religious writers with a certain degree of relish. Hence the overt "moralizing," the use of the word *sermon* to title his writings (*Lay Sermons*, "A Christmas Sermon"), and stories that often seem so strongly "moralistic" in their message or tone that modern readers are inclined to put them aside, or to dismiss them for that reason alone. Yet just as Hawthorne cannot be dismissed because of the moral message often attached to his stories, neither can Stevenson. His are no more moralistic, in the pejorative sense, than Haw-thorne's, perhaps even less so. And this is because he was in certain fundamental ways a more self-conscious artist than Hawthorne, as well as a more broadly intellectual one than Poe.

As for the French, it is virtually a commonplace that Stevenson's connection with French literature and culture was as deeply rooted as his attachment to the country itself. From his laudatory remarks on Victor Hugo at the beginning of his career to his dedication of *Across the Plains* to Paul Bourget near the end, Stevenson retained an unshaken admiration for French writers. He even incorporated them in his own fiction. In *The Rajah's Diamond*, for example, he calls attention to Emile Gaboriau, the novelist whose stories of the Paris underworld established the *roman policier*, and whose detective, Lecoq, was a model for Prince Florizel in the Arabian nights stories. The French provided Stevenson with an abundance of material for his work. Among his earliest essays were those on Charles of Orléans and François Villon, just as his best-known travel book charts his journey through the mountainous Cévennes in southern France (*Travels with a Donkey*). Of course,the old and deep ties between France and Scotland were central to Stevenson's cultural experience and formed the substance of his longer historical novels. But aspects of those ties surfaced as well in the shorter stories that were set in France, either in their entirety or only in part: *The Suicide Club* and *The Rajah's Diamond*, "A Lodging for the Night," "The Sire de Malétroit's Door," and "Providence and the Guitar." Certainly the intellectual and aesthetic quality and even the daily texture of French life quickened Stevenson's imagination. But as a student of art it was the writing that drew his closest attention.

The French *conte* was the only alternative to the American short story, the only other model available to a writer determined to craft a form that had no modern equivalent in England. For the French short story, as opposed to its American cousin, "revindicated . . . the supreme value of form in composition and of that unity of effect which is twin to structural completeness" (Una A. Taylor, "The Short Story in France," *Edinburgh Review*, July 1913, p. 137). Taylor's description of the French short story, and in particular the short fiction of Prosper Mérimée and Théophile Gautier, reads like a primer for Stevenson's art: "Gautier sought his end in concentration, Mérimée in elimination of detail. . . . In the hands of both . . . the art of the French *conte* remained for the most part definitely objective" (137, 141). Of his familiarity with Gautier, Stevenson himself told a San Francisco newspaper in June 1887: "My special distaste is the use of any foreign word. . . . The great instance of the folly of reading to get new words was Gautier."

Stevenson found in the French *conte* the elements that were essential to the construction of the modern short story in English: the economical use of language, an economy that invariably encouraged a highly conscious concern for diction and phrasing; the linkage of incidents in a logical, ineluctable chain so that the ending, as Stevenson said in a famous letter to Sidney Colvin, is always implicit in the beginning; the habit of telling the story from outside the events, through either a third-person narrator or a first-person narrator who is virtually an objective observer, even when he is intimately involved in the story; and, not least, the compression of incidents and details into a focused and self-contained unit. Stevenson's search for compression and economy was clearly recognized by his contemporaries, although they often disapproved of the end result. One review of *Jekyll and Hyde* took the story to task for its failure to develop what was seen as a brilliantly original conception: "Perhaps, however, a larger audience will be found, in these days of hurried reading, for the condensed narrative presented by Mr. Stevenson than for a more elaborate story" (*New York Tribune*, 24 January 1886, p. 6). Stevenson himself was very clear about this aim in his art:

When I am making a point I try to do it in the smallest possible space. I do not think a reader should be expected to plod through pages of print to find out what I mean. The great difficulty I have is in compressing my matter. I can always tell when an author does not write over and over again. The most rapid and fluent writer cannot arrange the mass of material that goes to make up a book without having it out of order here and there. Order is the basis, the charm and the end of literature. Literature is an art that takes place in time. Therefore the main point is to be certain that you have everything in proper order. That you can never get in the first shot. That is my experience. (*San Francisco Chronicle*, 17 December 1894, p. 1)

Stevenson was by temperament aligned with the French in their emphasis on form and style in the short story. This is nicely illustrated, albeit in a small way, in an interview he gave to a San Francisco reporter in 1887, when he observed that the only writer who was doing anything at all as artistically exciting as Henry James was Guy de Maupassant. Although the remark paid tribute to the new direction James's fiction had taken in the 1880s, it was also a compliment to the facility and originality of Maupassant, who began his career at the beginning of the decade and whose work Stevenson was clearly following. He was always attuned to what the French were doing, and his ability to draw from them ideas, both formal and thematic, was a constant reminder of the catholicity of his reading and his taste. If the nineteenth-century police novel of Emile Gaboriau provided a model for the Arabian nights stories, the fifteenth-century *ballades* (and life) of Villon offered him a means to explore issues of poverty and wealth, art and life, in "A Lodging for the Night."

Stevenson sought to combine the elements of the French *conte* and the American short story in order to construct a new form that exhibited the best features of both. It is not that either had wonderful qualities absent from the other; rather, each had elements that spoke directly to Stevenson's artistic imagination and intellectual interests. In effect, he was determined to exploit the potentialities inherent in both. What Stevenson required was a form that would maintain the detachment and objectivity of the French with the moral implicativeness, even discursiveness, of the Americans. In a sense he was attempting something that had not been done previously; he was trying to meld together two distinct and in some ways contradictory modes. For the French, the form was primary: the story was all, or rather the telling of the tale was the essential ingredient in the narrative, and there ought to be no impediment to that telling. The narrative is the embedded chain of incidents that controls and unifies the story from beginning to end. The narration is made as objective as possible in order to forestall the author's intrusion into the story, and the manner is polished in all its details—economy of expression, concision of incidents, and exclusion of all extraneous or irrelevant data. What the French *conte* provides is a story admirable in construction and powerful in effect, in short, a magnificent artifice. For Stevenson, the appeal of that kind of art was considerable, for the writer is challenged by the material, concerned with presentation, and committed almost exclusively to problems of technical mastery.

With the American model, on the other hand, the moral issues in the story were of primary consideration. This was certainly the case in Washington Irving's stories, just as it was obvious in Hawthorne's. Indeed, if the Americans were guilty of anything in their short fiction, it was of making too much of the issues, of making the story nothing more than a vehicle for the moral. While this may not be the most interesting way to read Irving, and certainly not Hawthorne, it is nonetheless an approach that readers and reviewers invariably adopted. In the case of Hawthorne in particular, the focus on sin and punishment made it convenient to read his short stories as moral exempla, aided by the summary conclusions often provided by the author. Although it is undeniable that the structural design of Hawthorne's fiction often concealed its complexity, rather like James's figure in the carpet, it is equally true that a reading of the exterior story frequently reduced it to a simple moral apothegm. Hawthorne, in effect, became the analyst of conscience. His subject and approach invariably focused attention on theme and deflected attention from technique. Even Poe, who everyone agreed was indifferent to moral issues, still paid them attention in tales like "The Cask of Amontillado," "The Fall of the House of Usher," and "The Masque of the Red Death."

Stevenson was at one and the same time the most deliberately artistic of new writers and the one most preoccupied with moral issues. The questions he confronted in his short stories were never without moral implications, whether it was equity and justice in "A Lodging for the Night" or prejudice and greed in *The Beach of Falesá*. Indeed, even his adoptions of particular forms of the short story, such as the folktale ("The Bottle Imp") or the parable ("Will O' the Mill"), exhibit the incorporation of moral issues within the form of the story itself. Stevenson (like Henry James) found himself with two fundamental inclinations: the one toward technical artistry, which he saw in the French, and the other toward moral analysis, which he found in Hawthorne. The problem was to amalgamate the two, creating a fiction that was both technically brilliant and thematically complex. Instead of highlighting one or the other, as the French and Americans did, Stevenson fashioned a short story that was moral in its impulse and artistic in its execution; he created, in effect, the "moral art story," or the art story with a moral.

Perhaps no other writer exhibits a greater dichotomy between play and purpose in fiction than Stevenson: fiction as play, and fiction as purpose; art as pleasure and art as instruction. Stevenson is the quintessential embodiment of the Horatian ideal—the function of art is to delight and instruct. The problem, of course, is that for most artists the one or the other takes prominence. In the nineteenth-century novel it appeared, for a time, as if the two purposes were united: in Dickens there was pleasure, even fun, and there was instruction, or more properly social outrage. Yet it is clear that as the great Victorians developed their art, they emphasized the one at the expense of the other: we think of Eliot as a great moralist; of Dickens as two people, the entertainer of *Pickwick Papers* and the justiciary of *Bleak House;* of Thackeray as a social satirist in the guise of a puppeteer. But in many ways these writers were working in an ad hoc manner; they were not consciously dividing their roles and determining the consequent effects on their fiction. Hawthorne illustrated the same phenomenon. His primary role was instructive in the widest sense. He may have complained about his lack of audience, but he did not write to entertain or delight that audience. As for Poe, if his conception of his role was complex, the consequence for his art was less so. His stories had calculated effects, and whether he constructed them for that purpose or whether the effects were simply a result of the stories' design is beside the point.

But Stevenson's position was more subtle. For one thing, he was extremely sophisticated and articulate about the artistic process. He was writing at a period when there was extraordinary ferment in France and even Britain about the nature of art, and particularly narrative art. He was involved in the historic debate that culminated in Henry James's "Art of Fiction" and his own "A Humble Remonstrance." That Stevenson's titles are so modest as to be virtually self-effacing is unfortunate, since they have encouraged critics to dismiss the arguments out of hand. Yet "A Humble Remonstrance" and "A Gossip on Romance" are far from modest inquiries into the nature of fictional art. Indeed, in "A Gossip on Romance" Stevenson anticipates Freud's commentary on creative writers and daydreaming, where the psychoanalyst argues that literature is nothing more than the legitimate expression of fantasies. When Stevenson says that fiction is play for grown-ups, he is merely using familiar language to describe the same idea. That perception of his—that fiction is an acceptable form of play for adults—is joined to another, that fiction is one of the few avenues for truth in the world because it is the only form that people will accept as entertainment, and therefore it is the only medium the truth teller has for his message.

Stevenson thus was caught in the position of wanting to entertain his readers, in that he realized he would have no readers without entertaining them, and at the same time was determined to convey his vision with the single-minded passion of a Hawthorne. Admittedly he had an arrogant and even patronizing view of his readers. Stevenson was under no illusions as to the abilities or interests or experience of the mass reading audience. And it is an open question whether his earliest fiction was even consciously written with that (or any) audience in mind. But there is no question whatever that he was always aware of what was owed his readers, and it is not for nothing that one of the central refrains that runs through Stevenson criticism is that he was a natural or born storyteller. The aptness of such a description was never in doubt during his lifetime, and it is that continued in force at least through the 1920s. Indeed, shortly after the news of his death, the *San Francisco Chronicle* headlined one of its biographical articles "Tales of the Prince of Storytellers" (23 December 1894). Stevenson's life had begun to assume a mythic quality; there were "tales" to be told of it that competed with—and indeed were bound and destined to compete with—the generated tales that constituted the work itself.

2

When we read Stevenson's short stories, we immediately sense the solitariness and loneliness of his characters. Francis Scrymgeour and Simon Rolles in *The Rajah's Diamond* are two early examples of figures who live in the midst of metropolitan centers but are nonetheless alone. Both are pursuing careers in the very center of European cities, one struggling against all odds for a secure position in an office in Edinburgh, the other driven by ambition for preferment in the church. They are intensely centered upon themselves and at the same time curiously unaware of the fact. Unlike James's "supersubtle fry," who know they are self-conscious and revel in that knowledge, Stevenson's figures (like those in classical tragedy) are largely unconscious of their obsessiveness. Even in a story like "The Pavilion on the Links," where the narrator admits to having been "a great solitary when . . . young" (181), the emphasis is not on the narrator's consciousness of his solitariness or even on his awareness of how distorting such a self-absorption might be. In *The Rajah's Diamond* there is a motif of voyeurism that functions as a mirror image for the voyeur's obsessive focus on himself, as if to gaze surreptitiously at others were the only escape from the prison of one's mind. That there is a sexual aspect to this gazing is clear in "The Physician and the Saratoga Trunk" when the young American cannot keep his eyes from the peephole. But on a deeper level Stevenson concentrates attention on an issue that was fundamental to a strict Protestant mind: the inward-looking self trying to discover an unblemished soul. It may be that the solitary and lonely self is the condition of the Calvinist mentality, a condition that was clearly reflected by the realities of Stevenson's Presbyterian upbringing and his Edinburgh experience. For him, the "long Scots faces" of the dour people he knew so well was a metonymy for their attitudes and their mentality.

A Stevenson story invariably has an individual at the center (either as character or narrator) and never seems to have more than one individual in it, even when there is a cast of characters who appear to fill out the pages. Moral issues, which are the heart of every Stevenson story, are always confronted in individual cases. From the start of "A Lodging for the Night," where Francis Villon is in a tavern carousing with his friends, to the end of the story, when he is alone in the street trying to toss off the experience of the evening, he is essentially alone in the world and forced to live with that condition. Philosophy, religion, art—all of which he is an adept at—can in no way alter or ameliorate his situation. Villon must live with himself, just as he has a vision of dying by himself, swinging from the gibbet like a piece of fruit on a tree. Part of the pain of Stevenson's depiction of the isolation of Villon, or of Cassilis or Northmour in "The Pavilion on the Links," is the realization that it is the inalterable condition of experience.

For Stevenson, mortality is destiny, inescapable, ineluctable—a vision that unquestionably drives many readers to attribute a distinctly morbid note to many of the stories. The doctor's speech in "The Physician and the Saratoga Trunk" spelling out his view of the flesh once the spirit has passed out of it can be read either as a cold-blooded commentary from a heartless materialist or as a plausible argument on the nature of man, an argument that must be acknowledged before one can determine how to address or answer it. The fact of death is so central to Stevenson's imagination that to shy from it at the start is to avoid wrestling with his subject and his art. Where is permanence? Over and over, he reflects upon this question through his surrogates. The young narrator in "The Merry Men," who discovers the shoe buckle at the bottom of the sea and silently discourses on the life of the man who wore the shoe, and in effect on human history, is another illustration of the way Stevenson promotes the idea of the transitoriness of life and perhaps the futility of all human pursuits. The contrast between life and death, which is another way of looking at this question, also recurs regularly in Stevenson's work. And it is the perception of death that makes the solitariness so bleak. It is curious, too, how little Stevenson's fiction is concerned with issues like ambition or success in the world in terms that would be recognizable to ordinary working people. Yet there is always an acute consciousness of the fact that these are indeed the issues that drive men's lives. The line in "Story of the Young Man in Holy Orders" about Rolles's struggle for success in the church and the recognition that his merits will have no effect on that success is only one of the wittier illustrations.

But the absence of incidents reflective of the ordinariness of life does not mean that Stevenson was simply trying to steal boys away from their Ovid and carry them into the world of romance, as he says in the dedication to *Kidnapped*. Rather, he preferred to concentrate on issues he considered more fundamental, or perhaps more revelatory of the human condition. The "adventures" in *The Suicide Club* and *The Rajah's Diamond* are merely the occasions for profound explorations of experience; they are certainly not the substance—let alone the meaning—of the stories. The swindling and fighting in "The Pavilion on the Links" are no more what that story is about than is the mystery surrounding the wrecked ship the subject of "The Merry Men."

This is not always apparent, because the engine that drives a Stevenson story is plot, moving forward through time with a series of incidents that are unpredictable and suspenseful. But for Stevenson plot is (on one level) just a technical device, a means to enthrall the reader while the serious issues are being explored. The excitement of a plot is the pleasure of the reading experience. Stevenson never denigrates that pleasure and always strives to sustain it, but it is finally an arbitrary, perhaps even a capricious, device. In *The Suicide Club* and *The Rajah's Diamond* the plots are extraordinary, straining credulity and calling attention to their own outrageousness. What is always at the center of the fiction is the idea. The core of a Stevenson story is intellect, either the intellect of a character or intellectual comprehension conveyed through the omniscient narrator. If we consider stories like *The Suicide Club*, *The Rajah's Diamond*, "A Lodging for the Night," "Markheim," and "The Merry Men," it is clear that intellectual issues are at bottom the meaning of the texts. It would indeed be surprising if one of the most widely read and scholarly of late Victorian writers were to suddenly park all his knowledge and wisdom outside the circle of his fiction. Stevenson can be called a philosopher in fiction with far more justness than virtually any of his contemporaries, including Hardy and James. This is why some of his texts assume the manner of discourses, as the dialogue between Villon and Brisetout in "A Lodging for the Night" illustrates. Does the debate between the two about poverty and riches, circumstance and fate, honor versus degradation, constitute an inauthentic or undramatic use of fiction? Or does it rather, given its rich visual and linguistic context, powerfully illustrate the irresolvability of those issues?

Stevenson, developing his story from the character of a historical figure, cannot take Villon and make him other than what he was: a creative genius whose rough life contrasted sharply with his natural gifts and in all probability ended briefly and painfully. Whether he might have had a different life under different circumstances is really beside the point. He had the life he had, and he was the man he was. Hence the brilliance of the ending: despite the long and contentious debate, the facing and challenging of complex philosophical questions, when Villon leaves and goes back out into the bitter-cold night, his first thought is for the loss of what he might have had: "A very dull old gentleman," he thought. "I wonder what his goblets may be worth" (253).

The opening sentence of "The Pavilion on the Links" ("I was a great solitary when I was young") introduces the retrospective narrative, a characteristic mode of Stevenson's first-person texts. This method of delivering a story invariably implies two stories, the one a story of past events told in sequential order, the other the present story, which remains untold, except for our awareness of its presentness. In other words, a typical retrospective narrative is a story about the past which feels as if it were happening at the moment, thus achieving the immediacy and suspense of present action. But in fact all the events have long since vanished into the world of time and memory, recalled partly as a means of reviving the experience, and partly as a way of holding on to life. For Stevenson's retrospective narrators, the past is often the only life that has any vivacity, perhaps even reality, and the stories are told with a vigor and excitement that entrances the reader and makes him imagine himself caught in a wonderful or terrifying web of suspense. Through retrospective narration, Stevenson gives a deeper dimension to past events, keeping them alive in the memory of the survivor-narrator.

The portrait of Frank Cassilis, the narrator of "The Pavilion on the Links," is one that Stevenson periodically produced—a figure alone in the world, virtually living in the wild, whose gypsy life is reflected in his physical surroundings. The description of the countryside surrounding the pavilion captures the mentalities of Cassilis and his equally solitary companion, Northmour: "But there stood in the northern part of the estate, in a wilderness of links and blowing sand-hills, and between a plantation and the sea, a small Pavilion or Belvidere, of modern design, which was exactly suited to our wants; and in this hermitage, speaking little, reading much, and rarely associating except at meals, Northmour and I spent four tempestuous winter months" (182). The image of a hermitage is an apt one, for in these situations Stevenson often identifies, or conflates, a disciplined, self-imposed isolation with a kind of religious asceticism. Indeed, along the sea wood not far from the pavilion, "one or two ruined cottages were dotted about the wood; and, according to Northmour, these were ecclesiastical foundations, and in their time had sheltered pious hermits" (184). There is a certain fascination with this life: a world where nothing but the sea and the links are to be encountered, a world with books for companions, this seems the ideal world sought by Cassilis.

It is hardly accidental that so many of Stevenson's protagonists are serious readers—Simon Rolles in *The Suicide Club* studies the patristic fathers, Villon in "A Lodging for the Night" is a student who quotes the Latin bible, and the Reverend Soulis in "Thrawn Janet" is immersed in theology. There is a complex association in Stevenson between the profound and disciplined study of deep books and the ascetic isolation of the (fictional) reader, a connection that leads to a kind of voyeurism, as if investigating the secrets of texts is the equivalent of surreptitiously looking into the secrets of others. It need hardly be remarked that the transference from the intense study of texts to the process of writing them is always present in Stevenson's consciousness, if not in the protagonist's or the narrator's. In some fundamental way there is an ineluctable connection between the self-imposed isolation of the fictional character, with all its attendant implications for personality and destiny, and the position of the creative artist in the world. The voyeurism referred to earlier that recurs in *The Suicide Club* and *The Rajah's Diamond* is nothing more than a fictional reality that inscribes the actual reality of the voyeurism that Stevenson practiced as a writer. It is a voyeurism that he himself viewed as a by-product of an obsessive self-absorption, a kind of narcissism that writers were prone to by the very nature of their work. If Stevenson deliberately fought against this tendency in his own life, it was through the ceaseless pursuit of friends. There is no other writer who worked so hard and so steadily to sustain his friendships—each of his books had its requisite dedicatee—and whose marriage itself may even have been an escape from the prison house of the self. Stevenson lived with the fullness of friends and family in order not to succumb to the tyranny of self. Yet the pace and intensity of the work produced in those last few years in the Pacific was so profound as to virtually ensure his early death, not of consumption, which might have been expected, but from a sudden cerebral hemorrhage.

Stevenson's Scottish stories always draw on the most rugged features of the beautiful and harsh landscape, features defined by sheer cliffs and craggy rocks, by cold winds and roiling seas. He creates a setting so unremittingly desolate in "Pavilion" that Frank Cassilis declares, "The place had an air of solitude that daunted even a solitary like myself" (183). It is almost impossible to read this story without experiencing the bleakness of the country. It is not for nothing that Stevenson was consistently invoked by twentieth-century writers of handbooks on short-story technique as an exemplary master of "atmosphere" or "description"—terms that highlighted his extraordinary gift for evoking a mood from the most extreme physical settings. But it is not mood alone that conditions the narrative. For Stevenson, place is character, and the windswept links, barren of all vegetation except evergreen shrub, are an appropriate counter for the reclusive Cassilis and Northmour.

The consequences of isolation are manifest in the mental condition and the social behavior of the characters, in Minister Soulis in "Thrawn Janet," or Gordon Darnaway in "The Merry Men." Villon declares that "man is not a solitary animal—*Cui Deus feminam tradit*" (to whom God gives woman) (251). Of course, in the mouth of Villon, who is both rogue and poet, the words have a mordancy that almost belies their meaning: Villon needs a woman in the same way he needs meat and drink, biblical citation notwithstanding. Nonetheless, the central idea of the assertion is in fact Stevenson's answer to the damage inflicted on the self by voluntary or enforced isolation—love with the proper woman. In "Pavilion" Frank Cassilis marries Clara Huddlestone and has children, to whom in fact he is relating the events of the story. But Clara is already dead when Cassilis begins his narrative, so the focus remains on the solitariness itself rather than on the love that becomes a salve for that solitariness. In truth, Stevenson's imagination was energized more by the sense of failure his figures experience than by their prospects for love. In a real sense Cassilis and Northmour are outcasts, people on the edge of society, whose lives are separated from intimacy and connection, people who have deliberately removed themselves from the norms of domestic social responsibilities. Although joined by their common love for Clara, which motivates them to protect her father, they are not really against the Italians and are in effect fighting a false battle. As the pavilion goes up in flames—their redoubt against the world—nothing is left but the links scarred "with little patches of burnt furze" (231). The land has gone back to itself, and all the intruders are expelled from its midst.

It is a nice question how an only child, growing up in an indulgent upper-class Edinburgh home, could have so compelling a vision of the loneliness of men and women in the world. But for whatever reasons, it is a vision that controls a substantial portion of his fiction, and creates the atmosphere and tone that dominate his greatest short stories. In a way that is nothing short of modern in its invention and execution, Stevenson made the landscape an element that heightens the loneliness endured by an individual. It came to symbolize both the condition and the consequence of experience. "The Reverend Murdoch Soulis . . . dwelt in the last years of his life, without relative or servant or any human company, in the small and lonely manse under the Hanging Shaw" (317). The fusion of character and place is so simple, yet so vivid, that it can more easily be understood in our time as a cinematic technique, a graphic and instantaneous representation of subject and form. It is a technique that readers intuitively understood but rarely analyzed. Part of its effectiveness lay in the simplicity of the language, part in the evocation of mood, part in the rhythm itself, with its building up of a sense of finality, and ultimate emptiness, by the suggestion of imminent death and the total absence of human contact. It is a method Stevenson continued through his career, so that by the 1890s he was using coral atolls in the South Seas to illustrate the same terrible loneliness that he earlier identified with the wet and dark rock fastnesses of the Scottish coastline.

3

In "A Lodging for the Night" Stevenson introduces a theme that was to figure prominently in his fiction—chance, or the capriciousness of life. It is a philosophical issue that he treated wryly in *The Suicide Club* and *The Rajah's Diamond*, and with deep sobriety in "The Merry Men" and "Markheim." It is an issue that focuses on a vision of the world, even of the universe, and of man's place in the world. How do we live our lives? How do we plan for our work, our children, our posterity? Stevenson was an intensely driven man: the thought that he might die and leave nothing behind, that his name would have been "writ in water" only, that it would disappear unremembered into the oblivion of time, this was the spur that impelled him to write wherever he was, traveling steerage on a transatlantic boat, on a train across the United States, or on a ninety-foot sloop across the Pacific, coughing blood or running a fever, but never to be without a notebook and pen in his pocket, or a board to write upon in bed. Perhaps the desire for immortality and the refusal to go quietly, however futile that notion to a man who had absorbed Darwin into his consciousness ("Pulvis et Umbra"), compelled him to write unremittingly. For Stevenson wanted to leave behind a small, indelible mark on a stick, so that whoever came after, so long as the stick lasted, would recall and in the process revivify his name. Of course, this is nothing more than the artist's desire for immortality, and there is certainly nothing new here. But with Stevenson it was joined to the late nineteenth century's recognition that in the context of geologic time, the very notion of immortality was something of an anachronism.

It is clear that Stevenson does not approach this issue from the point of view of religion. Like Hawthorne, he draws on the grammar of religion for his subject and his vocabulary, but everlasting perdition, like eternal glory, are simply tropes that enable us to enter the circle where true meaning is explored and debated. Part of that debate has to do with what Stevenson (through Villon) calls "the riddle of man's life." For the pursuit of fame and immortality through writing is as arbitrary as any other pursuit engaged in by people high and low in life.

In "A Lodging for the Night" Stevenson draws together issues of art and immortality, poverty and wealth, and the transiency of all worldly pursuits, with the central idea of a universe ruled by chance. He begins with the first of his memorable opening paragraphs, from which I quote just the first two lines: "It was late in November 1456. The snow fell over Paris with rigorous, relentless persistence; sometimes the wind made a sally and scattered it in flying vortices; sometimes there was a lull, and flake after flake descended out of the black night air, silent, circuitous, interminable" (234). The opening sentence cannot be bettered for its utter simplicity and modernity. The voice is as dateless today as it was in 1878, and it is only the insertion of the year "1456" that gives the sentence (and the reader) a jolt. It has the effect of bringing alive the late medieval city, as if we were in the midst of it, able to enter its *mentalité* while still living in our much later and more advanced time. Then Stevenson delivers one of the most powerful and evocative descriptions of a city covered in snow, whose whiteness provides a vivid contrast with the darkness of the night. And with the single word "vortices" he draws both on older theories of the universe that posited a rotational movement of cosmic matter around an axis and on nineteenth-century scientific theories that defined the term as a rapid movement of particles of matter around an axis. Thus the word itself merges the past with the present (just as historical fiction is a merger of different periods in time), while its meaning in each case is associated with natural laws or forces that are beyond man's control.

The snow, too, is beyond control, with its ceaseless and unpredictable falling, its complete sovereignty over the lives of the people. Francis Villon, who is educated, can speculate amusingly and just a bit blasphemously on its origins: "Pagan Jupiter plucking geese upon Olympus," or "the holy angels moulting" (234). But the illiterate poor, in contrast, have a sense of awe before natural phenomena, which is captured in a wonderful sentence: "To poor people, looking up under moist eyebrows, it seemed a wonder where it all came from." They are of course looking up to the heavens, and implicitly looking up to God. But Villon is too sophisticated for such absolute and unquestioning faith. He is a "Master of Arts," and his ability to mix classical and religious allusions identifies him as an intellectual who does not take wonders for signs, or at least not for signs of God. Of course Villon's sly humor borders on the blasphemous, and he does not pursue the joke. It is fine for an educated man to play with words and ideas, but it is also dangerous, and not something to treat cavalierly. But in even proposing the question, as Villon does, with a slight anticlerical edge, Stevenson opens up the prospect of religious questioning. Although the story is not one of specifically religious questioning, it is one of moral or ethical questioning, and one that addresses the "riddle of man's life" (241).

The phrase appears when Villon, searching for shelter in the middle of the night, stumbles upon the corpse of a woman who has frozen to death. He goes through her pockets, which are empty, and then discovers two small coins hidden in her stocking. Villon's search is clearly a violation of the woman's person, although the issue is problematic since it touches on a view of death that recurs in many of Stevenson's stories. Simply put, if the spirit is gone, how can one violate the flesh? In "The Physician and the Saratoga Trunk" Dr. Noel insists to the young American whom he cajoles into accompanying a dead body back to London that it is only a "boxful of dead flesh," and nothing to be concerned about. Once death occurs, all that remains is animal protein. Villon states this theme when he remarks upon the woman's bad luck at not being able to spend her coins: "It would have been one more good taste in the mouth, one more smack of the lips, before the devil got the soul, and the body was left to birds and vermin" (241).

Stevenson's picture of Villon searching the prostitute's garter and stocking functions on two levels: on the first, it draws on the historic Villon's well-known fondness for women of all classes, not excluding prostitutes. That the fictional Villon would automatically lift the dead woman's dress to search her stockings suggests that this is hardly a new experience for him. Stevenson builds his portrait from what his contemporaries commonly believed about Villon, deriving their knowledge from their reading of the poetry as well as from a recent French biography, which Stevenson had used as the source for his essay on the poet in *Familiar Studies*. One of Stevenson's methods for constructing character, which he followed in his greatest fictions, is introduced here for the first time. The fictional Villon is built up from the historical Villon, a libertine whose poetry is dense with images of sexuality and love, however complex and problematic its ultimate view. Stevenson never directly suggests here that sexuality is a subject. He uses two vivid and implicative words in a simple subordinate phrase ("but in her stocking, underneath the garter"), and the reader must interpret all else, must recognize that the only way the fictional Villon could have uncovered the coins would have been through the intimate knowledge of women's bodies that was presumably possessed by the real Villon. The small scene is instructive for what it tells us about Stevenson's artistic principles: never disclose more to the reader than is absolutely essential, which is in fact a dramatic method adapted to fiction; and, in historical fiction, always base a complete understanding of character on a contextual knowledge of the historical personage.

The act of searching the dead woman's body to uncover the coins is distinctly psychosexual, and akin to the psychosexuality illustrated in Silas Scuddamore's peering through the peephole for a view of Madame Zephyrine. From a thematic point of view the sexuality has a furtive and secretive aspect to it; from the point of view of presentation, however, it is so unobtrusively managed that its meaning might easily escape the reader. The story could serve as a model for the kind of objective narration that Kipling became famous for and that Hemingway identified with *Huck Finn* and Stephen Crane. That aside, Stevenson's association of sexuality and death, merely hinted at in this brief vignette, is further developed in *Jekyll and Hyde* and achieves a kind of climacteric in the death scene in *The Beach of Falesá*.

Of course death is such an overwhelming subject in Stevenson's fiction that there is hardly a story in this collection that does not contain a death within the narrative. The issue is one Stevenson places at the center of human existence: we cannot understand life until we recognize and acknowledge the fact of death, that it may come when life appears most indestructible, and that it happens to the "poor jade" in the middle of the night as quickly and unexpectedly as it does to that fine figure of a soldier, Colonel Geraldine's brother. The issue of death is so central in Stevenson that it has often been mistakenly attributed to the genre, viewed as simply part of the machinery of "adventure" or "romance" fiction. Yet it is a mistake to see in Stevenson's treatment nothing more than an early version of Hollywood's action-adventure films where the audience becomes immunized against the realities of death. Quite the contrary: in Stevenson the depiction is so vivid, so graphic, that a *Chicago Tribune* reviewer of *New Arabian Nights* considered the stories so repugnant as to warrant comparison with Emile Zola.

But let us return to one of the central points of this discussion: the idea that life is capricious, and that chance rules in place of fate, or individual will, and overrides the physical and mental endowments of being and personality. When Villon looks at the dead woman, and the coins in his hand, he shakes his head "over the riddle of man's life. Henry V. of England, dying at Vincennes just after he had conquered France, and this poor jade cut off by a cold draught in a great man's doorway, before she had time to spend her couple of whites—it seemed a cruel way to carry on the world" (241). Arbitrary, sudden death, which snatches the highest and the lowest at the moment of their smallest pleasures or their greatest triumphs, is the subject of Villon's thoughts. And the juxtaposition of a king with a prostitute, the conquest of a country with the fierce protection of two small coins, highlights the issue as a philosophical and religious question and gives it a universal application. It also obliterates the distinction between king and prostitute, for chance is an egalitarian ruler, running the world for good or ill, indifferent to high and low, without regard for cause or justice or charity. Stevenson's citation of Henry V adds an appropriate ironic touch since it keeps the allusion local—the English king dying in France a little over thirty years before the action of the story, an incident that

Villon could plausibly draw upon to illustrate the fortuitousness of fortune. But what Stevenson actually focuses on is not the casual nature of fortune but the tenuousness and fragility of life's glories or small pleasures. Villon reflects that it would be the better part of wisdom, or at least more satisfying, to leave this world in a moment of pleasure, for there is no guarantee that we will not be snuffed out before our long-prepared-for pleasure is enjoyed: "He would like to use all his tallow before the light was blown out and the lantern broken" (241).

Following the allusion and the reflection, "A Lodging for the Night" moves toward a dramatic debate concerning the nature of chance in individuals' lives. But the idea is there from the start of the story, in the depiction of Villon's debased and animal-like friend Tabary: "He had become a thief, just as he might have become the most decent of burgesses, by the imperious chance that rules the lives of human geese and human donkeys" (236). It is as if people are no different from animals, and certainly no better, and, what is most crucial, have absolutely no control over their lives: *imperious chance*, overbearing, dictatorial, domineering. Part of the brilliance of "A Lodging" is Stevenson's reconstitution in his own text of themes in Villon's poetry. Thus in Villon's *The Great Testament*: "The emperor asked him, 'Why are you a pirate?' The other replied, 'Why do you call me a pirate? If I could change my poor vessel for your throne, I would be an emperor, like you" (*The Poems of François Villon*, trans. H. De Vere Stackpoole [London: Hutchinson, 1913], p. 123). This observation is precisely the substance of the debate between Brisetout and Villon: "But if I had been born lord of Brisetout, and you had been the poor scholar Francis, would the difference have been any the less? . . . Should not I have been the soldier, and you the thief?" (249–50). Villon's argument throughout is that circumstances make people what they are. What is character but circumstance, or thievery but poverty, or virtue but the absence of hunger? The lord who takes Villon in from the cold, offers the hospitality of his home, addresses him with high sentiments, and extols the beauty of moral virtue believes that what he is saying is inherent in the structure of the world: that people are good or evil, follow truth or wrap themselves in falsehood, according to some preordained scheme by which absolute values like honor, integrity, and loyalty are rewarded. These beliefs are ingrained in the lord of Brisetout and fundamental to his vision of the world. Villon, who is intellectually more acute, better trained, and nimbler in argument, drives Brisetout to anger, for he undermines the nobleman's system of belief which assigns meaning and value, order and design to the world.

What Stevenson is doing here, and in other stories, is calling into relief a fundamental but unanswerable question about our experience: are we responsible for our lives or are they beyond our control? The question arises because so many elements of Stevenson's fiction appear to derive from it, or contribute to it. Thus the violence that is such a powerful and pervasive feature of Stevenson's work is frequently presented as impulsive and completely without warning. The murder of Thevenin is swift and unexpected: "Thevenin was just opening his mouth to claim another victory, when Montign leaped up, swift as an adder, and stabbed him to the heart. The blow took effect before he had time to utter a cry, before he had time to move" ("Lodging," 238). The rapidity of the act reveals something of the personality of the historical Montign, who was a hard case, older than Villon by two years, born into a noble family (a detail Stevenson quietly incorporates in his text), twice sentenced to death, once for murder. The violence in Stevenson's fiction is stitched into the narrative, with the aim of making it as functional, and surprising, as life itself. Stevenson does not focus on the experience of death so much as on the act of violence, along with the victim's physical response. It is a quintessentially modern method, and one that might profitably be compared with Hemingway's, particularly in the interchapters of *In Our Time*.

Stevenson can never stop ruminating upon the question of how we live in the world when our lives hang by the slimmest of threads, when nothing but the merest chance keeps our small personal triumphs from being taken away. It is bound up with his view of history and where we stand in the universe. We pass from this journey or voyage—two terms descriptive and reflective of Stevenson's most elemental plot structure—into nothingness. "Life is a little vapour that passeth away, as we are told by those in holy orders"

("The Sire de Malétroit's Door," *New Arabian Nights*, vol. 2 [London: Chatto & Windus, 1882], 173). Occasionally there are reminders of those long forgotten, such as the shoe buckle that the narrator discovers when he dives into the sea in "The Merry Men," a modern relic not all that different than Yorick's skull and one that poses the same question: is this all that remains of a man? If Stevenson were religious he might have had an easier time resolving the riddle. But Villon with his licentiate in theology, Simon Rolles with his church history, the Reverend Soulis with his sermons—none of them has an answer.

Of course, the question might be wrong; it need not be the one posed by Villon as to why there is suffering in the world, or why there are the hungry and the well fed, thieves and saints (or at least what approximate to saints, the righteous). There is no logic that explains why one suffers and another thrives, or why the two could not be switched, or why either's fortune can suddenly be snuffed out. In "The Sire de Malétroit's Door," for example, Denis's life is changed twice: first when he is caught inside the house and faces death in the morning, and second when he embarks on a new life with Blanche, having discovered his love for her in the course of the long evening. Critics who dismiss the story as sentimental would do well to see it in the context of Stevenson's other texts, for just as chance can destroy a life, so can it give a life, as it does for Denis. Similarly, there is no presumption as to what an individual may do in any specific situation. When Villon leaves Brisetout's house in the early hours of the morning, without robbing or murdering him, he reflects to himself, in a brilliant close to the story, "'A very dull old gentleman,' he thought. 'I wonder what his goblets may be worth'" ("Lodging," 253). That he leaves the house quietly may be a nice ending, but Villon could just as easily (and plausibly) have killed him. What is more to the point is that Stevenson, in the very design of his plot, allows for the open possibilities that constitute the realities of life: nothing is fixed or determined, and character and behavior, in fiction as in life, are conditioned by circumstances that are often beyond our control. Thus Stevenson might agree with Markheim that his life was bound at birth by the "giants" of circumstance and still reject the argument as nothing more than a plea for the failure of will. Character is not destiny, nor circumstance fate; but together they constitute life, and it is life that Stevenson's characters struggle valiantly, even desperately, to maintain.

4

"Jekyll and Hyde" has become a virtual synonym for good and evil, for the popular idea that every man has within himself an antithetical other self, and that the two selves exist in a state of unresolved tension or open conflict. The influence of Stevenson's story was powerful enough that as early as 1928 Funk and Wagnalls's *New Standard Dictionary* cited "Hyde" and "Jekyll" as separate entries, as if the fictional creation were two distinct characters, each of whom could then be referred to the other. By the time of *Webster's Third New International Dictionary* (1961) the phrase "Jekyll-and-Hyde" enjoyed its own definition as an adjective: "of, relating to, or resembling a person who leads a double life or who has two apparently distinct characters one of which is good and the other evil." No subject in Stevenson would appear to have a greater general recognition; indeed, *Jekyll-and-Hyde* is an eponym that everybody knows, even if not everyone could identify its source. What is the explanation for such a widespread "understanding"? There is of course the broad interest in the traditional literary device of the double. And the modern psychological concern with questions of individuation, split personality, and ego formation undoubtedly go far toward explaining the fascination with a late nineteenth-century story that was sold as nothing more than a cheap thriller but became the text for countless Sunday sermons.

Jekyll and Hyde, which Stevenson tells us came to him in a dream, dramatizes a subject that compelled the writer from the beginning of his career—the puzzle of duality in human nature. What is at the center of the exploration is the nature of human character itself or, put another way, the nature of the self. "Villon cringed, and brought up many servile words of apology; at a crisis of this sort, the beggar was uppermost in him, and the man of genius hid his head with confusion" ("Lodging," 246). And from "The Merry Men," the narrator's first view of his uncle Gordon Darnaway after many years: "He was a sour, small, bilious man, with a long face and very dark eyes; fifty-six years old, sound and active in body, and with an air somewhat between that of a shepherd and that of a man following the sea" (261). Each example reveals Stevenson's fundamental belief that identity is neither obvious nor singular. Clearly Villon has a variety of aspects to his personality and cannot be reduced to either artist or beggar, any more than he can be identified solely as thief or student or lover or philosopher. In a sense Stevenson shares Walt Whitman's conviction that each man is large and contains multitudes; indeed, it was his reading of Whitman's poetry, and in particular "Song of Myself," that inspired him to address issues of complex personality as directly as he does. The notion that men wear masks to cover up their inner selves can be traced as easily to Whitman as to Hawthorne, whose stories are rife with the image of the veil as a cover for the self.

Stevenson was always aware of the outer mask ("all men are better than this disguise that grows about and stifles them" ["Markheim," 311]). In the description of Villon quoted above, the poet adapts to the situation, presents himself as a mendicant, and plays on the charity of the noble lord. But the artist in him is far from a mendicant; he is arrogant, contentious, sarcastic, and disdainful. Is the beggar then mere disguise? The answer is no, for one of Stevenson's convictions is that we assume the personality we don or practice. Villon, as long as he begs, is a beggar; he is a poet as long as he composes *ballades*—just as Simon Rolles is both thief and theologian, ascetic scholar and avid pupil of the secrets of the underworld. One does not exist to the exclusion of the other; the criminal and the religious coexist within the same individual. We are, in other words, what we pretend to be.

In the sentence from "The Merry Men," Stevenson compares Gordon Darnaway to a shepherd and a sailor. The two could not be more dissimilar, the one rural, quiet, perhaps even contemplative, and the other placed in the middle of an active, violent, and perpetually changing world. The shepherd rarely wanders from his place, while the sailor is forever without a home. Stevenson builds up a complex picture of Darnaway in the paragraph, but here in an almost casual detail he divides his personality in such a way that he cannot easily be classified according to type. The elements of the shepherd are there in his rootedness, his care for his daughter, and his instinct for the isolation and quiet of his home. Yet he is also a man of the sea, surrounded by the sea, with potentialities for power that reveal themselves in the violent act that is at the center of the narrative. Although there may be qualities shared by shepherd and sailor, it is the stark contrast that is immediately called into question, a contrast reflective of Stevenson's portraiture. It is not always a division in personality that is crucial but the recognition that there are differing strands in any single personality, and that those strands cannot easily be separated. Stevenson's stylistic device ("between . . . a shepherd and . . . a man following the sea") is a linguistic fissure fundamental to his view of personality and, in a larger sense, to his perception of the world. By means of a simple preposition he exposes the modernist's sense of the world's uncertainty and ambiguity.

"The Pavilion on the Links" provides a striking illustration of Stevenson's presentation of personality:

My wife and I, a man and a woman, have often agreed to wonder how a person could be, at the same time, so handsome and so repulsive as Northmour. He had the appearance of a finished gentleman; his face bore every mark of intelligence and courage; but you had only to look at him, even in his most amiable moment, to see that he had the temper of a slaver captain. I never knew a character that was both explosive and revengeful to the same degree; he combined the vivacity of the south with the sustained and deadly hatreds of the north; and both traits were plainly written on his face, which was a sort of danger signal. In person, he was tall, strong, and active; his hair and complexion very dark; his features handsomely designed, but spoiled by a menacing expression. (190)

There could hardly be a more dramatic example of duality in the early fiction. Just five years later, in *Treasure Island*, Stevenson introduced Long John Silver, whose capacity for calculated evil was offset by charm, courage, and even a kind of verbal felicity. There is no question that some of Northmour's "traits" were carried over to

Silver. But the issue that is central to the portrait is the enigma of personality. How can Northmour be both handsome and repulsive, amiable and cruel? How can he possess the liveliness of the south and the remorseless vengeance of the north? What Stevenson does here is really quite simple: he adapts a divided personality to the larger aims of his narrative. Thus the division within Northmour mirrors the division that the text establishes between north and south, cold and warmth, dark and light, war and peace. A division within the self often reflects a division within the text, and the irreconcilable warfare taking place within the individual can only lead to a cataclysmic ending, in this case the fire that destroys the pavilion. Northmour's death, reported at the end in passing by the narrator, is symbolically identified with the demise of the pavilion, and his divided personality is nothing more than an image of the pavilion itself, a cold Scottish retreat of Italian design, a structure ill equipped and out of place yet curiously supportive of its residents and visitors. The visage is the visitation; perhaps we bring upon ourselves the destiny we seek to resist, just as we fail at the freedom we imagine we cherish.

Unquestionably the single story that most exemplifies duality in man, apart from *Jekyll and Hyde*, is "Markheim," originally published as part of a collection of "horror" stories in a volume titled *The Broken Shaft*. Stevenson used the form to focus attention on the divided self, and its implications for behavior and conscience. It is a story brilliant in its simplicity, its movement, and its psychological acuity. Markheim, a youngish man who has steadily resorted to more serious crimes as a result of his gambling debts, enters an antique dealer's shop on Christmas eve, engages the flinty old man in conversation, then murders him with a long knife. He sets about to rob the store, which is closed off from the afternoon light and filled with clocks and mirrors of all sizes and shapes. In the process of moving through the house, he suddenly encounters another presence. This presence, or "visitant," engages Markheim in conversation, and the two debate the path that the murderer's life has taken. The visitant offers to help the murderer escape, but after the long colloquy Markheim decides to give himself up. As the dealer's servant girl returns to the shop, he tells her, "Go for the police . . . I have killed your master." Simple enough on the surface, the story is a stunning achievement on a number of levels—as a psychological study of conscience; as a discourse on good and evil; as a textual compression of time and space, light and dark. It certainly looks back to Poe and E. T. A. Hoffman, just as it looks forward to Henry James's "The Jolly Corner." But this is not a ghost story where the protagonist is visited by images of his past and future selves; rather it is a story where *memory* renders visible the past. Markheim vividly recalls his experiences as a child, experiences in which the morbid alternated with the joyous, where the open fields were in contrast with the posters of notorious murderers hung up as sensational attractions at a Sunday fair. Stevenson takes for his subject memory and consciousness, twin images that generate the action and envelop the reader. Virtually the entire story takes place in the mind of the protagonist.

The question of duality can be readily placed in a modern context by substituting psychoanalytic concepts focusing on the ego, and in "Markheim" this approach would provide a plausible reading. Another way of examining duality is to approach it from the vantage point of good and evil—a common view of *Jekyll and Hyde*. But good and evil are more complicated, or perhaps more problematic, than a simple schematic division of the self suggests. Without question the nature of evil is one of Stevenson's major subjects, from his earliest fiction to his last unfinished texts. Although the treatment may not appear as profoundly philosophical as in Melville, where evil is immanent in the world, without origin or explanation, or as psychological as in Hawthorne, where the fall from grace is replicated in every individual's experience, it is in fact a fusion of both. Stevenson's focus on motivation and behavior foregrounds psychology, while his alternation of internal monologue with dialogic debate draws attention to the philosophical argument. Thus psychology and philosophy are joined for both dramatic and theoretic purposes.

What is the nature of evil? In "Thrawn Janet" the answer is complex. The devil is not the issue in this classic tale of witchcraft, but rather the minister's inability to perceive let alone acknowledge the fact of evil and its power in people's lives. This story, a masterpiece of dialectal realism, has always been considered among the strongest of Stevenson's achievements. He himself had a high regard for it, as he wrote to Lady Taylor, to whom he dedicated the volume of tales in which it appeared: "Of *Thrawn Janet* which I like very much myself, you say nothing, thus uttering volumes; but it is plain that people cannot always agree. I do not think it is a wholesome part of me that broods on the evil in the world and man; but I do not think that I get harm from it; possibly my readers may, which is more serious; but at any account, I do not purpose to write more in this vein" (undated letter to Lady Taylor, Parrish Collection, Princeton University Library). Stevenson, reflecting on the completed text, wonders about his preoccupation with a subject upon which no definitive conclusion can be drawn. It is also interesting to observe his view of the creative process, that although the subject may be oppressive, its working out has no deleterious effect on the artist. (He acknowledges that the same assurance may not so easily be granted his readers, thus inadvertently giving credence to Plato's fear that the artist is a dangerous person because his work cannot be controlled and its effect on audiences is unpredictable.) What is daunting about "Thrawn Janet" is not the diabolic (or the horror) but the unknown, and the realization that there is a core of evil in the world that can be denied only at one's peril. In effect, the diabolic served Stevenson as a convenient frame for focusing attention on an aspect of life that appears to resist rational explanation. Although the villagers have no evidence that Janet is a witch, and the minister is a learned man whose courage is sustained by his belief in his own rationality, in the end neither Janet hanging from the thin tape nor the minister's resort to a theology of unremitting Calvinism offers any rational explanation for what occurred. If one wants a modern parallel for "Thrawn Janet," one can do no better than to consider the films of Alfred Hitchcock.

In "Markheim" Stevenson melds the issues of duality and good and evil in a story of conscience, redemption, and the narcissism of consciousness. Confronted by the visitant who appears to know him, Markheim exclaims:

"Know me!" cried Markheim. "Who can do so? My life is but a travesty and slander on myself. I have lived to belie my nature. All men do; all men are better than this disguise that grows about and stifles them. You see each dragged away by life, like one whom bravos have seized and muffled in a cloak; if they had their own control—if you could see their faces, they would be altogether different, they would shine out for heroes and saints! I am worse than most; myself is more overlaid; my excuse is known to me and God. But had I the time, I could disclose myself." (311)

Markheim's plea is of course self-serving, blaming fate for his criminal conduct and his current condition. But if the argument appears nothing but an attempt at self-justification, it cannot be dismissed altogether. The belief that our outward life bears no relation to who we are is made with telling effect in this paragraph. It is as if "life" kidnaps us from our better selves, holds us in bondage to a behavior that is neither a genuine reflection nor an adequate expression of what we believe or feel. Markheim's cry is for the preservation of his own identity and against the false separation between our exterior and interior lives, of having our physical selves function as surrogates for our purer but captive spiritual beings. In a passage that has profound historical roots, Markheim declares the dilemma of his existence: "Evil and good run strong in me, haling me both ways. I do not love the one thing, I love all" (313–14). That sense of an individual at war with himself received its seminal expression in St. Paul's letter to the Romans ("But I see another law in my members, warring against the law of my mind, and bringing me into captivity to the law of sin which is in my members" [Rom. 7:23]), and in two telling descriptions in Sir Thomas Browne, whom Stevenson "sedulously" imitated when he was learning to write, and who as late as 1893 he continued to list in his private canon of revered writers ("With Mr Stevenson's compliments," undated letter, Parrish Collection, Princeton University Library): "The heart of man is the place the devill dwels in; I feele sometimes a hell within my selfe"; and "There is another man within mee that's angry with mee, rebukes, commands, and dastards me" (Browne, *Religio Medici and Other Works*, ed. L.C. Martin [Oxford: Clarendon, 1964], 49, 64).

This idea of inward division, that deep within the self there is a powerful disposition to evil that cannot be overcome simply by the mind's conscious desire for good—Milton's "hateful siege / Of contraries" (*Paradise Lost* 9:119–22)—is central in much of Stevenson's fiction. We have seen how pervasive the image of life as war is in Stevenson. Markheim's internal struggle represents a parallel version of the general struggle embodied in the social realm. In other words, just as life is a battlefield (in the words of Colonel Geraldine in *The Suicide Club*), Markheim and Gordon Darnaway and Northmour are engaged in a form of warfare within themselves, fighting to break out of the soul-destroying conflicts they face. There is a connection between the individual world and the social world, between the war within the self and the war in the larger world, for Stevenson's fiction is always set in the larger world and is never meant to be contained within the contours of the individual or egoistic consciousness. For the characters, the war within is frequently justified as the inevitable consequence of the war without, and the war without can be seen as a projection of the war within. Thus the battle royal between the "man-eaters" and the "voices" in "The Isle of Voices" serves symbolically as a clash between competing forms of ignorance and evil, and as a projection of the disturbed state of Keola's mind, his being torn between the laziness and greed that got him marooned on the island in the first place, and his desire to return home to his wife and his life in Hawaii.

It would be a mistake to think that there is ever a resolution, let alone a peaceful conclusion to the unending Darwinian battle that is life. One of the reasons the endings to Stevenson's fictions are so problematic is precisely because they are not envisioned in any way as conclusions. The stories are texts whose deeper narratives are still unfolding, or which take different directions, following the fortuitous details that "complete" the action proper. Stevenson's Villon goes out into the night, wondering to himself whether (at the very least) he should have robbed his host of his goblets. That the real Villon disappeared from Paris shortly after a major robbery in Christmas 1456, and that his final end remains a mystery, gives a curious historical veracity to the text's fictional and formal logic.

But as St. Paul and Sir Thomas Browne and Milton tell us, the mind is all, and in the conception lies the crime. Thus the devil (if that is indeed who the "visitant" represents) tells Markheim that he is indifferent to his subject's crime: "And it is not because you have killed a dealer, but because your name is Markheim, that I offer to forward your escape" (313). He then makes the declaration that directly echoes Satan's "Evil be thou my Good" (*Paradise Lost* 9:110): "Evil, for which I live, consists not in action but in character; the bad man is dear to me, not the bad act" (313). This attitude defines the idea of character and the position of good and evil in the world. If it is not the act that defines the evil, then it must be the perpetrator of the act; if it is not in the deed itself, then it is in its imagining. This serves to shift the attention away from the action and toward the conception. In effect, the action itself might be nothing more than a sophisticated decoy, a divertissement, entertaining in its own right but not really the main event. Good and evil then are exclusively centered in the mind of the individual, irrespective of whether or not he commits a crime. Conversely, if the individual is well loved by friends and family, no crime he may commit alters their judgment or their feeling for him. Dr. Noel's comment to the young man in "The Physician and the Saratoga Trunk" is a fair description of this position: "Credulous youth, the horror with which blind and unjust law regards an action never attaches to the doer in the eyes of those who love him; and if I saw the friend of my heart return to me out of seas of blood he would be in no way changed in my affection. . . . good and ill are a chimera; there is nought in life except destiny" (77).

Of course, this cannot be taken as an absolute statement of Stevenson's own position. But it is interesting for its philosophical dimension. Stevenson opens up the question of evil in terms of the nature of man, of his actions in the world, and of both in the context of time or "destiny." These issues are complicated, and neither the visitant nor Dr. Noel is a model for emulation. Yet their positions illustrate the kind of moral complexity that is articulated in all of Stevenson's texts. If good and evil are indeed a "chimera," then what is an individual's role in life? How are values like love, loyalty, honor, and courage maintained in a world devoid of meaning, yet one where evil is manifest? One answer is that the world is not empty, that evil does have its counterpart, and it is precisely that which gives Stevenson's characters their capacity to survive and their faith to continue living. If "Markheim" is a psychomachy, a struggle of good and evil for the soul of man, the ending is not on the side of evil: "If

I be condemned to evil acts . . . there is still one door of freedom open: I can cease from action. If my life be an ill thing, I can lay it down" (315).

In many ways this passage strikes at the heart of Stevenson's belief that it is *thought* that determines character, the mind that makes the man, rather than the acts performed. It is not recognized often enough how much of Stevenson's fiction turns on protagonists who use their intelligence to survive, who indeed survive only because of their intelligence. The best-known examples are Jim Hawkins and David Balfour, the latter getting some very simple advice from his minister upon leaving home: "Be soople, David, be soople." But it can be seen in the shorter fiction as well, in "The Merry Men," as Charlie unravels the mystery bit by bit; in "The Bottle Imp," as the resourceful wife figures out how to dispose of the bottle and save her husband's soul; or in "The Isle of Voices," where the presumably ignorant Hawaiian sizes up the white sailors' inability to believe anything but their own stories and thus decides that the better part of discretion is not to reveal the mystery of Kalamake's lantern. This focus on intelligence belies a common perception of Stevenson as an adventure writer whose compelling stories exist solely on the level of physical action. But Stevenson is nothing if not intellectual, and his dramatic texts represent the embodiment of his ideas.

Although Stevenson is commonly identified as a Late Victorian writer, his outlook was fundamentally modern. Both in the subjects that quickened his imagination and in the forms he devised for their expression, he stands at the very beginning of the modernist movement in literature. The individual isolated in a physical universe with no moral center; the fortuitousness that circumscribes and determines our lives, to the virtual exclusion of all will or desire; the existence of evil in the world and the mystery of its origin and nature—these are among the issues in Stevenson's fiction that can readily be seen as modernist. Running through all of these issues is Stevenson's fundamental doubt—a quintessential modernist doubt— regarding the reliability of our knowledge, particularly as it affects our judgment of peoples' motivation and behavior. He demonstrates repeatedly how large parts of our lives are shrouded in shadows and darkness, where the ability to see, let alone determine meaning, is either dubious or problematic. In the beginning paragraphs of "The Sire de Malétroit's Door" Denis de Beaulieu searches for a way home ("It is an eerie and mysterious position to be thus submerged in opaque blackness in an almost unknown town") and winds up caught in a trap he can neither escape nor understand. The sense of being caught up in shadows and half-lights is so pervasive in Stevenson that we almost come to assume this as the condition of his world, a condition reflected in the wonderful opening line of *The Beach of Falesá:* "I saw that island first when it was neither night nor morning." Yet he is one of the great open-air writers, one whose description of landscape, mountain, valley, and sea has little competition. We might expect the majesty of natural settings to detract from the darkness endemic to the stories, but in fact it contributes to deepening the tone, for in the midst of great clarity there is essential ambiguity.

Perhaps the most telling illustration comes in "The Merry Men," Stevenson's magnificent "fantasia" to the sea: "A great change passed at that moment over the appearance of the bay. It was no more that clear, visible interior, like a house roofed with glass, where the green, submarine sunshine slept so stilly" (275). This is not simply an example of the discrepancy between the appearance of things and their reality. It reflects a deeper, more complex idea: that material things change, that essential reality is not inalterably fixed and thus graspable in its essence. If Stevenson's stories teach us anything, it is exactly the opposite: that strive as we might to secure the truth, the truth escapes us, or is simply undiscoverable. In "The Merry Men" the ocean is at one and the same time a graveyard and a wonder of creation, depending upon the moment and the observer. So when the narrator, having dived down into the sea and come upon the shoe buckle of a drowned sailor, reflects at length on the symbolism of the artifact, on the wrecked ship and all the lost sailors, "the full horror of the charnel ocean burst upon my spirit." But when he returns to shore, and after a brief prayer is refreshed, he looks with calm "on that great bright creature, God's ocean" (276), and reinforces the profound paradox of terror and beauty.

This ambiguity, which discloses itself linguistically as well as structurally, is central to Stevenson's vision of the world. There are few, if any, plain truths, despite Stevenson's formidable effort to make everything plain to the reader. This is one of the defining features of his fiction, that the lucidity of the style conceals the complexity of the meaning. Inevitably, this feature deceived casual readers into believing that the stories were nothing more than the sum of their plots, sustained exercises in easy entertainment. It also accounts for the criticism that they often collapse at the end, that Stevenson could not maintain the intensity and suspense that mark the extraordinary openings of his narratives. If the stories are viewed from the perspective of a modernist, however, then the endings are perfectly consonant with the epistemological doubt that dominates the artist's imagination. Endings, in particular neat endings, are fundamentally false to the reality to which Stevenson adheres, a reality faithful to all the uncertainties and confusions that constitute our living in the world. Stevenson's stories often end abruptly, but that abruptness means only that the action goes no further, that the characters continue on, if they do, in other places along other paths. The inconclusiveness of these endings is both dramatic and symbolic—the completion of the action on one level, and its subversion on another. For despite the brilliance and propulsion of the narrative, Stevenson refuses to falsify a central idea, that uncertainty and ambiguity are not only part of our language but conditions of our existence.

THE SUICIDE CLUB

Story of the Young Man with the Cream Tarts

During his residence in London, the accomplished Prince Florizel of Bohemia gained the affection of all classes by the seduction of his manner and by a well-considered generosity. He was a remarkable man even by what was known of him; and that was but a small part of what he actually did. Although of a placid temper in ordinary circumstances, and accustomed to take the world with as much philosophy as any ploughman, the Prince of Bohemia was not without a taste for ways of life more adventurous and eccentric than that to which he was destined by his birth. Now and then, when he fell into a low humour, when there was no laughable play to witness in any of the London theatres, and when the season of the year was unsuitable to those field sports in which he excelled all competitors, he would summon his confidant and Master of the Horse, Colonel Geraldine, and bid him prepare himself against an evening ramble. The Master of the Horse was a young officer of a brave and even temerarious disposition. He greeted the news with delight, and hastened to make ready. Long practice and a varied acquaintance of life had given him a singular facility in disguise; he could adapt not only his face and bearing, but his voice and almost his thoughts, to those of any rank, character, or nation; and in this way he diverted attention from the Prince, and sometimes gained admission for the pair into strange societies. The civil authorities were never taken into the secret of these adventures; the imperturbable courage of the one and the ready invention and chivalrous devotion of the other had brought them through a score of dangerous passes; and they grew in confidence as time went on.

One evening in March they were driven by a sharp fall of sleet into an Oyster Bar in the immediate neighbourhood of Leicester Square. Colonel Geraldine was dressed and painted to represent a person connected with the Press in reduced circumstances; while the Prince had, as usual, travestied his appearance by the addition of false whiskers and a pair of large adhesive eyebrows. These lent him a shaggy and weather-beaten air, which, for one of his urbanity, formed the most impenetrable disguise. Thus equipped, the commander and his satellite sipped their brandy and soda in security.

The bar was full of guests, male and female; but though more than one of these offered to fall into talk with our adventurers, none of them promised to grow interesting upon a nearer acquaintance. There was nothing present but the lees of London and the commonplace of disrespectability; and the Prince had already fallen to yawning, and was beginning to grow weary of the whole excursion, when the swing doors were pushed violently open, and a young man, followed by a couple of commissionaires, entered the bar. Each of the commissionaires carried a large dish of cream tarts under a cover, which they at once removed; and the young man made the round of the company, and pressed these confections upon everyone's acceptance with an exaggerated courtesy. Sometimes his offer was laughingly accepted; sometimes it was firmly, or even harshly, rejected. In these latter cases the newcomer always ate the tart himself, with some more or less humorous commentary.

At last he accosted Prince Florizel.

"Sir," said he, with a profound obeisance, proffering the tart at the same time between his thumb and forefinger, "will you so far honour an entire stranger? I can answer for the quality of the pastry, having eaten two dozen and three of them myself since five o'clock."

"I am in the habit," replied the Prince, "of looking not so much to the nature of a gift as to the spirit in which it is offered."

"The spirit, sir," returned the young man, with another bow, "is one of mockery."

"Mockery?" repeated Florizel. "And whom do you propose to mock?"

"I am not here to expound my philosophy," replied the other, "but to distribute these cream tarts. If I mention that I heartily include myself in the ridicule of the transaction, I hope you will consider honour satisfied and condescend. If not, you will constrain me to eat my twenty-eighth, and I own to being weary of the exercise."

"You touch me," said the Prince, "and I have all the will in the world to rescue you from this dilemma, but upon one condition. If my friend and I eat your cakes—for which we have neither of us any natural inclination—we shall expect you to join us at supper by way of recompense."

The young man seemed to reflect.

"I have still several dozen upon hand," he said at last; "and that will make it necessary for me to visit several more bars before my great affair is concluded. This will take some time; and if you are hungry——"

The Prince interrupted him with a polite gesture.

"My friend and I will accompany you," he said; "for we have already a deep interest in your very agreeable mode of passing an evening. And now that the preliminaries of peace are settled, allow me to sign the treaty for both."

And the Prince swallowed the tart with the best grace imaginable.

"It is delicious," said he.

"I perceive you are a connoisseur," replied the young man.

Colonel Geraldine likewise did honour to the pastry; and everyone in that bar having now either accepted or refused his delicacies, the young man with the cream tarts led the way to another and similar establishment. The two commissionaires, who seemed to have grown accustomed to their absurd employment, followed immediately after; and the Prince and the Colonel brought up the rear, arm in arm, and smiling to each other as they went. In this order the company visited two other taverns, where scenes were enacted of a like nature to that already described—some refusing, some accepting, the favours of this vagabond hospitality, and the young man himself eating each rejected tart.

On leaving the third saloon the young man counted his store. There were but nine remaining, three in one tray and six in the other.

"Gentlemen," said he, addressing himself to his two new followers, "I am unwilling to delay your supper. I am positively sure you must be hungry. I feel that I owe you a special consideration. And on this great day for me, when I am closing a career of folly by my most conspicuously silly action, I wish to behave handsomely to all who give me countenance. Gentlemen, you shall wait no longer. Although my constitution is shattered by previous excesses, at the risk of my life I liquidate the suspensory condition."

With these words he crushed the nine remaining tarts into his mouth, and swallowed them at a single movement each. Then, turning to the commissionaires, he gave them a couple of sovereigns.

"I have to thank you," said he, "for your extraordinary patience."

And he dismissed them with a bow apiece. For some seconds he stood looking at the purse from which he had just paid his assistants, then, with a laugh, he tossed it into the middle of the street, and signified his readiness for supper.

In a small French restaurant in Soho, which had enjoyed an exaggerated reputation for some little while, but had already begun to be forgotten, and in a private room up two pair of stairs, the three companions made a very elegant supper, and drank three or four bottles of champagne, talking the while upon indifferent subjects. The young man was fluent and gay, but he laughed louder than was natural in a person of polite breeding; his hands trembled violently, and his voice took sudden and surprising inflections, which seemed to be independent of his will. The dessert had been cleared away, and all three had lighted their cigars, when the Prince addressed him in these words:

"You will, I am sure, pardon my curiosity. What I have seen of you has greatly pleased but even more puzzled me. And though I should be loth to seem indiscreet, I must tell you that my friend and I are persons very well worthy to be entrusted with a secret. We have many of our own, which we are continually revealing to improper ears. And if, as I suppose, your story is a silly one, you need have no delicacy with us, who are two of the silliest men in England. My name is Godall, Theophilus Godall; my friend is Major Alfred Hammersmith—or at least, such is the name by which he chooses to be known. We pass our lives entirely in the search for extravagant adventures; and there is no extravagance with which we are not capable of sympathy."

"I like you, Mr. Godall," returned the young man; "you inspire me with a natural confidence; and I have not the slightest objection to your friend the Major, whom I take to be a nobleman in masquerade. At least, I am sure he is no soldier."

The Colonel smiled at this compliment to the perfection of his art; and the young man went on in a more animated manner.

"There is every reason why I should not tell you my story. Perhaps that is just the reason why I am going to do so. At least, you seem so well prepared to hear a tale of silliness that I cannot find it in my heart to disappoint you. My name, in spite of your example, I shall keep to myself. My age is not essential to the narrative. I am descended from my ancestors by ordinary generation, and from them I inherited the very eligible human tenement which I still occupy and a fortune of three hundred pounds a year. I suppose they also handed on to me a harebrain humour, which it has been my chief delight to indulge. I received a good education. I can play the violin nearly well enough to earn money in the orchestra of a penny gaff, but not quite. The same remark applies to the flute and the French horn. I learned enough of whist to lose about a hundred a year at that scientific game. My acquaintance with French was sufficient to enable me to squander money in Paris with almost the same facility as in London. In short, I am a person full of manly accomplishments. I have had every sort of adventure, including a duel about nothing. Only two months ago I met a young lady exactly suited to my taste in mind and body; I found my heart melt; I saw that I had come upon my fate at last, and was in the way to fall in love. But when I came to reckon up what remained to me of my capital, I found it amounted to something less than four hundred pounds! I ask you fairly—can a man who respects himself fall in love on four hundred pounds? I concluded, certainly not; left the presence of my charmer, and slightly accelerating my usual rate of expenditure, came this morning to my last eighty pounds. This I divided into two equal parts; forty I reserved for a particular purpose; the remaining forty I was to dissipate before the night. I have passed a very entertaining day, and played many farces besides that of the cream tarts which procured me the advantage of your acquaintance; for I was determined, as I told you, to bring a foolish career to a still more foolish conclusion; and when you saw me throw my purse into the street, the forty pounds were at an end. Now you know me as well as I know myself: a fool but consistent in his folly; and, as I will ask you to believe, neither a whimperer nor a coward."

From the whole tone of the young man's statement it was plain that he harboured very bitter and contemptuous thoughts about himself. His auditors were led to imagine that his love affair was nearer his heart than he admitted, and that he had a design on his own life. The farce of the cream tarts began to have very much the air of a tragedy in disguise.

"Why, is this not odd," broke out Geraldine, giving a look to Prince Florizel, "that we three fellows should have met by the merest accident in so large a wilderness as London, and should be so nearly in the same condition?"

"How?" cried the young man. "Are you, too, ruined? Is this supper a folly like my cream tarts? Has the devil brought three of his own together for a last carouse?"

"The devil, depend upon it, can sometimes do a very gentlemanly thing," returned Prince Florizel; "and I am so much touched by this coincidence, that, although we are not entirely in the same case, I am going to put an end to the disparity. Let your heroic treatment of the last cream tarts be my example."

So saying, the Prince drew out his purse and took from it a small bundle of bank-notes.

"You see, I was a week or so behind you, but I mean to catch you up and come neck and neck into the winningpost," he continued. "This," laying one of the notes upon the table, "will suffice for the bill. As for the rest——"

He tossed them into the fire, and they went up the chimney in a single blaze.

The young man tried to catch his arm, but as the table was between them his interference came too late.

"Unhappy man," he cried, "you should not have burned them all! You should have kept forty pounds."

"Forty pounds!" repeated the Prince. "Why, in heaven's name, forty pounds?"

"Why not eighty?" cried the Colonel; "for to my certain knowledge there must have been a hundred in the bundle."

"It was only forty pounds he needed," said the young man gloomily. "But without them there is no admission. The rule is strict. Forty pounds for each. Accursed life, where a man cannot even die without money!"

The Prince and the Colonel exchanged glances.

"Explain yourself," said the latter. "I have still a pocket-book tolerably well lined, and I need not say how readily I should share my wealth with Godall. But I must know to what end: you must certainly tell us what you mean."

The young man seemed to awaken; he looked uneasily from one to the other, and his face flushed deeply.

"You are not fooling me?" he asked. "You are indeed ruined men like me?"

"Indeed, I am for my part," replied the Colonel.

"And for mine," said the Prince, "I have given you proof. Who but a ruined man would throw his notes into the fire? The action speaks for itself."

"A ruined man—yes," returned the other suspiciously, "or else a millionaire."

"Enough, sir," said the Prince; "I have said so, and I am not accustomed to have my word remain in doubt."

"Ruined?" said the young man. "Are you ruined, like me? Are you, after a life of indulgence, come to such a pass that you can only indulge yourself in one thing more? Are you"—he kept lowering his voice as he went on—"are you going to give yourselves that last indulgence? Are you going to avoid the consequences of your folly by the one infallible and easy path? Are you going to give the slip to the sheriff's officers of conscience by the one open door?"

Suddenly he broke off and attempted to laugh.

"Here is your health!" he cried, emptying his glass, "and good night to you, my merry ruined men."

Colonel Geraldine caught him by the arm as he was about to rise.

"You lack confidence in us," he said, "and you are wrong. To all your questions I make answer in the affirmative. But I am not so timid, and can speak the Queen's English plainly. We too, like yourself, have had enough of life, and are determined to die. Sooner or later, alone or together, we meant to seek out death and beard him where he lies ready. Since we have met you, and your case is more pressing, let it be tonight—and at once—and, if you will, all three together. Such a penniless trio," he cried, "should go arm in arm into the halls of Pluto, and give each other some countenance among the shades!"

Geraldine had hit exactly on the manners and intonations that became the part he was playing. The Prince himself was disturbed, and looked over at his confidant with a shade of doubt. As for the young man, the flush came back darkly into his cheek, and his eyes threw out a spark of light.

"You are the men for me!" he cried, with an almost terrible gaiety. "Shake hands upon the bargain!" (his hand was cold and wet). "You little know in what a company you will begin the march! You little know in what a happy moment for yourselves you partook of my cream tarts! I am only a unit, but I am a unit in an army. I know Death's private door. I am one of his familiars, and can show you into eternity without ceremony and yet without scandal."

They called upon him eagerly to explain his meaning.

"Can you muster eighty pounds between you?" he demanded.

Geraldine ostentatiously consulted his pocket-book, and replied in the affirmative.

"Fortunate beings!" cried the young man. "Forty pounds is the entry money of the Suicide Club."

"The Suicide Club," said the Prince, "why, what the devil is that?"

"Listen," said the young man; "this is the age of conveniences, and I have to tell you of the last perfection of the sort. We have affairs in different places; and hence railways were invented. Railways separated us infallibly from our friends; and so telegraphs were made that we might communicate speedily at great distances. Even in hotels we have lifts to spare us a climb of some hundred steps. Now, we know that life is only a stage to play the fool upon as long as the part amuses us. There was one more convenience lacking to modern comfort; a decent, easy way to quit that stage; the back stairs to liberty; or, as I said this moment, Death's private door. This, my two fellow rebels, is supplied by the Suicide Club. Do not suppose that you and I are alone, or even exceptional, in the highly reasonable desire that we profess. A large number of our fellowmen, who have grown heartily sick of the performance in which they are expected to join daily and all their lives long, are only kept from flight by one or two considerations. Some have families who would be shocked, or even blamed, if the matter became public; others have a weakness at heart and recoil from the circumstances of death. That is, to some extent, my own experience. I cannot put a pistol to my head and draw the trigger; for something stronger than myself withholds the act; and although I loathe life, I have not strength enough in my body to take hold of death and be done with it. For such as I, and for all who desire to be out of the coil without posthumous scandal, the Suicide Club has been inaugurated. How this has been managed, what is its history, or what may be its ramifications in other lands, I am myself uninformed; and what I know of its constitution, I am not at liberty to communicate to you. To this extent, however, I am at your service. If you are truly tired of life, I will introduce you tonight to a meeting; and if not to-night, at least some time within the week, you will be easily relieved of your existences. It is now (consulting his watch) eleven; by half-past, at latest, we must leave this place; so that you have half an hour before you to consider my proposal. It is more serious than a cream tart," he added, with a smile; "and I suspect more palatable."

"More serious, certainly," returned Colonel Geraldine; "and as it is so much more so, will you allow me five minutes' speech in private with my friend, Mr. Godall?"

"It is only fair," answered the young man. "If you will permit, I will retire."

"You will be very obliging," said the Colonel.

As soon as the two were alone—"What," said Prince Florizel, "is the use of this confabulation, Geraldine? I see you are flurried, whereas my mind is very tranquilly made up. I will see the end of this."

"Your Highness," said the Colonel turning pale; "let me ask you to consider the importance of your life, not only to your friends, but to the public interest. 'If not to-night,' said this madman; but supposing that to-night some irreparable disaster were to overtake your Highness's person, what, let me ask you, what would be my despair, and what the concern and disaster of a great nation?"

"I will see the end of this," repeated the Prince in his most deliberate tones; "and have the kindness, Colonel Geraldine, to remember and respect your word of honour as a gentleman. Under no circumstances, recollect, nor without my special authority, are you to betray the incognito under which I choose to go abroad. These were my commands, which I now reiterate. And now," he added, "let me ask you to call for the bill."

Colonel Geraldine bowed in submission; but he had a very white face as he summoned the young man of the cream tarts, and issued his directions to the waiter. The Prince preserved his undisturbed demeanour, and described a Palais Royal farce to the young suicide with great humour and gusto. He avoided the Colonel's appealing looks without ostentation, and selected another cheroot with more than usual care. Indeed, he was now the only man of the party who kept any command over his nerves.

The bill was discharged, the Prince giving the whole change of the note to the astonished waiter; and the three drove off in a four-wheeler. They were not long upon the way before the cab stopped at the entrance to a rather dark court. Here all descended.

After Geraldine had paid the fare, the young man turned, and addressed Prince Florizel as follows:

"It is still time, Mr. Godall, to make good your escape into thraldom. And for you too, Major Hammersmith. Reflect well before you take another step; and if your hearts say no—here are the crossroads."

"Lead on, sir," said the Prince. "I am not the man to go back from a thing once said."

"Your coolness does me good," replied their guide. "I have never seen anyone so unmoved at this conjuncture; and yet you are not the first whom I have escorted to this door. More than one of my friends has preceded me, where I knew I must shortly follow. But this is of no interest to you. Wait me here for only a few moments; I shall return as soon as I have arranged the preliminaries of your introduction."

And with that the young man, waving his hand to his companions, turned into the court, entered a doorway and disappeared.

"Of all our follies," said Colonel Geraldine in a low voice, "this is the wildest and most dangerous."

"I perfectly believe so," returned the Prince.

"We have still," pursued the Colonel, "a moment to ourselves. Let me beseech your Highness to profit by the opportunity and retire. The consequences of this step are so dark, and may be so grave, that I feel myself justified in pushing a little farther than usual the liberty which your Highness is so condescending as to allow me in private."

"Am I to understand that Colonel Geraldine is afraid?" asked his Highness, taking his cheroot from his lips, and looking keenly into the other's face.

"My fear is certainly not personal," replied the other proudly; "of that your Highness may rest well assured."

"I had supposed as much," returned the Prince, with undisturbed good humour; "but I was unwilling to remind you of the difference in our stations. No more—no more," he added, seeing Geraldine about to apologise, "you stand excused."

And he smoked placidly, leaning against a railing, until the young man returned.

"Well," he asked, "has our reception been arranged?"

"Follow me," was the reply. "The President will see you in the cabinet. And let me warn you to be frank in your answers. I have stood your guarantee; but the club requires a searching inquiry before admission; for the indiscretion of a single member would lead to the dispersion of the whole society for ever."

The Prince and Geraldine put their heads together for a moment. "Bear me out in this," said the one; and "bear me out in that," said the other; and by boldly taking up the characters of men with whom both were acquainted, they had come to an agreement in a twinkling, and were ready to follow their guide into the President's cabinet.

There were no formidable obstacles to pass. The outer door stood open; the door of the cabinet was ajar; and there, in a small but very high apartment, the young man left them once more.

"He will be here immediately," he said with a nod, as he disappeared.

Voices were audible in the cabinet through the folding doors which formed one end; and now and then the noise of a champagne cork, followed by a burst of laughter, intervened among the sounds of conversation. A single tall window looked out upon the river and the embankment; and by the disposition of the lights they judged themselves not far from Charing Cross station. The furniture was scanty, and the coverings worn to the thread; and there was nothing movable except a handbell in the centre of a round table, and the hats and coats of a considerable party hung round the wall on pegs.

"What sort of a den is this?" said Geraldine.

"That is what I have come to see," replied the Prince. "If they keep live devils on the premises, the thing may grow amusing."

Just then the folding door was opened no more than was necessary for the passage of a human body; and there entered at the same moment a louder buzz of talk, and the redoubtable President of the Suicide Club. The President was a man of fifty or upwards; large and rambling in his gait, with shaggy side whiskers, a bald top to his head, and a veiled grey eye, which now and then emitted a twinkle. His mouth, which embraced a large cigar, he kept continually screwing round and round and from side to side, as he looked sagaciously and coldly at the strangers. He was dressed in light tweeds, with his neck very open in a striped shirt collar; and carried a minute book under one arm.

"Good evening," said he, after he had closed the door behind him. "I am told you wish to speak with me."

"We have a desire, sir, to join the Suicide Club," replied the Colonel.

The President rolled his cigar about in his mouth.

"What is that?" he said abruptly.

"Pardon me," returned the Colonel, "but I believe you are the person best qualified to give us information on that point."

"I?" cried the President. "A Suicide Club? Come, come! this is a frolic for All Fools'-Day. I can make allowances for gentlemen who get merry in their liquor, but let there be an end to this."

"Call your Club what you will," said the Colonel, "you have some company behind these doors, and we insist on joining it."

"Sir," returned the President, curtly, "you have made a mistake. This is a private house, and you must leave it instantly."

The Prince had remained quietly in his seat throughout this little colloquy; but now, when the Colonel looked over to him, as much as to say, "Take your answer and come away, for God's sake!" he drew his cheroot from his mouth, and spoke—

"I have come here," said he, "upon the invitation of a friend of yours. He has doubtless informed you of my intention in thus intruding on your party. Let me remind you that a person in my circumstances has exceedingly little to bind him, and is not at all likely to tolerate much rudeness. I am a very quiet man, as a usual thing; but, my dear sir, you are either going to oblige me in the little matter of which you are aware, or you shall very bitterly repent that you ever admitted me to your antechamber."

The President laughed aloud.

"That is the way to speak," said he. "You are a man who is a man. You know the way to my heart, and can do what you like with me. Will you," he continued, addressing Geraldine, "will you step aside for a few minutes? I shall finish first with your companion, and some of the club's formalities require to be fulfilled in private."

With these words he opened the door of a small closet, into which he shut the colonel.

"I believe in you," he said to Florizel, as soon as they were alone; "but are you sure of your friend?"

"Not so sure as I am of myself, though he has more cogent reasons," answered Florizel, "but sure enough to bring him here without alarm. He has had enough to cure the most tenacious man of life. He was cashiered the other day for cheating at cards."

"A good reason, I daresay," replied the President; "at least, we have another in the same case, and I feel sure of him. Have you also been in the Service, may I ask?"

"I have," was the reply; "but I was too lazy, I left it early."

"What is your reason for being tired of life?" pursued the President.

"The same, as near as I can make out," answered the Prince; "unadulterated laziness."

The President started. "D—n it," said he, "you must have something better than that."

"I have no more money," added Florizel. "That is also a vexation, without doubt. It brings my sense of idleness to an acute point."

The President rolled his cigar round in his mouth for some seconds, directing his gaze straight into the eyes of this unusual neophyte; but the Prince supported his scrutiny with unabashed good temper.

"If I had not a deal of experience," said the President at last, "I should turn you off. But I know the world; and this much any way, that the most frivolous excuses for a suicide are often the toughest to stand by. And when I downright like a man, as I do you, sir, I would rather strain the regulation than deny him."

The Prince and the Colonel, one after the other, were subjected to a long and particular interrogatory: the Prince alone; but Geraldine in the presence of the Prince, so that the President might observe the countenance of the one while the other was being warmly cross-examined. The result was satisfactory; and the President, after having booked a few details of each case, produced a form of oath to be accepted. Nothing could be conceived more passive than the obedience promised, or more stringent than the terms by which the juror bound himself. The man who forfeited a pledge so awful could scarcely have a rag of honour or any of the consolations of religion left to him. Florizel signed the document, but not without a shudder; the Colonel followed his example with an air of great depression. Then the President received the entry money; and without more ado, introduced the two friends into the smoking-room of the Suicide Club.

The smoking room of the Suicide Club was the same height as the cabinet into which it opened, but much larger, and papered from top to bottom with an imitation of oak wainscot. A large and cheerful fire and a number of gas jets illuminated the company. The Prince and his follower made the number up to eighteen. Most of the party were smoking, and drinking champagne; a feverish hilarity reigned, with sudden and rather ghastly pauses.

"Is this a full meeting?" asked the Prince.

"Middling," said the President. "By the way," he added, "if you have any money, it is usual to offer some champagne. It keeps up a good spirit, and is one of my own little perquisites."

"Hammersmith," said Florizel, "I may leave the champagne to you."

And with that he turned away and began to go round among the guests. Accustomed to play the host in the highest circles, he charmed and dominated all whom he approached; there was something at once winning and authoritative in his address; and his extraordinary coolness gave him yet another distinction in this half maniacal society. As he went from one to another he kept both his eyes and ears open, and soon began to gain a general idea of the people among whom he found himself. As in all other places of resort, one type predominated: people in the prime of youth, with every show of intelligence and sensibility in their appearance, but with little promise of strength or the quality that makes success. Few were much above thirty, and not a few were still in their teens. They stood, leaning on tables and shifting on their feet; sometimes they smoked extraordinarily fast, and sometimes they let their cigars go out; some talked well, but the conversation of others was plainly the result of nervous tension, and was equally without wit or purport. As each new bottle of champagne was opened, there was a manifest improvement in gaiety. Only two were seated—one in a chair in the recess of the window, with his head hanging and his hands plunged deep into his trouser pockets, pale, visibly moist with perspiration, saying never a word, a very wreck of soul and body; the other sat on the divan close by the chimney, and attracted notice by a trenchant dissimilarity from all the rest. He was probably upwards of forty, but he looked fully ten years older; and Florizel thought he had never seen a man more naturally hideous, nor one more ravaged by disease and ruinous excitements. He was no more than skin and bone, was partly paralysed, and wore spectacles of such unusual power, that his eyes appeared through the glasses greatly magnified and distorted in shape. Except the Prince and the President, he was the only person in the room who preserved the composure of ordinary life.

There was little decency among the members of the club. Some boasted of the disgraceful actions, the consequences of which had reduced them to seek refuge in death; and the others listened without disapproval. There was a tacit understanding against moral judgments; and whoever passed the club doors enjoyed already some of the immunities of the tomb. They drank to each other's memories, and to those of notable suicides in the past. They compared and developed their different views of death—some declaring that it was no more than blackness and cessation; others full of a hope that that very night they should be scaling the stars and commercing with the mighty dead.

"To the eternal memory of Baron Trenck, the type of suicides!" cried one. "He went out of a small cell into a smaller, that he might come forth again to freedom."

"For my part," said a second, "I wish no more than a bandage for my eyes and cotton for my ears. Only they have no cotton thick enough in this world."

A third was for reading the mysteries of life in a future state; and a fourth professed that he would never have joined the club, if he had not been induced to believe in Mr. Darwin.

"I could not bear," said this remarkable suicide, "to be descended from an ape."

Altogether, the Prince was disappointed by the bearing and conversation of the members.

"It does not seem to me," he thought, "a matter for so much disturbance. If a man has made up his mind to kill himself, let him do it, in God's name, like a gentleman. This flutter and big talk is out of place."

In the meanwhile Colonel Geraldine was a prey to the blackest apprehensions; the club and its rules were still a mystery, and he looked round the room for some one who should be able to set his mind at rest. In this survey his eye lighted on the paralytic person with the strong spectacles; and seeing him so exceedingly tranquil, he besought the President, who was going in and out of the room under a pressure of business, to present him to the gentleman on the divan.

The functionary explained the needlessness of all such formalities within the club, but nevertheless presented Mr. Hammersmith to Mr. Malthus.

Mr. Malthus looked at the Colonel curiously, and then requested him to take a seat upon his right.

"You are a new comer," he said, "and wish information? You have come to the proper source. It is two years since I first visited this charming club."

The Colonel breathed again. If Mr. Malthus had frequented the place for two years there could be little danger for the Prince in a single evening. But Geraldine was none the less astonished, and began to suspect a mystification.

"What!" cried he, "two years! I thought—but indeed I see I have been made the subject of a pleasantry."

"By no means," replied Mr. Malthus mildly. "My case is peculiar. I am not, properly speaking, a suicide at all; but, as it were, an honorary member. I rarely visit the club twice in two months. My infirmity and the kindness of the President have procured me these little immunities, for which besides I pay at an advanced rate. Even as it is my luck has been extraordinary."

"I am afraid," said the Colonel, "that I must ask you to be more explicit. You must remember that I am still most imperfectly acquainted with the rules of the club."

"An ordinary member who comes here in search of death like yourself," replied the paralytic, "returns every evening until fortune favours him. He can even, if he is penniless, get board and lodging from the President: very fair, I believe, and clean, although, of course, not luxurious; that could hardly be, considering the exiguity (if I may so express myself) of the subscription. And then the President's company is a delicacy in itself."

"Indeed!" cried Geraldine, "he had not greatly prepossessed me."

"Ah!" said Mr. Malthus, "you do not know the man: the drollest fellow! What stories! What cynicism! He knows life to admiration and, between ourselves, is probably the most corrupt rogue in Christendom."

"And he also," asked the Colonel, "is a permanency—like yourself, if I may say so without offence?"

"Indeed, he is a permanency in a very different sense from me," replied Mr. Malthus. "I have been graciously spared, but I must go at last. Now he never plays. He shuffles and deals for the club, and makes the necessary arrangements. That man, my dear Mr. Hammersmith, is the very soul of ingenuity. For three years he has pursued in London his useful and, I think I may add, his artistic calling; and not so much as a whisper of suspicion has been once aroused. I believe him myself to be inspired. You doubtless remember the celebrated case, six months ago, of the gentleman who was accidentally poisoned in a chemist's shop? That was one of the least rich, one of the least racy, of his notions; but then, how simple! and how safe!"

"You astound me," said the Colonel. "Was that unfortunate gentleman one of the——" He was about to say "victims;" but bethinking himself in time, he substituted—"members of the club?"

In the same flash of thought, it occurred to him that Mr. Malthus himself had not at all spoken in the tone of one who is in love with death; and he added hurriedly:

"But I perceive I am still in the dark. You speak of shuffling and dealing; pray for what end? And since you seem rather unwilling to die than otherwise, I must own that I cannot conceive what brings you here at all."

"You say truly that you are in the dark," replied Mr. Malthus with more animation. "Why, my dear sir, this club is the temple of intoxication. If my enfeebled health could support the excitement more often, you may depend upon it I should be more often here. It requires all the sense of duty engendered by a long habit of ill-health and careful regimen, to keep me from excess in this, which is, I may say, my last dissipation. I have tried them all, sir," he went on, laying his hand on Geraldine's arm, "all without exception, and I declare to you, upon my honour, there is not one of them that has not been grossly and untruthfully overrated. People trifle with love. Now, I deny that love is a strong passion. Fear is the strong passion; it is with fear that you must trifle, if you wish to taste the intensest joys of living. Envy me—envy me, sir," he added with a chuckle, "I am a coward!"

Geraldine could scarcely repress a movement of repulsion for this deplorable wretch; but he commanded himself with an effort, and continued his inquiries.

"How, sir," he asked, "is the excitement so artfully prolonged? and where is there any element of uncertainty?"

"I must tell you how the victim for every evening is selected," returned Mr. Malthus; "and not only the victim, but another member, who is to be the instrument in the club's hands, and death's high priest for that occasion."

"Good God!" said the Colonel, "do they then kill each other?"

"The trouble of suicide is removed in that way," returned Malthus with a nod.

"Merciful Heavens!" ejaculated the Colonel, "and may you—may I—may the—my friend I mean—may any of us be pitched upon this evening as the slayer of another man's body and immortal spirit? Can such things be possible among men born of women? Oh! infamy of infamies!"

He was about to rise in his horror, when he caught the Prince's eye. It was fixed upon him from across the room with a frowning and angry stare. And in a moment Geraldine recovered his composure.

"After all," he added, "why not? And since you say the game is interesting, *vogue la galère*—I follow the club!"

Mr. Malthus had keenly enjoyed the Colonel's amazement and disgust. He had the vanity of wickedness; and it pleased him to see another man give way to a generous movement, while he felt himself, in his entire corruption, superior to such emotions.

"You now, after your first moment of surprise," said he, "are in a position to appreciate the delights of our society. You can see how it combines the excitement of a gaming table, a duel, and a Roman amphitheatre. The Pagans did well enough; I cordially admire the refinement of their minds; but it has been reserved for a Christian country to attain this extreme, this quintessence, this absolute of poignancy. You will understand how vapid are all amusements to a man who has acquired a taste for this one. The game we play," he continued, "is one of extreme simplicity. A full pack—but I perceive you are about to see the thing in progress. Will you lend me the help of your arm? I am unfortunately paralysed."

Indeed, just as Mr. Malthus was beginning his description, another pair of folding-doors was thrown open, and the whole club began to pass, not without some hurry, into the adjoining room. It was similar in every respect to the one from which it was entered, but somewhat differently furnished. The centre was occupied by a long green table, at which the President sat shuffling a pack of cards with great particularity. Even with the stick and the Colonel's arm, Mr. Malthus walked with so much difficulty that everyone was seated before this pair and the Prince, who had waited for them, entered the apartment; and, in consequence, the three took seats close together at the lower end of the board.

"It is a pack of fifty-two," whispered Mr. Malthus. "Watch for the ace of spades, which is the sign of death, and the ace of clubs, which designates the official of the night. Happy, happy young men!" he added. "You have good eyes, and can follow the game. Alas! I cannot tell an ace from a deuce across the table."

And he proceeded to equip himself with a second pair of spectacles.

"I must at least watch the faces," he explained.

The Colonel rapidly informed his friend of all that he had learned from the honorary member, and of the horrible alternative that lay before them. The Prince was conscious of a deadly chill and a contraction about his heart; he swallowed with difficulty, and looked from side to side like a man in a maze.

"One bold stroke," whispered the Colonel, "and we may still escape."

But the suggestion recalled the Prince's spirits.

"Silence!" said he. "Let me see that you can play like a gentleman for any stake, however serious."

And he looked about him, once more to all appearance at his ease, although his heart beat thickly, and he was conscious of an unpleasant heat in his bosom. The members were all very quiet and intent; everyone was pale, but none so pale as Mr. Malthus. His eyes protruded; his head kept nodding involuntarily upon his spine; his hands found their way, one after the other, to his mouth, where they made clutches at his tremulous and ashen lips. It was plain that the honorary member enjoyed his membership on very startling terms.

"Attention, gentlemen!" said the President.

And he began slowly dealing the cards about the table in the reverse direction, pausing until each man had shown his card. Nearly everyone hesitated; and sometimes you would see a player's fingers stumble more than once before he could turn over the momentous slip of pasteboard. As the Prince's turn drew nearer, he was conscious of a growing and almost suffocating excitement; but he had some-what of the gambler's nature, and recognised almost with astonish-ment that there was a degree of pleasure in his sensations. The nine of clubs fell to his lot; the three of spades was dealt to Geraldine; and the queen of hearts to Mr. Malthus, who was unable to suppress a sob of relief. The young man of the cream tarts almost immediately afterwards turned over the ace of clubs, and remained frozen with horror, the card still resting on his finger; he had not come there to kill, but to be killed; and the Prince in his generous sympathy with his position almost forgot the peril that still hung over himself and his friend.

The deal was coming round again, and still Death's card had not come out. The players held their respiration, and only breathed by gasps. The Prince received another club; Geraldine had a diamond; but when Mr. Malthus turned up his card a horrible noise, like that of something breaking, issued from his mouth; and he rose from his seat and sat down again, with no sign of his paralysis. It was the ace of spades. The honorary member had trifled once too often with his terrors.

Conversation broke out again almost at once. The players re-laxed their rigid attitudes, and began to rise from the table and stroll back by twos and threes into the smoking room. The President stretched his arms and yawned, like a man who has finished his day's work. But Mr. Malthus sat in his place, with his head in his hands, and his hands upon the table, drunk and motionless—a thing stricken down.

The Prince and Geraldine made their escape at once. In the

cold night air their horror of what they had witnessed was redoubled.

"Alas!" cried the Prince, "to be bound by an oath in such a matter! to allow this wholesale trade in murder to be continued with profit and impunity! If I but dared to forfeit my pledge!"

"That is impossible for your Highness," replied the Colonel, "whose honour is the honour of Bohemia. But I dare, and may with propriety, forfeit mine."

"Geraldine," said the Prince, "if your honour suffers in any of the adventures into which you follow me, not only will I never pardon you, but—what I believe will much more sensibly affect you—I should never forgive myself."

"I receive your Highness's commands," replied the Colonel. "Shall we go from this accursed spot?"

"Yes," said the Prince. "Call a cab in Heaven's name, and let me try to forget in slumber the memory of this night's disgrace."

But it was notable that he carefully read the name of the court before he left it.

The next morning, as soon as the Prince was stirring, Colonel Geraldine brought him a daily newspaper, with the following paragraph marked:

"MELANCHOLY ACCIDENT—This morning, about two o'clock, Mr. Bartholomew Malthus, of 16, Chepstow Place, Westbourne Grove, on his way home from a party at a friend's house, fell over the upper parapet in Trafalgar Square, fracturing his skull and breaking a leg and an arm. Death was instantaneous. Mr. Malthus, accompanied by a friend, was engaged in looking for a cab at the time of the unfortunate occurrence. As Mr. Malthus was paralytic, it is thought that his fall may have been occasioned by another seizure. The unhappy gentleman was well known in the most respectable circles, and his loss will be widely and deeply deplored."

"If ever a soul went straight to Hell," said Geraldine solemnly, "it was that paralytic man's."

The Prince buried his face in his hands, and remained silent.

"I am almost rejoiced," continued the Colonel, "to know that he is dead. But for our young man of the cream tarts I confess my heart bleeds."

"Geraldine," said the Prince, raising his face, "that unhappy lad was last night as innocent as you and I; and this morning the guilt of blood is on his soul. When I think of the President, my heart grows sick within me. I do not know how it shall be done, but I shall have that scoundrel at my mercy as there is a God in heaven. What an experience, what a lesson, was that game of cards!"

"One," said the Colonel, "never to be repeated."

The Prince remained so long without replying, that Geraldine grew alarmed.

"You cannot mean to return," he said. "You have suffered too much and seen too much horror already. The duties of your high position forbid the repetition of the hazard."

"There is much in what you say," replied Prince Florizel, "and I am not altogether pleased with my own determination. Alas! in the clothes of the greatest potentate, what is there but a man? I never felt my weakness more acutely than now, Geraldine, but it is stronger than I. Can I cease to interest myself in the fortunes of the unhappy young man who supped with us some hours ago? Can I leave the President to follow his nefarious career unwatched? Can I begin an adventure so entrancing, and not follow it to an end? No, Geraldine: you ask of the Prince more than the man is able to perform. To-night, once more, we take our places at the table of the Suicide Club."

Colonel Geraldine fell upon his knees.

"Will your Highness take my life?" he cried. "It is his—his freely; but do not, O do not! let him ask me to countenance so terrible a risk."

"Colonel Geraldine," replied the Prince, with some haughtiness of manner, "your life is absolutely your own. I only looked for obedience; and when that is unwillingly rendered, I shall look for that no longer. I add one word: your importunity in this affair has been sufficient."

The Master of the Horse regained his feet at once.

"Your Highness," he said, "may I be excused in my attendance this afternoon? I dare not, as an honourable man, venture a second time into that fatal house until I have perfectly ordered my affairs.

Your Highness shall meet, I promise him, with no more opposition from the most devoted and grateful of his servants."

"My dear Geraldine," returned Prince Florizel, "I always regret when you oblige me to remember my rank. Dispose of your day as you think fit, but be here before eleven in the same disguise."

The club, on this second evening, was not so fully attended; and when Geraldine and the Prince arrived, there were not above half-a-dozen persons in the smoking-room. His Highness took the President aside and congratulated him warmly on the demise of Mr. Malthus.

"I like," he said, "to meet with capacity, and certainly find much of it in you. Your profession is of a very delicate nature, but I see you are well qualified to conduct it with success and secresy."

The President was somewhat affected by these compliments from one of his Highness's superior bearing. He acknowledged them almost with humility.

"Poor Malthy!" he added, "I shall hardly know the club without him. The most of my patrons are boys, sir, and poetical boys, who are not much company for me. Not but what Malthy had some poetry, too; but it was of a kind that I could understand."

"I can readily imagine you should find yourself in sympathy with Mr. Malthus," returned the Prince. "He struck me as a man of a very original disposition."

The young man of the cream tarts was in the room, but painfully depressed and silent. His late companions sought in vain to lead him into conversation.

"How bitterly I wish," he cried, "that I had never brought you to this infamous abode! Begone, while you are clean-handed. If you could have heard the old man scream as he fell, and the noise of his bones upon the pavement! Wish me, if you have any kindness to so fallen a being—wish the ace of spades for me tonight!"

A few more members dropped in as the evening went on, but the club did not muster more than the devil's dozen when they took their places at the table. The prince was again conscious of a certain joy in his alarms; but he was astonished to see Geraldine so much more self-possessed than on the night before.

"It is extraordinary," thought the Prince, "that a will, made or unmade, should so greatly influence a young man's spirit."

"Attention, gentlemen!" said the President, and he began to deal.

Three times the cards went all round the table, and neither of the marked cards had yet fallen from his hand. The excitement as he began the fourth distribution was overwhelming. There were just cards enough to go once more entirely round. The Prince, who sat second from the dealer's left, would receive, in the reverse mode of dealing practised at the club, the second last card. The third player turned up a black ace—it was the ace of clubs. The next received a diamond, the next a heart, and so on; but the ace of spades was still undelivered. At last Geraldine, who sat upon the Prince's left, turned his card; it was an ace, but the ace of hearts.

When Prince Florizel saw his fate upon the table in front of him, his heart stood still. He was a brave man, but the sweat poured off his face. There were exactly fifty chances out of a hundred that he was doomed. He reversed the card; it was the ace of spades. A loud roaring filled his brain, and the table swam before his eyes. He heard the player on his right break into a fit of laughter that sounded between mirth and disappointment; he saw the company rapidly dispersing, but his mind was full of other thoughts. He recognised how foolish, how criminal, had been his conduct. In perfect health, in the prime of his years, the heir to a throne, he had gambled away his future and that of a brave and loyal country. "God," he cried, "God forgive me!" And with that, the confusion of his senses passed away, and he regained his self-possession in a moment.

To his surprise Geraldine had disappeared. There was no one in the cardroom but his destined butcher consulting with the President, and the young man of the cream tarts, who slipped up to the Prince and whispered in his ear:

"I would give a million, if I had it, for your luck."

His Highness could not help reflecting, as the young man departed, that he would have sold his opportunity for a much more moderate sum.

The whispered conference now came to an end. The holder of the ace of clubs left the room with a look of intelligence, and the

President, approaching the unfortunate Prince, proffered him his hand.

"I am pleased to have met you, sir," said he, "and pleased to have been in a position to do you this trifling service. At least, you cannot complain of delay. On the second evening—what a stroke of luck!"

The Prince endeavoured in vain to articulate something in response, but his mouth was dry and his tongue seemed paralysed.

"You feel a little sickish?" asked the President, with some show of solicitude. "Most gentlemen do. Will you take a little brandy?"

The Prince signified in the affirmative, and the other immediately filled some of the spirit into a tumbler.

"Poor old Malthy!" ejaculated the President, as the Prince drained the glass. "He drank near upon a pint, and little enough good it seemed to do him!"

"I am more amenable to treatment," said the Prince, a good deal revived. "I am my own man again at once, as you perceive. And so, let me ask you, what are my directions?"

"You will proceed along the Strand in the direction of the City, and on the left-hand pavement, until you meet the gentleman who has just left the room. He will continue your instructions, and him you will have the kindness to obey; the authority of the club is vested in his person for the night. And now," added the President, "I wish you a pleasant walk."

Florizel acknowledged the salutation rather awkwardly, and took his leave. He passed through the smoking room, where the bulk of the players were still consuming champagne, some of which he had himself ordered and paid for; and he was surprised to find himself cursing them in his heart. He put on his hat and greatcoat in the cabinet, and selected his umbrella from a corner. The familiarity of these acts, and the thought that he was about them for the last time, betrayed him into a fit of laughter which sounded unpleasantly in his own ears. He conceived a reluctance to leave the cabinet, and turned instead to the window. The sight of the lamps and the darkness recalled him to himself.

"Come, come, I must be a man," he thought, "and tear myself away."

At the corner of Box Court three men fell upon Prince Florizel and he was unceremoniously thrust into a carriage, which at once drove rapidly away. There was already an occupant.

"Will your Highness pardon my zeal?" said a well-known voice.

The Prince threw himself upon the Colonel's neck in a passion of relief.

"How can I ever thank you?" he cried. "And how was this effected?"

Although he had been willing to march upon his doom, he was overjoyed to yield to friendly violence, and return once more to life and hope.

"You can thank me effectually enough," replied the Colonel, "by avoiding all such dangers in the future. And as for your second question, all has been managed by the simplest means. I arranged this afternoon with a celebrated detective. Secrecy has been promised and paid for. Your own servants have been principally engaged in the affair. The house in Box Court has been surrounded since nightfall, and this, which is one of your own carriages, has been awaiting you for nearly an hour."

"And the miserable creature who was to have slain me—what of him?" inquired the Prince.

"He was pinioned as he left the club," replied the Colonel, "and now awaits your sentence at the Palace, where he will soon be joined by his accomplices."

"Geraldine," said the Prince, "you have saved me against my explicit orders, and you have done well. I owe you not only my life, but a lesson; and I should be unworthy of my rank if I did not show myself grateful to my teacher. Let it be yours to choose the manner."

There was a pause, during which the carriage continued to speed through the streets, and the two men were each buried in his own reflections. The silence was broken by Colonel Geraldine.

"Your Highness," said he, "has by this time a considerable body of prisoners. There is at least one criminal among the number to whom justice should be dealt. Our oath forbids us all recourse to law; and discretion would forbid it equally if the oath were loosened. May I inquire your Highness's intention?"

"It is decided," answered Florizel; "the President must fall in duel. It only remains to choose his adversary."

"Your Highness has permitted me to name my own recompense," said the Colonel. "Will he permit me to ask the appointment of my brother? It is an honourable post, but I dare assure your Highness that the lad will acquit himself with credit."

"You ask me an ungracious favour," said the Prince, "but I must refuse you nothing."

The Colonel kissed his hand with the greatest affection; and at that moment the carriage rolled under the archway of the Prince's splendid residence.

An hour after, Florizel in his official robes, and covered with all the orders of Bohemia, received the members of the Suicide Club.

"Foolish and wicked men," said he, "as many of you as have been driven into this strait by the lack of fortune shall receive employment and remuneration from my officers. Those who suffer under a sense of guilt must have recourse to a higher and more generous Potentate than I. I feel pity for all of you, deeper than you can imagine; tomorrow you shall tell me your stories; and as you answer more frankly, I shall be the more able to remedy your misfortunes. As for you," he added, turning to the President, "I should only offend a person of your parts by any offer of assistance; but I have instead a piece of diversion to propose to you. Here," laying his hand on the shoulder of Colonel Geraldine's young brother, "is an officer of mine who desires to make a little tour upon the Continent; and I ask you, as a favour, to accompany him on this excursion. Do you," he went on, changing his tone, "do you shoot well with the pistol? Because you may have need of that accomplishment. When two men go travelling together, it is best to be prepared for all. Let me add that, if by any chance you should lose young Mr. Geraldine upon the way, I shall always have another member of my household to place at your disposal; and I am known, Mr. President, to have long eyesight, and as long an arm."

With these words, said with much sternness, the Prince concluded his address. Next morning the members of the club were suitably provided for by his munificence, and the President set forth upon his travels, under the supervision of Mr. Geraldine, and a pair of faithful and adroit lackeys, well trained in the Prince's household. Not content with this, discreet agents were put in possession of the house in Box Court, and all letters or visitors for the Suicide Club or its officials were to be examined by Prince Florizel in person.

Here (says my Arabian author) *ends* THE STORY OF THE YOUNG MAN WITH THE CREAM TARTS, *who is now a comfortable householder in Wigmore Street, Cavendish Square. The number, for obvious reasons, I suppress. Those who care to pursue the adventures of Prince Florizel and the President of the Suicide Club, may read the* HISTORY OF THE PHYSICIAN AND THE SARATOGA TRUNK.

Story of the Physician and the Saratoga Trunk

Mr. Silas Q. Scuddamore was a young American of a simple and harmless disposition, which was the more to his credit as he came from New England—a quarter of the New World not precisely famous for those qualities. Although he was exceedingly rich, he kept a note of all his expenses in a little paper pocketbook; and he had chosen to study the attractions of Paris from the seventh story of what is called a furnished hotel, in the Latin Quarter. There was a great deal of habit in his penuriousness; and his virtue, which was very remarkable among his associates, was principally founded upon diffidence and youth.

The next room to his was inhabited by a lady, very attractive in her air and very elegant in toilette, whom, on his first arrival, he had taken for a Countess. In course of time he had learned that she was known by the name of Madame Zéphyrine, and that whatever station she occupied in life it was not that of a person of title. Madame Zéphyrine, probably in the hope of enchanting the young American, used to flaunt by him on the stairs with a civil inclination, a word of course, and a knock-down look out of her black eyes, and disappear in a rustle of silk, and with the revelation of an admirable foot and ankle. But these advances, so far from encouraging Mr. Scuddamore, plunged him into the depths of depression and bashfulness. She had come to him several times for a light, or to apologise for the imaginary depredations of her poodle; but his mouth was closed in the presence of so superior a being, his French promptly left him, and he could only stare and stammer until she was gone. The slenderness of their intercourse did not prevent him from throwing out insinuations of a very glorious order when he was safely alone with a few males.

The room on the other side of the American's—for there were three rooms on a floor in the hotel—was tenanted by an old English physician of rather doubtful reputation. Dr. Noel, for that was his name, had been forced to leave London, where he enjoyed a large and increasing practice; and it was hinted that the police had been the instigators of this change of scene. At least he, who had made something of a figure in earlier life, now dwelt in the Latin Quarter in great simplicity and solitude, and devoted much of his time to study. Mr. Scuddamore had made his acquaintance, and the pair would now and then dine together frugally in a restaurant across the street.

Silas Q. Scuddamore had many little vices of the more respectable order, and was not restrained by delicacy from indulging them in many rather doubtful ways. Chief among his foibles stood curiosity. He was a born gossip; and life, and especially those parts of it in which he had no experience, interested him to the degree of passion. He was a pert, invincible questioner, pushing his inquiries with equal pertinacity and indiscretion; he had been observed, when he took a letter to the post, to weigh it in his hand, to turn it over and over, and to study the address with care; and when he found a flaw in the partition between his room and Madame Zéphyrine's, instead of filling it up, he enlarged and improved the opening, and made use of it as a spy-hole on his neighbour's affairs.

One day, in the end of March, his curiosity growing as it was indulged, he enlarged the hole a little further, so that he might command another corner of the room. That evening, when he went as usual to inspect Madame Zéphyrine's movements, he was astonished to find the aperture obscured in an odd manner on the other side, and still more abashed when the obstacle was suddenly withdrawn and a titter of laughter reached his ears. Some of the plaster had evidently betrayed the secret of his spy-hole, and his neighbour had been returning the compliment in kind. Mr. Scuddamore was moved to a very acute feeling of annoyance; he condemned Madame Zéphyrine unmercifully; he even blamed himself; but when he found, next day, that she had taken no means to baulk him of his favourite pastime, he continued to profit by her carelessness, and gratify his idle curiosity.

That next day Madame Zéphyrine received a long visit from a tall, loosely-built man of fifty or upwards, whom Silas had not hitherto seen. His tweed suit and coloured shirt, no less than his shaggy side whiskers, identified him as a Britisher, and his dull grey eye affected Silas with a sense of cold. He kept screwing his mouth from side to side and round and round during the whole colloquy, which was carried on in whispers. More than once it seemed to the young New Englander as if their gestures indicated his own apartment; but the only thing definite he could gather by the most scrupulous attention was this remark made by the Englishman in a somewhat higher key, as if in answer to some reluctance or opposition.

"I have studied his taste to a nicety, and I tell you again and again you are the only woman of the sort that I can lay my hands on."

In answer to this, Madame Zéphyrine sighed, and appeared by a gesture to resign herself, like one yielding to unqualified authority.

That afternoon the observatory was finally blinded, a wardrobe having been drawn in front of it upon the other side; and while Silas was still lamenting over this misfortune, which he attributed to the Britisher's malign suggestion, the concierge brought him up a letter in a female handwriting. It was conceived in French of no very rigorous orthography, bore no signature, and in the most encouraging terms invited the young American to be present in a certain part of the Bullier Ball at eleven o'clock that night. Curiosity and timidity fought a long battle in his heart; sometimes he was all virtue, sometimes all fire and daring; and the result of it was that, long before ten, Mr. Silas Q. Scuddamore presented himself in unimpeachable attire at the door of the Bullier Ball Rooms, and paid his entry money with a sense of reckless deviltry that was not without its charm.

It was Carnival time, and the Ball was very full and noisy. The lights and the crowd at first rather abashed our young adventurer, and then, mounting to his brain with a sort of intoxication, put him in possession of more than his own share of manhood. He felt ready to face the devil, and strutted in the ballroom with the swagger of a cavalier. While he was thus parading, he became aware of Madame Zéphyrine and her Britisher in conference behind a pillar. The cat-like spirit of eavesdropping overcame him at once. He stole nearer and nearer on the couple from behind, until he was within earshot.

"That is the man," the Britisher was saying; "there—with the long blond hair—speaking to a girl in green."

Silas identified a very handsome young fellow of small stature, who was plainly the object of this designation.

"It is well," said Madame Zéphyrine. "I shall do my utmost. But, remember, the best of us may fail in such a matter."

"Tut!" returned her companion; "I answer for the result. Have I not chosen you from thirty? Go; but be wary of the Prince. I cannot think what cursed accident has brought him here tonight. As if there were not a dozen balls in Paris better worth his notice than this riot of students and counterjumpers! See him where he sits, more like a reigning Emperor at home than a Prince upon his holidays!"

Silas was again lucky. He observed a person of rather a full build, strikingly handsome, and of a very stately and courteous demeanour, seated at table with another handsome young man, several years his junior, who addressed him with conspicuous deference. The name of Prince struck gratefully on Silas's Republican hearing, and the aspect of the person to whom that name was applied exercised its usual charm upon his mind. He left Madame Zéphyrine and her English-man to take care of each other, and threading his way through the assembly, approached the table which the Prince and his confidant had honoured with their choice.

"I tell you, Geraldine," the former was saying, "the action is madness. Yourself (I am glad to remember it) chose your brother for this perilous service, and you are bound in duty to have a guard upon his conduct. He has consented to delay so many days in Paris; that was already an imprudence, considering the character of the man he has to deal with; but now, when he is within eight-and-forty hours of his departure, when he is within two or three days of the decisive trial, I ask you, is this a place for him to spend his time? He should be in a gallery at practice; he should be sleeping long hours and taking moderate exercise on foot; he should be on a rigorous diet, without white wines or brandy. Does the dog imagine we are all playing comedy? The thing is deadly earnest, Geraldine."

"I know the lad too well to interfere," replied Colonel Geraldine, "and well enough not to be alarmed. He is more cautious than you fancy, and of an indomitable spirit. If it had been a woman I should not say so much, but I trust the President to him and the two valets without an instant's apprehension."

"I am gratified to hear you say so," replied the Prince; "but my mind is not at rest. These servants are well-trained spies, and already has not this miscreant succeeded three times in eluding their observation and spending several hours on end in private, and most likely dangerous affairs? An amateur might have lost him by accident, but if Rudolph and Jérome were thrown off the scent, it must have been done on purpose, and by a man who had a cogent reason and exceptional resources."

"I believe the question is now one between my brother and myself," replied Geraldine, with a shade of offence in his tone.

"I permit it to be so, Colonel Geraldine," returned Prince Florizel. "Perhaps, for that very reason, you should be all the more ready to accept my counsels. But enough. That girl in yellow dances well."

And the talk veered into the ordinary topics of a Paris ballroom in the Carnival.

Silas remembered where he was, and that the hour was already near at hand when he ought to be upon the scene of his assignation. The more he reflected the less he liked the prospect, and as at that moment an eddy in the crowd began to draw him in the direction of the door, he suffered it to carry him away without resistance. The eddy stranded him in a corner under the gallery, where his ear was immediately struck with the voice of Madame Zéphyrine. She was speaking in French with the young man of the blond locks who had been pointed out by the strange Britisher not half an hour before.

"I have a character at stake," she said, "or I would put no other condition than my heart recommends. But you have only to say so much to the porter, and he will let you go by without a word."

"But why this talk of debt?" objected her companion.

"Heavens!" said she, "do you think I do not understand my own hotel?"

And she went by, clinging affectionately to her companion's arm.

This put Silas in mind of his billet.

"Ten minutes hence," thought he, "and I may be walking with as beautiful a woman as that, and even better dressed—perhaps a real lady, possibly a woman of title."

And then he remembered the spelling, and was a little downcast.

"But it may have been written by her maid," he imagined.

The clock was only a few minutes from the hour, and this immediate proximity set his heart beating at a curious and rather disagreeable speed. He reflected with relief that he was in no way bound to put in an appearance. Virtue and cowardice were together, and he made once more for the door, but this time of his own accord, and battling against the stream of people which was now moving in a contrary direction. Perhaps this prolonged resistance wearied him, or perhaps he was in that frame of mind when merely to continue in the same determination for a certain number of minutes produces a reaction and a different purpose. Certainly, at least, he wheeled about for a third time, and did not stop until he had found a place of concealment within a few yards of the appointed place.

Here he went through an agony of spirit, in which he several times prayed to God for help, for Silas had been devoutly educated. He had now not the least inclination for the meeting; nothing kept him from flight but a silly fear lest he should be thought unmanly; but this was so powerful that it kept head against all other motives; and although it could not decide him to advance, prevented him from definitely running away. At last the clock indicated ten minutes past the hour. Young Scuddamore's spirit began to rise; he peered round the corner and saw no one at the place of meeting; doubtless his unknown correspondent had wearied and gone away. He became as bold as he had formerly been timid. It seemed to him that if he came at all to the appointment, however late, he was clear from the charge of cowardice. Nay, now he began to suspect a hoax, and actually complimented himself on his shrewdness in having suspected and outmanoeuvered his mystifiers. So very idle a thing is a boy's mind!

Armed with these reflections, he advanced boldly from his corner; but he had not taken above a couple of steps before a hand was laid upon his arm. He turned and beheld a lady cast in a very large mould and with somewhat stately features, but bearing no mark of severity in her looks.

"I see that you are a very self-confident lady-killer," said she; "for you make yourself expected. But I was determined to meet you. When a woman has once so far forgotten herself as to make the first advance, she has long ago left behind her all considerations of petty pride."

Silas was overwhelmed by the size and attractions of his correspondent and the suddenness with which she had fallen upon him. But she soon set him at his ease. She was very towardly and lenient in her behaviour; she led him on to make pleasantries, and then applauded him to the echo; and in a very short time, between blandishments and a liberal exhibition of warm brandy, she had not only induced him to fancy himself in love, but to declare his passion with the greatest vehemence.

"Alas!" she said; "I do not know whether I ought not to deplore this moment, great as is the pleasure you give me by your words. Hitherto I was alone to suffer; now, poor boy, there will be two. I am not my own mistress. I dare not ask you to visit me at my own house, for I am watched by jealous eyes. Let me see," she added; "I am older than you, although so much weaker; and while I trust in your courage and determination, I must employ my own knowledge of the world for our mutual benefit. Where do you live?"

He told her that he lodged in a furnished hotel, and named the street and number.

She seemed to reflect for some minutes, with an effort of mind.

"I see," she said at last. "You will be faithful and obedient, will you not?"

Silas assured her eagerly of his fidelity.

"Tomorrow night, then," she continued, with an encouraging smile, "you must remain at home all the evening; and if any friends should visit you, dismiss them at once on any pretext that most readily presents itself. Your door is probably shut by ten?" she asked.

"By eleven," answered Silas.

"At a quarter past eleven," pursued the lady, "leave the house. Merely cry for the door to be opened, and be sure you fall into no talk with the porter, as that might ruin everything. Go straight to the corner where the Luxembourg Gardens join the Boulevard; there you will find me waiting you. I trust you to follow my advice from point to point: and remember, if you fail me in only one particular, you will bring the sharpest trouble on a woman whose only fault is to have seen and loved you."

"I cannot see the use of all these instructions," said Silas.

"I believe you are already beginning to treat me as a master," she cried, tapping him with her fan upon the arm. "Patience, patience! that should come in time. A woman loves to be obeyed at first, although afterwards she finds her pleasure in obeying. Do as I ask you, for Heaven's sake, or I will answer for nothing. Indeed, now I think of it," she added, with the manner of one who has just seen further into a difficulty, "I find a better plan of keeping importunate visitors away. Tell the porter to admit no one for you, except a person who may come that night to claim a debt; and speak with some feeling, as though you feared the interview, so that he may take your words in earnest."

"I think you may trust me to protect myself against intruders," he said, not without a little pique.

"That is how I should prefer the thing arranged," she answered, coldly. "I know you men; you think nothing of a woman's reputation."

Silas blushed and somewhat hung his head; for the scheme he had in view had involved a little vainglorying before his acquaintances.

"Above all," she added, "do not speak to the porter as you come out."

"And why?" said he. "Of all your instructions, that seems to me the least important."

"You at first doubted the wisdom of some of the others, which you now see to be very necessary," she replied. "Believe me, this also has its uses; in time you will see them; and what am I to think of your affection, if you refuse me such trifles at our first interview?"

Silas confounded himself in explanations and apologies; in the middle of these she looked up at the clock and clapped her hands together with a suppressed scream.

"Heavens!" she cried, "is it so late? I have not an instant to lose. Alas, we poor women, what slaves we are! What have I not risked for you already?"

And after repeating her directions, which she artfully combined with caresses and the most abandoned looks, she bade him farewell and disappeared among the crowd.

The whole of the next day Silas was filled with a sense of great importance; he was now sure she was a countess; and when evening came he minutely obeyed her orders and was at the corner of the Luxembourg Gardens by the hour appointed. No one was there. He waited nearly half an hour, looking in the face of everyone who passed or loitered near the spot; he even visited the neighbouring corners of the Boulevard and made a complete circuit of the garden railings; but there was no beautiful countess to throw herself into his arms. At last, and most reluctantly, he began to retrace his steps towards his hotel. On the way he remembered the words he had heard pass between Madame Zéphyrine and the blond young man, and they gave him an indefinite uneasiness.

"It appears," he reflected, "that everyone has to tell lies to our porter."

He rang the bell, the door opened before him, and the porter in his bedclothes came to offer him a light.

"Has he gone?" inquired the porter.

"He? Whom do you mean?" asked Silas, somewhat sharply, for he was irritated by his disappointment.

"I did not notice him go out," continued the porter, "but I trust you paid him. We do not care, in this house, to have lodgers who cannot meet their liabilities."

"What the devil do you mean?" demanded Silas, rudely. "I cannot understand a word of this farrago."

"The short, blond young man who came for his debt," returned the other. "Him it is I mean. Who else should it be, when I had your orders to admit no one else?"

"Why, good God, of course he never came," retorted Silas.

"I believe what I believe," returned the porter, putting his tongue into his cheek with a most roguish air.

"You are an insolent scoundrel," cried Silas, and, feeling that he had made a ridiculous exhibition of asperity, and at the same time bewildered by a dozen alarms, he turned and began to run upstairs.

"Do you not want a light then?" cried the porter.

But Silas only hurried the faster, and did not pause until he had reached the seventh landing and stood in front of his own door. There he waited a moment to recover his breath, assailed by the worst forebodings and almost dreading to enter the room.

When at last he did so he was relieved to find it dark, and to all appearance, untenanted. He drew a long breath. Here he was, home again in safety, and this should be his last folly as certainly as it had been his first. The matches stood on a little table by the bed, and he began to grope his way in that direction. As he moved, his apprehensions grew upon him once more, and he was pleased, when his foot encountered an obstacle, to find it nothing more alarming than a chair. At last he touched curtains. From the position of the window, which was faintly visible, he knew he must be at the foot of the bed, and had only to feel his way along it in order to reach the table in question.

He lowered his hand, but what it touched was not simply a counterpane—it was a counterpane with something underneath it like the outline of a human leg. Silas withdrew his arm and stood a moment petrified.

"What, what," he thought, "can this betoken?"

He listened intently, but there was no sound of breathing. Once more, with a great effort, he reached out the end of his finger to the spot he had already touched; but this time he leaped back half a yard, and stood shivering and fixed with terror. There was something in his bed. What it was he knew not, but there was something there.

It was some seconds before he could move. Then, guided by an instinct, he fell straight upon the matches, and keeping his back towards the bed lighted a candle. As soon as the flame had kindled, he turned slowly round and looked for what he feared to see. Sure enough, there was the worst of his imaginations realised. The coverlid was drawn carefully up over the pillow, but it moulded the outline of a human body lying motionless; and when he dashed forward and flung aside the sheets, he beheld the blond young man whom he had seen in the Bullier Ball the night before, his eyes open and without speculation, his face swollen and blackened, and a thin stream of blood trickling from his nostrils.

Silas uttered a long, tremulous wail, dropped the candle, and fell on his knees beside the bed.

Silas was awakened from the stupor into which his terrible discovery had plunged him, by a prolonged but discreet tapping at the door. It took him some seconds to remember his position; and when he hastened to prevent anyone from entering it was already too late. Dr. Noel, in a tall nightcap, carrying a lamp which lighted up his long white countenance, sidling in his gait, and peering and cocking his head like some sort of bird, pushed the door slowly open, and advanced into the middle of the room.

"I thought I heard a cry," began the Doctor, "and fearing you might be unwell I did not hesitate to offer this intrusion."

Silas, with a flushed face and a fearful beating heart, kept between the Doctor and the bed; but he found no voice to answer.

"You are in the dark," pursued the Doctor; "and yet you have not even begun to prepare for rest. You will not easily persuade me against my own eyesight; and your face declares most eloquently that you require either a friend or a physician—which is it to be? Let me feel your pulse, for that is often a just reporter of the heart."

He advanced to Silas, who still retreated before him backwards, and sought to take him by the wrist; but the strain on the young American's nerves had become too great for endurance. He avoided the Doctor with a febrile movement, and, throwing himself upon the floor, burst into a flood of weeping.

As soon as Dr. Noel perceived the dead man in the bed his face darkened; and hurrying back to the door which he had left ajar, he hastily closed and double-locked it.

"Up!" he cried, addressing Silas in strident tones; "this is no time for weeping. What have you done? How came this body in your room? Speak freely to one who may be helpful. Do you imagine I would ruin you? Do you think this piece of dead flesh on your pillow can alter in any degree the sympathy with which you have inspired me? Credulous youth, the horror with which blind and unjust law regards an action never attaches to the doer in the eyes of those who love him; and if I saw the friend of my heart return to me out of seas of blood he would be in no way changed in my affection. Raise yourself," he said; "good and ill are a chimera; there is nought in life except destiny, and however you may be circumstanced there is one at your side who will help you to the last."

Thus encouraged, Silas gathered himself together, and in a broken voice, and helped out by the Doctor's interrogations, contrived at last to put him in possession of the facts. But the conversation between the Prince and Geraldine he altogether omitted, as he had understood little of its purport, and had no idea that it was in any way related to his own misadventure.

"Alas!" cried Dr. Noel, "I am much abused, or you have fallen innocently into the most dangerous hands in Europe. Poor boy, what a pit has been dug for your simplicity! into what a deadly peril have your unwary feet been conducted! This man," he said, "this Englishman, whom you twice saw, and whom I suspect to be the soul of the contrivance, can you describe him? Was he young or old? tall or short?"

But Silas, who, for all his curiosity, had not a seeing eye in his head, was able to supply nothing but meagre generalities, which it was impossible to recognise.

"I would have it a piece of education in all schools!" cried the Doctor angrily. "Where is the use of eyesight and articulate speech if a man cannot observe and recollect the features of his enemy? I, who know all the gangs of Europe, might have identified him, and gained new weapons for your defence. Cultivate this art in future, my poor boy; you may find it of momentous service."

"The future!" repeated Silas. "What future is there left for me except the gallows?"

"Youth is but a cowardly season," returned the Doctor; "and a man's own troubles look blacker than they are. I am old, and yet I never despair."

"Can I tell such a story to the police?" demanded Silas.

"Assuredly not," replied the Doctor. "From what I see already of the machination in which you have been involved, your case is desperate upon that side; and for the narrow eye of the authorities you are infallibly the guilty person. And remember that we only know a portion of the plot; and the same infamous contrivers have doubtless arranged many other circumstances which would be elicited by a police inquiry, and help to fix the guilt more certainly upon your innocence."

"I am then lost, indeed!" cried Silas.

"I have not said so," answered Dr. Noel, "for I am a cautious man."

"But look at this!" objected Silas, pointing to the body. "Here is this object in my bed: not to be explained, not to be disposed of, not to be regarded without horror."

"Horror?" replied the Doctor. "No. When this sort of clock has run down, it is no more to me than an ingenious piece of mechanism, to be investigated with the bistery. When blood is once cold and stagnant, it is no longer human blood; when flesh is once dead, it is no longer that flesh which we desire in our lovers and respect in our friends. The grace, the attraction, the terror, have all gone from it with the animating spirit. Accustom yourself to look upon it with composure; for if my scheme is practicable you will have to live some days in constant proximity to that which now so greatly horrifies you."

"Your scheme?" cried Silas. "What is that? Tell me speedily, Doctor; for I have scarcely courage enough to continue to exist."

Without replying, Dr. Noel turned towards the bed, and proceeded to examine the corpse.

"Quite dead," he murmured. "Yes, as I had supposed, the pockets empty. Yes, and the name cut off the shirt. Their work has been done thoroughly and well. Fortunately, he is of small stature."

Silas followed these words with an extreme anxiety. At last the Doctor, his autopsy completed, took a chair and addressed the young American with a smile.

"Since I came into your room," said he, "although my ears and my tongue have been so busy, I have not suffered my eyes to remain idle. I noted a little while ago that you have there, in the corner, one of those monstrous constructions which your fellow countrymen carry with them into all quarters of the globe—in a word, a Saratoga trunk. Until this moment I have never been able to conceive the utility of these erections; but then I began to have a glimmer. Whether it was for convenience in the slave trade, or to obviate the results of too ready an employment of the bowie knife, I cannot bring myself to decide. But one thing I see plainly—the object of such a box is to contain a human body."

"Surely," cried Silas, "surely this is not a time for jesting."

"Although I may express myself with some degree of pleasantry," replied the Doctor, "the purport of my words is entirely serious. And the first thing we have to do, my young friend, is to empty your coffer of all that it contains."

Silas, obeying the authority of Doctor Noel, put himself at his disposition. The Saratoga trunk was soon gutted of its contents, which made a considerable litter on the floor; and then—Silas taking the heels and the Doctor supporting the shoulders—the body of the murdered man was carried from the bed, and, after some difficulty, doubled up and inserted whole into the empty box. With an effort on the part of both, the lid was forced down upon this unusual baggage, and the trunk was locked and corded by the Doctor's own hand, while Silas disposed of what had been taken out between the closet and a chest of drawers.

"Now," said the Doctor, "the first step has been taken on the way to your deliverance. Tomorrow, or rather today, it must be your task to allay the suspicions of your porter, paying him all that you owe; while you may trust me to make the arrangements necessary to a safe conclusion. Meantime, follow me to my room, where I shall give you a safe and powerful opiate; for, whatever you do, you must have rest."

The next day was the longest in Silas's memory; it seemed as if it would never be done. He denied himself to his friends, and sat in a corner with his eyes fixed upon the Saratoga trunk in dismal contemplation. His own former indiscretions were now returned upon him in kind; for the observatory had been once more opened, and he was conscious of an almost continual study from Madame Zéphyrine's apartment. So distressing did this become, that he was at last obliged to block up the spy-hole from his own side; and when he was thus secured from observation he spent a considerable portion of his time in contrite tears and prayer.

Late in the evening Dr. Noel entered the room carrying in his hand a pair of sealed envelopes without address, one somewhat bulky, and the other so slim as to seem without enclosure.

"Silas," he said, seating himself at the table, "the time has now come for me to explain my plan for your salvation. Tomorrow morning, at an early hour, Prince Florizel of Bohemia returns to London, after having diverted himself for a few days with the Parisian carnival. It was my fortune, a good while ago, to do Colonel Geraldine, his Master of the Horse, one of those services, so common in my profession, which are never forgotten upon either side. I have no need to explain to you the nature of the obligation under which he was laid; suffice it to say that I knew him ready to serve me in any practicable manner. Now, it was necessary for you to gain London with your trunk unopened. To this the Custom House seemed to oppose a fatal difficulty; but I bethought me that the baggage of so considerable a person as the Prince, is, as a matter of courtesy, passed without examination by the officers of Custom. I applied to Colonel Geraldine, and succeeded in obtaining a favourable answer. Tomorrow, if you go before six to the hotel where the Prince lodges, your baggage will be passed over as a part of his, and you yourself will make the journey as a member of his suite."

"It seems to me, as you speak, that I have already seen both the Prince and Colonel Geraldine; I even overheard some of their conversation the other evening at the Bullier Ball."

"It is probable enough; for the Prince loves to mix with all societies," replied the Doctor. "Once arrived in London," he pursued, "your task is nearly ended. In this more bulky envelope I have given you a letter which I dare not address; but in the other you will find the designation of the house to which you must carry it along with your box, which will there be taken from you and not trouble you any more."

"Alas!" said Silas, "I have every wish to believe you; but how is it possible? You open up to me a bright prospect, but, I ask you, is my mind capable of receiving so unlikely a solution? Be more generous, and let me farther understand your meaning."

The Doctor seemed painfully impressed.

"Boy," he answered, "you do not know how hard a thing you ask of me. But be it so. I am now inured to humiliation; and it would be strange if I refused you this, after having granted you so much. Know, then, that although I now make so quiet an appearance— frugal, solitary, addicted to study—when I was younger, my name was once a rallying cry among the most astute and dangerous spirits of London; and while I was outwardly an object for respect and consideration, my true power resided in the most secret, terrible, and criminal relations. It is to one of the persons who then obeyed me that I now address myself to deliver you from your burden. They were men of many different nations and dexterities, all bound together by a formidable oath, and working to the same purposes; the trade of the association was in murder; and I who speak to you, innocent as I appear, was the chieftain of this redoubtable crew."

"What?" cried Silas. "A murderer? And one with whom murder was a trade? Can I take your hand? Ought I so much as to accept your services? Dark and criminal old man, would you make an accomplice of my youth and my distress?"

The Doctor bitterly laughed.

"You are difficult to please, Mr. Scuddamore," said he; "but I now offer you your choice of company between the murdered man and the murderer. If your conscience is too nice to accept my aid, say so, and I will immediately leave you. Thenceforward you can deal with your trunk and its belongings as best suits your upright conscience."

"I own myself wrong," replied Silas. "I should have remembered how generously you offered to shield me, even before I had convinced you of my innocence, and I continue to listen to your counsels with gratitude."

"That is well," returned the Doctor; "and I perceive you are beginning to learn some of the lessons of experience."

"At the same time," resumed the New Englander, "as you confess yourself accustomed to this tragical business, and the people to whom you recommend me are your own former associates and friends, could you not yourself undertake the transport of the box, and rid me at once of its detested presence?"

"Upon my word," replied the Doctor, "I admire you cordially. If you do not think I have already meddled sufficiently in your concerns, believe me, from my heart I think the contrary. Take or leave my services as I offer them; and trouble me with no more words of gratitude, for I value your consideration even more lightly than I do your intellect. A time will come, if you should be spared to see a number of years in health of mind, when you will think differently of all this, and blush for your tonight's behaviour."

So saying, the Doctor arose from his chair, repeated his directions briefly and clearly, and departed from the room without permitting Silas any time to answer.

The next morning Silas presented himself at the hotel, where he was politely received by Colonel Geraldine, and relieved, from that moment, of all immediate alarm about his trunk and its grisly contents. The journey passed over without much incident, although the young man was horrified to overhear the sailors and railway porters complaining among themselves about the unusual weight of the Prince's baggage. Silas travelled in a carriage with the valets, for Prince Florizel chose to be alone with his Master of the Horse. On board the steamer, however, Silas attracted his Highness's attention by the melancholy of his air and attitude as he stood gazing at the pile of baggage; for he was still full of disquietude about the future.

"There is a young man," observed the Prince, "who must have some cause for sorrow."

"That," replied Geraldine, "is the American for whom I obtained permission to travel with your suite."

"You remind me that I have been remiss in courtesy," said Prince Florizel, and advancing to Silas, he addressed him with the most exquisite condescension in these words:

"I was charmed, young sir, to be able to gratify the desire you made known to me through Colonel Geraldine. Remember, if you please, that I shall be glad at any future time to lay you under a more serious obligation."

And he then put some questions as to the political condition of America, which Silas answered with sense and propriety.

"You are still a young man," said the Prince; "but I observe you to be very serious for your years. Perhaps you allow your attention to be too much occupied with grave studies. But, perhaps, on the other hand, I am myself indiscreet and touch upon a painful subject."

"I have certainly cause to be the most miserable of men," said Silas; "never has a more innocent person been more dismally abused."

"I will not ask you for your confidence," returned Prince Florizel. "But do not forget that Colonel Geraldine's recommendation is an unfailing passport; and that I am not only willing, but possibly more able than many others, to do you a service."

Silas was delighted with the amiability of this great personage; but his mind soon returned upon its gloomy preoccupations; for not even the favour of a prince to a Republican can discharge a brooding spirit of its cares.

The train arrived at Charing Cross, where the officers of the Revenue respected the baggage of Prince Florizel in the usual manner. The most elegant equipages were in waiting; and Silas was driven, along with the rest, to the Prince's residence. There Colonel Geraldine sought him out, and expressed himself pleased to have been of any service to a friend of the physician's, for whom he professed a great consideration.

"I hope," he added, "that you will find none of your porcelain injured. Special orders were given along the line to deal tenderly with the Prince's effects."

And then, directing the servants to place one of the carriages at the young gentleman's disposal, and at once to charge the Saratoga trunk upon the dickey, the Colonel shook hands and excused himself on account of his occupations in the princely household.

Silas now broke the seal of the envelope containing the address, and directed the stately footman to drive him to Box Court, opening off the Strand. It seemed as if the place were not at all unknown to the man, for he looked startled and begged a repetition of the order. It was with a heart full of alarms, that Silas mounted into the luxurious vehicle, and was driven to his destination. The entrance to Box Court was too narrow for the passage of a coach; it was a mere footway between railings, with a post at either end. On one of these posts was seated a man, who at once jumped down and exchanged a friendly sign with the driver, while the footman opened the door and inquired of Silas whether he should take down the Saratoga trunk, and to what number it should be carried.

"If you please," said Silas. "To number three."

The footman and the man who had been sitting on the post, even with the aid of Silas himself, had hard work to carry in the trunk; and before it was deposited at the door of the house in question, the young American was horrified to find a score of loiterers looking on. But he knocked with as good a countenance as he could muster up, and presented the other envelope to him who opened.

"He is not at home," said he, "but if you will leave your letter and return tomorrow early, I shall be able to inform you whether and when he can receive your visit. Would you like to leave your box?" he added.

"Dearly," cried Silas; and the next moment he repented his precipitation, and declared, with equal emphasis, that he would carry the box along with him to the hotel.

The crowd jeered at his indecision and followed him to the carriage with insulting remarks; and Silas, covered with shame and terror, implored the servants to conduct him to some quiet and comfortable house of entertainment in the immediate neighbourhood.

The Prince's equipage deposited Silas at the Craven Hotel in Craven Street, and immediately drove away, leaving him alone with the servants of the inn. The only vacant room, it appeared, was a little den up four pairs of stairs, and looking towards the back. To this hermitage, with infinite trouble and complaint, a pair of stout porters carried the Saratoga trunk. It is needless to mention that Silas kept closely at their heels throughout the ascent, and had his heart in his mouth at every corner. A single false step, he reflected, and the box might go over the bannisters and land its fatal contents, plainly discovered, on the pavement of the hall.

Arrived in the room, he sat down on the edge of his bed to recover from the agony that he had just endured; but he had hardly taken his position when he was recalled to a sense of his peril by the action of the boots, who had knelt beside the trunk, and was proceeding officiously to undo its elaborate fastenings.

"Let it be!" cried Silas. "I shall want nothing from it while I stay here."

"You might have let it lie in the hall, then," growled the man; "a thing as big and heavy as a church. What you have inside, I cannot fancy. If it is all money, you are a richer man than me."

"Money?" repeated Silas, in a sudden perturbation. "What do you mean by money? I have no money, and you are speaking like a fool."

"All right, captain," retorted the boots with a wink. "There's nobody will touch your lordship's money. I'm as safe as the bank," he added; "but as the box is heavy, I shouldn't mind drinking something to your lordship's health."

Silas pressed two Napoleons upon his acceptance, apologising, at the same time, for being obliged to trouble him with foreign money, and pleading his recent arrival for excuse. And the man, grumbling with even greater fervour, and looking contemptuously from the money in his hand to the Saratoga trunk and back again from the one to the other, at last consented to withdraw.

For nearly two days the dead body had been packed into Silas's box; and as soon as he was alone the unfortunate New Englander nosed all the cracks and openings with the most passionate attention. But the weather was cool, and the trunk still managed to contain his shocking secret.

He took a chair beside it, and buried his face in his hands, and his mind in the most profound reflection. If he were not speedily relieved, no question but he must be speedily discovered. Alone in a strange city, without friends or accomplices, if the Doctor's introduction failed him, he was indubitably a lost New Englander. He reflected pathetically over his ambitious designs for the future; he should not now become the hero and spokesman of his native place of Bangor, Maine; he should not, as he had fondly anticipated, move on from office to office, from honour to honour; he might as well divest himself at once of all hope of being acclaimed President of the United States, and leaving behind him a statue, in the worst possible style of art, to adorn the Capitol at Washington. Here he was, chained to a dead Englishman doubled up inside a Saratoga trunk; whom he must get rid of, or perish from the rolls of national glory!

I should be afraid to chronicle the language employed by this young man to the Doctor, to the murdered man, to Madame Zéphyrine, to the boots of the hotel, to the Prince's servants, and, in a word, to all who had been ever so remotely connected with his horrible misfortune.

He slunk down to dinner about seven at night; but the yellow coffee room appalled him, the eyes of the other diners seemed to rest on his with suspicion, and his mind remained upstairs with the Saratoga trunk. When the waiter came to offer him cheese, his nerves were already so much on edge that he leaped halfway out of his chair and upset the remainder of a pint of ale upon the tablecloth.

The fellow offered to show him to the smoking room when he had done; and although he would have much preferred to return at once to his perilous treasure, he had not the courage to refuse, and was shown downstairs to the black, gas-lit cellar, which formed, and possibly still forms, the divan of the Craven Hotel.

Two very sad betting men were playing billiards, attended by a moist, consumptive marker; and for the moment Silas imagined that these were the only occupants of the apartment. But at the next glance his eye fell upon a person smoking in the farthest corner, with lowered eyes and a most respectable and modest aspect. He knew at once that he had seen the face before; and, in spite of the entire change of clothes, recognised the man whom he had found seated on a post at the entrance to Box Court, and who had helped him to carry the trunk to and from the carriage. The New Englander simply turned and ran, nor did he pause until he had locked and bolted himself into his bedroom.

There, all night long, a prey to the most terrible imaginations, he watched beside the fatal boxful of dead flesh. The suggestion of the boots that his trunk was full of gold inspired him with all manner of new terrors, if he so much as dared to close an eye; and the presence in the smoking room, and under an obvious disguise, of the loiterer from Box Court convinced him that he was once more the centre of obscure machinations.

Midnight had sounded some time, when, impelled by uneasy suspicions, Silas opened his bedroom door and peered into the passage. It was dimly illuminated by a single jet of gas; and some distance off he perceived a man sleeping on the floor in the costume of an hotel underservant. Silas drew near the man on tiptoe. He lay partly on his back, partly on his side, and his right forearm concealed his face from recognition. Suddenly, while the American was still bending over him, the sleeper removed his arm and opened his eyes, and Silas found himself once more face to face with the loiterer of Box Court.

"Good night, sir," said the man, pleasantly.

But Silas was too profoundly moved to find an answer, and regained his room in silence.

Towards morning, worn out by apprehension, he fell asleep on his chair, with his head forward on the trunk. In spite of so constrained an attitude and such a grisly pillow, his slumber was sound and prolonged, and he was only awakened at a late hour and by a sharp tapping at the door.

He hurried to open, and found the boots without.

"You are the gentleman who called yesterday at Box Court?" he asked.

Silas, with a quaver, admitted that he had done so.

"Then this note is for you," added the servant, proffering a sealed envelope.

Silas tore it open, and found inside the words: "Twelve o'clock."

He was punctual to the hour; the trunk was carried before him by several stout servants; and he was himself ushered into a room, where a man sat warming himself before the fire with his back towards the door. The sound of so many persons entering and leaving, and the scraping of the trunk as it was deposited upon the bare boards, were alike unable to attract the notice of the occupant; and Silas stood waiting, in an agony of fear, until he should deign to recognise his presence.

Perhaps five minutes had elapsed before the man turned leisurely about, and disclosed the features of Prince Florizel of Bohemia.

"So, sir," he said, with great severity, "this is the manner in which you abuse my politeness. You join yourselves to persons of condition, I perceive, for no other purpose than to escape the consequences of your crimes; and I can readily understand your embarrassment when I addressed myself to you yesterday."

"Indeed," cried Silas, "I am innocent of everything except misfortune."

And in a hurried voice, and with the greatest ingenuousness, he recounted to the Prince the whole history of his calamity.

"I see I have been mistaken," said his Highness, when he had heard him to an end. "You are no other than a victim, and since I am not to punish you may be sure I shall do my utmost to help. And now," he continued, "to business. Open your box at once, and let me see what it contains."

Silas changed colour.

"I almost fear to look upon it," he exclaimed.

"Nay," replied the Prince, "have you not looked at it already? This is a form of sentimentality to be resisted. The sight of a sick man, whom we can still help, should appeal more directly to the feelings than that of a dead man who is equally beyond help or harm, love or hatred. Nerve yourself, Mr. Scuddamore," and then, seeing that Silas still hesitated, "I do not desire to give another name to my request," he added.

The young American awoke as if out of a dream, and with a shiver of repugnance addressed himself to loose the straps and open the lock of the Saratoga trunk. The Prince stood by, watching with a composed countenance and his hands behind his back. The body was quite stiff, and it cost Silas a great effort, both moral and physical, to dislodge it from its position, and discover the face.

Prince Florizel started back with an exclamation of painful surprise.

"Alas!" he cried, "you little know, Mr. Scuddamore, what a cruel gift you have brought me. This is a young man of my own suite, the brother of my trusted friend; and it was upon matters of my own service that he has thus perished at the hands of violent and treacherous men. Poor Geraldine," he went on, as if to himself, "in what words am I to tell you of your brother's fate? How can I excuse myself in your eyes, or in the eyes of God, for the presumptuous schemes that led him to this bloody and unnatural death? Ah, Florizel! Florizel! when will you learn the discretion that suits mortal life, and be no longer dazzled with the image of power at your disposal? Power!" he cried; "who is more powerless? I look upon this young man whom I have sacrificed, Mr. Scuddamore, and feel how small a thing it is to be a Prince."

Silas was moved at the sight of his emotion. He tried to murmur some consolatory words, and burst into tears. The Prince, touched by his obvious intention, came up to him and took him by the hand.

"Command yourself," said he. "We have both much to learn, and we shall both be better men for today's meeting."

Silas thanked him in silence with an affectionate look.

"Write me the address of Doctor Noel on this piece of paper," continued the Prince, leading him towards the table; "and let me recommend you, when you are again in Paris, to avoid the society of that dangerous man. He has acted in this matter on a generous inspiration; that I must believe; had he been privy to young Geraldine's death he would never have despatched the body to the care of the actual criminal."

"The actual criminal!" repeated Silas in astonishment.

"Even so," returned the Prince. "This letter, which the disposition of Almighty Providence has so strangely delivered into my hands, was addressed to no less a person than the criminal himself, the infamous President of the Suicide Club. Seek to pry no farther in these perilous affairs, but content yourself with your own miraculous escape, and leave this house at once. I have pressing affairs, and must arrange at once about this poor clay, which was so lately a gallant and handsome youth."

Silas took a grateful and submissive leave of Prince Florizel, but he lingered in Box Court until he saw him depart in a splendid carriage on a visit to Colonel Henderson of the police. Republican as he was, the young American took off his hat with almost a sentiment of devotion to the retreating carriage. And the same night he started by rail on his return to Paris.

Here (observes my Arabian author) *is the end of* THE HISTORY OF THE PHYSICIAN AND THE SARATOGA TRUNK. *Omitting some reflections on the power of Providence, highly pertinent in the original, but little suited to our occidental taste, I shall only add that Mr. Scuddamore has already begun to mount the ladder of political fame, and by last advices was the Sheriff of his native town.*

The Adventure of the Hansom Cabs

Lieutenant Brackenbury Rich had greatly distinguished himself in one of the lesser Indian hill wars. He it was who took the chieftain prisoner with his own hand; his gallantry was universally applauded; and when he came home, prostrated by an ugly sabre cut and a protracted jungle fever, society was prepared to welcome the Lieutenant as a celebrity of minor lustre. But his was a character remarkable for unaffected modesty; adventure was dear to his heart, but he cared little for adulation; and he waited at foreign watering places and in Algiers until the fame of his exploits had run through its nine days' vitality and begun to be forgotten. He arrived in London at last, in the early season, with as little observation as he could desire; and as he was an orphan and had none but distant relatives who lived in the provinces, it was almost as a foreigner that he installed himself in the capital of the country for which he had shed his blood.

On the day following his arrival he dined alone at a military club. He shook hands with a few old comrades, and received their warm congratulations; but as one and all had some engagement for the evening, he found himself left entirely to his own resources. He was in dress, for he had entertained the notion of visiting a theatre. But the great city was new to him; he had gone from a provincial school to a military college, and thence direct to the Eastern Empire; and he promised himself a variety of delights in this world for exploration. Swinging his cane, he took his way westward. It was a mild evening, already dark, and now and then threatening rain. The succession of faces in the lamplight stirred the Lieutenant's imagination; and it seemed to him as if he could walk for ever in that stimulating city atmosphere and surrounded by the mystery of four million private lives. He glanced at the houses, and marvelled what was passing behind those warmly lighted windows; he looked into face after face, and saw them each intent upon some unknown interest, criminal or kindly.

"They talk of war," he thought, "but this is the great battlefield of mankind."

And then he began to wonder that he should walk so long in this complicated scene, and not chance upon so much as the shadow of an adventure for himself.

"All in good time," he reflected. "I am still a stranger, and perhaps wear a strange air. But I must be drawn into the eddy before long."

The night was already well advanced when a plump of cold rain fell suddenly out of the darkness. Brackenbury paused under some trees, and as he did so he caught sight of a hansom cabman making him a sign that he was disengaged. The circumstance fell in so happily to the occasion that he at once raised his cane in answer, and had soon ensconced himself in the London gondola.

"Where to, sir?" asked the driver.

"Where you please," said Brackenbury.

And immediately, at a pace of surprising swiftness, the hansom drove off through the rain into a maze of villas. One villa was so like another, each with its front garden, and there was so little to distinguish the deserted lamp-lit streets and crescents through which the flying hansom took its way, that Brackenbury soon lost all idea of direction. He would have been tempted to believe that the cabman was amusing himself by driving him round and round and in and out about a small quarter, but there was something businesslike in the speed which convinced him of the contrary. The man had an object in view, he was hastening towards a definite end; and Brackenbury was at once astonished at the fellow's skill in picking a way through such a labyrinth, and a little concerned to imagine what was the occasion of his hurry. He had heard tales of strangers falling ill in London. Did the driver belong to some bloody and treacherous association? and was he himself being whirled to a murderous death?

The thought had scarcely presented itself, when the cab swung sharply round a corner and pulled up before the garden gate of a villa in a long and wide road. The house was brilliantly lighted up. Another hansom had just driven away, and Brackenbury could see a gentleman being admitted at the front door and received by several liveried servants. He was surprised that the cabman should have stopped so immediately in front of a house where a reception was being held; but he did not doubt it was the result of accident, and sat placidly smoking where he was, until he heard the trap thrown open over his head.

"Here we are, sir," said the driver.

"Here!" repeated Brackenbury. "Where?"

"You told me to take you where I pleased, sir," returned the man with a chuckle, "and here we are."

It struck Brackenbury that the voice was wonderfully smooth and courteous for a man in so inferior a position; he remembered the speed at which he had been driven; and now it occurred to him that the hansom was more luxuriously appointed than the common run of public conveyances.

"I must ask you to explain," said he. "Do you mean to turn me out into the rain? My good man, I suspect the choice is mine."

"The choice is certainly yours," replied the driver; "but when I tell you all, I believe I know how a gentleman of your figure will decide. There is a gentlemen's party in this house. I do not know whether the master be a stranger to London and without acquaintances of his own; or whether he is a man of odd notions. But certainly I was hired to kidnap single gentlemen in evening dress, as many as I pleased, but military officers by preference. You have simply to go in and say that Mr. Morris invited you."

"Are you Mr. Morris?" inquired the Lieutenant.

"Oh, no," replied the cabman. "Mr. Morris is the person of the house."

"It is not a common way of collecting guests," said Brackenbury:

"but an eccentric man might very well indulge the whim without any intention to offend. And suppose that I refuse Mr. Morris's invitation," he went on, "what then?"

"My orders are to drive you back where I took you from," replied the man, "and set out to look for others up to midnight. Those who have no fancy for such an adventure, Mr. Morris said, were not the guests for him."

These words decided the Lieutenant on the spot.

"After all," he reflected, as he descended from the hansom, "I have not had long to wait for my adventure."

He had barely found footing on the sidewalk, and was still feeling in his pocket for the fare, when the cab swung about and drove off by the way it came at the former breakneck velocity. Brackenbury shouted after the man, who paid no heed, and continued to drive away; but the sound of his voice was overheard in the house, the door was again thrown open, emitting a flood of light upon the garden, and a servant ran down to meet him holding an umbrella.

"The cabman has been paid," observed the servant in a very civil tone; and he proceeded to escort Brackenbury along the path and up the steps. In the hall several other attendants relieved him of his hat, cane, and paletot, gave him a ticket with a number in return, and politely hurried him up a stair adorned with tropical flowers, to the door of an apartment on the first storey. Here a grave butler inquired his name, and announcing "Lieutenant Brackenbury Rich," ushered him into the drawing room of the house.

A young man, slender and singularly handsome, came forward and greeted him with an air at once courtly and affectionate. Hundreds of candles, of the finest wax, lit up a room that was perfumed, like the staircase, with a profusion of rare and beautiful flowering shrubs. A side table was loaded with tempting viands. Several servants went to and fro with fruits and goblets of champagne. The company was perhaps sixteen in number, all men, few beyond the prime of life, and with hardly an exception, of a dashing and capable exterior. They were divided into two groups, one about a roulette board, and the other surrounding a table at which one of their number held a bank of baccarat.

"I see," thought Brackenbury, "I am in a private gambling saloon, and the cabman was a tout."

His eye had embraced the details, and his mind formed the conclusion, while his host was still holding him by the hand; and to him his looks returned from this rapid survey. At a second view Mr. Morris surprised him still more than on the first. The easy elegance of his manners, the distinction, amiability, and courage that appeared upon his features, fitted very ill with the Lieutenant's preconceptions on the subject of the proprietor of a hell; and the tone of his conversation seemed to mark him out for a man of position and merit. Brackenbury found he had an instinctive liking for his entertainer; and though he chid himself for the weakness, he was unable to resist a sort of friendly attraction for Mr. Morris's person and character.

"I have heard of you, Lieutenant Rich," said Mr. Morris, lowering his tone; "and believe me I am gratified to make your acquaintance. Your looks accord with the reputation that has preceded you from India. And if you will forget for a while the irregularity of your presentation in my house, I shall feel it not only an honour, but a genuine pleasure besides. A man who makes a mouthful of barbarian cavaliers," he added with a laugh, "should not be appalled by a breach of etiquette, however serious."

And he led him towards the sideboard and pressed him to partake of some refreshment.

"Upon my word," the Lieutenant reflected, "this is one of the pleasantest fellows and, I do not doubt, one of the most agreeable societies in London."

He partook of some champagne, which he found excellent; and observing that many of the company were already smoking, he lit one of his own Manillas, and strolled up to the roulette board, where he sometimes made a stake and sometimes looked on smilingly on the fortune of others. It was while he was thus idling that he became aware of a sharp scrutiny to which the whole of the guests were subjected. Mr. Morris went here and there, ostensibly busied on hospitable concerns; but he had ever a shrewd glance at disposal; not a man of the party escaped his sudden, searching looks; he took stock of the bearing of heavy losers, he valued the amount of the stakes, he paused behind couples who were deep in conversation; and, in a word, there was hardly a characteristic of anyone present but he seemed to catch and make a note of it. Brackenbury began to wonder if this were indeed a gambling hell: it had so much the air of a private inquisition. He followed Mr. Morris in all his movements; and although the man had a ready smile, he seemed to perceive, as it were under a mask, a haggard, careworn, and preoccupied spirit. The fellows around him laughed and made their game; but Brackenbury had lost interest in the guests.

"This Morris," thought he, "is no idler in the room. Some deep purpose inspires him; let it be mine to fathom it."

Now and then Mr. Morris would call one of his visitors aside; and after a brief colloquy in an anteroom, he would return alone, and the visitors in question reappeared no more. After a certain number of repetitions, this performance excited Brackenbury's curiosity to a high degree. He determined to be at the bottom of this minor mystery at once; and strolling into the anteroom, found a deep window recess concealed by curtains of the fashionable green. Here he hurriedly ensconced himself; nor had he to wait long before the sound of steps and voices drew near him from the principal apartment. Peering through the division, he saw Mr. Morris escorting a fat and ruddy personage, with somewhat the look of a commercial traveller, whom Brackenbury had already remarked for his coarse laugh and underbred behaviour at the table. The pair halted immediately before the window, so that Brackenbury lost not a word of the following discourse:

"I beg you a thousand pardons!" began Mr. Morris, with the most conciliatory manner; "and, if I appear rude, I am sure you will readily forgive me. In a place so great as London accidents must continually happen; and the best that we can hope is to remedy them with as small delay as possible. I will not deny that I fear you have made a mistake and honoured my poor house by inadvertence; for, to speak openly, I cannot at all remember your appearance. Let me put the question without unnecessary circumlocution—between gentlemen of honour a word will suffice—Under whose roof do you suppose yourself to be?"

"That of Mr. Morris," replied the other, with a prodigious display of confusion, which had been visibly growing upon him throughout the last few words.

"Mr. John or Mr. James Morris?" inquired the host.

"I really cannot tell you," returned the unfortunate guest. "I am not personally acquainted with the gentleman, any more than I am with yourself."

"I see," said Mr. Morris. "There is another person of the same name farther down the street; and I have no doubt the policeman will be able to supply you with his number. Believe me, I felicitate myself on the misunderstanding which has procured me the pleasure of your company for so long; and let me express a hope that we may meet again upon a more regular footing. Meantime, I would not for the world detain you longer from your friends. John," he added, raising his voice, "will you see that this gentleman finds his great-coat?"

And with the most agreeable air Mr. Morris escorted his visitor as far as the anteroom door, where he left him under the conduct of the butler. As he passed the window, on his return to the drawing room, Brackenbury could hear him utter a profound sigh, as though his mind was loaded with a great anxiety, and his nerves already fatigued with the task on which he was engaged.

For perhaps an hour the hansoms kept arriving with such frequency, that Mr. Morris had to receive a new guest for every old one that he sent away, and the company preserved its number undiminished. But towards the end of that time the arrivals grew few and far between, and at length ceased entirely, while the process of elimination was continued with unimpaired activity. The drawing-room began to look empty: the baccarat was discontinued for lack of a banker; more than one person said good night of his own accord, and was suffered to part without expostulation; and in the meanwhile Mr. Morris redoubled in agreeable attentions to those who stayed behind. He went from group to group and from person to person with looks of the readiest sympathy and the most pertinent and pleasing talk; he was not so much like a host as like a hostess, and there was a feminine coquetry and condescension in his manner which charmed the hearts of all.

As the guests grew thinner, Lieutenant Rich strolled for a moment out of the drawing room into the hall in quest of fresher air. But he had no sooner passed the threshold of the antechamber than he was brought to a dead halt by a discovery of the most surprising nature. The flowering shrubs had disappeared from the staircase; three large furniture waggons stood beside the garden gate; the servants were busy dismantling the house upon all sides; and some of them had already donned their greatcoats and were preparing to depart. It was like the end of a country ball, where everything has been supplied by contract. Brackenbury had indeed some matter for reflection. First, the guests, who were no real guests after all, had been dismissed; and now the servants, who could hardly be genuine servants, were actively dispersing.

"Was the whole establishment a sham?" he asked himself. "The mushroom of a single night which should disappear before morning?"

Watching a favourable opportunity, Brackenbury dashed upstairs to the higher regions of the house. It was as he had expected. He ran from room to room, and saw not a stick of furniture nor so much as a picture on the walls. Although the house had been painted and papered, it was not only uninhabited at present, but plainly had never been inhabited at all. The young officer remembered with astonishment its specious, settled, and hospitable air on his arrival. It was only at a prodigious cost that the imposture could have been carried out upon so great a scale.

Who, then, was Mr. Morris? What was his intention in thus playing the householder for a single night in the remote west of London? And why did he collect his visitors at hazard from the streets?

Brackenbury remembered that he had already delayed too long, and hastened to join the company. Many had left during his absence; and counting the Lieutenant and his host, there were not more than five persons in the drawing-room—recently so thronged. Mr. Morris greeted him, as he reentered the apartment, with a smile, and immediately rose to his feet.

"It is now time, gentlemen," said he, "to explain my purpose in decoying you from your amusements. I trust you did not find the evening hang very dully on your hands; but my object, I will confess it, was not to entertain your leisure, but to help myself in an unfortunate necessity. You are all gentlemen," he continued, "your appearance does you that much justice, and I ask for no better security. Hence, I speak it without concealment, I ask you to render me a dangerous and delicate service; dangerous because you may run the hazard of your lives, and delicate because I must ask an absolute discretion upon all that you shall see or hear. From an utter stranger the request is almost comically extravagant; I am well aware of this; and I would add at once, if there be anyone present who has heard enough, if there be one among the party who recoils from a dangerous confidence and a piece of Quixotic devotion to he knows not whom—here is my hand ready, and I shall wish him good night and Godspeed with all the sincerity in the world."

A very tall, black man, with a heavy stoop, immediately responded to this appeal.

"I commend your frankness, Sir," said he; "and, for my part, I go. I make no reflections; but I cannot deny that you fill me with suspicious thoughts. I go myself, as I say; and perhaps you will think I have no right to add words to my example."

"On the contrary," replied Mr. Morris, "I am obliged to you for all you say. It would be impossible to exaggerate the gravity of my proposal."

"Well, gentlemen, what do you say?" said the tall man, addressing the others. "We have had our evening's frolic; shall we all go homeward peaceably in a body? You will think well of my suggestion in the morning, when you see the sun again in innocence and safety."

The speaker pronounced the last words with an intonation which added to their force; and his face wore a singular expression, full of gravity and significance. Another of the company rose hastily, and, with some appearance of alarm, prepared to take his leave. There were only two who held their ground, Brackenbury and an old red-nosed cavalry Major; but these two preserved a nonchalant demeanour, and, beyond a look of intelligence which they rapidly exchanged, appeared entirely foreign to the discussion that had just been terminated.

Mr. Morris conducted the deserters as far as the door, which he closed upon their heels; then he turned round, disclosing a countenance of mingled relief and animation, and addressed the two officers as follows.

"I have chosen my men like Joshua in the Bible," said Mr. Morris, "and I now believe I have the pick of London. Your appearance pleased my hansom cabmen; then it delighted me; I have watched your behaviour in a strange company, and under the most unusual circumstances: I have studied how you played and how you bore your losses; lastly, I have put you to the test of a staggering announcement, and you received it like an invitation to dinner. It is not for nothing," he cried, "that I have been for years the companion and the pupil of the bravest and wisest potentate in Europe."

"At the affair of Bunderchang," observed the Major, "I asked for twelve volunteers, and every trooper in the ranks replied to my appeal. But a gaming party is not the same thing as a regiment under fire. You may be pleased, I suppose, to have found two, and two who will not fail you at a push. As for the pair who ran away, I count them among the most pitiful hounds I ever met with. Lieutenant Rich," he added, addressing Brackenbury, "I have heard much of you of late; and I cannot doubt but you have also heard of me. I am Major O'Rooke."

And the veteran tendered his hand, which was red and tremulous, to the young Lieutenant.

"Who has not?" answered Brackenbury.

"When this little matter is settled," said Mr. Morris, "you will think I have sufficiently rewarded you; for I could offer neither a more valuable service than to make him acquainted with the other."

"And now," said Major O'Rooke, "is it a duel?"

"A duel after a fashion," replied Mr. Morris, "a duel with unknown and dangerous enemies, and, as I gravely fear, a duel to the death. I must ask you," he continued, "to call me Morris no longer; call me, if you please, Hammersmith; my real name, as well as that of another person to whom I hope to present you before long, you will gratify me by not asking and not seeking to discover for yourselves. Three days ago the person of whom I speak disappeared suddenly from home; and, until this morning, I received no hint of his situation. You will fancy my alarm when I tell you that he is engaged upon a work of private justice. Bound by an unhappy oath, too lightly sworn, he finds it necessary, without the help of law, to rid the earth of an insidious and bloody villain. Already two of our friends, and one of them my own born brother, have perished in the enterprise. He himself, or I am much deceived, is taken in the same fatal toils. But at least he still lives and still hopes, as this billet sufficiently proves."

And the speaker, no other than Colonel Geraldine, proffered a letter, thus conceived:

"Major Hammersmith,—On Wednesday, at 3 A.M., you will be admitted by the small door to the gardens of Rochester House, Regent's Park, by a man who is entirely in my interest. I must request you not to fail me by a second. Pray bring my case of swords, and, if you can find them, one or two gentlemen of conduct and discretion to whom my person is unknown. My name must not be used in this affair.   T. GODALL."

"From his wisdom alone, if he had no other title," pursued Colonel Geraldine, when the others had each satisfied his curiosity, "my friend is a man whose directions should implicitly be followed. I need not tell you, therefore, that I have not so much as visited the neighbourhood of Rochester House; and that I am still as wholly in the dark as either of yourselves as to the nature of my friend's dilemma. I betook myself, as soon as I had received this order, to a furnishing contractor, and, in a few hours, the house in which we now are had assumed its late air of festival. My scheme was at least original; and I am far from regretting an action which has procured me the services of Major O'Rooke and Lieutenant Brackenbury Rich. But the servants in the street will have a strange awakening. The house which this evening was full of lights and visitors they will find uninhabited and for sale tomorrow morning. Thus even the most serious concerns," added the Colonel, "have a merry side."

"And let us add a merry ending," said Brackenbury.

The Colonel consulted his watch.

"It is now hard on two," he said. "We have an hour before us, and a swift cab is at the door. Tell me if I may count upon your help."

"During a long life," replied Major O'Rooke, "I never took back my hand from anything, nor so much as hedged a bet."

Brackenbury signified his readiness in the most becoming terms; and after they had drunk a glass or two of wine, the Colonel gave each of them a loaded revolver, and the three mounted into the cab and drove off for the address in question.

Rochester House was a magnificent residence on the banks of the canal. The large extent of the garden isolated it in an unusual degree from the annoyances of neighbourhood. It seemed the *parc aux cerfs* of some great nobleman or millionaire. As far as could be seen from the street, there was not a glimmer of light in any of the numerous windows of the mansion; and the place had a look of neglect, as though the master had been long from home.

The cab was discharged, and the three gentlemen were not long in discovering the small door, which was a sort of postern in a lane between two garden walls. It still wanted ten or fifteen minutes of the appointed time; the rain fell heavily, and the adventurers sheltered themselves below some pendant ivy, and spoke in low tones of the approaching trial.

Suddenly Geraldine raised his finger to command silence, and all three bent their hearing to the utmost. Through the continuous noise of the rain, the steps and voices of two men became audible from the other side of the wall; and, as they drew nearer, Brackenbury, whose sense of hearing was remarkably acute, could even distinguish some fragments of their talk.

"Is the grave dug?" asked one.

"It is," replied the other; "behind the laurel hedge. When the job is done, we can cover it with a pile of stakes."

The first speaker laughed, and the sound of his merriment was shocking to the listeners on the other side.

"In an hour from now," he said.

And by the sound of the steps it was obvious that the pair had separated, and were proceeding in contrary directions.

Almost immediately after the postern door was cautiously

opened, a white face was protruded into the lane, and a hand was seen beckoning to the watchers. In dead silence the three passed the door, which was immediately locked behind them, and followed their guide through several garden alleys to the kitchen entrance of the house. A single candle burned in the great paved kitchen, which was destitute of the customary furniture; and as the party proceeded to ascend from thence by a flight of winding stairs, a prodigious noise of rats testified still more plainly to the dilapidation of the house.

Their conductor preceded them, carrying the candle. He was a lean man, much bent, but still agile; and he turned from time to time and admonished silence and caution by his gestures. Colonel Geraldine followed on his heels, the case of swords under one arm, and a pistol ready in the other. Brackenbury's heart beat thickly. He perceived that they were still in time; but he judged from the alacrity of the old man that the hour of action must be near at hand; and the circumstances of this adventure were so obscure and menacing, the place seemed so well chosen for the darkest acts, that an older man than Brackenbury might have been pardoned a measure of emotion as he closed the procession up the winding stair.

At the top the guide threw open a door and ushered the three officers before him into a small apartment, lighted by a smoky lamp and the glow of a modest fire. At the chimney corner sat a man in the early prime of life, and of a stout but courtly and commanding appearance. His attitude and expression were those of the most unmoved composure; he was smoking a cheroot with much enjoyment and deliberation, and on a table by his elbow stood a long glass of some effervescing beverage which diffused an agreeable odour through the room.

"Welcome," said he, extending his hand to Colonel Geraldine. "I knew I might count on your exactitude."

"On my devotion," replied the Colonel, with a bow.

"Present me to your friends," continued the first; and, when that ceremony had been performed, "I wish, gentlemen," he added, with the most exquisite affability, "that I could offer you a more cheerful programme; it is ungracious to inaugurate an acquaintance upon serious affairs; but the compulsion of events is stronger than the obligations of good-fellowship. I hope and believe you will be able to forgive me this unpleasant evening; and for men of your stamp it will be enough to know that you are conferring a considerable favour."

"Your Highness," said the Major, "must pardon my bluntness. I am unable to hide what I know. For some time back I have suspected Major Hammersmith, but Mr. Godall is unmistakable. To seek two men in London unacquainted with Prince Florizel of Bohemia was to ask too much at Fortune's hands."

"Prince Florizel!" cried Brackenbury in amazement.

And he gazed with the deepest interest on the features of the celebrated personage before him.

"I shall not lament the loss of my incognito," remarked the Prince, "for it enables me to thank you with the more authority. You would have done as much for Mr. Godall, I feel sure, as for the Prince of Bohemia; but the latter can perhaps do more for you. The gain is mine," he added, with a courteous gesture.

And the next moment he was conversing with the two officers about the Indian army and the native troops, a subject on which, as on all others, he had a remarkable fund of information and the soundest views.

There was something so striking in this man's attitude at a moment of deadly peril that Brackenbury was overcome with respectful admiration; nor was he less sensible to the charm of his conversation or the surprising amenity of his address. Every gesture, every intonation, was not only noble in itself, but seemed to ennoble the fortunate mortal for whom it was intended; and Brackenbury confessed to himself with enthusiasm that this was a sovereign for whom a brave man might thankfully lay down his life.

Many minutes had thus passed, when the person who had introduced them into the house, and who had sat ever since in a corner, and with his watch in his hand, arose and whispered a word into the Prince's ear.

"It is well, Dr. Noel," replied Florizel, aloud; and then addressing the others, "You will excuse me, gentlemen," he added, "if I have to leave you in the dark. The moment now approaches."

Dr. Noel extinguished the lamp. A faint, gray light, premonitory of the dawn, illuminated the window, but was not sufficient to illuminate the room; and when the Prince rose to his feet, it was impossible to distinguish his features or to make a guess at the nature of the emotion which obviously affected him as he spoke. He moved towards the door, and placed himself at one side of it in an attitude of the wariest attention.

"You will have the kindness," he said, "to maintain the strictest silence, and to conceal yourselves in the densest of the shadow."

The three officers and the physician hastened to obey, and for nearly ten minutes the only sound in Rochester House was occasioned by the excursions of the rats behind the woodwork. At the end of that period, a loud creak of a hinge broke in with surprising distinctness on the silence; and shortly after, the watchers could distinguish a slow and cautious tread approaching up the kitchen stair. At every second step the intruder seemed to pause and lend an ear, and during these intervals, which seemed of an incalculable duration, a profound disquiet possessed the spirit of the listeners. Dr. Noel, accustomed as he was to dangerous emotions, suffered an almost pitiful physical prostration; his breath whistled in his lungs, his teeth grated one upon another, and his joints cracked aloud as he nervously shifted his position.

At last a hand was laid upon the door, and the bolt shot back with a slight report. There followed another pause, during which Brackenbury could see the Prince draw himself together noiselessly as if for some unusual exertion. Then the door opened, letting in a little more of the light of the morning; and the figure of a man appeared upon the threshold and stood motionless. He was tall, and carried a knife in his hand. Even in the twilight they could see his upper teeth bare and glistening, for his mouth was open like that of a hound about to leap. The man had evidently been over the head in water but a minute or two before; and even while he stood there the drops kept falling from his wet clothes and pattered on the floor.

The next moment he crossed the threshold. There was a leap, a stifled cry, an instantaneous struggle; and before Colonel Geraldine could spring to his aid, the Prince held the man, disarmed and helpless, by the shoulders.

"Dr. Noel," he said, "you will be so good as to relight the lamp."

And relinquishing the charge of his prisoner to Geraldine and Brackenbury, he crossed the room and set his back against the chimneypiece. As soon as the lamp had kindled, the party beheld an unaccustomed sternness on the Prince's features. It was no longer Florizel, the careless gentleman; it was the Prince of Bohemia, justly incensed and full of deadly purpose, who now raised his head and addressed the captive President of the Suicide Club.

"President," he said, "you have laid your last snare, and your own feet are taken in it. The day is beginning; it is your last morning. You have just swum the Regent's Canal; it is your last bathe in this world. Your old accomplice, Dr. Noel, so far from betraying me, has delivered you into my hands for judgment. And the grave you had dug for me this afternoon shall serve, in God's almighty providence, to hide your own just doom from the curiosity of mankind. Kneel and pray, sir, if you have a mind that way; for your time is short, and God is weary of your iniquities."

The President made no answer either by word or sign; but continued to hang his head and gaze sullenly on the floor, as though he were conscious of the Prince's prolonged and unsparing regard.

"Gentlemen," continued Florizel, resuming the ordinary tone of his conversation, "this is a fellow who has long eluded me, but whom, thanks to Dr. Noel, I now have tightly by the heels. To tell the story of his misdeeds would occupy more time than we can now afford; but if the canal had contained nothing but the blood of his victims, I believe the wretch would have been no drier than you see him. Even in an affair of this sort I desire to preserve the forms of honour. But I make you the judges, gentlemen—this is more an execution than a duel; and to give the rogue his choice of weapons would be to push too far a point of etiquette. I cannot afford to lose my life in such a business," he continued, unlocking the case of swords; "and as a pistol bullet travels so often on the wings of chance, and skill and courage may fall by the most trembling marksman, I have decided, and I feel sure you will approve my determination, to put this question to the touch of swords."

When Brackenbury and Major O'Rooke, to whom these remarks were particularly addressed, had each intimated his approval, "Quick, sir," added Prince Florizel to the President, "choose a blade and do not keep me waiting; I have an impatience to be done with you for ever."

For the first time since he was captured and disarmed the President raised his head, and it was plain that he began instantly to pluck up courage.

"Is it to be stand up?" he asked eagerly, "and between you and me?"

"I mean so far to honour you," replied the Prince.

"Oh, come!" cried the President. "With a fair field, who knows how things may happen? I must add that I consider it handsome behaviour on your Highness's part; and if the worst comes to the worst I shall die by one of the most gallant gentlemen in Europe."

And the President, liberated by those who had detained him, stepped up to the table and began, with minute attention, to select a sword. He was highly elated, and seemed to feel no doubt that he should issue victorious from the contest. The spectators grew alarmed in the face of so entire a confidence, and adjured Prince Florizel to reconsider his intention.

"It is but a farce," he answered; "and I think I can promise you, gentlemen, that it will not be long a-playing."

"Your Highness will be careful not to overreach," said Colonel Geraldine.

"Geraldine," returned the Prince, "did you ever know me fail in a debt of honour? I owe you this man's death, and you shall have it."

The President at last satisfied himself with one of the rapiers, and signified his readiness by a gesture that was not devoid of a rude nobility. The nearness of peril, and the sense of courage, even to this obnoxious villain, lent an air of manhood and a certain grace.

The Prince helped himself at random to a sword.

"Colonel Geraldine and Doctor Noel," he said, "will have the goodness to await me in this room. I wish no personal friend of mine to be involved in this transaction. Major O'Rooke, you are a man of some years and a settled reputation—let me recommend the President to your good graces. Lieutenant Rich will be so good as lend me his attentions: a young man cannot have too much experience in such affairs."

"Your Highness," replied Brackenbury, "it is an honour I shall prize extremely."

"It is well," returned Prince Florizel; "I shall hope to stand your friend in more important circumstances."

And so saying he led the way out of the apartment and down the kitchen stairs.

The two men who were thus left alone threw open the window and leaned out, straining every sense to catch an indication of the tragical events that were about to follow. The rain was now over; day had almost come, and the birds were piping in the shrubbery and on the forest trees of the garden. The Prince and his companions were visible for a moment as they followed an alley between two flowering thickets; but at the first corner a clump of foliage intervened, and they were again concealed from view. This was all that the Colonel and the Physician had an opportunity to see, and the garden was so vast, and the place of combat evidently so remote from the house, that not even the noise of swordplay reached their ears.

"He has taken him towards the grave," said Dr. Noel, with a shudder.

"God," cried the Colonel, "God defend the right!"

And they awaited the event in silence, the Doctor shaking with fear, the Colonel in an agony of sweat. Many minutes must have elapsed, the day was sensibly broader, and the birds were singing more heartily in the garden before a sound of returning footsteps recalled their glances towards the door. It was the Prince and the two Indian officers who entered. God had defended the right.

"I am ashamed of my emotion," said Prince Florizel; "I feel it is a weakness unworthy of my station, but the continued existence of that hound of hell had begun to prey upon me like a disease, and his death has more refreshed me than a night of slumber. Look, Geraldine," he continued, throwing his sword upon the floor, "there is the blood of the man who killed your brother. It should be a welcome sight. And yet," he added, "see how strangely we men are made! my revenge is not yet five minutes old, and already I am beginning to ask myself if even revenge be attainable on this precarious stage of life. The ill he did, who can undo it? The career in which he amassed a huge fortune (for the house itself in which we stand belonged to him)—that career is now a part of the destiny of mankind for ever; and I might weary myself making thrusts in carte until the crack of judgment, and Geraldine's brother would be none the less dead, and a thousand other innocent persons would be none the less dishonoured and debauched! The existence of a man is so small a thing to take, so mighty a thing to employ! Alas!" he cried, "is there anything in life so disenchanting as attainment?"

"God's justice has been done," replied the Doctor. "So much I behold. The lesson, your Highness, has been a cruel one for me; and I await my own turn with deadly apprehension."

"What was I saying?" cried the Prince. "I have punished, and here is the man beside us who can help me to undo. Ah, Dr. Noel! you and I have before us many a day of hard and honourable toil; and perhaps, before we have done, you may have more than redeemed your early errors."

"And in the meantime," said the Doctor, "let me go and bury my oldest friend."

(*And this,* observes the erudite Arabian, *is the fortunate conclusion of the tale. The Prince, it is superfluous to mention, forgot none of those who served him in this great exploit; and to this day his authority and influence help them forward in their public career, while his condescending friendship adds a charm to their private life. To collect,* continues my author, *all the strange events in which this Prince has played the part of Providence were to fill the habitable globe with books. But the stories which relate to the fortunes of* THE RAJAH'S DIAMOND *are of too entertaining a description,* says he, *to be omitted. Following prudently in the footsteps of this Oriental, we shall now begin the series to which he refers with the* STORY OF THE BANDBOX.)

THE RAJAH'S DIAMOND

Story of the Bandbox

U p to the age of sixteen, at a private school and afterwards at one of those great institutions for which England is justly famous, Mr. Harry Hartley had received the ordinary education of a gentleman. At that period, he manifested a remarkable distaste for study; and his only surviving parent being both weak and ignorant, he was permitted thenceforward to spend his time in the attainment of petty and purely elegant accomplishments. Two years later, he was left an orphan and almost a beggar. For all active and industrious pursuits, Harry was unfitted alike by nature and training. He could sing romantic ditties, and accompany himself with discretion on the piano; he was a graceful although a timid cavalier; he had a pronounced taste for chess; and nature had sent him into the world with one of the most engaging exteriors that can well be fancied. Blond and pink, with dove's eyes and a gentle smile, he had an air of agreeable tenderness and melancholy, and the most submissive and caressing manners. But when all is said, he was not the man to lead armaments of war, or direct the councils of a State.

A fortunate chance and some influence obtained for Harry, at the time of his bereavement, the position of private secretary to Major-General Sir Thomas Vandeleur, C.B. Sir Thomas was a man of sixty, loud-spoken, boisterous, and domineering. For some reason, some service the nature of which had been often whispered and repeatedly denied, the Rajah of Kashgar had presented this officer with the sixth known diamond of the world. The gift transformed General Vandeleur from a poor into a wealthy man, from an obscure and unpopular soldier into one of the lions of London society; the possessor of the Rajah's Diamond was welcome in the most exclusive circles; and he had found a lady, young, beautiful, and well-born, who was willing to call the diamond hers even at the price of marriage with Sir Thomas Vandeleur. It was commonly said at the time that, as like draws to like, one jewel had attracted another; certainly Lady Vandeleur was not only a gem of the finest water in her own person, but she showed herself to the world in a very costly setting; and she was considered by many respectable authorities, as one among the three or four best-dressed women in England.

Harry's duty as secretary was not particularly onerous; but he had a dislike for all prolonged work; it gave him pain to ink his fingers; and the charms of Lady Vandeleur and her toilettes drew him often from the library to the boudoir. He had the prettiest ways among women, could talk fashions with enjoyment, and was never more happy than when criticising a shade of ribbon, or running on an errand to the milliner's. In short, Sir Thomas's correspondence fell into pitiful arrears, and my Lady had another lady's maid.

At last the General, who was one of the least patient of military commanders, arose from his place in a violent access of passion, and indicated to his secretary that he had no further need for his services, with one of those explanatory gestures which are most rarely employed between gentlemen. The door being unfortunately open, Mr. Hartley fell downstairs head foremost.

He arose somewhat hurt and very deeply aggrieved. The life in the General's house precisely suited him; he moved, on a more or less doubtful footing, in very genteel company, he did little, he ate of the best, and he had a lukewarm satisfaction in the presence of Lady Vandeleur, which, in his own heart, he dubbed by a more emphatic name.

Immediately after he had been outraged by the military foot, he hurried to the boudoir and recounted his sorrows.

"You know very well, my dear Harry," replied Lady Vandeleur, for she called him by name like a child or a domestic servant, "that you never by any chance do what the General tells you. No more do I, you may say. But that is different. A woman can earn her pardon for a good year of disobedience by a single adroit submission; and, besides, no one is married to his private secretary. I shall be sorry to lose you; but since you cannot stay longer in a house where you have been insulted, I shall wish you good-bye, and I promise you to make the General smart for his behaviour."

Harry's countenance fell; tears came into his eyes, and he gazed on Lady Vandeleur with a tender reproach.

"My Lady," said he, "what is an insult? I should think little indeed of anyone who could not forgive them by the score. But to leave one's friends; to tear up the bonds of affection——"

He was unable to continue, for his emotion choked him, and he began to weep.

Lady Vandeleur looked at him with a curious expression.

"This little fool," she thought, "imagines himself to be in love with me. Why should he not become my servant instead of the General's? He is good-natured, obliging, and understands dress; and besides it will keep him out of mischief. He is positively too pretty to be unattached."

That night she talked over the General, who was already somewhat ashamed of his vivacity; and Harry was transferred to the feminine department, where his life was little short of heavenly. He was always dressed with uncommon nicety, wore delicate flowers in his buttonhole, and could entertain a visitor with tact and pleasantry. He took a pride in servility to a beautiful woman; received Lady Vandeleur's commands as so many marks of favour; and was pleased to exhibit himself before other men, who derided and despised him, in his character of male lady's maid and man milliner. Nor could he think enough of his existence from a moral point of view. Wickedness seemed to him an essentially male attribute, and to pass one's days with a delicate woman, and principally occupied about trimmings, was to inhabit an enchanted isle among the storms of life.

One fine morning he came into the drawing room and began to arrange some music on the top of the piano. Lady Vandeleur, at the other end of the apartment, was speaking somewhat eagerly with her brother, Charlie Pendragon, an elderly young man, much broken with dissipation, and very lame of one foot. The private secretary, to whose entrance they paid no regard, could not avoid overhearing a part of their conversation.

"Today or never," said the lady. "Once and for all, it shall be done today."

"Today, if it must be," replied the brother, with a sigh. "But it is a false step, a ruinous step, Clara; and we shall live to repent it dismally."

Lady Vandeleur looked her brother steadily and somewhat strangely in the face.

"You forget," she said; "the man must die at last."

"Upon my word, Clara," said Pendragon, "I believe you are the most heartless rascal in England."

"You men," she returned, "are so coarsely built, that you can never appreciate a shade of meaning. You are yourselves rapacious, violent, immodest, careless of distinction; and yet the least thought for the future shocks you in a woman. I have no patience with such stuff. You would despise in a common banker the imbecility that you expect to find in us."

"You are very likely right," replied her brother; "you were always cleverer than I. And, anyway, you know my motto: The family before all."

"Yes, Charlie," she returned, taking his hand in hers, "I know your motto better than you know it yourself. "And Clara before the family!" Is not that the second part of it? Indeed, you are the best of brothers, and I love you dearly."

Mr. Pendragon got up, looking a little confused by these family endearments.

"I had better not be seen," said he. "I understand my part to a miracle, and I'll keep an eye on the Tame Cat."

"Do," she replied. "He is an abject creature, and might ruin all."

She kissed the tips of her fingers to him daintily; and the brother withdrew by the boudoir and the back stair.

"Harry," said Lady Vandeleur, turning towards the secretary as soon as they were alone, "I have a commission for you this morning. But you shall take a cab; I cannot have my secretary freckled."

She spoke the last words with emphasis and a look of half-motherly pride that caused great contentment to poor Harry; and he professed himself charmed to find an opportunity of serving her.

"It is another of our great secrets," she went on, archly, "and no one must know of it but my secretary and me. Sir Thomas would make the saddest disturbance; and if you only knew how weary I am of these scenes! Oh, Harry, Harry, can you explain to me what makes you men so violent and unjust? But, indeed, I know you cannot; you are the only man in the world who knows nothing of these shameful passions; you are so good, Harry, and so kind; you, at least, can be a woman's friend; and, do you know? I think you make the others more ugly by comparison."

"It is you," said Harry, gallantly, "who are so kind to me. You treat me like——"

"Like a mother," interposed Lady Vandeleur, "I try to be a mother to you. Or, at least," she corrected herself with a smile, "almost a mother. I am afraid I am too young to be your mother really. Let us say a friend—a dear friend."

She paused long enough to let her words take effect in Harry's sentimental quarters, but not long enough to allow him a reply.

"But all this is beside our purpose," she resumed. "You will find a bandbox in the left-hand side of the oak wardrobe; it is underneath the pink slip that I wore on Wednesday with my Mechlin. You will take it immediately to this address," and she gave him a paper, "but do not, on any account, let it out of your hands until you have received a receipt written by myself. Do you understand? Answer, if you please—answer! This is extremely important, and I must ask you to pay some attention.

Harry pacified her by repeating her instructions perfectly; and she was just going to tell him more when General Vandeleur flung into the apartment, scarlet with anger, and holding a long and elaborate milliner's bill in his hand.

"Will you look at this, madam?" cried he. "Will you have the goodness to look at this document? I know well enough you married me for my money, and I hope I can make as great allowances as any other man in the service; but, as sure as God made me, I mean to put a period to this disreputable prodigality."

"Mr. Hartley," said Lady Vandeleur, "I think you understand what you have to do. May I ask you to see to it at once?"

"Stop," said the General, addressing Harry, "one word before you go." And then, turning again to Lady Vandeleur, "What is this precious fellow's errand?" he demanded. "I trust him no further than I do yourself, let me tell you. If he had as much as the rudiments of honesty, he would scorn to stay in this house; and what he does for his wages is a mystery to all the world. What is his errand, madam? and why are you hurrying him away?"

"I supposed you had something to say to me in private," replied the lady.

"You spoke about an errand," insisted the General. "Do not attempt to deceive me in my present state of temper. You certainly spoke about an errand."

"If you insist on making your servants privy to our humiliating dissensions," replied Lady Vandeleur, "perhaps I had better ask Mr. Hartley to sit down. No?" she continued; "then you may go, Mr. Hartley. I trust you may remember all that you have heard in this room; it may be useful to you."

Harry at once made his escape from the drawing room; and as he ran upstairs he could hear the General's voice upraised in declamation, and the thin tones of Lady Vandeleur planting icy repartees at every opening. How cordially he admired the wife! How skilfully she could evade an awkward question! with what secure effrontery she repeated her instructions under the very guns of the enemy! and on the other hand, how he detested the husband!

There had been nothing unfamiliar in the morning's events, for he was continually in the habit of serving Lady Vandeleur on secret missions, principally connected with millinery. There was a skeleton in the house, as he well knew. The bottomless extravagance and the unknown liabilities of the wife had long since swallowed her own fortune, and threatened day by day to engulf that of the husband. Once or twice in every year exposure and ruin seemed imminent, and Harry kept trotting round to all sorts of furnishers' shops, telling small fibs, and paying small advances on the gross amount, until another term was tided over, and the lady and her faithful secretary breathed again. For Harry, in a double capacity, was heart and soul upon that side of the war: not only did he adore Lady Vandeleur and fear and dislike her husband, but he naturally sympathised with the love of finery, and his own single extravagance was at the tailor's.

He found the bandbox where it had been described, arranged

his toilette with care, and left the house. The sun shone brightly; the distance he had to travel was considerable, and he remembered with dismay that the General's sudden irruption had prevented Lady Vandeleur from giving him money for a cab. On this sultry day there was every chance that his complexion would suffer severely; and to walk through so much of London with a bandbox on his arm was a humiliation almost insupportable to a youth of his character. He paused, and took counsel with himself. The Vandeleurs lived in Eaton Place; his destination was near Notting Hill; plainly, he might cross the Park by keeping well in the open and avoiding populous alleys; and he thanked his stars when he reflected that it was still comparatively early in the day.

Anxious to be rid of his incubus, he walked somewhat faster than his ordinary, and he was already some way through Kensington Gardens when, in a solitary spot among trees, he found himself confronted by the General.

"I beg your pardon, Sir Thomas," observed Harry, politely falling on one side; for the other stood directly in his path.

"Where are you going, sir?" asked the General.

"I am taking a little walk among the trees," replied the lad.

The general struck the bandbox with his cane.

"With that thing?" he cried; "you lie, sir, and you know you lie!"

"Indeed, Sir Thomas," returned Harry, "I am not accustomed to be questioned in so high a key."

"You do not understand your position," said the General. "You are my servant, and a servant of whom I have conceived the most serious suspicions. How do I know but that your box is full of teaspoons?"

"It contains a silk hat belonging to a friend," said Harry.

"Very well," replied General Vandeleur. "Then I want to see your friend's silk hat. I have," he added, grimly, "a singular curiosity for hats; and I believe you know me to be somewhat positive."

"I beg your pardon, Sir Thomas, I am exceedingly grieved," Harry apologised; "but indeed this is a private affair."

The General caught him roughly by the shoulder with one hand, while he raised his cane in the most menacing manner with the other. Harry gave himself up for lost; but at the same moment

Heaven vouchsafed him an unexpected defender in the person of Charlie Pendragon, who now strode forward from behind the trees.

"Come, come, General, hold your hand," said he, "this is neither courteous nor manly."

"Aha!" cried the General, wheeling round upon his new antagonist, "Mr. Pendragon! And do you suppose, Mr. Pendragon, that because I have had the misfortune to marry your sister, I shall suffer myself to be dogged and thwarted by a discredited and bankrupt libertine like you? My acquaintance with Lady Vandeleur, sir, has taken away all my appetite for the other members of her family."

"And do you fancy, General Vandeleur," retorted Charlie, "that because my sister has had the misfortune to marry you, she there and then forfeited her rights and privileges as a lady? I own, sir, that by the action she did as much as anybody could to derogate from her position; but to me she is still a Pendragon. I make it my business to protect her from ungentlemanly outrage, and if you were ten times her husband I would not permit her liberty to be restrained, nor her private messengers to be violently arrested."

"How is that, Mr. Hartley?" interrogated the General. "Mr. Pendragon is of my opinion, it appears. He too suspects that Lady Vandeleur has something to do with your friend's silk hat."

Charlie saw that he had committed an unpardonable blunder, which he hastened to repair.

"How, sir?" he cried; "I suspect, do you say? I suspect nothing. Only where I find strength abused and a man brutalising his inferiors, I take the liberty to interfere."

As he said these words he made a sign to Harry, which the latter was too dull or too much troubled to understand.

"In what way am I to construe your attitude, sir?" demanded Vandeleur.

"Why, sir, as you please," returned Pendragon.

The General once more raised his cane, and made a cut for Charlie's head; but the latter, lame foot and all, evaded the blow with his umbrella, ran in, and immediately closed with his formidable adversary.

"Run, Harry, run!" he cried; "run, you dolt!"

Harry stood petrified for a moment, watching the two men

sway together in this fierce embrace; then he turned and took to his heels. When he cast a glance over his shoulder he saw the General prostrate under Charlie's knee, but still making desperate efforts to reverse the situation; and the Gardens seemed to have filled with people, who were running from all directions towards the scene of fight. This spectacle lent the secretary wings; and he did not relax his pace until he had gained the Bayswater road, and plunged at random into an unfrequented bystreet.

To see two gentlemen of his acquaintance thus brutally mauling each other was deeply shocking to Harry. He desired to forget the sight; he desired, above all, to put as great a distance as possible between himself and General Vandeleur; and in his eagerness for this he forgot everything about his destination, and hurried before him headlong and trembling. When he remembered that Lady Vandeleur was the wife of one and the sister of the other of these gladiators, his heart was touched with sympathy for a woman so distressingly misplaced in life. Even his own situation in the General's household looked hardly so pleasing as usual in the light of these violent transactions.

He had walked some little distance, busied with these meditations, before a slight collision with another passenger reminded him of the bandbox on his arm.

"Heavens!" cried he, "where was my head? and whither have I wandered?"

Thereupon he consulted the envelope which Lady Vandeleur had given him. The address was there, but without a name. Harry was simply directed to ask for "the gentleman who expected a parcel from Lady Vandeleur," and if he were not at home to await his return. The gentleman, added the note, should present a receipt in the handwriting of the lady herself. All this seemed mightily mysterious, and Harry was above all astonished at the omission of the name and the formality of the receipt. He had thought little of this last when he heard it dropped in conversation; but reading it in cold blood, and taking it in connection with the other strange particulars, he became convinced that he was engaged in perilous affairs. For half a moment he had a doubt of Lady Vandeleur herself; for he found these obscure proceedings somewhat unworthy of so high a lady, and became more critical when her secrets were preserved against himself. But her empire over his spirit was too complete, he dismissed his suspicions, and blamed himself roundly for having so much as entertained them.

In one thing, however, his duty and interest, his generosity and his terrors, coincided—to get rid of the bandbox with the greatest possible despatch.

He accosted the first policeman and courteously inquired his way. It turned out that he was already not far from his destination, and a walk of a few minutes brought him to a small house in a lane, freshly painted, and kept with the most scrupulous attention. The knocker and bellpull were highly polished; flowering pot-herbs garnished the sills of the different windows; and curtains of some rich material concealed the interior from the eyes of curious passengers. The place had an air of repose and secrecy; and Harry was so far caught with this spirit that he knocked with more than usual discretion, and was more than usually careful to remove all impurity from his boots.

A servant maid of some personal attractions immediately opened the door, and seemed to regard the secretary with no unkind eyes.

"This is the parcel from Lady Vandeleur," said Harry.

"I know," replied the maid, with a nod. "But the gentleman is from home. Will you leave it with me?"

"I cannot," answered Harry. "I am directed not to part with it but upon a certain condition, and I must ask you, I am afraid, to let me wait."

"Well," said she, "I suppose I may let you wait. I am lonely enough, I can tell you, and you do not look as though you would eat a girl. But be sure and do not ask the gentleman's name, for that I am not to tell you."

"Do you say so?" cried Harry. "Why, how strange! But indeed for some time back I walk among surprises. One question I think I may surely ask without indiscretion: Is he the master of this house?"

"He is a lodger, and not eight days old at that," returned the maid. "And now a question for a question: Do you know Lady Vandeleur?"

"I am her private secretary," replied Harry with a glow of modest pride.

"She is pretty, is she not?" pursued the servant.

"Oh, beautiful!" cried Harry; "wonderfully lovely, and not less good and kind!"

"You look kind enough yourself," she retorted; "and I wager you are worth a dozen Lady Vandeleurs."

Harry was properly scandalised.

"I!" he cried. "I am only a secretary!"

"Do you mean that for me?" said the girl. "Because I am only a housemaid, if you please." And then, relenting at the sight of Harry's obvious confusion, "I know you mean nothing of the sort," she added; "and I like your looks; but I think nothing of your Lady Vandeleur. Oh, these mistresses!" she cried. "To send out a real gentleman like you—with a bandbox—in broad day!"

During this talk they had remained in their original positions—she on the doorstep, he on the sidewalk, bareheaded for the sake of coolness, and with the bandbox on his arm. But upon this last speech Harry, who was unable to support such point-blank compliments to his appearance, nor the encouraging look with which they were accompanied, began to change his attitude, and glance from left to right in perturbation. In so doing he turned his face towards the lower end of the lane, and there, to his indescribable dismay, his eyes encountered those of General Vandeleur. The General, in a prodigious fluster of heat, hurry, and indignation, had been scouring the streets in chase of his brother-in-law; but so soon as he caught a glimpse of the delinquent secretary, his purpose changed, his anger flowed into a new channel, and he turned on his heel and came tearing up the lane with truculent gestures and vociferations.

Harry made but one bolt of it into the house, driving the maid before him; and the door was slammed in his pursuer's countenance.

"Is there a bar? Will it lock?" asked Harry, while a salvo on the knocker made the house echo from wall to wall.

"Why, what is wrong with you?" asked the maid. "Is it this old gentleman?"

"If he gets hold of me," whispered Harry, "I am as good as dead.

He has been pursuing me all day, carries a sword stick, and is an Indian military officer."

"These are fine manners," cried the maid. "And what, if you please, may be his name?"

"It is the General, my master," answered Harry. "He is after this bandbox."

"Did not I tell you?" cried the maid in triumph. "I told you I thought worse than nothing of your Lady Vandeleur; and if you had an eye in your head you might see what she is for yourself. An ungrateful minx, I will be bound for that!"

The General renewed his attack upon the knocker, and his passion growing with delay, began to kick and beat upon the panels of the door.

"It is lucky," observed the girl, "that I am alone in the house; your General may hammer until he is weary, and there is none to open for him. Follow me!"

So saying she led Harry into the kitchen, where she made him sit down, and stood by him herself in an affectionate attitude, with a hand upon his shoulder. The din at the door, so far from abating, continued to increase in volume, and at each blow the unhappy secretary was shaken to the heart.

"What is your name?" asked the girl.

"Harry Hartley," he replied.

"Mine," she went on, "is Prudence. Do you like it?"

"Very much," said Harry. "But hear for a moment how the General beats upon the door. He will certainly break it in, and then, in heaven's name, what have I to look for but death?"

"You put yourself very much about with no occasion," answered Prudence. "Let your General knock, he will do no more than blister his hands. Do you think I would keep you here if I were not sure to save you? Oh, no, I am a good friend to those that please me! and we have a back door upon another lane. But," she added, checking him, for he had got upon his feet immediately on this welcome news, "but I will not show where it is unless you kiss me. Will you, Harry?"

"That I will," he cried, remembering his gallantry, "not for your back door, but because you are good and pretty."

And he administered two or three cordial salutes, which were returned to him in kind.

Then Prudence led him to the back gate, and put her hand upon the key.

"Will you come and see me?" she asked.

"I will indeed," said Harry. "Do not I owe you my life?"

"And now," she added, opening the door, "run as hard as you can, for I shall let in the General."

Harry scarcely required this advice; fear had him by the fore-lock; and he addressed himself diligently to flight. A few steps, and he believed he would escape from his trials, and return to Lady Vandeleur in honour and safety. But these few steps had not been taken before he heard a man's voice hailing him by name with many execrations, and, looking over his shoulder, he beheld Charlie Pendragon waving him with both arms to return. The shock of this new incident was so sudden and profound, and Harry was already worked into so high a state of nervous tension, that he could think of nothing better than to accelerate his pace, and continue running. He should certainly have remembered the scene in Kensington Gardens; he should certainly have concluded that, where the General was his enemy, Charlie Pendragon could be no other than a friend. But such was the fever and perturbation of his mind that he was struck by none of these considerations, and only continued to run the faster up the lane.

Charlie, by the sound of his voice and the vile terms that he hurled after the secretary, was obviously beside himself with rage. He, too, ran his very best; but, try as he might, the physical advantages were not upon his side, and his outcries and the fall of his lame foot on the macadam began to fall farther and farther into the wake.

Harry's hopes began once more to arise. The lane was both steep and narrow, but it was exceedingly solitary, bordered on either hand by garden walls, overhung with foliage; and, for as far as the fugitive could see in front of him, there was neither a creature moving nor an open door. Providence, weary of persecution, was now offering him an open field for his escape.

Alas! as he came abreast of a garden door under a tuft of chestnuts, it was suddenly drawn back, and he could see inside, upon a garden path, the figure of a butcher's boy with his tray upon his arm. He had hardly recognised the fact before he was some steps beyond upon the other side. But the fellow had had time to observe him; he was evidently much surprised to see a gentleman go by at so unusual a pace; and he came out into the lane and began to call after Harry with shouts of ironical encouragement.

His appearance gave a new idea to Charlie Pendragon, who, although he was now sadly out of breath, once more upraised his voice.

"Stop, thief!" he cried.

And immediately the butcher's boy had taken up the cry and joined in the pursuit.

This was a bitter moment for the hunted secretary. It is true that his terror enabled him once more to improve his pace, and gain with every step on his pursuers; but he was well aware that he was near the end of his resources, and should he meet anyone coming the other way, his predicament in the narrow lane would be desperate indeed.

"I must find a place of concealment," he thought, "and that within the next few seconds, or all is over with me in this world."

Scarcely had the thought crossed his mind than the lane took a sudden turning; and he found himself hidden from his enemies. There are circumstances in which even the least energetic of mankind learn to behave with vigour and decision; and the most cautious forget their prudence and embrace foolhardy resolutions. This was one of those occasions for Harry Hartley; and those who knew him best would have been the most astonished at the lad's audacity. He stopped dead, flung the bandbox over a garden wall, and leaping upward with incredible agility and seizing the copestone with his hands, he tumbled headlong after it into the garden.

He came to himself a moment afterwards, seated in a border of small rosebushes. His hands and knees were cut and bleeding, for the wall had been protected against such an escalade by a liberal provision of old bottles; and he was conscious of a general dislocation and a painful swimming in the head. Facing him across the garden, which was in admirable order, and set with flowers of the most delicious perfume, he beheld the back of a house. It was of considerable extent, and plainly habitable; but, in odd contrast to the grounds, it was crazy, ill-kept, and of a mean appearance. On all other sides the circuit of the garden wall appeared unbroken.

He took in these features of the scene with mechanical glances, but his mind was still unable to piece together or draw a rational conclusion from what he saw. And when he heard footsteps advancing on the gravel, although he turned his eyes in that direction, it was with no thought either for defence or flight.

The new comer was a large, coarse, and very sordid personage, in gardening clothes, and with a watering pot in his left hand. One less confused would have been affected with some alarm at the sight of this man's huge proportions and black and lowering eyes. But Harry was too gravely shaken by his fall to be so much as terrified; and if he was unable to divert his glances from the gardener, he remained absolutely passive, and suffered him to draw near, to take him by the shoulder, and to plant him roughly on his feet, without a motion of resistance.

For a moment the two stared into each other's eyes, Harry fascinated, the man filled with wrath and a cruel, sneering humour.

"Who are you?" he demanded at last. "Who are you to come flying over my wall and break my *Gloire de Dijons*? What is your name?" he added, shaking him; "and what may be your business here?"

Harry could not as much as proffer a word in explanation.

But just at that moment Pendragon and the butcher's boy went clumping past, and the sound of their feet and their hoarse cries echoed loudly in the narrow lane. The gardener had received his answer; and he looked down into Harry's face with an obnoxious smile.

"A thief!" he said. "Upon my word, and a very good thing you must make of it; for I see you dressed like a gentleman from top to toe. Are you not ashamed to go about the world in such a trim, with honest folk, I dare say, glad to buy your cast-off finery secondhand? Speak up, you dog," the man went on; "you can understand English, I suppose; and I mean to have a bit of talk with you before I march you to the station."

"Indeed, sir," said Harry, "this is all a dreadful misconception;

and if you will go with me to Sir Thomas Vandeleur's in Eaton Place, I can promise that all will be made plain. The most upright person, as I now perceive, can be led into suspicious positions."

"My little man," replied the gardener, "I will go with you no farther than the station-house in the next street. The inspector, no doubt, will be glad to take a stroll with you as far as Eaton Place, and have a bit of afternoon tea with your great acquaintances. Or would you prefer to go direct to the Home Secretary? Sir Thomas Vandeleur, indeed! Perhaps you think I don't know a gentleman when I see one, from a common run-the-hedge like you? Clothes or no clothes, I can read you like a book. Here is a shirt that maybe cost as much as my Sunday hat; and that coat, I take it, has never seen the inside of Rag-fair, and then your boots——"

The man, whose eyes had fallen upon the ground, stopped short in his insulting commentary, and remained for a moment looking intently upon something at his feet. When he spoke his voice was strangely altered.

"What, in God's name," said he, "is all this?"

Harry, following the direction of the man's eyes, beheld a spectacle that struck him dumb with terror and amazement. In his fall he had descended vertically upon the bandbox and burst it open from end to end; thence a great treasure of diamonds had poured forth, and now lay abroad, part trodden in the soil, part scattered on the surface in regal and glittering profusion. There was a magnificent coronet which he had often admired on Lady Vandeleur; there were rings and brooches, ear-drops and bracelets, and even unset brilliants rolling here and there among the rosebushes like drops of morning dew. A princely fortune lay between the two men upon the ground—a fortune in the most inviting, solid, and durable form, capable of being carried in an apron, beautiful in itself, and scattering the sunlight in a million rainbow flashes.

"Good God!" said Harry, "I am lost!"

His mind raced backwards into the past with the incalculable velocity of thought, and he began to comprehend his day's adventures, to conceive them as a whole, and to recognise the sad imbroglio in which his own character and fortunes had become involved. He looked round him, as if for help, but he was alone in the garden, with his scattered diamonds and his redoubtable interlocutor; and when he gave ear, there was no sound but the rustle of the leaves and the hurried pulsation of his heart. It was little wonder if the young man felt himself deserted by his spirits, and with a broken voice repeated his last ejaculation——

"I am lost!"

The gardener peered in all directions with an air of guilt; but there was no face at any of the windows, and he seemed to breathe again.

"Pick up a heart," he said, "you fool! The worst of it is done. Why could you not say at first there was enough for two? Two?" he repeated, "aye, and for two hundred! But come away from here, where we may be observed; and, for the love of wisdom, straighten out your hat and brush your clothes. You could not travel two steps the figure of fun you look just now."

While Harry mechanically adopted these suggestions, the gardener, getting upon his knees, hastily drew together the scattered jewels and returned them to the bandbox. The touch of these costly crystals sent a shiver of emotion through the man's stalwart frame; his face was transfigured, and his eyes shone with concupiscence; indeed it seemed as if he luxuriously prolonged his occupation, and dallied with every diamond that he handled. At last, however, it was done; and, concealing the bandbox in his smock, the gardener beckoned to Harry and preceded him in the direction of the house.

Near the door they were met by a young man evidently in holy orders, dark and strikingly handsome, with a look of mingled weakness and resolution, and very neatly attired after the manner of his caste. The gardener was plainly annoyed by this encounter; but he put as good a face upon it as he could, and accosted the clergyman with an obsequious and smiling air.

"Here is a fine afternoon, Mr. Rolles," said he: "a fine afternoon, as sure as God made it! And here is a young friend of mine who had a fancy to look at my roses. I took the liberty to bring him in, for I thought none of the lodgers would object."

"Speaking for myself," replied the Reverend Mr. Rolles, "I do not; nor do I fancy any of the rest of us would be more difficult upon so small a matter. The garden is your own, Mr. Raeburn; we must none of us forget that; and because you give us liberty to walk there we should be indeed ungracious if we so far presumed upon your politeness as to interfere with the convenience of your friends. But, on second thoughts," he added, "I believe that this gentleman and I have met before. Mr. Hartley, I think. I regret to observe that you have had a fall."

And he offered his hand.

A sort of maiden dignity and a desire to delay as long as possible the necessity for explanation moved Harry to refuse this chance of help, and to deny his own identity. He chose the tender mercies of the gardener, who was at least unknown to him, rather than the curiosity and perhaps the doubts of an acquaintance.

"I fear there is some mistake," said he. "My name is Thomlinson and I am a friend of Mr. Raeburn's."

"Indeed?" said Mr. Rolles. "The likeness is amazing."

Mr. Raeburn, who had been upon thorns throughout this colloquy, now felt it high time to bring it to a period.

"I wish you a pleasant saunter sir," said he.

And with that he dragged Harry after him into the house, and then into a chamber on the garden. His first care was to draw down the blind, for Mr. Rolles still remained where they had left him, in an attitude of perplexity and thought. Then he emptied the broken bandbox on the table, and stood before the treasure, thus fully displayed, with an expression of rapturous greed, and rubbing his hands upon his thighs. For Harry, the sight of the man's face under the influence of this base emotion, added another pang to those he was already suffering. It seemed incredible that, from his life of pure and delicate trifling, he should be plunged in a breath among sordid and criminal relations. He could reproach his conscience with no sinful act; and yet he was now suffering the punishment of sin in its most acute and cruel forms—the dread of punishment, the suspicions of the good, and the companionship and contamination of vile and brutal natures. He felt he could lay his life down with gladness to escape from the room and the society of Mr. Raeburn.

"And now," said the latter, after he had separated the jewels into two nearly equal parts, and drawn one of them nearer to himself;

"and now," said he, "everything in this world has to be paid for, and some things sweetly. You must know, Mr. Hartley, if such be your name, that I am a man of a very easy temper, and good nature has been my stumbling block from first to last. I could pocket the whole of these pretty pebbles, if I chose, and I should like to see you dare to say a word; but I think I must have taken a liking to you; for I declare I have not the heart to shave you so close. So, do you see, in pure kind feeling, I propose that we divide; and these," indicating the two heaps, "are the proportions that seem to me just and friendly. Do you see any objection, Mr. Hartley, may I ask? I am not the man to stick upon a brooch."

"But, sir," cried Harry, "what you propose to me is impossible. The jewels are not mine, and I cannot share what is another's, no matter with whom, nor in what proportions."

"They are not yours, are they not?" returned Raeburn. "And you could not share them with anybody, couldn't you? Well now, that is what I call a pity; for here am I obliged to take you to the station. The police—think of that," he continued; "think of the disgrace for your respectable parents; think," he went on, taking Harry by the wrist; "think of the Colonies and the Day of Judgment."

"I cannot help it," wailed Harry. "It is not my fault. You will not come with me to Eaton Place."

"No," replied the man, "I will not, that is certain. And I mean to divide these playthings with you here."

And so saying he applied a sudden and severe torsion to the lad's wrist.

Harry could not suppress a scream, and the perspiration burst forth upon his face. Perhaps pain and terror quickened his intelligence, but certainly at that moment the whole business flashed across him in another light; and he saw that there was nothing for it but to accede to the ruffian's proposal, and trust to find the house and force him to disgorge, under more favourable circumstances, and when he himself was clear from all suspicion.

"I agree," he said.

"There is a lamb," sneered the gardener. "I thought you would recognise your interests at last. This bandbox," he continued, "I shall burn with my rubbish; it is a thing that curious folk might recognise; and as for you, scrape up your gaieties and put them in your pocket."

Harry proceeded to obey, Raeburn watching him, and every now and again his greed rekindled by some bright scintillation, abstracting another jewel from the secretary's share, and adding it to his own.

When this was finished, both proceeded to the front door, which Raeburn cautiously opened to observe the street. This was apparently clear of passengers; for he suddenly seized Harry by the nape of the neck, and holding his face downward so that he could see nothing but the roadway and the doorsteps of the houses, pushed him violently before him down one street and up another for the space of perhaps a minute and a half. Harry had counted three corners before the bully relaxed his grasp, and crying, "Now be off with you!" sent the lad flying headforemost with a well-directed and athletic kick.

When Harry gathered himself up, half-stunned and bleeding freely at the nose, Mr. Raeburn had entirely disappeared. For the first time, anger and pain so completely overcame the lad's spirits that he burst into a fit of tears and remained sobbing in the middle of the road.

After he had thus somewhat assuaged his emotion, he began to look about him and read the names of the streets at whose intersection he had been deserted by the gardener. He was still in an unfrequented portion of West London, among villas and large gardens; but he could see some persons at a window who had evidently witnessed his misfortune; and almost immediately after a servant came running from the house and offered him a glass of water. At the same time, a dirty rogue, who had been slouching somewhere in the neighbourhood, drew near him from the other side.

"Poor fellow," said the maid, "how vilely you have been handled, to be sure! Why, your knees are all cut, and your clothes ruined! Do you know the wretch who used you so?"

"That I do!" cried Harry, who was somewhat refreshed by the water; "and shall run him home in spite of his precautions. He shall pay dearly for this day's work, I promise you."

"You had better come into the house and have yourself washed and brushed," continued the maid. "My mistress will make you welcome, never fear. And see, I will pick up your hat. Why, love of mercy!" she screamed, "if you have not dropped diamonds all over the street!"

Such was the case; a good half of what remained to him after the depredations of Mr. Raeburn, had been shaken out of his pockets by the somersault and once more lay glittering on the ground. He blessed his fortune that the maid had been so quick of eye; "there is nothing so bad but it might be worse," thought he; and the recovery of these few seemed to him almost as great an affair as the loss of all the rest. But, alas! as he stooped to pick up his treasures, the loiterer made a rapid onslaught, overset both Harry and the maid with a movement of his arms, swept up a double handful of the diamonds, and made off along the street with an amazing swiftness.

Harry, as soon as he could get upon his feet, gave chase to the miscreant with many cries, but the latter was too fleet of foot, and probably too well acquainted with the locality; for turn where the pursuer would he could find no traces of the fugitive.

In the deepest despondency, Harry revisited the scene of his mishap, where the maid, who was still waiting, very honestly returned him his hat and the remainder of the fallen diamonds. Harry thanked her from his heart, and being now in no humour for economy, made his way to the nearest cabstand and set off for Eaton Place by coach.

The house, on his arrival, seemed in some confusion, as if a catastrophe had happened in the family; and the servants clustered together in the hall, and were unable, or perhaps not altogether anxious, to suppress their merriment at the tatterdemalion figure of the secretary. He passed them with as good an air of dignity as he could assume, and made directly for the boudoir. When he opened the door an astonishing and even menacing spectacle presented itself to his eyes; for he beheld the General and his wife and, of all people, Charlie Pendragon, closeted together and speaking with earnestness and gravity on some important subject. Harry saw at once that there was little left for him to explain—plenary confession had plainly been made to the General of the intended fraud upon his pocket, and the unfortunate miscarriage of the scheme; and they had all made common cause against a common danger.

"Thank Heaven!" cried Lady Vandeleur, "here he is! The bandbox, Harry—the bandbox!"

But Harry stood before them silent and downcast.

"Speak!" she cried. "Speak! Where is the bandbox?"

And the men, with threatening gestures, repeated the demand.

Harry drew a handful of jewels from his pocket. He was very white.

"This is all that remains," said he. "I declare before Heaven it was through no fault of mine; and if you will have patience, although some are lost, I am afraid, for ever, others, I am sure, may be still recovered."

"Alas!" cried Lady Vandeleur, "all our diamonds are gone, and I owe ninety thousand pounds for dress!"

"Madam," said the General, "you might have paved the gutter with your own trash; you might have made debts to fifty times the sum you mention; you might have robbed me of my mother's coronet and ring; and Nature might have still so far prevailed that I could have forgiven you at last. But, madam, you have taken the Rajah's Diamond—the Eye of Light, as the Orientals poetically termed it— the Pride of Kashgar! You have taken from me the Rajah's Diamond," he cried, raising his hands, "and all, madam, all is at an end between us!"

"Believe me, General Vandeleur," she replied, "that is one of the most agreeable speeches that ever I heard from your lips; and since we are to be ruined, I could almost welcome the change, if it delivers me from you. You have told me often enough that I married you for your money; let me tell you now that I always bitterly repented the bargain; and if you were still marriageable, and had a diamond bigger than your head, I should counsel even my maid against a union so uninviting and disastrous. As for you, Mr. Hartley," she continued, turning on the secretary, "you have sufficiently exhibited your valuable qualities in this house; we are now persuaded that you equally lack manhood, sense, and self-respect; and I can see only one course open for you—to withdraw instanter, and, if possible, return no more. For your wages you may rank as a creditor in my late husband's bankruptcy."

Harry had scarcely comprehended this insulting address before the General was down upon him with another.

"And in the meantime," said that personage, "follow me before the nearest Inspector of Police. You may impose upon a simple-minded soldier, sir, but the eye of the law will read your disreputable secret. If I must spend my old age in poverty through your underhand intriguing with my wife, I mean at least that you shall not remain unpunished for your pains; and God, sir, will deny me a very considerable satisfaction if you do not pick oakum from now until your dying day."

With that, the General dragged Harry from the apartment, and hurried him downstairs and along the street to the police station of the district.

Here (says my Arabian author) *ended this deplorable business of the bandbox. But to the unfortunate Secretary the whole affair was the beginning of a new and manlier life. The police were easily persuaded of his innocence; and, after he had given what help he could in the subsequent investigations, he was even complimented by one of the chiefs of the detective department on the probity and simplicity of his behaviour. Several persons interested themselves in one so unfortunate; and soon after he inherited a sum of money from a maiden aunt in Worcestershire. With this he married Prudence, and set sail for Bendigo, or according to another account, for Trincomalee, exceedingly content, and with the best of prospects.*

Story of the Young Man in Holy Orders

The Reverend Mr. Simon Rolles had distinguished himself in the Moral Sciences, and was more than usually proficient in the study of Divinity. His essay "On the Christian Doctrine of the Social Obligations" obtained for him, at the moment of its production, a certain celebrity in the University of Oxford; and it was understood in clerical and learned circles that young Mr. Rolles had in contemplation a considerable work—a folio, it was said—on the authority of the Fathers of the Church. These attainments, these ambitious designs, however, were far from helping him to any preferment; and he was still in quest of his first curacy when a chance ramble in that part of London, the peaceful and rich aspect of the garden, a desire for solitude and study, and the cheapness of the lodging, led him to take up his abode with Mr. Raeburn, the nurseryman of Stockdove Lane.

It was his habit every afternoon, after he had worked seven or eight hours on St. Ambrose or St. Chrysostom, to walk for a while in meditation among the roses. And this was usually one of the most productive moments of his day. But even a sincere appetite for thought, and the excitement of grave problems awaiting solution, are not always sufficient to preserve the mind of the philosopher against the petty shocks and contacts of the world. And when Mr. Rolles found General Vandeleur's secretary, ragged and bleeding, in the company of his landlord; when he saw both change colour and seek to avoid his questions; and, above all, when the former denied his own identity with the most unmoved assurance, he speedily forgot the Saints and Fathers in the vulgar interest of curiosity.

"I cannot be mistaken," thought he. "That is Mr. Hartley beyond a doubt. How comes he in such a pickle? why does he deny his name? and what can be his business with that black-looking ruffian, my landlord?"

As he was thus reflecting, another peculiar circumstance attracted his attention. The face of Mr. Raeburn appeared at a low window next the door; and, as chance directed, his eyes met those of Mr. Rolles. The nurseryman seemed disconcerted, and even alarmed; and immediately after the blind of the apartment was pulled sharply down.

"This may all be very well," reflected Mr. Rolles; "it may be all excellently well; but I confess freely that I do not think so. Suspicious, underhand, untruthful, fearful of observation—I believe upon my soul," he thought, "the pair are plotting some disgraceful action."

The detective that there is in all of us awoke and became clamant in the bosom of Mr. Rolles; and with a brisk, eager step, that bore no resemblance to his usual gait, he proceeded to make the circuit of the garden. When he came to the scene of Harry's escalade, his eye was at once arrested by a broken rosebush and marks of trampling on the mould. He looked up, and saw scratches on the brick, and a rag of trouser floating from a broken bottle. This, then, was the mode of entrance chosen by Mr. Raeburn's particular friend! It was thus that General Vandeleur's secretary came to admire a flower garden! The young clergyman whistled softly to himself as he stooped to examine the ground. He could make out where Harry had landed from his perilous leap; he recognised the flat foot of Mr. Raeburn where it had sunk deeply in the soil as he pulled up the Secretary by the collar; nay, on a closer inspection, he seemed to distinguish the marks of groping fingers, as though something had been spilt abroad and eagerly collected.

"Upon my word," he thought, "the thing grows vastly interesting."

And just then he caught sight of something almost entirely buried in the earth. In an instant he had disinterred a dainty morocco case, ornamented and clasped in gilt. It had been trodden heavily underfoot, and thus escaped the hurried search of Mr. Raeburn. Mr. Rolles opened the case, and drew a long breath of almost horrified astonishment; for there lay before him, in a cradle of green velvet, a diamond of prodigious magnitude and of the finest water. It was of the bigness of a duck's egg; beautifully shaped, and without a flaw; and as the sun shone upon it, it gave forth a lustre like that of electricity, and seemed to burn in his hand with a thousand internal fires.

He knew little of previous stones; but the Rajah's Diamond was a wonder that explained itself; a village child, if he found it, would run screaming for the nearest cottage; and a savage would prostrate himself in adoration before so imposing a fetish. The beauty of the stone flattered the young clergyman's eyes; the thought of its incalculable value overpowered his intellect. He knew that what he held in his hand was worth more than many years' purchase of an archiepiscopal see; that it would build cathedrals more stately than Ely or Cologne; that he who possessed it was set free for ever from the primal curse, and might follow his own inclinations without concern or hurry, without let or hindrance. And as he suddenly turned it, the rays leaped forth again with renewed brilliancy, and seemed to pierce his very heart.

Decisive actions are often taken in a moment and without any conscious deliverance from the rational parts of man. So it was now with Mr. Rolles. He glanced hurriedly round; beheld, like Mr. Raeburn before him, nothing but the sunlit flower garden, the tall treetops, and the house with blinded windows; and in a trice he had shut the case, thrust it into his pocket, and was hastening to his study with the speed of guilt.

The Reverend Simon Rolles had stolen the Rajah's Diamond.

Early in the afternoon the police arrived with Harry Hartley. The nurseryman, who was beside himself with terror, readily discovered his hoard; and the jewels were identified and inventoried in the presence of the Secretary. As for Mr. Rolles, he showed himself in a most obliging temper, communicated what he knew with freedom, and professed regret that he could do no more to help the officers in their duty.

"Still," he added, "I suppose your business is nearly at an end."

"By no means," replied the man from Scotland Yard; and he narrated the second robbery of which Harry had been the immediate victim, and gave the young clergyman a description of the more important jewels that were still not found, dilating particularly on the Rajah's Diamond.

"It must be worth a fortune," observed Mr. Rolles.

"Ten fortunes—twenty fortunes," cried the officer.

"The more it is worth," remarked Simon, shrewdly, "the more difficult it must be to sell. Such a thing has a physiognomy not to be disguised, and I should fancy a man might as easily negotiate St. Paul's Cathedral."

"Oh, truly!" said the officer; "but if the thief be a man of any intelligence, he will cut it into three or four, and there will be still enough to make him rich."

"Thank you," said the clergyman. "You cannot imagine how much your conversation interests me."

Whereupon the functionary admitted that they knew many strange things in his profession, and immediately after took his leave.

Mr. Rolles regained his apartment. It seemed smaller and barer than usual; the materials for his great work had never presented so little interest; and he looked upon his library with the eyes of scorn. He took down, volume by volume, several Fathers of the Church, and glanced them through; but they contained nothing to his purpose.

"These old gentlemen," thought he, "are no doubt very valuable writers, but they seem to me conspicuously ignorant of life. Here am I, with learning enough to be a Bishop, and I positively do not know how to dispose of a stolen diamond. I glean a hint from a common policeman, and, with all my folios, I cannot so much as put it into execution. This inspires me with very low ideas of University training."

Herewith he kicked over his bookshelf and, putting on his hat, hastened from the house to the club of which he was a member. In such a place of mundane resort he hoped to find some man of good counsel and a shrewd experience in life. In the reading room he saw many of the country clergy and an Archdeacon; there were three journalists and a writer upon the Higher Metaphysic, playing pool; and at dinner only the raff of ordinary club frequenters showed their commonplace and obliterated countenances. None of these, thought Mr. Rolles, would know more on dangerous topics than he knew himself; none of them were fit to give him guidance in his present strait. At length, in the smoking room, up many weary stairs, he hit upon a gentleman of somewhat portly build and dressed with conspicuous plainness. He was smoking a cigar and reading the *Fortnightly Review;* his face was singularly free from all sign of preoccupation or fatigue; and there was something in his air which seemed to invite confidence and to expect submission. The more the young clergyman scrutinised his features, the more he was convinced that he had fallen on one capable of giving pertinent advice.

"Sir," said he, "you will excuse my abruptness; but I judge you from your appearance to be preeminently a man of the world."

"I have indeed considerable claims to that distinction," replied the stranger, laying aside his magazine with a look of mingled amusement and surprise.

"I, sir," continued the Curate, "am a recluse, a student, a creature of ink bottles and patristic folios. A recent event has brought my folly vividly before my eyes, and I desire to instruct myself in life. By life," he added, "I do not mean Thackeray's novels; but the crimes and secret possibilities of our society, and the principles of wise conduct among exceptional events. I am a patient reader; can the thing be learnt in books?"

"You put me in a difficulty," said the stranger. "I confess I have no great notion of the use of books, except to amuse a railway journey; although, I believe, there are some very exact treatises on astronomy, the use of the globes, agriculture, and the art of making paper flowers. Upon the less apparent provinces of life I fear you will find nothing truthful. Yet stay," he added, "have you read Gaboriau?"

Mr. Rolles admitted he had never even heard the name.

"You may gather some notions from Gaboriau," resumed the stranger. "He is at least suggestive; and as he is an author much studied by Prince Bismarck, you will, at the worst, lose your time in good society."

"Sir," said the Curate, "I am infinitely obliged by your politeness."

"You have already more than repaid me," returned the other.

"How?" inquired Simon.

"By the novelty of your request," replied the gentleman; and with a polite gesture, as though to ask permission, he resumed the study of the *Fortnightly Review.*

On his way home Mr. Rolles purchased a work on precious stones and several of Gaboriau's novels. These last he eagerly skimmed until an advanced hour in the morning; but although they introduced him to many new ideas, he could nowhere discover what to do with a stolen diamond. He was annoyed, moreover, to find the information scattered amongst romantic storytelling, instead of soberly set forth after the manner of a manual; and he concluded that, even if the writer had thought much upon these subjects, he was totally lacking in educational method. For the character and attainments of Lecoq, however, he was unable to contain his admiration.

"He was truly a great creature," ruminated Mr. Rolles. "He knew the world as I know Paley's Evidences. There was nothing that he could not carry to a termination with his own hand, and against the largest odds. Heavens!" he broke out suddenly, "is not this the lesson? Must I not learn to cut diamonds for myself?"

It seemed to him as if he had sailed at once out of his perplexities; he remembered that he knew a jeweller, one B. Macculloch, in Edinburgh, who would be glad to put him in the way of the necessary training; a few months, perhaps a few years, of sordid toil, and he would be sufficiently expert to divide and sufficiently cunning to dispose with advantage of the Rajah's Diamond. That done, he might return to pursue his researches at leisure, a wealthy and luxurious student, envied and respected by all. Golden visions attended him through his slumber, and he awoke refreshed and lighthearted with the morning sun.

Mr. Raeburn's house was on that day to be closed by the police, and this afforded a pretext for his departure. He cheerfully prepared his baggage, transported it to King's Cross, where he left it in the cloakroom, and returned to the club to while away the afternoon and dine.

"If you dine here today, Rolles," observed an acquaintance, "you may see two of the most remarkable men in England—Prince Florizel of Bohemia, and old Jack Vandeleur."

"I have heard of the Prince," replied Mr. Rolles; "and General Vandeleur I have even met in society."

"General Vandeleur is an ass!" returned the other. "This is his brother John, the biggest adventurer, the best judge of precious stones, and one of the most acute diplomatists in Europe. Have you never heard of his duel with the Duc de Val d'Orge? of his exploits and atrocities when he was Dictator of Paraguay? of his dexterity in recovering Sir Samuel Levi's jewellery? nor of his services in the Indian Mutiny—services by which the Government profited, but which the Government dared not recognise? You make me wonder what we mean by fame, or even by infamy; for Jack Vandeleur has prodigious claims to both. Run down stairs," he continued, "take a table near them, and keep your ears open. You will hear some strange talk, or I am much misled."

"But how shall I know them?" inquired the clergyman.

"Know them!" cried his friend; "why, the Prince is the finest gentleman in Europe, the only living creature who looks like a king; and as for Jack Vandeleur, if you can imagine Ulysses at seventy years of age, and with a sabre cut across his face, you have the man before you! Know them, indeed! Why, you could pick either of them out of a Derby day!"

Rolles eagerly hurried to the dining room. It was as his friend had asserted; it was impossible to mistake the pair in question. Old John Vandeleur was of a remarkable force of body, and obviously broken to the most difficult exercises. He had neither the carriage of a swordsman, nor of a sailor, nor yet of one much inured to the saddle; but something made up of all these, and the result and expression of many different habits and dexterities. His features were bold and aquiline; his expression arrogant and predatory; his whole appearance that of a swift, violent, unscrupulous man of action; and his copious white hair and the deep sabre cut that traversed his nose and temple added a note of savagery to a head already remarkable and menacing in itself.

In his companion, the Prince of Bohemia, Mr. Rolles was astonished to recognise the gentleman who had recommended him the study of Gaboriau. Doubtless Prince Florizel, who rarely visited the club, of which, as of most others, he was an honorary member, had been waiting for John Vandeleur when Simon accosted him on the previous evening.

The other diners had modestly retired into the angles of the room, and left the distinguished pair in a certain isolation, but the young clergyman was unrestrained by any sentiment of awe, and, marching boldly up, took his place at the nearest table.

The conversation was, indeed, new to the student's ears. The ex-Dictator of Paraguay stated many extraordinary experiences in different quarters of the world; and the Prince supplied a commentary which, to a man of thought, was even more interesting than the events themselves. Two forms of experience were thus brought together and laid before the young clergyman; and he did not know which to admire the most—the desperate actor or the skilled expert in life; the man who spoke boldly of his own deeds and perils, or the man who seemed, like a god, to know all things and to have suffered nothing. The manner of each aptly fitted with his part in the discourse. The Dictator indulged in brutalities alike of speech and gesture; his hand opened and shut and fell roughly on the table; and his voice was loud and heady. The Prince, on the other hand, seemed the very type of urbane docility and quiet; the least movement, the least inflection, had with him a weightier significance than all the shouts and pantomime of his companion; and if ever, as must frequently have been the case, he described some experience personal to himself, it was so aptly dissimulated as to pass unnoticed with the rest.

At length the talk wandered on to the late robberies and the Rajah's Diamond.

"That diamond would be better in the sea," observed Prince Florizel.

"As a Vandeleur," replied the Dictator, "your Highness may imagine my dissent."

"I speak on grounds of public policy," pursued the Prince. "Jewels so valuable should be reserved for the collection of a Prince or the treasury of a great nation. To hand them about among the common sort of men is to set a price on Virtue's head; and if the Rajah of Kashgar—a Prince, I understand, of great enlightenment—desired vengeance upon the men of Europe, he could hardly have gone more efficaciously about his purpose than by sending us this apple of discord. There is no honesty too robust for such a trial. I myself, who have many duties and many privileges of my own—I myself, Mr. Vandeleur, could scarce handle the intoxicating crystal and be safe. As for you, who are a diamond hunter by taste and profession, I do not believe there is a crime in the calendar you would not perpetrate—I do not believe you have a friend in the world whom you would not eagerly betray—I do not know if you have a family, but if you have I declare you would sacrifice your children—and all this for what? Not to be richer, nor to have more comforts or more respect, but simply to call this diamond yours for a year or two until you die, and now and again to open a safe and look at it as one looks at a picture."

"It is true," replied Vandeleur. "I have hunted most things, from men and women down to mosquitos; I have dived for coral; I have followed both whales and tigers; and a diamond is the tallest quarry of the lot. It has beauty and worth; it alone can properly reward the ardours of the chase. At this moment, as your Highness may fancy, I am upon the trail; I have a sure knack, a wide experience; I know every stone of price in my brother's collection as a shepherd knows his sheep; and I wish I may die if I do not recover them every one!"

"Sir Thomas Vandeleur will have great cause to thank you," said the prince.

"I am not so sure," returned the Dictator, with a laugh. "One of the Vandeleurs will. Thomas or John—Peter or Paul—we are all apostles."

"I did not catch your observation," said the Prince with some disgust.

And at the same moment the waiter informed Mr. Vandeleur that his cab was at the door.

Mr. Rolles glanced at the clock, and saw that he also must be moving; and the coincidence struck him sharply and unpleasantly, for he desired to see no more of the diamond hunter.

Much study having somewhat shaken the young man's nerves, he was in the habit of travelling in the most luxurious manner; and for the present journey he had taken a sofa in the sleeping carriage.

"You will be very comfortable," said the guard; "there is no one in your compartment, and only one old gentleman in the other end."

It was close upon the hour, and the tickets were being examined, when Mr. Rolles beheld this other fellow passenger ushered by several porters into his place; certainly, there was not another man in the world whom he would not have preferred—for it was old John Vandeleur, the ex-Dictator.

The sleeping carriages on the Great Northern line were divided into three compartments—one at each end for travellers, and one in the centre fitted with the conveniences of a lavatory. A door running in grooves separated each of the others from the lavatory; but as there were neither bolts nor locks, the whole suite was practically common ground.

When Mr. Rolles had studied his position, he perceived himself without defence. If the Dictator chose to pay him a visit in the course of the night, he could do no less than receive it; he had no means of fortification, and lay open to attack as if he had been lying in the fields. This situation caused him some agony of mind. He recalled with alarm the boastful statements of his fellow traveller across the dining table, and the professions of immorality which he had heard him offering to the disgusted Prince. Some persons, he remembered to have read, are endowed with a singular quickness of perception for the neighbourhood of precious metals; through walls and even at considerable distances they are said to divine the presence of gold. Might it not be the same with diamonds? he wondered; and if so, who was more likely to enjoy this transcendental sense than the person who gloried in the appellation of the Diamond Hunter? From such a man he recognised that he had everything to fear, and longed eagerly for the arrival of the day.

In the meantime he neglected no precaution, concealed his diamond in the most internal pocket of a system of greatcoats, and devoutly recommended himself to the care of Providence.

The train pursued its usual even and rapid course; and nearly half the journey had been accomplished before slumber began to triumph over uneasiness in the breast of Mr. Rolles. For some time he resisted its influence; but it grew upon him more and more, and a little before York he was fain to stretch himself upon one of the couches and suffer his eyes to close; and almost at the same instant consciousness deserted the young clergyman. His last thought was of his terrifying neighbour.

When he awoke it was still pitch dark, except for the flicker of the veiled lamp; and the continual roaring and oscillation testified to the unrelaxed velocity of the train. He sat upright in a panic, for he had been tormented by the most uneasy dreams; it was some seconds before he recovered his self-command; and even after he had resumed a recumbent attitude sleep continued to flee him, and he lay awake with his brain in a state of violent agitation, and his eyes fixed upon the lavatory door. He pulled his clerical felt hat over his brow still farther to shield him from the light; and he adopted the usual expedients, such as counting a thousand or banishing thought, by which experienced invalids are accustomed to woo the approach of sleep. In the case of Mr. Rolles they proved one and all vain; he was harassed by a dozen different anxieties—the old man in the other end of the carriage haunted him in the most alarming shapes; and in whatever attitude he chose to lie the diamond in his pocket occasioned him a sensible physical distress. It burned, it was too large, it bruised his ribs; and there were infinitesimal fractions of a second in which he had half a mind to throw it from the window.

While he was thus lying, a strange incident took place.

The sliding door into the lavatory stirred a little, and then a little more, and was finally drawn back for the space of about twenty inches. The lamp in the lavatory was unshaded, and in the lighted aperture thus disclosed, Mr. Rolles could see the head of Mr. Vandeleur in an attitude of deep attention. He was conscious that the gaze of the Dictator rested intently on his own face; and the instinct of self-preservation moved him to hold his breath, to refrain from the least movement, and keeping his eyes lowered, to watch his visitor from underneath the lashes. After about a moment, the head was withdrawn and the door of the lavatory replaced.

The Dictator had not come to attack, but to observe; his action was not that of a man threatening another, but that of a man who was himself threatened; if Mr. Rolles was afraid of him, it appeared that he, in his turn, was not quite easy on the score of Mr. Rolles. He had come, it would seem, to make sure that his only fellow traveller was asleep; and, when satisfied on that point, he had at once withdrawn.

The clergyman leaped to his feet. The extreme of terror had given place to a reaction of foolhardy daring. He reflected that the rattle of the flying train concealed all other sounds, and determined, come what might, to return the visit he had just received. Divesting himself of his cloak, which might have interfered with the freedom of his action, he entered the lavatory and paused to listen. As he had expected, there was nothing to be heard above the roar of the train's progress; and laying his hand on the door at the farther side, he proceeded cautiously to draw it back for about six inches. Then he stopped, and could not contain an ejaculation of surprise.

John Vandeleur wore a fur travelling cap with lappets to protect his ears; and this may have combined with the sound of the express to keep him in ignorance of what was going forward. It is certain, at least, that he did not raise his head, but continued without interruption to pursue his strange employment. Between his feet stood an open hatbox; in one hand he held the sleeve of his sealskin greatcoat, in the other a formidable knife, with which he had just slit up the lining of the sleeve. Mr. Rolles had read of persons carrying money in a belt; and as he had no acquaintance with any but cricketbelts, he had never been able rightly to conceive how this was managed. But here was a stranger thing before his eyes; for John Vandeleur, it appeared, carried diamonds in the lining of his sleeve; and even as the young clergyman gazed, he could see one glittering brilliant drop after another into the hatbox.

He stood riveted to the spot, following this unusual business with his eyes. The diamonds were, for the most part, small, and not easily distinguishable either in shape or fire. Suddenly the Dictator appeared to find a difficulty; he employed both hands and stooped over his task; but it was not until after considerable manoeuvering that he extricated a large tiara of diamonds from the lining, and held it up for some seconds' examination before he placed it with the others in the hatbox. The tiara was a ray of light to Mr. Rolles; he immediately recognised it for a part of the treasure stolen from Harry Hartley by the loiterer. There was no room for mistake; it was exactly as the detective had described it; there were the ruby stars, with a great emerald in the centre; there were the interlacing crescents; and there were the pear-shaped pendants, each a single stone, which gave a special value to Lady Vandeleur's tiara.

Mr. Rolles was hugely relieved. The Dictator was as deeply in the affair as he was; neither could tell tales upon the other. In the first glow of happiness, the clergyman suffered a deep sigh to escape him; and as his bosom had become choked and his throat dry during his previous suspense, the sigh was followed by a cough.

Mr. Vandeleur looked up; his face contracted with the blackest and most deadly passion; his eyes opened widely, and his under jaw dropped in an astonishment that was upon the brink of fury. By an instinctive movement he had covered the hatbox with the coat. For half a minute the two men stared upon each other in silence. It was not a long interval, but it sufficed for Mr. Rolles; he was one of those who think swiftly on dangerous occasions; he decided on a course of action of a singularly daring nature; and although he felt he was setting his life upon the hazard, he was the first to break silence.

"I beg your pardon," said he.

The Dictator shivered slightly, and when he spoke his voice was hoarse.

"What do you want here?" he asked.

"I take a particular interest in diamonds," replied Mr. Rolles, with an air of perfect self-possession. "Two connoisseurs should be acquainted. I have here a trifle of my own which may perhaps serve for an introduction."

And so saying, he quietly took the case from his pocket, showed the Rajah's Diamond to the Dictator for an instant, and replaced it in security.

"It was once your brother's," he added.

John Vandeleur continued to regard him with a look of almost painful amazement; but he neither spoke nor moved.

"I was pleased to observe," resumed the young man, "that we have gems from the same collection."

The Dictator's surprise overpowered him.

"I beg your pardon," he said; "I begin to perceive that I am growing old! I am positively not prepared for little incidents like this. But set my mind at rest upon one point: do my eyes deceive me, or are you indeed a parson?"

"I am in holy orders," answered Mr. Rolles.

"Well," cried the other, "as long as I live I will never hear another word against the cloth!"

"You flatter me," said Mr. Rolles.

"Pardon me," replied Vandeleur; "pardon me, young man. You are no coward, but it still remains to be seen whether you are not the worst of fools. Perhaps," he continued, leaning back upon his seat, "perhaps you would oblige me with a few particulars. I must suppose you had some object in the stupefying impudence of your proceedings, and I confess I have a curiosity to know it."

"It is very simple," replied the clergyman; "it proceeds from my great inexperience of life."

"I shall be glad to be persuaded," answered Vandeleur.

Whereupon Mr. Rolles told him the whole story of his connection with the Rajah's Diamond, from the time he found it in Raeburn's garden to the time when he left London in the Flying Scotchman. He added a brief sketch of his feelings and thoughts during the journey, and concluded in these words:

"When I recognised the tiara I knew we were in the same attitude towards Society, and this inspired me with a hope, which I trust you will say was not ill-founded, that you might become in some sense my partner in the difficulties and, of course, the profits of my situation. To one of your special knowledge and obviously great experience the negotiation of the diamond would give but little trouble, while to me it was a matter of impossibility. On the other part, I judged that I might lose nearly as much by cutting the diamond, and that not improbably with an unskilful hand, as might enable me to pay you with proper generosity for your assistance. The subject was a delicate one to broach; and perhaps I fell short in delicacy. But I must ask you to remember that for me the situation was a new one, and I was entirely unacquainted with the etiquette in use. I believe without vanity that I could have married or baptised you in a very acceptable manner; but every man has his own aptitudes, and this sort of bargain was not among the list of my accomplishments."

"I do not wish to flatter you," replied Vandeleur; "but upon my word, you have an unusual disposition for a life of crime. You have more accomplishments than you imagine; and though I have encountered a number of rogues in different quarters of the world, I never met with one so unblushing as yourself. Cheer up, Mr. Rolles, you are in the right profession at last! As for helping you, you may command me as you will. I have only a day's business in Edinburgh on a little matter for my brother; and once that is concluded, I return to Paris, where I usually reside. If you please, you may accompany me thither. And before the end of a month I believe I shall have brought your little business to a satisfactory conclusion."

(At this point, contrary to all the canons of his art, our Arabian Author breaks off the STORY OF THE YOUNG MAN IN HOLY ORDERS. *I regret and condemn such practices; but I must follow my original, and*

refer the reader for the conclusion of Mr. Rolles' adventures to the next number of the cycle, the STORY OF THE HOUSE WITH THE GREEN BLINDS.)

Story of the House with the Green Blinds

Francis Scrymgeour, a clerk in the Bank of Scotland at Edinburgh, had attained the age of twenty-five in a sphere of quiet, creditable, and domestic life. His mother died while he was young; but his father, a man of sense and probity, had given him an excellent education at school, and brought him up at home to orderly and frugal habits. Francis, who was of a docile and affectionate disposition, profited by these advantages with zeal, and devoted himself heart and soul to his employment. A walk upon Saturday afternoon, an occasional dinner with members of his family, and a yearly tour of a fortnight in the Highlands or even on the continent of Europe, were his principal distractions, and he grew rapidly in favour with his superiors, and enjoyed already a salary of nearly two hundred pounds a year, with the prospect of an ultimate advance to almost double that amount. Few young men were more contented, few more willing and laborious than Francis Scrymgeour. Sometimes at night, when he had read the daily paper, he would play upon the flute to amuse his father, for whose qualities he entertained a great respect.

One day he received a note from a well-known firm of Writers to the Signet, requesting the favour of an immediate interview with him. The letter was marked "Private and Confidential," and had been addressed to him at the bank, instead of at home—two unusual circumstances which made him obey the summons with the more alacrity. The senior member of the firm, a man of much austerity of manner, made him gravely welcome, requested him to take a seat, and proceeded to explain the matter in hand in the picked expressions of a veteran man of business. A person, who must remain nameless, but of whom the lawyer had every reason to think well—a man, in short, of some station in the country—desired to make Francis an annual allowance of five hundred pounds. The capital was to be placed under the control of the lawyer's firm and two trustees who must also remain anonymous. There were conditions annexed to this liberality, but he was of opinion that his new client would find nothing either excessive or dishonourable in the terms; and he repeated these two words with emphasis, as though he desired to commit himself to nothing more.

Francis asked their nature.

"The conditions," said the Writer to the Signet, "are, as I have twice remarked, neither dishonourable nor excessive. At the same time I cannot conceal from you that they are most unusual. Indeed, the whole case is very much out of our way; and I should certainly have refused it had it not been for the reputation of the gentleman who entrusted it to my care, and, let me add, Mr. Scrymgeour, the interest I have been led to take in yourself by many complimentary and, I have no doubt, well-deserved reports."

Francis entreated him to be more specific.

"You cannot picture my uneasiness as to these conditions," he said.

"They are two," replied the lawyer, "only two; and the sum, as you will remember, is five hundred a year—and unburdened, I forgot to add, unburdened."

And the lawyer raised his eyebrows at him with solemn gusto.

"The first," he resumed, "is of remarkable simplicity. You must be in Paris by the afternoon of Sunday, the 15th; there you will find, at the box office of the Comédie Française, a ticket for admission taken in your name and waiting you. You are requested to sit out the whole performance in the seat provided, and that is all."

"I should certainly have preferred a weekday," replied Francis. "But, after all, once in a way——"

"And in Paris, my dear sir," added the lawyer, soothingly. "I believe I am something of a precisian myself, but upon such a consideration, and in Paris, I should not hesitate an instant."

And the pair laughed pleasantly together.

"The other is of more importance," continued the Writer to the

Signet. "It regards your marriage. My client, taking a deep interest in your welfare, desires to advise you absolutely in the choice of a wife. Absolutely, you understand," he repeated.

"Let us be more explicit, if you please," returned Francis. "Am I to marry anyone, maid or widow, black or white, whom this invisible person chooses to propose?"

"I was to assure you that suitability of age and position should be a principle with your benefactor," replied the lawyer. "As to race, I confess the difficulty had not occurred to me, and I failed to inquire; but if you like I will make a note of it at once, and advise you on the earliest opportunity."

"Sir," said Francis, "it remains to be seen whether this whole affair is not a most unworthy fraud. The circumstances are inexplicable—I had almost said incredible; and until I see a little more daylight, and some plausible motive, I confess I should be very sorry to put a hand to the transaction. I appeal to you in this difficulty for information. I must learn what is at the bottom of it all. If you do not know, cannot guess, or are not at liberty to tell me, I shall take my hat and go back to my bank as I came."

"I do not know," answered the lawyer, "but I have an excellent guess. Your father, and no one else, is at the root of this apparently unnatural business."

"My father!" cried Francis, in extreme disdain. "Worthy man, I know every thought of his mind, every penny of his fortune!"

"You misinterpret my words," said the lawyer. "I do not refer to Mr. Scrymgeour, senior; for he is not your father. When he and his wife came to Edinburgh, you were already nearly one year old, and you had not yet been three months in their care. The secret has been well kept; but such is the fact. Your father is unknown, and I say again that I believe him to be the original of the offers I am charged at present to transmit to you."

It would be impossible to exaggerate the astonishment of Francis Scrymgeour at this unexpected information. He pled this confusion to the lawyer.

"Sir," said he, "after a piece of news so startling, you must grant me some hours for thought. You shall know this evening what conclusion I have reached."

The lawyer commended his prudence; and Francis, excusing himself upon some pretext at the bank, took a long walk into the country, and fully considered the different steps and aspects of the case. A pleasant sense of his own importance rendered him the more deliberate: but the issue was from the first not doubtful. His whole carnal man leaned irresistibly towards the five hundred a year, and the strange conditions with which it was burdened; he discovered in his heart an invincible repugnance to the name of Scrymgeour, which he had never hitherto disliked; he began to despise the narrow and unromantic interests of his former life; and when once his mind was fairly made up, he walked with a new feeling of strength and freedom, and nourished himself with the gayest anticipations.

He said but a word to the lawyer, and immediately received a cheque for two quarters' arrears; for the allowance was antedated from the first of January. With this in his pocket, he walked home. The flat in Scotland Street looked mean in his eyes; his nostrils, for the first time, rebelled against the odour of broth; and he observed little defects of manner in his adoptive father which filled him with surprise and almost with disgust. The next day, he determined, should see him on his way to Paris.

In that city, where he arrived long before the appointed date, he put up at a modest hotel frequented by English and Italians, and devoted himself to improvement in the French tongue; for this purpose he had a master twice a week, entered into conversation with loiterers in the Champs Elysées, and nightly frequented the theatre. He had his whole toilette fashionably renewed; and was shaved and had his hair dressed every morning by a barber in a neighbouring street. This gave him something of a foreign air, and seemed to wipe off the reproach of his past years.

At length, on the Saturday afternoon, he betook himself to the box office of the theatre in the Rue Richelieu. No sooner had he mentioned his name than the clerk produced the order in an envelope of which the address was scarcely dry.

"It has been taken this moment," said the clerk.

"Indeed!" said Francis. "May I ask what the gentleman was like?"

"Your friend is easy to describe," replied the official. "He is old and strong and beautiful, with white hair and a sabre cut across his face. You cannot fail to recognise so marked a person."

"No, indeed," returned Francis; "and I thank you for your politeness."

"He cannot yet be far distant," added the clerk. "If you make haste you might still overtake him."

Francis did not wait to be twice told; he ran precipitately from the theatre into the middle of the street and looked in all directions. More than one white-haired man was within sight; but though he overtook each of them in succession, all wanted the sabre cut. For nearly half an hour he tried one street after another in the neighbourhood, until at length, recognising the folly of continued search, he started on a walk to compose his agitated feelings; for this proximity of an encounter with him to whom he could not doubt he owed the day had profoundly moved the young man.

It chanced that his way lay up the Rue Drouot and thence up the Rue des Martyrs; and chance, in this case, served him better than all the forethought in the world. For on the outer boulevard he saw two men in earnest colloquy upon a seat. One was dark, young, and handsome, secularly dressed, but with an indelible clerical stamp; the other answered in every particular to the description given him by the clerk. Francis felt his heart beat high in his bosom; he knew he was now about to hear the voice of his father; and making a wide circuit, he noiselessly took his place behind the couple in question, who were too much interested in their talk to observe much else. As Francis had expected, the conversation was conducted in the English language.

"Your suspicions begin to annoy me, Rolles," said the older man. "I tell you I am doing my utmost; a man cannot lay his hand on millions in a moment. Have I not taken you up, a mere stranger, out of pure good will? Are you not living largely on my bounty?"

"On your advances, Mr. Vandeleur," corrected the other.

"Advances, if you choose; and interest instead of goodwill, if you prefer it," returned Vandeleur, angrily. "I am not here to pick expressions. Business is business; and your business, let me remind you, is too muddy for such airs. Trust me, or leave me alone and find someone else; but let us have an end, for God's sake, of your jeremiads."

"I am beginning to learn the world," replied the other, "and I see that you have every reason to play me false, and not one to deal honestly. I am not here to pick expressions either; you wish the diamond for yourself; you know you do—you dare not deny it. Have you not already forged my name, and searched my lodging in my absence? I understand the cause of your delays; you are lying in wait; you are the diamond hunter, forsooth; and sooner or later, by fair means or foul, you'll lay your hands upon it. I tell you, it must stop; push me much further and I promise you a surprise."

"It does not become you to use threats," returned Vandeleur. "Two can play at that. My brother is here in Paris; the police are on the alert; and if you persist in wearying me with your caterwauling, I will arrange a little astonishment for you, Mr. Rolles. But mine shall be once and for all. Do you understand, or would you prefer me to tell it you in Hebrew? There is an end to all things, and you have come to the end of my patience. Tuesday, at seven; not a day, not an hour sooner, not the least part of a second, if it were to save your life. And if you do not choose to wait, you may go to the bottomless pit for me, and welcome."

And so saying, the Dictator arose from the bench, and marched off in the direction of Montmartre, shaking his head and swinging his cane with a most furious air; while his companion remained where he was, in an attitude of great dejection.

Francis was at the pitch of surprise and horror; his sentiments had been shocked to the last degree; the hopeful tenderness with which he had taken his place upon the bench was transformed into repulsion and despair; old Mr. Scrymgeour, he reflected, was a far more kindly and creditable parent than this dangerous and violent intriguer; but he retained his presence of mind, and suffered not a moment to elapse before he was on the trail of the Dictator.

That gentleman's fury carried him forward at a brisk pace, and he was so completely occupied in his angry thoughts that he never so much as cast a look behind him till he reached his own door.

His house stood high up in the Rue Lepic, commanding a view

of all Paris and enjoying the pure air of the heights. It was two stories high, with green blinds and shutters; and all the windows looking on the street were hermetically closed. Tops of trees showed over the high garden wall, and the wall was protected by *chevaux-de-frise*. The Dictator paused a moment while he searched his pocket for a key; and then, opening a gate, disappeared within the enclosure.

Francis looked about him; the neighbourhood was very lonely; the house isolated in its garden. It seemed as if his observation must here come to an abrupt end. A second glance, however, showed him a tall house next door presenting a gable to the garden, and in this gable a single window. He passed to the front and saw a ticket offering unfurnished lodgings by the month; and, on inquiry, the room which commanded the Dictator's garden proved to be one of those to let. Francis did not hesitate a moment; he took the room, paid an advance upon the rent, and returned to his hotel to seek his baggage.

The old man with the sabre cut might or might not be his father; he might or he might not be upon the true scent; but he was certainly on the edge of an exciting mystery, and he promised himself that he would not relax his observation until he had got to the bottom of the secret.

From the window of his new apartment Francis Scrymgeour commanded a complete view into the garden of the house with the green blinds. Immediately below him a very comely chestnut with wide boughs sheltered a pair of rustic tables where people might dine in the height of summer. On all sides save one a dense vegetation concealed the soil; but there, between the tables and the house, he saw a patch of gravel walk leading from the verandah to the garden gate. Studying the place from between the boards of the Venetian shutters, which he durst not open for fear of attracting attention, Francis observed but little to indicate the manners of the inhabitants, and that little argued no more than a close reserve and a taste for solitude. The garden was conventual, the house had the air of a prison. The green blinds were all drawn down upon the outside; the door into the verandah was closed; the garden, as far as he could see it, was left entirely to itself in the evening sunshine. A modest curl of smoke from a single chimney alone testified to the presence of living people.

In order that he might not be entirely idle, and to give a certain colour to his way of life, Francis had purchased Euclid's Geometry in French, which he set himself to copy and translate on the top of his portmanteau and seated on the floor against the wall; for he was equally without chair or table. From time to time he would rise and cast a glance into the enclosure of the house with the green blinds; but the windows remained obstinately closed and the garden empty.

Only late in the evening did anything occur to reward his continued attention. Between nine and ten the sharp tinkle of a bell aroused him from a fit of dozing; and he sprang to his observatory in time to hear an important noise of locks being opened and bars removed, and to see Mr. Vandeleur, carrying a lantern and clothed in a flowing robe of black velvet with a skullcap to match, issue from under the verandah and proceed leisurely towards the garden gate. The sound of bolts and bars was then repeated; and a moment after Francis perceived the Dictator escorting into the house, in the mobile light of the lantern, an individual of the lowest and most despicable appearance.

Half an hour afterwards the visitor was reconducted to the street; and Mr. Vandeleur, setting his light upon one of the rustic tables, finished a cigar with great deliberation under the foliage of the chestnut. Francis, peering through a clear space among the leaves, was able to follow his gestures as he threw away the ash or enjoyed a copious inhalation; and beheld a cloud upon the old man's brow and a forcible action of the lips, which testified to some deep and probably painful train of thought. The cigar was already almost at an end, when the voice of a young girl was heard suddenly crying the hour from the interior of the house.

"In a moment," replied John Vandeleur.

And, with that, he threw away the stump and, taking up the lantern, sailed away under the verandah for the night. As soon as the door was closed, absolute darkness fell upon the house; Francis might try his eyesight as much as he pleased, he could not detect so much as a single chink of light below a blind; and he concluded, with great good sense, that the bedchambers were all upon the other side.

Early the next morning (for he was early awake after an uncomfortable night upon the floor), he saw cause to adopt a different explanation. The blinds rose, one after another, by means of a spring in the interior, and disclosed steel shutters such as we see on the front of shops; these in their turn were rolled up by a similar contrivance; and for the space of about an hour, the chambers were left open to the morning air. At the end of that time, Mr. Vandeleur, with his own hand, once more closed the shutters and replaced the blinds from within.

While Francis was still marvelling at these precautions, the door opened and a young girl came forth to look about her in the garden. It was not two minutes before she reentered the house, but even in that short time he saw enough to convince him that she possessed the most unusual attractions. His curiosity was not only highly excited by this incident, but his spirits were improved to a still more notable degree. The alarming manners and more than equivocal life of his father ceased from that moment to prey upon his mind; from that moment he embraced his new family with ardour; and whether the young lady should prove his sister or his wife, he felt convinced she was an angel in disguise. So much was this the case that he was seized with a sudden horror when he reflected how little he really knew, and how possible it was that he had followed the wrong person when he followed Mr. Vandeleur.

The porter, whom he consulted, could afford him little information; but, such as it was, it had a mysterious and questionable sound. The person next door was an English gentleman of extraordinary wealth, and proportionately eccentric in his tastes and habits. He possessed great collections, which he kept in the house beside him; and it was to protect these that he had fitted the place with steel shutters, elaborate fastenings, and *chevaux-de-frise* along the garden wall. He lived much alone, in spite of some strange visitors with whom, it seemed, he had business to transact; and there was no one else in the house, except Mademoiselle and an old woman servant.

"Is Mademoiselle his daughter?" inquired Francis.

"Certainly," replied the porter. "Mademoiselle is the daughter of the house; and strange it is to see how she is made to work. For all his riches, it is she who goes to market; and every day in the week you may see her going by with a basket on her arm."

"And the collections?" asked the other.

"Sir," said the man, "they are immensely valuable. More I cannot tell you. Since M. de Vandeleur's arrival no one in the quarter has so much as passed the door."

"Suppose not," returned Francis, "you must surely have some notion what these famous galleries contain. Is it pictures, silks, statues, jewels, or what?"

"My faith, sir," said the fellow with a shrug, "it might be carrots, and still I could not tell you. How should I know? The house is kept like a garrison, as you perceive."

And then as Francis was returning disappointed to his room, the porter called him back.

"I have just remembered, sir," said he. "M. de Vandeleur has been in all parts of the world, and I once heard the old woman declare that he had brought many diamonds back with him. If that be the truth, there must be a fine show behind those shutters."

By an early hour on Sunday Francis was in his place at the theatre. The seat which had been taken for him was only two or three numbers from the left-hand side, and directly opposite one of the lower boxes. As the seat had been specially chosen there was doubtless something to be learned from its position; and he judged by an instinct that the box upon his right was, in some way or other, to be connected with the drama in which he ignorantly played a part. Indeed it was so situated that its occupants could safely observe him from beginning to end of the piece, if they were so minded; while, profiting by the depth, they could screen themselves sufficiently well from any counterexamination on his side. He promised himself not to leave it for a moment out of sight; and whilst he scanned the rest of the theatre, or made a show of attending to the business of the stage, he always kept a corner of an eye upon the empty box.

The second act had been some time in progress, and was even drawing towards a close, when the door opened and two persons entered and ensconced themselves in the darkest of the shade.

Francis could hardly control his emotion. It was Mr. Vandeleur and his daughter. The blood came and went in his arteries and veins with stunning activity; his ears sang; his head turned. He dared not look lest he should awake suspicion; his playbill, which he kept reading from end to end and over and over again, turned from white to red before his eyes; and when he cast a glance upon the stage, it seemed incalculably far away, and he found the voices and gestures of the actors to the last degree impertinent and absurd.

From time to time he risked a momentary look in the direction which principally interested him; and once at least he felt certain that his eyes encountered those of the young girl. A shock passed over his body, and he saw all the colours of the rainbow. What would he not have given to overhear what passed between the Vandeleurs? What would he not have given for the courage to take up his opera glass and steadily inspect their attitude and expression? There, for aught he knew, his whole life was being decided—and he not able to interfere, not able even to follow the debate, but condemned to sit and suffer where he was, in impotent anxiety.

At last the act came to an end. The curtain fell, and the people around him began to leave their places for the interval. It was only natural that he should follow their example; and if he did so, it was not only natural but necessary that he should pass immediately in front of the box in question. Summoning all his courage, but keeping his eyes lowered, Francis drew near the spot. His progress was slow, for the old gentleman before him moved with incredible deliberation, wheezing as he went. What was he to do? Should he address the Vandeleurs by name as he went by? Should he take the flower from his buttonhole and throw it into the box? Should he raise his face and direct one long and affectionate look upon the lady who was either his sister or his betrothed? As he found himself thus struggling among so many alternatives, he had a vision of his old equable existence in the bank, and was assailed by a thought of regret for the past.

By this time he had arrived directly opposite the box; and although he was still undetermined what to do or whether to do anything, he turned his head and lifted his eyes. No sooner had he done so than he uttered a cry of disappointment and remained rooted to the spot. The box was empty. During his slow advance Mr. Vandeleur and his daughter had quietly slipped away.

A polite person in his rear reminded him that he was stopping the path; and he moved on again with mechanical footsteps, and suffered the crowd to carry him unresisting out of the theatre. Once in the street, the pressure ceasing, he came to a halt, and the cool night air speedily restored him to the possession of his faculties. He was surprised to find that his head ached violently, and that he remembered not one word of the two acts which he had witnessed. As the excitement wore away, it was succeeded by an overweening appetite for sleep, and he hailed a cab and drove to his lodging in a state of extreme exhaustion and some disgust of life.

Next morning he lay in wait for Miss Vandeleur on her road to market, and by eight o'clock beheld her stepping down a lane. She was simply, and even poorly, attired; but in the carriage of her head and body there was something flexible and noble that would have lent distinction to the meanest toilette. Even her basket, so aptly did she carry it, became her like an ornament. It seemed to Francis, as he slipped into a doorway, that the sunshine followed and the shadows fled before her as she walked; and he was conscious, for the first time, of a bird singing in a cage above the lane.

He suffered her to pass the doorway, and then, coming forth once more, addressed her by name from behind.

"Miss Vandeleur," said he.

She turned and, when she saw who he was, became deadly pale.

"Pardon me," he continued; "Heaven knows I had no will to startle you; and, indeed, there should be nothing startling in the presence of one who wishes you so well as I do. And, believe me, I am acting rather from necessity than choice. We have many things in common, and I am sadly in the dark. There is much that I should be doing, and my hands are tied. I do not know even what to feel, nor who are my friends and enemies."

She found her voice with an effort.

"I do not know who you are," she said.

"Ah, yes! Miss Vandeleur, you do," returned Francis; "better than I do myself. Indeed it is on that, above all, that I seek light. Tell me what you know," he pleaded. "Tell me who I am, who you are, and how our destinies are intermixed. Give me a little help with my life, Miss Vandeleur—only a word or two to guide me, only the name of my father, if you will—and I shall be grateful and content."

"I will not attempt to deceive you," she replied. "I know who you are, but I am not at liberty to say."

"Tell me, at least, that you have forgiven my presumption, and I shall wait with all the patience I have," he said. "If I am not to know, I must do without. It is cruel, but I can bear more upon a push. Only do not add to my troubles the thought that I have made an enemy of you."

"You did only what was natural," she said, "and I have nothing to forgive you. Farewell."

"Is it to be *farewell*?" he asked.

"Nay, that I do not know myself," she answered. "Farewell for the present, if you like."

And with these words she was gone.

Francis returned to his lodging in a state of considerable commotion of mind. He made the most trifling progress with his Euclid for that forenoon, and was more often at the window than at his improvised writing table. But beyond seeing the return of Miss Vandeleur, and the meeting between her and her father, who was smoking a Trichinopoli cigar in the verandah, there was nothing notable in the neighbourhood of the house with the green blinds before the time of the midday meal. The young man hastily allayed his appetite in a neighbouring restaurant, and returned with the speed of unallayed curiosity to the house in the Rue Lepic. A mounted servant was leading a saddle horse to and fro before the garden wall; and the porter of Francis's lodging was smoking a pipe against the doorpost, absorbed in contemplation of the livery and the steeds.

"Look!" he cried to the young man, "what fine cattle! what an elegant costume! They belong to the brother of M. de Vandeleur, who is now within upon a visit. He is a great man, a general, in your country; and you doubtless know him well by reputation."

"I confess," returned Francis, "that I have never heard of General Vandeleur before. We have many officers of that grade, and my pursuits have been exclusively civil."

"It is he," replied the porter, "who lost the great diamond of the Indies. Of that at least you must have read often in the papers."

As soon as Francis could disengage himself from the porter he ran upstairs and hurried to the window. Immediately below the clear space in the chestnut leaves, the two gentlemen were seated in conversation over a cigar. The General, a red, military-looking man, offered some traces of a family resemblance to his brother; he had something of the same features, something, although very little, of the same free and powerful carriage; but he was older, smaller, and more common in air; his likeness was that of a caricature, and he seemed altogether a poor and debile being by the side of the Dictator.

They spoke in tones so low, leaning over the table with every appearance of interest, that Francis could catch no more than a word or two on an occasion. For as little as he heard, he was convinced that the conversation turned upon himself and his own career; several times the name of Scrymgeour reached his ear, for it was easy to distinguish, and still more frequently he fancied he could distinguish the name Francis.

At length the General, as if in a hot anger, broke forth into several violent exclamations.

"Francis Vandeleur!" he cried, accentuating the last word. "Francis Vandeleur, I tell you."

The Dictator made a movement of his whole body, half affirmative, half contemptuous, but his answer was inaudible to the young man.

Was he the Francis Vandeleur in question? he wondered. Were they discussing the name under which he was to be married? Or was the whole affair a dream and a delusion of his own conceit and self-absorption?

After another interval of inaudible talk, dissension seemed again to arise between the couple underneath the chestnut, and again the General raised his voice angrily so as to be audible to Francis.

"My wife?" he cried. "I have done with my wife for good. I will not hear her name. I am sick of her very name."

And he swore aloud and beat the table with his fist.

The Dictator appeared, by his gestures, to pacify him after a paternal fashion; and a little after he conducted him to the garden gate. The pair shook hands affectionately enough; but as soon as the door had closed behind his visitor, John Vandeleur fell into a fit of laughter which sounded unkindly and even devilish in the ears of Francis Scrymgeour.

So another day had passed, and little more learnt. But the young man remembered that the morrow was Tuesday, and promised himself some curious discoveries; all might be well, or all might be ill; he was sure, at least, to glean some curious information, and, perhaps, by good luck, get at the heart of the mystery which surrounded his father and his family.

As the hour of the dinner drew near many preparations were made in the garden of the house with the green blinds. That table which was partly visible to Francis through the chestnut leaves was destined to serve as a sideboard, and carried relays of plates and the materials for salad: the other, which was almost entirely concealed, had been set apart for the diners, and Francis could catch glimpses of white cloth and silver plate.

Mr. Rolles arrived, punctual to the minute; he looked like a man upon his guard, and spoke low and sparingly. The Dictator, on the other hand, appeared to enjoy an unusual flow of spirits; his laugh, which was youthful and pleasant to hear, sounded frequently from the garden; by the modulation and the changes of his voice it was obvious that he told many droll stories and imitated the accents of a variety of different nations; and before he and the young clergyman had finished their vermouth all feeling of distrust was at an end, and they were talking together like a pair of school companions.

At length Miss Vandeleur made her appearance, carrying the soup tureen. Mr. Rolles ran to offer her assistance which she laughingly refused; and there was an interchange of pleasantries among the trio which seemed to have reference to this primitive manner of waiting by one of the company.

"One is more at one's ease," Mr. Vandeleur was heard to declare.

Next moment they were all three in their places, and Francis could see as little as he could hear of what passed. But the dinner seemed to go merrily; there was a perpetual babble of voices and sound of knives and forks below the chestnut; and Francis, who had no more than a roll to gnaw, was affected with envy by the comfort and deliberation of the meal. The party lingered over one dish after another, and then over a delicate dessert, with a bottle of old wine carefully uncorked by the hand of the Dictator himself. As it began to grow dark a lamp was set upon the table and a couple of candles on the sideboard; for the night was perfectly pure, starry, and windless. Light overflowed besides from the door and window in the verandah, so that the garden was fairly illuminated and the leaves twinkled in the darkness.

For perhaps the tenth time Miss Vandeleur entered the house; and on this occasion she returned with the coffee tray, which she placed upon the sideboard. At the same moment her father rose from his seat.

"The coffee is my province," Francis heard him say.

And next moment he saw his supposed father standing by the sideboard in the light of the candles.

Talking over his shoulder all the while, Mr. Vandeleur poured out two cups of the brown stimulant, and then, by a rapid act of prestidigitation, emptied the contents of a tiny phial into the smaller of the two. The thing was so swiftly done that even Francis, who looked straight into his face, had hardly time to perceive the movement before it was completed. And next instant, and still laughing, Mr. Vandeleur had turned again towards the table with a cup in either hand.

"Ere we have done with this," said he, "we may expect our famous Hebrew."

It would be impossible to depict the confusion and distress of Francis Scrymgeour. He saw foul play going forward before his eyes, and he felt bound to interfere, but knew not how. It might be a mere pleasantry, and then how should he look if he were to offer an unnecessary warning? Or again, if it were serious, the criminal might be his own father, and then how should he not lament if he were to bring ruin on the author of his days? For the first time he became conscious of his own position as a spy. To wait inactive at such a juncture and with such a conflict of sentiments in his bosom was to suffer the most acute torture; he clung to the bars of the shutters, his heart beat fast and with irregularity, and he felt a strong sweat break forth upon his body.

Several minutes passed.

He seemed to perceive the conversation die away and grow less and less in vivacity and volume; but still no sign of any alarming or even notable event.

Suddenly the ring of a glass breaking was followed by a faint and dull sound, as of a person who should have fallen forward with his head upon the table. At the same moment a piercing scream rose from the garden.

"What have you done?" cried Miss Vandeleur. "He is dead!"

The Dictator replied in a violent whisper, so strong and sibilant that every word was audible to the watcher at the window.

"Silence!" said Mr. Vandeleur; "the man is as well as I am. Take him by the heels whilst I carry him by the shoulders."

Francis heard Miss Vandeleur break forth into a passion of tears.

"Do you hear what I say?" resumed the Dictator, in the same tones. "Or do you wish to quarrel with me? I give you your choice, Miss Vandeleur."

There was another pause, and the Dictator spoke again.

"Take that man by the heels," he said. "I must have him brought into the house. If I were a little younger, I could help myself against the world. But now that years and dangers are upon me and my hands are weakened, I must turn to you for aid."

"It is a crime," replied the girl.

"I am your father," said Mr. Vandeleur.

This appeal seemed to produce its effect. A scuffling noise followed upon the gravel, a chair was overset, and then Francis saw the father and daughter stagger across the walk and disappear under the verandah, bearing the inanimate body of Mr. Rolles embraced about the knees and shoulders. The young clergyman was limp and pallid, and his head rolled upon his shoulders at every step.

Was he alive or dead? Francis, in spite of the Dictator's declaration, inclined to the latter view. A great crime had been committed; a great calamity had fallen upon the inhabitants of the house with the green blinds. To his surprise, Francis found all horror for the deed swallowed up in sorrow for a girl and an old man whom he judged to be in the height of peril. A tide of generous feeling swept into his heart; he, too, would help his father against man and mankind, against fate and justice; and casting open the shutters he closed his eyes and threw himself with outstretched arms into the foliage of the chestnut.

Branch after branch slipped from his grasp or broke under his weight; then he caught a stalwart bough under his armpit, and hung suspended for a second; and then he let himself drop and fell heavily against the table. A cry of alarm from the house warned him that his entrance had not been effected unobserved. He recovered himself with a stagger, and in three bounds crossed the intervening space and stood before the door in the verandah.

In a small apartment, carpeted with matting and surrounded by glazed cabinets full of rare and costly curios, Mr. Vandeleur was stooping over the body of Mr. Rolles. He raised himself as Francis entered, and there was an instantaneous passage of hands. It was the business of a second; as fast as an eye can wink the thing was done; the young man had not the time to be sure, but it seemed to him as if the Dictator had taken something from the curate's breast, looked at it for the least fraction of time as it lay in his hand, and then suddenly and swiftly passed it to his daughter.

All this was over while Francis had still one foot upon the threshold, and the other raised in air. The next instant he was on his knees to Mr. Vandeleur.

"Father!" he cried. "Let me too help you. I will do what you wish and ask no questions; I will obey you with my life; treat me as a son, and you will find I have a son's devotion."

A deplorable explosion of oaths was the Dictator's first reply.

"Son and father?" he cried. "Father and son? What d—d unnatural comedy is all this? How do you come in my garden? What do you want? And who, in God's name, are you?"

Francis, with a stunned and shamefaced aspect, got upon his feet again, and stood in silence.

Then a light seemed to break upon Mr. Vandeleur, and he laughed aloud.

"I see," cried he. "It is the Scrymgeour. Very well, Mr. Scrymgeour. Let me tell you in a few words how you stand. You have entered my private residence by force, or perhaps by fraud, but certainly with no encouragement from me; and you come at a moment of some annoyance, a guest having fainted at my table, to besiege me with your protestations. You are no son of mine. You are my brother's bastard by a fishwife, if you want to know. I regard you with an indifference closely bordering on aversion; and from what I now see of your conduct, I judge your mind to be exactly suitable to your exterior. I recommend you these mortifying reflections for your leisure; and, in the meantime, let me beseech you to rid us of your presence. If I were not occupied," added the Dictator, with a terrifying oath, "I should give you the unholiest drubbing ere you went!"

Francis listened in profound humiliation. He would have fled had it been possible; but as he had no means of leaving the residence into which he had so unfortunately penetrated, he could do no more than stand foolishly where he was.

It was Miss Vandeleur who broke the silence.

"Father," she said, "you speak in anger. Mr. Scrymgeour may have been mistaken, but he meant well and kindly."

"Thank you for speaking," returned the Dictator. "You remind me of some other observations which I hold it a point of honour to make to Mr. Scrymgeour. My brother," he continued, addressing the young man, "has been foolish enough to give you an allowance; he was foolish enough and presumptuous enough to propose a match between you and this young lady. You were exhibited to her two nights ago; and I rejoice to tell you that she rejected the idea with disgust. Let me add that I have considerable influence with your father; and it shall not be my fault if you are not beggared of your allowance and sent back to your scrivening ere the week be out."

The tones of the old man's voice were, if possible, more wounding than his language; Francis felt himself exposed to the most cruel, blighting, and unbearable contempt; his head turned, and he covered his face with his hands, uttering at the same time a tearless sob of agony. But Miss Vandeleur once again interfered in his behalf.

"Mr. Scrymgeour," she said, speaking in clear and even tones, "you must not be concerned at my father's harsh expressions. I felt no disgust for you; on the contrary, I asked an opportunity to make your better acquaintance. As for what has passed tonight, believe me it has filled my mind with both pity and esteem."

Just then Mr. Rolles made a convulsive movement with his arm, which convinced Francis that he was only drugged, and was beginning to throw off the influence of the opiate. Mr. Vandeleur stooped over him and examined his face for an instant.

"Come, come!" cried he, raising his head. "Let there be an end of this. And since you are so pleased with his conduct, Miss Vandeleur, take a candle and show the bastard out."

The young lady hastened to obey.

"Thank you," said Francis, as soon as he was alone with her in the garden. "I thank you from my soul. This has been the bitterest evening of my life, but it will have always one pleasant recollection."

"I spoke as I felt," she replied, "and in justice to you. It made my heart sorry that you should be so unkindly used."

By this time they had reached the garden gate; and Miss Vandeleur, having set the candle on the ground, was already unfastening the bolts.

"One word more," said Francis. "This is not for the last time—I shall see you again, shall I not?"

"Alas!" she answered. "You have heard my father. What can I do but obey?"

"Tell me at least that it is not with your consent," returned Francis; "tell me that you have no wish to see the last of me."

"Indeed," replied she, "I have none. You seem to me both brave and honest."

"Then," said Francis, "give me a keepsake."

She paused for a moment, with her hand upon the key; for the various bars and bolts were all undone, and there was nothing left but to open the lock.

"If I agree," she said, "will you promise to do as I tell you from point to point?"

"Can you ask?" replied Francis. "I would do so willingly on your bare word."

She turned the key and threw open the door.

"Be it so," said she. "You do not know what you ask, but be it so.

Whatever you hear," she continued, "whatever happens, do not return to this house; hurry fast until you reach the lighted and populous quarters of the city; even there be upon your guard. You are in a greater danger than you fancy. Promise me you will not so much as look at my keepsake until you are in a place of safety."

"I promise," replied Frances.

She put something loosely wrapped in a handkerchief into the young man's hand; and at the same time, with more strength than he could have anticipated, she pushed him into the street.

"Now, run!" she cried.

He heard the door close behind him, and the noise of the bolts being replaced.

"My faith," said he, "since I have promised!"

And he took to his heels down the lane that leads into the Rue Ravignan.

He was not fifty paces from the house with the green blinds when the most diabolical outcry suddenly arose out of the stillness of the night. Mechanically he stood still; another passenger followed his example; in the neighbouring floors he saw people crowding to the windows; a conflagration could not have produced more disturbance in this empty quarter. And yet it seemed to be all the work of a single man, roaring between grief and rage, like a lioness robbed of her whelps; and Francis was surprised and alarmed to hear his own name shouted with English imprecations to the wind.

His first movement was to return to the house; his second, as he remembered Miss Vandeleur's advice, to continue his flight with greater expedition than before; and he was in the act of turning to put his thought in action, when the Dictator, bareheaded, bawling aloud, his white hair blowing about his head, shot past him like a ball out of the cannon's mouth, and went careering down the street.

"That was a close shave," thought Francis to himself. "What he wants with me, and why he should be so disturbed, I cannot think; but he is plainly not good company for the moment, and I cannot do better than follow Miss Vandeleur's advice."

So saying, he turned to retrace his steps, thinking to double and descend by the Rue Lepic itself while his pursuer should continue to follow after him on the other line of street. The plan was ill-devised: as a matter of fact, he should have taken his seat in the nearest café, and waited there until the first heat of the pursuit was over. But besides that Francis had no experience and little natural aptitude for the small war of private life, he was so unconscious of any evil on his part, that he saw nothing to fear beyond a disagreeable interview. And to disagreeable interviews he felt he had already served his apprenticeship that evening; nor could he suppose that Miss Vandeleur had left anything unsaid. Indeed, the young man was sore both in body and mind—the one was all bruised, the other was full of smarting arrows; and he owned to himself that Mr. Vandeleur was master of a very deadly tongue.

The thought of his bruises reminded him that he had not only come without a hat, but that his clothes had considerably suffered in his descent through the chestnut. At the first magazine he purchased a cheap wideawake, and had the disorder of his toilet summarily repaired. The keepsake, still rolled in the handkerchief, he thrust in the meanwhile into his trousers pocket.

Not many steps beyond the shop he was conscious of a sudden shock, a hand upon his throat, an infuriated face close to his own, and an open mouth bawling curses in his ear. The Dictator, having found no trace of his quarry, was returning by the other way. Francis was a stalwart young fellow; but he was no match for his adversary whether in strength or skill; and after a few ineffectual struggles he resigned himself entirely to his captor.

"What do you want with me?" said he.

"We will talk of that at home," returned the Dictator, grimly.

And he continued to march the young man up hill in the direction of the house with the green blinds.

But Francis, although he no longer struggled, was only waiting an opportunity to make a bold push for freedom. With a sudden jerk he left the collar of his coat in the hands of Mr. Vandeleur, and once more made off at his best speed in the direction of the Boulevards.

The tables were now turned. If the Dictator was the stronger, Francis, in the top of his youth, was the more fleet of foot, and he had soon effected his escape among the crowds. Relieved for a moment, but with a growing sentiment of alarm and wonder in his mind, he walked briskly until he debouched upon the Place de l'Opéra, lit up like day with electric lamps.

"This, at least," thought he, "should satisfy Miss Vandeleur."

And turning to his right along the Boulevards, he entered the Café Américain and ordered some beer. It was both late and early for the majority of the frequenters of the establishment. Only two or three persons, all men, were dotted here and there at separate tables in the hall; and Francis was too much occupied by his own thoughts to observe their presence.

He drew the handkerchief from his pocket. The object wrapped in it proved to be a morocco case, clasped and ornamented in gilt, which opened by means of a spring, and disclosed to the horrified young man a diamond of monstrous bigness and extraordinary brilliancy. The circumstance was so inexplicable, the value of the stone was plainly so enormous, that Francis sat staring into the open casket without movement, without conscious thought, like a man stricken suddenly with idiocy.

A hand was laid upon his shoulder, lightly but firmly, and a quiet voice, which yet had in it the ring of command, uttered these words in his ear—

"Close the casket, and compose your face."

Looking up, he beheld a man, still young, of an urbane and tranquil presence, and dressed with rich simplicity. This personage had risen from a neighbouring table, and, bringing his glass with him, had taken a seat beside Francis.

"Close the casket," repeated the stranger, "and put it quietly back into your pocket, where I feel persuaded it should never have been. Try, if you please, to throw off your bewildered air, and act as though I were one of your acquaintances whom you had met by chance. So! Touch glasses with me. That is better. I fear, sir, you must be an amateur."

And the stranger pronounced these last words with a smile of peculiar meaning, leaned back in his seat and enjoyed a deep inhalation of tobacco.

"For God's sake," said Francis, "tell me who you are and what this means? Why I should obey your most unusual suggestions I am sure I know not; but the truth is, I have fallen this evening into so many perplexing adventures, and all I meet conduct themselves so strangely, that I think I must either have gone mad or wandered into another planet. Your face inspires me with confidence; you seem wise, good, and experienced; tell me, for heaven's sake, why you accost me in so odd a fashion?"

"All in due time," replied the stranger. "But I have the first hand, and you must begin by telling me how the Rajah's Diamond is in your possession."

"The Rajah's Diamond!" echoed Francis.

"I would not speak so loud, if I were you," returned the other. "But most certainly you have the Rajah's Diamond in your pocket. I have seen and handled it a score of times in Sir Thomas Vandeleur's collection."

"Sir Thomas Vandeleur! The General! My father!" cried Francis.

"Your father?" repeated the stranger. "I was not aware the General had any family."

"I am illegitimate, sir," replied Francis, with a flush.

The other bowed with gravity. It was a respectful bow, as of a man silently apologising to his equal; and Francis felt relieved and comforted, he scarce knew why. The society of this person did him good; he seemed to touch firm ground; a strong feeling of respect grew up in his bosom, and mechanically he removed his wideawake as though in the presence of a superior.

"I perceive," said the stranger, "that your adventures have not all been peaceful. Your collar is torn, your face is scratched, you have a cut upon your temple; you will, perhaps, pardon my curiosity when I ask you to explain how you came by these injuries, and how you happen to have stolen property to an enormous value in your pocket."

"I must differ from you!" returned Francis, hotly. "I possess no stolen property. And if you refer to the diamond, it was given to me not an hour ago by Miss Vandeleur in the Rue Lepic."

"By Miss Vandeleur of the Rue Lepic!" repeated the other. "You interest me more than you suppose. Pray continue."

"Heavens!" cried Francis.

His memory had made a sudden bound. He had seen Mr. Vandeleur take an article from the breast of his drugged visitor, and that article, he was now persuaded, was a morocco case.

"You have a light?" inquired the stranger.

"Listen," replied Francis. " I know not who you are, but I believe you to be worthy of confidence and helpful; I find myself in strange waters; I must have counsel and support, and since you invite me I shall tell you all."

And he briefly recounted his experiences since the day when he was summoned from the bank by his lawyer.

"Yours is indeed a remarkable history," said the stranger, after the young man had made an end of his narrative; "and your position is full of difficulty and peril. Many would counsel you to seek out your father, and give the diamond to him; but I have other views. Waiter!" he cried.

The waiter drew near.

"Will you ask the manager to speak with me a moment?" said he; and Francis observed once more, both in his tone and manner, the evidence of a habit of command.

The waiter withdrew, and returned in a moment with the manager, who bowed with obsequious respect.

"What," said he, "can I do to serve you?"

"Have the goodness," replied the stranger, indicating Francis, "to tell this gentleman my name."

"You have the honour, sir," said the functionary, addressing young Scrymgeour, "to occupy the same table with His Highness Prince Florizel of Bohemia."

Francis rose with precipitation, and made a grateful reverence to the Prince, who bade him resume his seat.

"I thank you," said Florizel, once more addressing the functionary; "I am sorry to have deranged you for so small a matter."

And he dismissed him with a movement of his hand.

"And now," added the Prince, turning to Francis, "give me the diamond."

Without a word the casket was handed over.

"You have done right," said Florizel; "your sentiments have properly inspired you, and you will live to be grateful for the misfortunes of tonight. A man, Mr. Scrymgeour, may fall into a thousand perplexities, but if his heart be upright and his intelligence unclouded, he will issue from them all without dishonour. Let your mind be at rest; your affairs are in my hand; and with the aid of heaven I am strong enough to bring them to a good end. Follow me, if you please, to my carriage."

So saying the Prince arose and, having left a piece of gold for the waiter, conducted the young man from the café and along the Boulevard to where an unpretentious brougham and a couple of servants out of livery awaited his arrival.

"This carriage," said he, "is at your disposal; collect your baggage as rapidly as you can make it convenient, and my servants will conduct you to a villa in the neighbourhood of Paris where you can wait in some degree of comfort until I have had time to arrange your situation. You will find there a pleasant garden, a library of good authors, a cook, a cellar, and some good cigars, which I recommend to your attention. Jérome," he added, turning to one of the servants, "you have heard what I say; I leave Mr. Scrymgeour in your charge; you will, I know, be careful of my friend."

Francis uttered some broken phrases of gratitude.

"It will be time enough to thank me," said the Prince, "when you are acknowledged by your father and married to Miss Vandeleur."

And with that the Prince turned away and strolled leisurely in the direction of Montmartre. He hailed the first passing cab, gave an address, and a quarter of an hour afterwards, having discharged the driver some distance lower, he was knocking at Mr. Vandeleur's garden gate.

It was opened with singular precautions by the Dictator in person.

"Who are you?" he demanded.

"You must pardon me this late visit, Mr. Vandeleur," replied the Prince.

"Your Highness is always welcome," returned Mr. Vandeleur, stepping back.

The Prince profited by the open space, and without waiting for his host walked right into the house and opened the door of the *salon.* Two people were seated there; one was Miss Vandeleur, who bore the marks of weeping about her eyes, and was still shaken from time to time by a sob; in the other the Prince recognised the young man who had consulted him on literary matters about a month before, in a club smoking room.

"Good evening, Miss Vandeleur," said Florizel; "you look fatigued. Mr. Rolles, I believe? I hope you have profited by the study of Gaboriau, Mr. Rolles."

But the young clergyman's temper was too much embittered for speech; and he contented himself with bowing stiffly, and continued to gnaw his lip.

"To what good wind," said Mr. Vandeleur, following his guest, "am I to attribute the honour of your Highness's presence?"

"I am come on business," returned the Prince; "on business with you; as soon as that is settled I shall request Mr.Rolles to accompany me for a walk. Mr. Rolles," he added, with severity, "let me remind you that I have not yet sat down."

The clergyman sprang to his feet with an apology; whereupon the Prince took an armchair beside the table, handed his hat to Mr. Vandeleur, his cane to Mr. Rolles, and, leaving them standing and thus menially employed upon his service, spoke as follows:

"I have come here, as I said, upon business; but, had I come looking for pleasure, I could not have been more displeased with my reception nor more dissatisfied with my company. You, sir," addressing Mr. Rolles, "you have treated your superior in station with discourtesy; you, Vandeleur, receive me with a smile, but you know right well that your hands are not yet cleansed from misconduct. I do not desire to be interrupted, sir," he added, imperiously; "I am here to speak, and not to listen; and I have to ask you to hear me with respect, and to obey punctiliously. At the earliest possible date your daughter shall be married at the Embassy to my friend, Francis Scrymgeour, your brother's acknowledged son. You will oblige me by offering not less than ten thousand pounds dowry. For yourself, I will indicate to you in writing a mission of some importance in Siam which I destine to your care. And now, sir, you will answer me in two words whether or not you agree to these conditions."

"Your Highness will pardon me," said Mr. Vandeleur, "and permit me, with all respect, to submit to him two queries?"

"The permission is granted," replied the Prince.

"Your Highness," resumed the Dictator, "has called Mr. Scrymgeour his friend. Believe me, had I known he was thus honoured, I should have treated him with proportional respect."

"You interrogate adroitly," said the Prince; "but it will not serve your turn. You have my commands; if I had never seen that gentleman before tonight, it would not render them less absolute."

"Your Highness interprets my meaning with his usual subtlety," returned Vandeleur. "Once more: I have, unfortunately, put the police upon the track of Mr. Scrymgeour on a charge of theft; am I to withdraw or to uphold the accusation?"

"You will please yourself," replied Florizel. "The question is one between your conscience and the laws of this land. Give me my hat; and you, Mr. Rolles, give me my cane and follow me. Miss Vandeleur, I wish you good evening. I judge," he added to Vandeleur, "that your silence means unqualified assent."

"If I can do no better," replied the old man, "I shall submit; but I warn you openly it shall not be without a struggle."

"You are old," said the Prince; "but years are disgraceful to the wicked. Your age is more unwise than the youth of others. Do not provoke me, or you may find me harder than you dream. This is the first time that I have fallen across your path in anger; take care that it be the last."

With these words, motioning the clergyman to follow, Florizel left the apartment and directed his steps towards the garden gate; and the Dictator, following with a candle, gave them light, and once more undid the elaborate fastenings with which he sought to protect himself from intrusion.

"Your daughter is no longer present," said the Prince, turning on the threshold. "Let me tell you that I understand your threats; and you have only to lift your hand to bring upon yourself sudden and irremediable ruin."

The Dictator made no reply; but as the Prince turned his back upon him in the lamplight he made a gesture full of menace and insane fury; and the next moment, slipping round a corner, he was running at full speed for the nearest cabstand.

(*Here,* says my Arabian, *the thread of events is finally diverted from* THE HOUSE WITH THE GREEN BLINDS. *One more adventure,* he adds, *and we have done with* THE RAJAH'S DIAMOND. *That last link in the chain is known among the inhabitants of Bagdad by the name of* THE ADVENTURE OF PRINCE FLORIZEL AND A DETECTIVE.)

The Adventure of Prince Florizel and a Detective

Prince Florizel walked with Mr. Rolles to the door of a small hotel where the latter resided. They spoke much together, and the clergyman was more than once affected to tears by the mingled severity and tenderness of Florizel's reproaches.

"I have made ruin of my life," he said at last. "Help me; tell me what I am to do; I have, alas! neither the virtues of a priest nor the dexterity of a rogue."

"Now that you are humbled," said the Prince, "I command no longer; the repentant have to do with God and not with princes. But if you will let me advise you, go to Australia as a colonist, seek menial labour in the open air, and try to forget that you have ever been a clergyman, or that you ever set eyes on that accursed stone."

"Accurst indeed!" replied Mr. Rolles. "Where is it now? What further hurt is it not working for mankind?"

"It will do no more evil," returned the Prince. "It is here in my pocket. And this," he added, kindly, "will show that I place some faith in your penitence, young as it is."

"Suffer me to touch your hand," pleaded Mr. Rolles.

"No," replied Prince Florizel, "not yet."

The tone in which he uttered these last words was eloquent in the ears of the young clergyman; and for some minutes after the Prince had turned away he stood on the threshold following with his eyes the retreating figure and invoking the blessing of heaven upon a man so excellent in counsel.

For several hours the Prince walked alone in unfrequented streets. His mind was full of concern; what to do with the diamond, whether to return it to its owner, whom he judged unworthy of this rare possession, or to take some sweeping and courageous measure and put it out of the reach of all mankind at once and for ever, was a problem too grave to be decided in a moment. The manner in which it had come into his hands appeared manifestly providential; and as he took out the jewel and looked at it under the street lamps, its size and surprising brilliancy inclined him more and more to think of it as of an unmixed and dangerous evil for the world.

"God help me!" he thought; "if I look at it much oftener I shall begin to grow covetous myself."

At last, though still uncertain in his mind, he turned his steps towards the small but elegant mansion on the riverside which had belonged for centuries to his royal family. The arms of Bohemia are deeply graved over the door and upon the tall chimneys; passengers have a look into a green court set with the most costly flowers, and a stork, the only one in Paris, perches on the gable all day long and keeps a crowd before the house. Grave servants are seen passing to and fro within; and from time to time the great gate is thrown open and a carriage rolls below the arch. For many reasons this residence was especially dear to the heart of Prince Florizel; he never drew near to it without enjoying that sentiment of homecoming so rare in the lives of the great; and on the present evening he beheld its tall roof and mildly illuminated windows with unfeigned relief and satisfaction.

As he was approaching the postern door by which he always entered when alone, a man stepped forth from the shadow and presented himself with an obeisance in the Prince's path.

"I have the honour of addressing Prince Florizel of Bohemia?" said he.

"Such is my title," replied the Prince. "What do you want with me?"

"I am," said the man, "a detective, and I have to present your Highness with this billet from the Prefect of Police."

The Prince took the letter and glanced it through by the light of the street lamp. It was highly apologetic, but requested him to follow the bearer to the Prefecture without delay.

"In short," said Florizel, "I am arrested."

"Your Highness," replied the officer, "nothing, I am certain, could be further from the intention of the Prefect. You will observe that he has not granted a warrant. It is mere formality, or call it, if you prefer, an obligation that your Highness lays on the authorities."

"At the same time," asked the Prince, "if I were to refuse to follow you?"

"I will not conceal from your Highness that a considerable discretion has been granted me," replied the detective with a bow.

"Upon my word," cried Florizel, "your effrontery astounds me! Yourself, as an agent, I must pardon; but your superiors shall dearly smart for their misconduct. What, have you any idea, is the cause of this impolitic and unconstitutional act? You will observe that I have as yet neither refused nor consented, and much may depend on your prompt and ingenuous answer. Let me remind you, officer, that this is an affair of some gravity."

"Your Highness," said the detective humbly, "General Vandeleur and his brother have had the incredible presumption to accuse you of theft. The famous diamond, they declare, is in your hands. A word from you in denial will most amply satisfy the Prefect; nay, I go farther: if your Highness would so far honour a subaltern as to declare his ignorance of the matter even to myself, I should ask permission to retire upon the spot."

Florizel, up to the last moment, had regarded his adventure in the light of a trifle, only serious upon international considerations. At the name of Vandeleur the horrible truth broke upon him in a moment; he was not only arrested, but he was guilty. This was not only an annoying incident—it was a peril to his honour. What was he to say? What was he to do? The Rajah's Diamond was indeed an accursed stone; and it seemed as if he were to be the last victim to its influence.

One thing was certain. He could not give the required assurance to the detective. He must gain time.

His hesitation had not lasted a second.

"Be it so," said he, "let us walk together to the Prefecture."

The man once more bowed, and proceeded to follow Florizel at a respectful distance in the rear.

"Approach," said the Prince. "I am in a humour to talk, and, if I mistake not, now I look at you again, this is not the first time that we have met."

"I count it an honour," replied the officer, "that your Highness should recollect my face. It is eight years since I had the pleasure of an interview."

"To remember faces," returned Florizel, "is as much a part of my profession as it is of yours. Indeed, rightly looked upon, a Prince and a detective serve in the same corps. We are both combatants against crime; only mine is the more lucrative and yours the more dangerous rank, and there is a sense in which both may be made equally honourable to a good man. I had rather, strange as you may think it, be a detective of character and parts than a weak and ignoble sovereign."

The officer was overwhelmed.

"Your Highness returns good for evil," said he. "To an act of presumption he replies by the most amiable condescension."

"How do you know," replied Florizel, "that I am not seeking to corrupt you?"

"Heaven preserve me from the temptation!" cried the detective.

"I applaud your answer," returned the Prince. "It is that of a wise and honest man. The world is a great place and stocked with wealth and beauty, and there is no limit to the rewards that may be offered. Such an one who would refuse a million of money may sell his honour for an empire or the love of a woman; and I myself, who speak to you, have seen occasions so tempting, provocations so irresistible to the strength of human virtue, that I have been glad to tread in your steps and recommend myself to the grace of God. It is thus, thanks to that modest and becoming habit alone," he added, "that you and I can walk this town together with untarnished hearts."

"I had always heard that you were brave," replied the officer, "but I was not aware that you were wise and pious. You speak the truth, and you speak it with an accent that moves me to the heart. This world is indeed a place of trial."

"We are now," said Florizel, "in the middle of the bridge. Lean your elbows on the parapet and look over. As the water rushing below, so the passions and complications of life carry away the honesty of weak men. Let me tell you a story."

"I receive your Highness's commands," replied the man.

And, imitating the Prince, he leaned against the parapet, and disposed himself to listen. The city was already sunk in slumber; had it not been for the infinity of lights and the outline of buildings on the starry sky, they might have been alone beside some country river.

"An officer," began Prince Florizel, "a man of courage and conduct, who had already risen by merit to an eminent rank, and won not only admiration but respect, visited, in an unfortunate hour for his peace of mind, the collections of an Indian Prince. Here he beheld a diamond so extraordinary for size and beauty that from that instant he had only one desire in life: honour, reputation, friendship, the love of country, he was ready to sacrifice all for this lump of sparkling crystal. For three years he served this semi-barbarian potentate as Jacob served Laban; he falsified frontiers, he connived at murders, he unjustly condemned and executed a brother officer who had the misfortune to displease the Rajah by some honest freedoms; lastly, at a time of great danger to his native land, he betrayed a body of his fellow soldiers, and suffered them to be defeated and massacred by thousands. In the end, he had amassed a magnificent fortune, and brought home with him the coveted diamond.

"Years passed," continued the Prince, "and at length the diamond is accidentally lost. It falls into the hands of a simple and laborious youth, a student, a minister of God, just entering on a career of usefulness and even distinction. Upon him also the spell is cast; he deserts everything, his holy calling, his studies, and flees with the gem into a foreign country. The officer has a brother, an astute, daring, unscrupulous man, who learns the clergyman's secret. What does he do? Tell his brother, inform the police? No; upon this man also the Satanic charm has fallen; he must have the stone for himself. At the risk of murder, he drugs the young priest and seizes the prey. And now, by an accident which is not important to my moral, the jewel passes out of his custody into that of another, who, terrified at what he sees, gives it into the keeping of a man in high station and above reproach.

"The officer's name is Thomas Vandeleur," continued Florizel.

"The stone is called the Rajah's Diamond. And"—suddenly opening his hand—"you behold it here before your eyes."

The officer started back with a cry.

"We have spoken of corruption," said the Prince. "To me this nugget of bright crystal is as loathsome as though it were crawling with the worms of death; it is as shocking as though it were compacted out of innocent blood. I see it here in my hand, and I know it is shining with hellfire. I have told you but a hundredth part of its story; what passed in former ages, to what crimes and treacheries it incited men of yore, the imagination trembles to conceive; for years and years it has faithfully served the powers of hell; enough, I say, of blood, enough of disgrace, enough of broken lives and friendships; all things come to an end, the evil like the good; pestilence as well as beautiful music; and as for this diamond, God forgive me if I do wrong, but its empire ends tonight."

The Prince made a sudden movement with his hand, and the jewel, describing an arc of light, dived with a splash into the flowing river.

"Amen," said Florizel, with gravity. "I have slain a cockatrice!"

"God pardon me!" cried the detective. "What have you done? I am a ruined man."

"I think," returned the Prince with a smile, "that many well-to-do people in this city might envy you your ruin."

"Alas! your Highness!" said the officer, "and you corrupt me after all?"

"It seems there was no help for it," replied Florizel. "And now let us go forward to the Prefecture."

Not long after, the marriage of Francis Scrymgeour and Miss Vandeleur was celebrated in great privacy; and the Prince acted on that occasion as groom's man. The two Vandeleurs surprised some rumour of what had happened to the diamond; and their vast diving operations on the River Seine are the wonder and amusement of the idle. It is true that through some miscalculation they have chosen the wrong branch of the river. As for the Prince, that sublime person, having now served his turn, may go, along with the *Arabian Author*, topsy-turvy into space. But if the reader insists on more specific information, I am happy to say that a recent revolution hurled him from the throne of Bohemia, in consequence of his continued absence and edifying neglect of public business; and that his Highness now keeps a cigar store in Rupert Street, much frequented by other foreign refugees. I go there from time to time to smoke and have a chat, and find him as great a creature as in the days of his prosperity; he has an Olympian air behind the counter; and although a sedentary life is beginning to tell upon his waistcoat, he is probably, take him for all in all, the handsomest tobacconist in London.

THE PAVILION ON
THE LINKS

INSCRIBED TO D.A.S. IN MEMORY OF DAYS NEAR FIDRA

Chapter One
Tells how I camped in Graden Sea-Wood, and beheld a light in the pavilion

I was a great solitary when I was young. I made it my pride to keep aloof and suffice for my own entertainment; and I may say that I had neither friends nor acquaintances until I met that friend who became my wife and the mother of my children. With one man only was I on private terms; this was R. Northmour, Esquire, of Graden Easter, in Scotland. We had met at college; and though there was not much liking between us, nor even much intimacy, we were so nearly of a humour that we could associate with ease to both. Misanthropes, we believed ourselves to be; but I have thought since that we were only sulky fellows. It was scarcely a companionship, but a coexistence in unsociability. Northmour's exceptional violence of temper made it no easy affair for him to keep the peace with anyone but me; and as he respected my silent ways, and let me come and go as I pleased, I could tolerate his presence without concern. I think we called each other friends.

When Northmour took his degree and I decided to leave the university without one, he invited me on a long visit to Graden Easter; and it was thus that I first became acquainted with the scene of my adventures. The mansion house of Graden stood in a bleak stretch of country some three miles from the shore of the German Ocean. It was as large as a barrack; and as it had been built of a soft stone, liable to consume in the eager air of the seaside, it was damp and draughty within and half ruinous without. It was impossible for two young men to lodge with comfort in such a dwelling. But there stood in the northern part of the estate, in a wilderness of links and blowing sandhills, and between a plantation and the sea, a small Pavilion or Belvidere, of modern design, which was exactly suited to our wants; and in this hermitage, speaking little, reading much, and rarely associating except at meals, Northmour and I spent four tempestuous winter months. I might have stayed longer; but one March night there sprang up between us a dispute, which rendered my departure necessary. Northmour spoke hotly, I remember, and I suppose I must have made some tart rejoinder. He leaped from his chair and grappled me; I had to fight, without exaggeration, for my life; and it was only with a great effort that I mastered him, for he was near as strong in body as myself, and seemed filled with the devil. The next morning, we met on our usual terms; but I judged it more delicate to withdraw; nor did he attempt to dissuade me.

It was nine years before I revisited the neighbourhood. I travelled at that time with a tilt cart, a tent, and a cooking stove, tramping all day beside the waggon, and at night, whenever it was possible, gipsying in a cove of the hills, or by the side of a wood. I believe I visited in this manner most of the wild and desolate regions both in England and Scotland; and, as I had neither friends nor relations, I was troubled with no correspondence, and had nothing in the nature of headquarters, unless it was the office of my solicitors, from whom I drew my income twice a year. It was a life in which I delighted; and I fully thought to have grown old upon the march, and at last died in a ditch.

It was my whole business to find desolate corners, where I could camp without the fear of interruption; and hence, being in another part of the same shire, I bethought me suddenly of the Pavilion on the Links. No thoroughfare passed within three miles of it. The nearest town, and that was but a fisher village, was at a distance of six or seven. For ten miles of length, and from a depth varying from three miles to half a mile, this belt of barren country lay along the sea. The beach, which was the natural approach, was full of quicksands. Indeed I may say there is hardly a better place of concealment in the United Kingdom. I determined to pass a week in the Sea-Wood of Graden-Easter, and making a long stage, reached it about sundown on a wild September day.

The country, I have said, was mixed sandhill and links; *links* being a Scottish name for sand which has ceased drifting and become more or less solidly covered with turf. The pavilion stood on an even space; a little behind it, the wood began in a hedge of elders huddled together by the wind; in front, a few tumbled sandhills stood between it and the sea. An outcropping of rock had formed a bastion for the sand, so that there was here a promontory in the coastline between two shallow bays; and just beyond the tides, the rock again cropped out and formed an islet of small dimensions but strikingly designed. The quicksands were of great extent at low water, and had an infamous reputation in the country. Close in shore, between the islet and the promontory, it was said they would swallow a man in four minutes and a half; but there may have been little ground for this precision. The district was alive with rabbits, and haunted by gulls which made a continual piping about the pavilion. On summer days the outlook was bright and even gladsome; but at sundown in September, with a high wind, and a heavy surf rolling in close along the links, the place told of nothing but dead mariners and sea disaster. A ship beating to windward on the horizon, and a huge truncheon of wreck half buried in the sands at my feet, completed the innuendo of the scene.

The pavilion—it had been built by the last proprietor, Northmour's uncle, a silly and prodigal virtuoso—presented little signs of age. It was two stories in height, Italian in design, surrounded by a patch of garden in which nothing had prospered but a few coarse flowers; and looked, with its shuttered windows, not like a house that had been deserted, but like one that had never been tenanted by man. Northmour was plainly from home; whether, as usual, sulking in the cabin of his yacht, or in one of his fitful and extravagant appearances in the world of society, I had, of course, no means of guessing. The place had an air of solitude that daunted even a solitary like myself; the wind cried in the chimneys with a strange and wailing note; and it was with a sense of escape, as if I were going indoors, that I turned away and, driving my cart before me, entered the skirts of the wood.

The Sea-Wood of Graden had been planted to shelter the cultivated fields behind, and check the encroachments of the blowing sand. As you advanced into it from coastward, elders were succeeded by other hardy shrubs; but the timber was all stunted and bushy; it led a life of conflict; the trees were accustomed to swing there all night long in fierce winter tempests; and even in early spring, the leaves were already flying, and autumn was beginning, in this exposed plantation. Inland the ground rose into a little hill, which, along with the islet, served as a sailing mark for seamen. When the hill was open of the islet to the north, vessels must bear well to the eastward to clear Graden Ness and the Graden Bullers. In the lower ground, a streamlet ran among the trees, and, being dammed with dead leaves and clay of its own carrying, spread out every here and there, and lay in stagnant pools. One or two ruined cottages were dotted about the wood; and, according to Northmour, these were ecclesiastical foundations, and in their time had sheltered pious hermits.

I found a den, or small hollow, where there was a spring of pure water; and there, clearing away the brambles, I pitched the tent, and made a fire to cook my supper. My horse I picketed farther in the wood where there was a patch of sward. The banks of the den not only concealed the light of my fire, but sheltered me from the wind, which was cold as well as high.

The life I was leading made me both hardy and frugal. I never drank but water and rarely ate anything more costly than oatmeal; and I required so little sleep, that, although I rose with the peep of day, I would often lie long awake in the dark or starry watches of the night. Thus in Graden Sea-Wood, although I fell thankfully asleep by eight in the evening I was awake again before eleven with a full possession of my faculties, and no sense of drowsiness or fatigue. I rose and sat by the fire, watching the trees and clouds tumultuously tossing and fleeing overhead, and hearkening to the wind and the rollers along the shore; till at length, growing weary of inaction, I quitted the den, and strolled towards the borders of the wood. A young moon, buried in mist, gave a faint illumination to my steps; and the light grew brighter as I walked forth into the links. At the same moment, the wind, smelling salt of the open ocean and carrying particles of sand, struck me with its full force, so that I had to bow my head.

When I raised it again to look about me, I was aware of a light in the pavilion. It was not stationary; but passed from one window to another, as though someone were reviewing the different apartments with a lamp or candle. I watched it for some seconds in great surprise. When I had arrived in the afternoon the house had been plainly deserted; now it was as plainly occupied. It was my first idea that a gang of thieves might have broken in and be now ransacking Northmour's cupboards, which were many and not ill supplied. But what should bring thieves to Graden Easter? And, again, all the shutters had been thrown open, and it would have been more in the character of such gentry to close them. I dismissed the notion, and fell back upon another. Northmour himself must have arrived, and was now airing and inspecting the pavilion.

I have said that there was no real affection between this man and me; but, had I loved him like a brother, I was then so much more in love with solitude that I should none the less have shunned his company. As it was, I turned and ran for it; and it was with genuine satisfaction that I found myself safely back beside the fire. I had escaped an acquaintance; I should have one more night in comfort. In the morning, I might either slip away before Northmour was abroad, or pay him as short a visit as I chose.

But when morning came, I thought the situation so diverting that I forgot my shyness. Northmour was at my mercy; I arranged a good practical jest, though I knew well that my neighbour was not the man to jest with in security; and, chuckling beforehand over its success, took my place among the elders at the edge of the wood, whence I could command the door of the pavilion. The shutters were all once more closed, which I remember thinking odd; and the house, with its white walls and green venetians, looked spruce and habitable in the morning light. Hour after hour passed, and still no sign of Northmour. I knew him for a sluggard in the morning; but, as it drew on towards noon, I lost my patience. To say the truth, I had promised myself to break my fast in the pavilion, and hunger began to prick me sharply. It was a pity to let the opportunity go by without some cause for mirth; but the grosser appetite prevailed, and I relinquished my jest with regret, and sallied from the wood.

The appearance of the house affected me, as I drew near, with disquietude. It seemed unchanged since last evening; and I had expected it, I scarce knew why, to wear some external signs of habitation. But no: the windows were all closely shuttered, the chimneys breathed no smoke, and the front door itself was closely padlocked. Northmour, therefore, had entered by the back; this was the natural, and indeed, the necessary conclusion; and you may judge of my surprise when, on turning the house, I found the back door similarly secured.

My mind at once reverted to the original theory of thieves; and I blamed myself sharply for my last night's inaction. I examined all the windows on the lower story, but none of them had been tampered with; I tried the padlocks, but they were both secure. It thus became a problem how the thieves, if thieves they were, had managed to enter the house. They must have got, I reasoned, upon the roof of the outhouse where Northmour used to keep his photographic battery; and from thence, either by the window of the study or that of my old bedroom, completed their burglarious entry.

I followed what I supposed was their example; and, getting on the roof, tried the shutters of each room. Both were secure; but I was not to be beaten; and, with a little force, one of them flew open, grazing, as it did so, the back of my hand. I remember, I put the wound to my mouth, and stood for perhaps half a minute licking it like a dog, and mechanically gazing behind me over the waste links and the sea; and, in that space of time, my eye made note of a large schooner yacht some miles to the northeast. Then I threw up the window and climbed in.

I went over the house, and nothing can express my mystification. There was no sign of disorder, but, on the contrary, the rooms were unusually clean and pleasant. I found fires laid, ready for lighting; three bedrooms prepared with a luxury quite foreign to Northmour's habits, and with water in the ewers and the beds turned down; a table set for three in the dining room; and an ample supply of cold meats, game, and vegetables on the pantry shelves. There were guests expected, that was plain; but why guests, when Northmour hated society? And, above all, why was the house thus stealthily prepared at dead of night? and why were the shutters closed and the doors padlocked?

I effaced all traces of my visit, and came forth from the window feeling sobered and concerned.

The schooner yacht was still in the same place; and it flashed for a moment through my mind that this might be the *Red Earl* bringing the owner of the pavilion and his guests. But the vessel's head was set the other way.

Chapter Two
Tells of the nocturnal landing from the yacht

I returned to the den to cook myself a meal, of which I stood in great need, as well as to care for my horse, whom I had somewhat neglected in the morning. From time to time I went down to the edge of the wood; but there was no change in the pavilion, and not a human creature was seen all day upon the links. The schooner in the offing was the one touch of life within my range of vision. She, apparently with no set object, stood off and on or lay to, hour after hour; but as the evening deepened, she drew steadily nearer. I became more convinced that she carried Northmour and his friends, and that they would probably come ashore after dark; not only because that was of a piece with the secrecy of the preparations, but because the tide would not have flowed sufficiently before eleven to cover Graden Floe and the other sea quags that fortified the shore against invaders.

All day the wind had been going down, and the sea along with it; but there was a return towards sunset of the heavy weather of the day before. The night set in pitch dark. The wind came off the sea in squalls, like the firing of a battery of cannon; now and then there was a flaw of rain, and the surf rolled heavier with the rising tide. I was down at my observatory among the elders, when a light was run up to the masthead of the schooner, and showed she was closer in than when I had last seen her by the dying daylight. I concluded that this must be a signal to Northmour's associates on shore; and, stepping forth into the links, looked around me for something in response.

A small footpath ran along the margin of the wood, and formed the most direct communication between the pavilion and the mansion house; and, as I cast my eyes to that side, I saw a spark of light, not a quarter of a mile away, and rapidly approaching. From its uneven course it appeared to be the light of a lantern carried by a person who followed the windings of the path, and was often staggered and taken aback by the more violent squalls. I concealed myself once more among the elders, and waited eagerly for the newcomer's advance. It proved to be a woman; and, as she passed within half a rod of my ambush, I was able to recognise the features. The deaf and silent old dame, who had nursed Northmour in his childhood, was his associate in this underhand affair.

I followed her at a little distance, taking advantage of the innumerable heights and hollows, concealed by the darkness, and favoured not only by the nurse's deafness, but by the uproar of the wind and surf. She entered the pavilion, and, going at once to the upper story, opened and set a light in one of the windows that looked towards the sea. Immediately afterwards the light at the schooner's masthead was run down and extinguished. Its purpose had been attained, and those on board were sure that they were expected. The old woman resumed her preparations; although the other shutters remained closed, I could see a glimmer going to and fro about the house; and a gush of sparks from one chimney after another soon told me that the fires were being kindled.

Northmour and his guests, I was now persuaded, would come ashore as soon there was water on the floe. It was a wild night for boat service; and I felt some alarm mingle with my curiosity as I reflected on the danger of the landing. My old acquaintance, it was true, was the most eccentric of men; but the present eccentricity was both disquieting and lugubrious to consider. A variety of feelings thus led me towards the beach, where I lay flat on my face in a hollow within six feet of the track that led to the pavilion. Thence, I should have the satisfaction of recognising the arrivals, and, if they should prove to be acquaintances, greeting them as soon as they had landed.

Some time before eleven, while the tide was still dangerously low, a boat's lantern appeared close in shore; and, my attention being thus awakened, I could perceive another still far to seaward, violently tossed, and sometimes hidden by the billows. The weather, which was getting dirtier as the night went on, and the perilous situation of the yacht upon a leeshore, had probably driven them to attempt a landing at the earliest possible moment.

A little afterwards, four yachtsmen carrying a very heavy chest, and guided by a fifth with a lantern, passed close in front of me as I lay, and were admitted to the pavilion by the nurse. They returned to the beach, and passed me a third time with another chest, larger but apparently not so heavy as the first. A third time they made the transit; and on this occasion one of the yachtsmen carried a leather portmanteau, and the others a lady's trunk and carriage bag. My curiosity was sharply excited. If a woman were among the guests of Northmour, it would show a change in his habits and an apostasy from his pet theories of life, well calculated to fill me with surprise. When he and I dwelt there together, the pavilion had been a temple of misogyny. And now, one of the detested sex was to be installed under its roof. I remembered one or two particulars, a few notes of daintiness and almost of coquetry which had struck me the day before as I surveyed the preparations in the house; their purpose was now clear, and I thought myself dull not to have perceived it from the first.

While I was thus reflecting, a second lantern drew near me from the beach. It was carried by a yachtsman whom I had not yet seen, and who was conducting two other persons to the pavilion. These two persons were unquestionably the guests for whom the house was made ready; and, straining eye and ear, I set myself to watch them as they passed. One was an unusually tall man, in a travelling hat slouched over his eyes, and a highland cape closely buttoned and turned up so as to conceal his face. You could make out no more of him than that he was, as I have said, unusually tall, and walked feebly with a heavy stoop. By his side, and either clinging to him or giving him support—I could not make out which—was a young, tall, and slender figure of a woman. She was extremely pale; but in the light of the lantern her face was so marred by strong and changing shadows, that she might equally well have been as ugly as sin or as beautiful as I afterwards found her to be.

When they were just abreast of me, the girl made some remark which was drowned by the noise of the wind.

"Hush!" said her companion; and there was something in the tone with which the word was uttered that thrilled and rather shook my spirits. It seemed to breathe from a bosom labouring under the deadliest terror; I have never heard another syllable so expressive; and I still hear it again when I am feverish at night, and my mind runs upon old times. The man turned towards the girl as he spoke; I had a glimpse of much red beard and a nose which seemed to have been broken in youth; and his light eyes seemed shining in his face with some strong and unpleasant emotion.

But these two passed on and were admitted in their turn to the pavilion.

One by one, or in groups, the seamen returned to the beach. The wind brought me the sound of a rough voice crying, "Shove off!" Then, after a pause, another lantern drew near. It was Northmour alone.

My wife and I, a man and a woman, have often agreed to wonder how a person could be, at the same time, so handsome and so repulsive as Northmour. He had the appearance of a finished gentleman; his face bore every mark of intelligence and courage; but you had only to look at him, even in his most amiable moment, to see that he had the temper of a slaver captain. I never knew a character that was both explosive and revengeful to the same degree; he combined the vivacity of the south with the sustained and deadly hatreds of the north; and both traits were plainly written on his face, which was a sort of danger signal. In person, he was tall, strong, and active; his hair and complexion very dark; his features handsomely designed, but spoiled by a menacing expression.

At that moment he was somewhat paler than by nature; he wore a heavy frown; and his lips worked, and he looked sharply round him as he walked, like a man besieged with apprehensions. And yet I thought he had a look of triumph underlying all, as though he had already done much, and was near the end of an achievement.

Partly from a scruple of delicacy—which I daresay came too late—partly from the pleasure of startling an acquaintance, I desired to make my presence known to him without delay.

I got suddenly to my feet, and stepped forward.

"Northmour!" said I.

I have never had so shocking a surprise in all my days. He leaped on me without a word; something shone in his hand; and he struck for my heart with a dagger. At the same moment I knocked him head over heels. Whether it was my quickness, or his own uncertainty, I know not; but the blade only grazed my shoulder, while the hilt and his fist struck me violently on the mouth.

I fled, but not far. I had often and often observed the capabilities of the sandhills for protracted ambush or stealthy advances and retreats; and, not ten yards from the scene of the scuffle, plumped down again upon the grass. The lantern had fallen and gone out. But what was my astonishment to see Northmour slip at a bound into the pavilion, and hear him bar the door behind him with a clang of iron!

He had not pursued me. He had run away. Northmour, whom I knew for the most implacable and daring of men, had run away! I could scarce believe my reason; and yet in this strange business, where all was incredible, there was nothing to make a work about in an incredibility more or less. For why was the pavilion secretly prepared? Why had Northmour landed with his guests at dead of night, in half a gale of wind, and with the floe scarce covered? Why had he sought to kill me? Had he not recognised my voice? I wondered. And, above all, how had he come to have a dagger ready in his hand? A dagger, or even a sharp knife, seemed out of keeping with the age in which we lived; and a gentleman landing from his yacht on the shore of his own estate, even although it was at night and with some mysterious circumstances, does not usually, as a matter of fact, walk thus prepared for deadly onslaught. The more I reflected, the further I felt at sea. I recapitulated the elements of mystery, counting them on my fingers: the pavilion secretly prepared for guests; the guests landed at the risk of their lives and to the imminent peril of the yacht; the guests, or at least one of them, in undisguised and seemingly causeless terror; Northmour with a naked weapon; Northmour stabbing his most intimate acquaintance at a word; last, and not least strange, Northmour fleeing from the man whom he had sought to murder, and barricading himself, like a hunted creature, behind the door of the pavilion. Here were at least six separate causes for extreme surprise; each part and parcel with the others, and forming all together one consistent story. I felt almost ashamed to believe my own senses.

As I thus stood, transfixed with wonder, I began to grow painfully conscious of the injuries I had received in the scuffle; skulked round among the sandhills; and, by a devious path, regained the shelter of the wood. On the way, the old nurse passed again within several yards of me, still carrying her lantern, on the return journey to the mansion house of Graden. This made a seventh suspicious feature in the case. Northmour and his guests, it appeared, were to cook and do the cleaning for themselves, while the old woman continued to inhabit the big empty barrack among the policies. There must surely be great cause for secrecy, when so many inconveniences were confronted to preserve it.

So thinking, I made my way to the den. For greater security, I trod out the embers of the fire, and lit my lantern to examine the wound upon my shoulder. It was a trifling hurt, although it bled somewhat freely, and I dressed it as well as I could (for its position made it difficult to reach) with some rag and cold water from the spring. While I was thus busied, I mentally declared war against Northmour and his mystery. I am not an angry man by nature, and I believe there was more curiosity than resentment in my heart. But war I certainly declared; and, by way of preparation, I got out my revolver, and, having drawn the charges, cleaned and reloaded it with scrupulous care. Next I became preoccupied about my horse. It might break loose, or fall to neighing, and so betray my camp in the Sea-Wood. I determined to rid myself of its neighbourhood; and long before dawn I was leading it over the links in the direction of the fisher village.

Chapter Three
Tells how I became acquainted with my wife

For two days I skulked round the pavilion, profiting by the uneven surface of the links. I became an adept in the necessary tactics. These low hillocks and shallow dells, running one into another, became a kind of cloak of darkness for my enthralling, but perhaps dishonourable, pursuit. Yet, in spite of this advantage, I could learn but little of Northmour or his guests.

Fresh provisions were brought under cover of darkness by the old woman from the mansion house. Northmour, and the young lady, sometimes together, but more often singly, would walk for an hour or two at a time on the beach beside the quicksand. I could not but conclude that this promenade was chosen with an eye to secrecy; for the spot was open only to the seaward. But it suited me not less excellently; the highest and most accidented of the sandhills immediately adjoined; and from these, lying flat in a hollow, I could overlook Northmour or the young lady as they walked.

The tall man seemed to have disappeared. Not only did he never cross the threshold, but he never so much as showed face at a window; or, at least, not so far as I could see; for I dared not creep forward beyond a certain distance in the day, since the upper floor commanded the bottoms of the links; and at night, when I could venture farther, the lower windows were barricaded as if to stand a siege. Sometimes I thought the tall man must be confined to bed, for I remembered the feebleness of his gait; and sometimes I thought he must have gone clear away, and that Northmour and the young lady remained alone together in the pavilion. The idea, even then, displeased me.

Whether or not this pair were man and wife, I had seen abundant reason to doubt the friendliness of their relation. Although I could hear nothing of what they said, and rarely so much as glean a decided expression on the face of either, there was a distance, almost a stiffness, in their bearing which showed them to be either unfamiliar or at enmity. The girl walked faster when she was with Northmour than when she was alone; and I conceived that any inclination between a man and a woman would rather delay than accelerate the step. Moreover, she kept a good yard free of him, and trailed her umbrella, as if it were a barrier, on the side between them. Northmour kept sidling closer; and, as the girl retired from his advance, their course lay at a sort of diagonal across the beach, and would have landed them in the surf had it been long enough continued. But, when this was imminent, the girl would unostentatiously change sides and put Northmour between her and the sea. I watched these manoeuvers, for my part, with high enjoyment and approval, and chuckled to myself at every move.

On the morning of the third day, she walked alone for some time, and I perceived, to my great concern, that she was more than once in tears. You will see that my heart was already interested more than I supposed. She had a firm yet airy motion of the body, and carried her head with unimaginable grace; every step was a thing to look at, and she seemed in my eyes to breathe sweetness and distinction.

The day was so agreeable, being calm and sunshiny, with a tranquil sea, and yet with a healthful piquancy and vigour in the air, that, contrary to custom, she was tempted forth a second time to walk. On this occasion she was accompanied by Northmour, and they had been but a short while on the beach, when I saw him take forcible possession of her hand. She struggled, and uttered a cry that was almost a scream. I sprang to my feet, unmindful of my strange position; but, ere I had taken a step, I saw Northmour bareheaded and bowing very low, as if to apologise; and dropped again at once into my ambush. A few words were interchanged; and then, with another bow, he left the beach to return to the pavilion. He passed not far from me, and I could see him, flushed and lowering, and cutting savagely with his cane among the grass. It was not without satisfaction that I recognised my own handiwork in a great cut under his right eye, and a considerable discolouration round the socket.

For some time the girl remained where he had left her, looking out past the islet and over the bright sea. Then with a start, as one who throws off preoccupation and puts energy again upon its mettle, she broke into a rapid and decisive walk. She also was much incensed by what had passed. She had forgotten where she was. And I beheld her walk straight into the borders of the quicksand where it is most abrupt and dangerous. Two or three steps farther and her life would have been in serious jeopardy, when I slid down the face of the sand-hill, which is there precipitous, and, running halfway forward, called to her to stop.

She did so, and turned round. There was not a tremor of fear in her behaviour, and she marched directly up to me like a queen. I was barefoot, and clad like a common sailor, save for an Egyptian scarf round my waist; and she probably took me at first for some one from the fisher village, straying after bait. As for her, when I thus saw her face to face, her eyes set steadily and imperiously upon mine, I was filled with admiration and astonishment, and thought her even more beautiful than I had looked to find her. Nor could I think enough of one who, acting with so much boldness, yet preserved a maidenly air that was both quaint and engaging; for my wife kept an old-fashioned precision of manner through all her admirable life—an excellent thing in woman, since it sets another value on her sweet familiarities.

"What does this mean?" she asked.

"You were walking," I told her, "directly into Graden Floe."

"You do not belong to these parts," she said again. "You speak like an educated man."

"I believe I have right to that name," said I, "although in this disguise."

But her woman's eye had already detected the sash.

"Oh!" she said; "your sash betrays you."

"You have said the word *betray*," I resumed. "May I ask you not to betray me? I was obliged to disclose myself in your interest; but if Northmour learned my presence it might be worse than disagreeable for me."

"Do you know," she asked, "to whom you are speaking?"

"Not to Mr. Northmour's wife?" I asked, by way of answer.

She shook her head. All this while she was studying my face with an embarrassing intentness. Then she broke out—

"You have an honest face. Be honest like your face, sir, and tell me what you want and what you are afraid of. Do you think I could hurt you? I believe you have far more power to injure me! And yet you do not look unkind. What do you mean—you, a gentleman—by skulking like a spy about this desolate place? Tell me," she said, "who is it you hate?"

"I hate no one," I answered; "and I fear no one face to face. My name is Cassilis—Frank Cassilis. I lead the life of a vagabond for my own good pleasure. I am one of Northmour's oldest friends; and three nights ago, when I addressed him on these links, he stabbed me in the shoulder with a knife."

"It was you!" she said.

"Why he did so," I continued, disregarding the interruption, "is more than I can guess, and more than I care to know. I have not many friends, nor am I very susceptible to friendship; but no man shall drive me from a place by terror. I had camped in Graden Sea-Wood ere he came; I camp in it still. If you think I mean harm to you or yours, madam, the remedy is in your hand. Tell him that my camp is in the Hemlock Den, and tonight he can stab me in safety while I sleep."

With this I doffed my cap to her, and scrambled up once more among the sandhills. I do not know why, but I felt a prodigious sense of injustice, and felt like a hero and a martyr; while, as a matter of fact, I had not a word to say in my defence, nor so much as one plausible reason to offer for my conduct. I had stayed at Graden out of a curiosity natural enough, but undignified; and though there was another motive growing in along with the first, it was not one which, at that period, I could have properly explained to the lady of my heart.

Certainly, that night, I thought of no one else; and, though her whole conduct and position seemed suspicious, I could not find it in my heart to entertain a doubt of her integrity. I could have staked my life that she was clear of blame, and, though all was dark at the present, that the explanation of the mystery would show her part in these events to be both right and needful. It was true, let me cudgel my imagination as I pleased, that I could invent no theory of her relations to Northmour; but I felt none the less sure of my conclusion because it was founded on instinct in place of reason, and, as I may say, went to sleep that night with the thought of her under my pillow.

Next day she came out about the same hour alone, and, as soon as the sandhills concealed her from the pavilion, drew nearer to the edge, and called me by name in guarded tones. I was astonished to observe that she was deadly pale, and seemingly under the influence of strong emotion.

"Mr. Cassilis!" she cried; "Mr. Cassilis!"

I appeared at once, and leaped down upon the beach. A remarkable air of relief overspread her countenance as soon as she saw me.

"Oh!" she cried, with a hoarse sound, like one whose bosom has been lightened of a weight. And then, "Thank God you are still safe!" she added; "I knew, if you were, you would be here." (Was not this strange? So swiftly and wisely does Nature prepare our hearts for these great lifelong intimacies, that both my wife and I had been given a presentiment on this the second day of our acquaintance. I had even then hoped that she would seek me; she had felt sure that she would find me.) "Do not," she went on swiftly, "do not stay in this place. Promise me that you will sleep no longer in that wood. You do not know how I suffer; all last night I could not sleep for thinking of your peril."

"Peril?" I repeated. "Peril from whom? From Northmour?"

"Not so," she said. "Did you think I would tell him after what you said?"

"Not from Northmour?" I repeated. "Then how? From whom? I see none to be afraid of."

"You must not ask me," was her reply, "for I am not free to tell you. Only believe me, and go hence—believe me, and go away quickly, quickly, for your life!"

An appeal to his alarm is never a good plan to rid oneself of a spirited young man. My obstinacy was but increased by what she said, and I made it a point of honour to remain. And her solicitude for my safety still more confirmed me in the resolve.

"You must not think me inquisitive, madam," I replied; "but, if Graden is so dangerous a place, you yourself perhaps remain here at some risk."

She only looked at me reproachfully.

"You and your father——" I resumed; but she interrupted me almost with a gasp.

"My father! How do you know that?" she cried.

"I saw you together when you landed," was my answer; and I do not know why, but it seemed satisfactory to both of us, as indeed it was the truth. "But," I continued, "you need have no fear from me. I see you have some reason to be secret, and, you may believe me, your secret is as safe with me as if I were in Graden Floe. I have scarce spoken to anyone for years; my horse is my only companion, and even he, poor beast, is not beside me. You see, then, you may count on me for silence. So tell me the truth, my dear young lady, are you not in danger?"

"Mr. Northmour says you are an honourable man," she returned, "and I believe it when I see you. I will tell you so much; you are right; we are in dreadful, dreadful danger, and you share it by remaining where you are."

"Ah!" said I; "you have heard of me from Northmour? And he gives me a good character?"

"I asked him about you last night," was her reply. "I pretended," she hesitated, "I pretended to have met you long ago, and spoken to you of him. It was not true; but I could not help myself without betraying you, and you had put me in a difficulty. He praised you highly."

"And—you may permit me one question—does this danger come from Northmour?" I asked.

"From Mr. Northmour?" she cried. "Oh, no; he stays with us to share it."

"While you propose that I should run away?" I said. "You do not rate me very high."

"Why should you stay?" she asked. "You are no friend of ours."

I know not what came over me, for I had not been conscious of a similar weakness since I was a child, but I was so mortified by this retort that my eyes pricked and filled with tears, as I continued to gaze upon her face.

"No, no," she said, in a changed voice; "I did not mean the words unkindly."

"It was I who offended," I said; and I held out my hand with a look of appeal that somehow touched her, for she gave me hers at once, and even eagerly. I held it for awhile in mine, and gazed into her eyes. It was she who first tore her hand away, and, forgetting all about her request and the promise she had sought to extort, ran at the top of her speed, and without turning, till she was out of sight. And then I knew that I loved her, and thought in my glad heart that she—she herself—was not indifferent to my suit. Many a time she has denied it in after days, but it was with a smiling and not a serious denial. For my part, I am sure our hands would not have lain so closely in each other if she had not begun to melt to me already. And, when all is said, it is no great contention, since, by her own avowal, she began to love me on the morrow.

And yet on the morrow very little took place. She came and called me down as on the day before, upbraided me for lingering at Graden, and, when she found I was still obdurate, began to ask me more particularly as to my arrival. I told her by what series of accidents I had come to witness their disembarkation, and how I had determined to remain, partly from the interest which had been wakened in me by Northmour's guests, and partly because of his own murderous attack. As to the former, I fear I was disingenuous, and led her to regard herself as having been an attraction to me from the first moment that I saw her on the links. It relieves my heart to make this confession even now, when my wife is with God, and already knows all things, and the honesty of my purpose even in this; for while she lived, although it often pricked my conscience, I had never the hardihood to undeceive her. Even a little secret, in such a married life as ours, is like the rose leaf which kept the Princess from her sleep.

From this the talk branched into other subjects, and I told her much about my lonely and wandering existence; she, for her part, giving ear, and saying little. Although we spoke very naturally, and latterly on topics that might seem indifferent, we were both sweetly agitated. Too soon it was time for her to go; and we separated, as if by mutual consent, without shaking hands, for both knew that, between us, it was no idle ceremony.

The next, and that was the fourth day of our acquaintance, we met in the same spot, but early in the morning, with much familiarity and yet much timidity on either side. When she had once more spoken about my danger—and that, I understood, was her excuse for coming—I, who had prepared a great deal of talk during the night, began to tell her how highly I valued her kind interest, and how no one had ever cared to hear about my life, nor had I ever cared to relate it, before yesterday. Suddenly she interrupted me, saying with vehemence—

"And yet, if you knew who I was, you would not so much as speak to me!"

I told her such a thought was madness, and, little as we had met, I counted her already a dear friend; but my protestations seemed only to make her more desperate.

"My father is in hiding!" she cried.

"My dear," I said, forgetting for the first time to add "young lady," "what do I care? If he were in hiding twenty times over, would it make one thought of change in you?"

"Ah, but the cause!" she cried, "the cause! It is——" she faltered for a second——"it is disgraceful to us!"

Chapter Four
Tells in what a startling manner I learned that I was not alone in Graden Sea-Wood

This was my wife's story, as I drew it from her among tears and sobs. Her name was Clara Huddlestone: it sounded very beautiful in my ears; but not so beautiful as that other name of Clara Cassilis, which she wore during the longer and, I thank God, the happier portion of her life. Her father, Bernard Huddlestone, had been a private banker in a very large way of business. Many years before, his affairs becoming disordered, he had been led to try dangerous, and at last criminal, expedients to retrieve himself from ruin. All was in vain; he became more and more cruelly involved, and found his honour lost at the same moment with his fortune. About this period, Northmour had been courting his daughter with great assiduity, though with small encouragement; and to him, knowing him thus disposed in his favour, Bernard Huddlestone turned for help in his extremity. It was not merely ruin and dishonour, nor merely a legal condemnation, that the unhappy man had brought upon his head. It seems he could have gone to prison with a light heart. What he feared, what kept him awake at night or recalled him from slumber into frenzy, was some secret, sudden, and unlawful attempt upon his life. Hence, he desired to bury his existence and escape to one of the islands in the South Pacific, and it was in Northmour's yacht, the *Red Earl,* that he designed to go. The yacht picked them up clandestinely upon the coast of Wales, and had once more deposited them at Graden, till she could be refitted and provisioned for the longer voyage. Nor could Clara doubt that her hand had been stipulated as the price of passage. For, although Northmour was neither unkind nor even discourteous, he had shown himself in several instances somewhat overbold in speech and manner.

I listened, I need not say, with fixed attention, and put many questions as to the more mysterious part. It was in vain. She had no clear idea of what the blow was, nor of how it was expected to fall. Her father's alarm was unfeigned and physically prostrating, and he had thought more than once of making an unconditional surrender to the police. But the scheme was finally abandoned, for he was convinced that not even the strength of our English prisons could shelter him from his pursuers. He had had many affairs with Italy, and with Italians resident in London, in the later years of his business; and these last, as Clara fancied, were somehow connected with the doom that threatened him. He had shown great terror at the presence of an Italian seaman on board the *Red Earl,* and had bitterly and repeatedly accused Northmour in consequence. The latter had protested that Beppo (that was the seaman's name) was a capital fellow, and could be trusted to the death; but Mr. Huddlestone had continued ever since to declare that all was lost, that it was only a question of days, and that Beppo would be the ruin of him yet.

I regarded the whole story as the hallucination of a mind shaken by calamity. He had suffered heavy loss by his Italian transactions; and hence the sight of an Italian was hateful to him, and the principal part in his nightmare would naturally enough be played by one of that nation.

"What your father wants," I said, "is a good doctor and some calming medicine."

"But Mr. Northmour?" objected your mother. "He is untroubled by losses, and yet he shares in this terror."

I could not help laughing at what I considered her simplicity.

"My dear," said I, "you have told me yourself what reward he has to look for. All is fair in love, you must remember; and if Northmour foments your father's terrors, it is not at all because he is afraid of any Italian man, but simply because he is infatuated with a charming English woman."

She reminded me of his attack upon myself on the night of the disembarkation, and this I was unable to explain. In short, and from one thing to another, it was agreed between us, that I should set out at once for the fisher village, Graden Wester, as it was called, look up all the newspapers I could find, and see for myself if there seemed any basis of fact for these continued alarms. The next morning, at the same hour and place, I was to make my report to Clara. She said no more on that occasion about my departure; nor, indeed, did she make it a secret that she clung to the thought of my proximity as something helpful and pleasant; and, for my part, I could not have left her, if she had gone upon her knees to ask it.

I reached Graden Wester before ten in the forenoon; for in those days I was an excellent pedestrian, and the distance, as I think I have said, was little over seven miles; fine walking all the way upon the springy turf. The village is one of the bleakest on that coast, which is saying much: there is a church in a hollow; a miserable haven in the rocks, where many boats have been lost as they returned from fishing; two or three score of stone houses arranged along the beach and in two streets, one leading from the harbour, and another striking out from it at right angles; and, at the corner of these two, a very dark and cheerless tavern, by way of principal hotel.

I had dressed myself somewhat more suitably to my station in life, and at once called upon the minister in his little manse beside the graveyard. He knew me, although it was more than nine years since we had met; and when I told him that I had been long upon a walking tour, and was behind with the news, readily lent me an armful of newspapers, dating from a month back to the day before. With these I sought the tavern, and, ordering some breakfast, sat down to study the "Huddlestone Failure."

It had been, it appeared, a very flagrant case. Thousands of persons were reduced to poverty; and one in particular had blown out his brains as soon as payment was suspended. It was strange to myself that, while I read these details, I continued rather to sympathise with Mr. Huddlestone than with his victims; so complete already was the empire of my love for my wife. A price was naturally set upon the banker's head; and, as the case was inexcusable and the public indignation thoroughly aroused, the unusual figure of 750*l.* was offered for his capture. He was reported to have large sums of money in his possession. One day, he had been heard of in Spain; the next, there was sure intelligence that he was still lurking between Manchester and Liverpool, or along the border of Wales; and the day after, a telegram would announce his arrival in Cuba or Yucatan. But in all this there was no word of an Italian, nor any sign of mystery.

In the very last paper, however, there was one item not so clear. The accountants who were charged to verify the failure had, it seemed, come upon the traces of a very large number of thousands, which figured for some time in the transactions of the house of Huddlestone; but which came from nowhere, and disappeared in the same mysterious fashion. It was only once referred to by name, and then under the initials "X. X."; but it had plainly been floated for the first time into the business at a period of great depression some six years ago. The name of a distinguished Royal personage had been mentioned by rumour in connection with this sum. "The cowardly desperado"—such, I remember, was the editorial expression—was supposed to have escaped with a large part of this mysterious fund still in his possession.

I was still brooding over the fact, and trying to torture it into some connection with Mr. Huddlestone's danger, when a man entered the tavern and asked for some bread and cheese with a decided foreign accent.

"*Siete Italiano?*" said I.

"*Sì signor*," was his reply.

I said it was unusually far north to find one of his compatriots; at which he shrugged his shoulders, and replied that a man would go anywhere to find work. What work he could hope to find at Graden Wester, I was totally unable to conceive; and the incident struck so unpleasantly upon my mind, that I asked the landlord, while he was counting me some change, whether he had ever before seen an Italian in the village. He said he had once seen some Norwegians, who had been shipwrecked on the other side of Graden Ness and rescued by the lifeboat from Cauld-haven.

"No!" said I; "but an Italian, like the man who has just had bread and cheese."

"What?" cried he, "yon black-avised fellow wi' the teeth? Was he an I-talian? Weel, yon's the first that ever I saw, an' I dare say he's like to be the last."

Even as he was speaking, I raised my eyes, and, casting a glance into the street, beheld three men in earnest conversation together, and not thirty yards away. One of them was my recent companion in the tavern parlour; the other two, by their handsome, sallow features and soft hats, should evidently belong to the same race. A crowd of village children stood around them, gesticulating and talking gibberish in imitation. The trio looked singularly foreign to the bleak dirty street in which they were standing, and the dark grey heaven that overspread them; and I confess my incredulity received at that moment a shock from which it never recovered. I might reason with myself as I pleased, but I could not argue down the effect of what I had seen, and I began to share in the Italian terror.

It was already drawing towards the close of the day before I had returned the newspapers at the manse, and got well forward on to the links on my way home. I shall never forget that walk. It grew very cold and boisterous; the wind sang in the short grass about my feet; thin rain showers came running on the gusts; and an immense mountain range of clouds began to arise out of the bosom of the sea. It would be hard to imagine a more dismal evening; and whether it was from these external influences, or because my nerves were already affected by what I had heard and seen, my thoughts were as gloomy as the weather.

The upper windows of the pavilion commanded a considerable spread of links in the direction of Graden Wester. To avoid observation, it was necessary to hug the beach until I had gained cover from the higher sandhills on the little headland, when I might strike across, through the hollows, for the margin of the wood. The sun was about setting; the tide was low, and all the quicksands uncovered; and I was moving along, lost in unpleasant thought, when I was suddenly thunderstruck to perceive the prints of human feet. They ran parallel to my own course, but low down upon the beach instead of along the border of the turf; and, when I examined them, I saw at once, by the size and coarseness of the impression, that it was a stranger to me and to those in the pavilion who had recently passed that way. Not only so; but from the recklessness of the course which he had followed, steering near to the most formidable portions of the sand, he was as evidently a stranger to the country and to the ill-repute of Graden beach.

Step by step I followed the prints; until, a quarter of a mile farther, I beheld them die away into the southeastern boundary of Graden Floe. There, whoever he was, the miserable man had perished. One or two gulls, who had, perhaps, seen him disappear, wheeled over his sepulchre with their usual melancholy piping. The sun had broken through the clouds by a last effort, and coloured the wide level of quicksands with a dusky purple. I stood for some time gazing at the spot, chilled and disheartened by my own reflections, and with a strong and commanding consciousness of death. I remember wondering how long the tragedy had taken, and whether his screams had been audible at the pavilion. And then, making a strong resolution, I was about to tear myself away, when a gust fiercer than usual fell upon this quarter of the beach, and I saw now, whirling high in air, now skimming lightly across the surface of the sands, a soft, black, felt hat, somewhat conical in shape, such as I had remarked already on the heads of the Italians.

I believe, but I am not sure, that I uttered a cry. The wind was driving the hat shoreward, and I ran round the border of the floe to be ready against its arrival. The gust fell, dropping the hat for a while upon the quicksand, and then, once more freshening, landed it a few yards from where I stood. I seized it with the interest you may imagine. It had seen some service; indeed, it was rustier than either of those I had seen that day upon the street. The lining was red, stamped with the name of the maker, which I have forgotten, and that of the place of manufacture, *Venedig*. This (it is not yet forgotten) was the name given by the Austrians to the beautiful city of Venice, then, and for long after, a part of their dominions.

The shock was complete. I saw imaginary Italians upon every side; and for the first, and, I may say, for the last time in my experience, became overpowered by what is called a panic terror. I knew nothing, that is, to be afraid of, and yet I admit that I was heartily afraid; and it was with a sensible reluctance that I returned to my exposed and solitary camp in the Sea-Wood.

There I ate some cold porridge which had been left over from the night before, for I was disinclined to make a fire; and, feeling strengthened and reassured, dismissed all these fanciful terrors from my mind, and lay down to sleep with composure.

How long I may have slept it is impossible for me to guess; but I was awakened at last by a sudden, blinding flash of light into my face. It woke me like a blow. In an instant I was upon my knees. But the light had gone as suddenly as it came. The darkness was intense. And, as it was blowing great guns from the sea and pouring with rain, the noises of the storm effectually concealed all others.

It was, I dare say, half a minute before I regained my self-possession. But for two circumstances, I should have thought I had been awakened by some new and vivid form of nightmare. First, the flap of my tent, which I had shut carefully when I retired, was now unfastened; and, second, I could still perceive, with a sharpness that excluded any theory of hallucination, the smell of hot metal and of burning oil. The conclusion was obvious. I had been wakened by someone flashing a bull's-eye lantern in my face. It had been but a flash, and away. He had seen my face, and then gone. I asked myself the object of so strange a proceeding, and the answer came pat. The man, whoever he was, had thought to recognise me, and he had not. There was yet another question unresolved; and to this, I may say, I feared to give an answer; if he had recognised me, what would he have done?

My fears were immediately diverted from myself, for I saw that I had been visited in a mistake; and I became persuaded that some dreadful danger threatened the pavilion. It required some nerve to issue forth into the black and intricate thicket which surrounded and overhung the den; but I groped my way to the links, drenched with rain, beaten upon and deafened by the gusts, and fearing at every step to lay my hand upon some lurking adversary. The darkness was so complete that I might have been surrounded by an army and yet none the wiser, and the uproar of the gale so loud that my hearing was as useless as my sight.

For the rest of that night, which seemed interminably long, I patrolled the vicinity of the pavilion, without seeing a living creature or hearing any noise but the concert of the wind, the sea, and the rain. A light in the upper story filtered through a cranny of the shutter, and kept me company till the approach of dawn.

Chapter Five
Tells of an interview between Northmour, Clara, and myself

With the first peep of day, I retired from the open to my old lair among the sandhills, there to await the coming of my wife. The morning was grey, wild, and melancholy; the wind moderated before sunrise, and then went about, and blew in puffs from the shore; the sea began to go down, but the rain still fell without mercy. Over all the wilderness of links there was not a creature to be seen. Yet I felt sure the neighbourhood was alive with skulking foes. The light had been so suddenly and surprisingly flashed upon my face as I lay sleeping, and the hat that had been blown ashore by the wind from over Graden Floe, were two speaking signals of the peril that environed Clara and the party in the pavilion.

It was, perhaps, half past seven, or nearer eight, before I saw the door open, and that dear figure come towards me in the rain. I was waiting for her on the beach before she had crossed the sandhills.

"I have had such trouble to come!" she cried. "They did not wish me to go walking in the rain."

"Clara," I said, "you are not frightened!"

"No," said she, with a simplicity that filled my heart with confidence. For my wife was the bravest as well as the best of women; in my experience, I have not found the two go always together, but with her they did; and she combined the extreme of fortitude with the most endearing and beautiful virtues.

I told her what had happened; and, though her cheek grew visibly paler, she retained perfect control over her senses.

"You see now that I am safe," said I, in conclusion. "They do not mean to harm me; for, had they chosen, I was a dead man last night."

She laid her hand upon my arm.

"And I had no presentiment!" she cried.

Her accent thrilled me with delight. I put my arm about her, and strained her to my side; and, before either of us was aware, her hands were on my shoulders and my lips upon her mouth. Yet up to that moment no word of love had passed between us. To this day I remember the touch of her cheek, which was wet and cold with the rain; and many a time since, when she has been washing her face, I have kissed it again for the sake of that morning on the beach. Now that she is taken from me, and I finish my pilgrimage alone, I recall our old lovingkindnesses and the deep honesty and affection which united us, and my present loss seems but a trifle in comparison.

We may have thus stood for some seconds—for time passes quickly with lovers—before we were startled by a peal of laughter close at hand. It was not natural mirth, but seemed to be affected in order to conceal an angrier feeling. We both turned, though I still kept my left arm about Clara's waist; nor did she seek to withdraw herself; and there, a few paces off upon the beach, stood Northmour, his head lowered, his hands behind his back, his nostrils white with passion.

"Ah! Cassilis!" he said, as I disclosed my face.

"That same," said I; for I was not at all put about.

"And so, Miss Huddlestone," he continued slowly but savagely, "this is how you keep your faith to your father and to me? This is the value you set upon your father's life? And you are so infatuated with this young gentleman that you must brave ruin, and decency, and common human caution——"

"Miss Huddlestone——" I was beginning to interrupt him, when he, in his turn, cut in brutally——

"You hold your tongue," said he; "I am speaking to that girl."

"That girl, as you call her, is my wife," said I; and my wife only leaned a little nearer, so that I knew she had affirmed my words.

"Your what?" he cried. "You lie!"

"Northmour," I said, "we all know you have a bad temper, and I am the last man to be irritated by words. For all that, I propose that you speak lower, for I am convinced that we are not alone."

He looked round him, and it was plain my remark had in some degree sobered his passion. "What do you mean!" he asked.

I only said one word: "Italians."

He swore a round oath, and looked at us, from one to the other.

"Mr. Cassilis knows all that I know," said my wife.

"What I want to know," he broke out, "is where the devil Mr. Cassilis comes from, and what the devil Mr. Cassilis is doing here. You say you are married; that I do not believe. If you were, Graden Floe would soon divorce you; four minutes and a half, Cassilis. I keep my private cemetery for my friends."

"It took somewhat longer," said I, "for that Italian."

He looked at me for a moment half daunted, and then, almost civilly, asked me to tell my story. "You have too much the advantage of me, Cassilis," he added. I complied of course; and he listened, with several ejaculations, while I told him how I had come to Graden: that it was I whom he had tried to murder on the night of landing; and what I had subsequently seen and heard of the Italians.

"Well," said he, when I had done, "it is here at last; there is no mistake about that. And what, may I ask, do you propose to do?"

"I propose to stay with you and lend a hand," said I.

"You are a brave man," he returned, with a peculiar intonation.

"I am not afraid," said I.

"And so," he continued, "I am to understand that you two are married? And you stand up to it before my face, Miss Huddlestone?"

"We are not yet married," said Clara; "but we shall be as soon as we can."

"Bravo!" cried Northmour. "And the bargain? D—n it, you're not a fool, young woman; I may call a spade a spade with you. How about the bargain? You know as well as I do what your father's life depends upon. I have only to put my hands under my coattails and walk away, and his throat would be cut before the evening."

"Yes, Mr. Northmour," returned Clara, with great spirit; "but that is what you will never do. You made a bargain that was unworthy of a gentleman; but you are gentleman for all that, and you will never desert a man whom you have begun to help."

"Aha!" said he. "You think I will give my yacht for nothing? You think I will risk my life and liberty for love of the old gentleman; and then, I suppose, be best man at the wedding, to wind up? Well," he added, with an odd smile, "perhaps you are not altogether wrong. But ask Cassilis here. *He* knows me. Am I a man to trust? Am I safe and scrupulous? Am I kind?"

"I know you talk a great deal, and sometimes, I think, very foolishly," replied Clara, "but I know you are a gentleman, and I am not the least afraid."

He looked at her with a peculiar approval and admiration; then, turning to me, "Do you think I would give her up without a struggle, Frank?" said he. "I tell you plainly, you look out. The next time we come to blows——"

"Will make the third," I interrupted, smiling.

"Aye, true; so it will," he said. "I had forgotten. Well, the third time's lucky."

"The third time, you mean, you will have the crew of the *Red Earl* to help," I said.

"Do you hear him?" he asked, turning to my wife.

"I hear two men speaking like cowards," said she. "I should despise myself either to think or speak like that. And neither of you believe one word that you are saying, which makes it the more wicked and silly."

"She's a trump!" cried Northmour. "But she's not yet Mrs. Cassilis. I say no more. The present is not for me."

Then my wife surprised me.

"I leave you here," she said suddenly. "My father has been too long alone. But remember this: you are to be friends, for you are both good friends to me."

She has since told me her reason for this step. As long as she remained, she declares that we two would have continued to quarrel; and I suppose that she was right, for when she was gone we fell at once into a sort of confidentiality.

Northmour stared after her as she went away over the sandhill.

"She is the only woman in the world!" he exclaimed with an oath. "Look at her action."

I, for my part, leaped at this opportunity for a little further light.

"See here, Northmour," said I; "we are all in a tight place, are we not?"

"I believe you, my boy," he answered, looking me in the eyes, and with great emphasis. "We have all hell upon us, that's the truth. You may believe me or not, but I'm afraid of my life."

"Tell me one thing," said I. "What are they after, these Italians? What do they want with Mr. Huddlestone?"

"Don't you know?" he cried. "The black old scamp had *carbonaro* funds on a deposit—two hundred and eighty thousand; and of course he gambled it away on stocks. There was to have been a revolution in the Tridentino, or Parma; but the revolution is off, and the whole wasp's nest is after Huddlestone. We shall all be lucky if we can save our skins."

"The *carbonari*!" I exclaimed; "God help him indeed!"

"Amen!" said Northmour. "And now, look here: I have said that we are in a fix; and, frankly, I shall be glad of your help. If I can't save Huddlestone, I want at least to save the girl. Come and stay in the pavilion; and, there's my hand on it, I shall act as your friend until the old man is either clear or dead. But," he added, "once that is settled, you become my rival once again, and I warn you—mind yourself."

"Done!" said I; and we shook hands.

"And now let us go directly to the fort," said Northmour; and he began to lead the way through the rain.

Chapter Six
Tells of my introduction to the tall man

We were admitted to the pavilion by Clara, and I was surprised by the completeness and security of the defences. A barricade of great strength, and yet easy to displace, supported the door against any violence from without; and the shutters of the dining room, into which I was led directly, and which was feebly illuminated by a lamp, were even more elaborately fortified. The panels were strengthened by bars and crossbars; and these, in their turn, were kept in position by a system of braces and struts, some abutting on the floor, some on the roof, and others, in fine, against the opposite wall of the apartment. It was at once a solid and well-designed piece of carpentry; and I did not seek to conceal my admiration.

"I am the engineer," said Northmour. "You remember the planks in the garden? Behold them!"

"I did not know you had so many talents," said I.

"Are you armed?" he continued, pointing to an array of guns and pistols, all in admirable order, which stood in line against the wall or were displayed upon the sideboard.

"Thank you," I returned; "I have gone armed since our last encounter. But, to tell you the truth, I have had nothing to eat since early yesterday evening."

Northmour produced some cold meat, to which I eagerly set myself, and a bottle of good Burgundy, by which, wet as I was, I did not scruple to profit. I have always been an extreme temperance man on principle; but it is useless to push principle to excess, and on this occasion I believe that I finished three-quarters of the bottle. As I ate, I still continued to admire the preparations for defence.

"We could stand a siege," I said at length.

"Ye—es," drawled Northmour; "a very little one, per—haps. It is not so much the strength of the pavilion I misdoubt; it is the double danger that kills me. If we get to shooting, wild as the country is some one is sure to hear it, and then—why then it's the same thing, only different, as they say: caged by law, or killed by *carbonari*. There's the choice. It is a devilish bad thing to have the law against you in this world, and so I tell the old gentleman upstairs. He is quite of my way of thinking."

"Speaking of that," said I, "what kind of person is he?"

"Oh, he!" cried the other; "he's a rancid fellow, as far as he goes. I should like to have his neck wrung tomorrow by all the devils in Italy. I am not in this affair for him. You take me? I made a bargain for Missy's hand, and I mean to have it too."

"That, by the way," said I. "I understand. But how will Mr. Huddlestone take my intrusion?"

"Leave that to Clara," returned Northmour.

I could have struck him in the face for this coarse familiarity; but I respected the truce, as, I am bound to say, did Northmour, and so long as the danger continued not a cloud arose in our relation. I bear him this testimony with the most unfeigned satisfaction; nor am I without pride when I look back upon my own behaviour. For surely no two men were ever left in a position so invidious and irritating.

As soon as I had done eating, we proceeded to inspect the lower floor. Window by window we tried the different supports, now and then making an inconsiderable change; and the strokes of the hammer sounded with startling loudness through the house. I proposed, I remember, to make loopholes; but he told me they were already made in the windows of the upper story. It was an anxious business this inspection, and left me downhearted. There were two doors and and five windows to protect, and, counting Clara, only four of us to defend them against an unknown number of foes. I communicated my doubts to Northmour, who assured me, with unmoved composure, that he entirely shared them.

"Before morning," said he, "we shall all be butchered and buried in Graden Floe. For me, that is written."

I could not help shuddering at the mention of the quicksand, but reminded Northmour that our enemies had spared me in the wood.

"Do not flatter yourself," said he. "Then you were not in the same boat with the old gentleman; now you are. It's the floe for all of us, mark my words."

I trembled for Clara; and just then her dear voice was heard calling us to come upstairs. Northmour showed me the way, and, when he had reached the landing, knocked at the door of what used to be called *My Uncle's Bedroom*, as the founder of the pavilion had designed it especially for himself.

"Come in, Northmour; come in, dear Mr. Cassilis," said a voice from within.

Pushing open the door, Northmour admitted me before him

into the apartment. As I came in I could see the daughter slipping out by the side door into the study, which had been prepared as her bedroom. In the bed, which was drawn back against the wall, instead of standing, as I had last seen it, boldly across the window, sat Bernard Huddlestone, the defaulting banker. Little as I had seen of him by the shifting light of the lantern on the links, I had no difficulty in recognising him for the same. He had a long and sallow countenance, surrounded by a long red beard and side-whiskers. His broken nose and high cheekbones gave him somewhat the air of a Kalmuck, and his light eyes shone with the excitement of a high fever. He wore a skullcap of black silk; a huge Bible lay open before him on the bed, with a pair of gold spectacles in the place, and a pile of other books lay on the stand by his side. The green curtains lent a cadaverous shade to his cheek; and, as he sat propped on pillows, his great stature was painfully hunched, and his head protruded till it overhung his knees. I believe if he had not died otherwise, he must have fallen a victim to consumption in the course of but a very few weeks.

He held out to me a hand, long, thin, and disagreeably hairy.

"Come in, come in, Mr. Cassilis," said he. "Another protector—ahem!—another protector. Always welcome as a friend of my daughter's, Mr. Cassilis. How they have rallied about me, my daughter's friends! May God in heaven bless and reward them for it!"

I gave him my hand, of course, because I could not help it; but the sympathy I had been prepared to feel for Clara's father was immediately soured by his appearance, and the wheedling, unreal tones in which he spoke.

"Cassilis is a good man," said Northmour; "worth ten."

"So I hear," cried Mr. Huddlestone eagerly; "so my girl tells me. Ah, Mr. Cassilis, my sin has found me out, you see! I am very low, very low; but I hope equally penitent. We must all come to the throne of grace at last, Mr. Cassilis. For my part, I come late indeed; but with unfeigned humility, I trust."

"Fiddle-de-dee!" said Northmour roughly.

"No, no, dear Northmour!" cried the banker. "You must not say that; you must not try to shake me. You forget, my dear, good boy, you forget I may be called this very night before my Maker."

His excitement was pitiful to behold; and I felt myself grow indignant with Northmour, whose infidel opinions I well knew, and heartily derided, as he continued to taunt the poor sinner out of his humour of repentance.

"Pooh, my dear Huddlestone!" said he. "You do yourself injustice. You are a man of the world inside and out, and were up to all kinds of mischief before I was born. Your conscience is tanned like South American leather—only you forgot to tan your liver, and that, if you will believe me, is the seat of the annoyance."

"Rogue, rogue! bad boy!" said Mr. Huddlestone, shaking his finger. "I am no precisian, if you come to that; I always hated a precisian; but I never lost hold of something better through it all. I have been a bad boy, Mr. Cassilis; I do not seek to deny that; but it was after my wife's death, and you know, with a widower, it's a different thing: sinful—I won't say no; but there is a gradation, we shall hope. And talking of that—— Hark!" he broke out suddenly, his hand raised, his fingers spread, his face racked with interest and terror. "Only the rain, bless God!" he added, after a pause, and with indescribable relief.

For some seconds he lay back among the pillows like a man near to fainting; then he gathered himself together, and, in somewhat tremulous tones, began once more to thank me for the share I was prepared to take in his defence.

"One question, sir," said I, when he had paused. "Is it true that you have money with you?"

He seemed annoyed by the question, but admitted with reluctance that he had a little.

"Well," I continued, "it is their money they are after, is it not? Why not give it up to them?"

"Ah!" replied he, shaking his head, "I have tried that already, Mr. Cassilis; and alas! that it should be so, but it is blood they want."

"Huddlestone, that's a little less than fair," said Northmour. "You should mention that what you offered them was upwards of two hundred thousand short. The deficit is worth a reference; it is for what they call a cool sum, Frank. Then, you see, the fellows reason in their clear Italian way; and it seems to them, as indeed it seems to me, that they may just as well have both while they're about it—money and blood together, by George, and no more trouble for the extra pleasure."

"Is it in the pavilion?" I asked.

"It is; and I wish it were in the bottom of the sea instead," said Northmour; and then suddenly—"What are you making faces at me for?" he cried to Mr. Huddlestone, on whom I had unconsciously turned my back. "Do you think Cassilis would sell you?"

Mr. Huddlestone protested that nothing had been further from his mind.

"It is a good thing," retorted Northmour in his ugliest manner. "You might end by wearying us. What were you going to say?" he added, turning to me.

"I was going to propose an occupation for the afternoon," said I. "Let us carry that money out, piece by piece, and lay it down before the pavilion door. If the *carbonari* come, why, it's theirs at any rate."

"No, no," cried Mr. Huddlestone; "it does not, it cannot belong to them! It should be distributed *pro rata* among all my creditors."

"Come now, Huddlestone," said Northmour, "none of that."

"Well, but my daughter," moaned the wretched man.

"Your daughter will do well enough. Here are two suitors, Cassilis and I, neither of us beggars, between whom she has to choose. And as for yourself, to make an end of arguments, you have no right to a farthing, and, unless I'm much mistaken, you are going to die."

It was certainly very cruelly said; but Mr. Huddlestone was a man who attracted little sympathy; and, although I saw him wince and shudder, I mentally endorsed the rebuke; nay, I added a contribution of my own.

"Northmour and I," I said, "are willing enough to help you to save your life, but not to escape with stolen property."

He struggled for a while with himself, as though he were on the point of giving way to anger, but prudence had the best of the controversy.

"My dear boys," he said, "do with me or my money what you will. I leave all in your hands. Let me compose myself."

And so we left him, gladly enough I am sure. The last that I saw, he had once more taken up his great Bible, and with tremulous hands was adjusting his spectacles to read.

Chapter Seven
Tells how a word was cried through the pavilion window

The recollection of that afternoon will always be graven on my mind. Northmour and I were persuaded that an attack was imminent; and if it had been in our power to alter in any way the order of events, that power would have been used to precipitate rather than delay the critical moment. The worst was to be anticipated; yet we could conceive no extremity so miserable as the suspense we were now suffering. I have never been an eager, though always a great, reader; but I never knew books so insipid as those which I took up and cast aside that afternoon in the pavilion. Even talk became impossible, as the hours went on. One or other was always listening for some sound, or peering from an upstairs window over the links. And yet not a sign indicated the presence of our foes.

We debated over and over again my proposal with regard to the money; and had we been in complete possession of our faculties, I am sure we should have condemned it as unwise; but we were flustered with alarm, grasped at a straw, and determined, although it was as much as advertising Mr. Huddlestone's presence in the pavilion, to carry my proposal into effect.

The sum was part in specie, part in bank paper, and part in circular notes payable to the name of James Gregory. We took it out, counted it, enclosed it once more in a dispatch box belonging to Northmour, and prepared a letter in Italian which he tied to the handle. It was signed by both of us under oath, and declared that this was all the money which had escaped the failure of the house of Huddlestone. This was, perhaps, the maddest action ever perpetrated by two persons professing to be sane. Had the dispatch box fallen into other hands than those for which it was intended, we stood criminally convicted on our own written testimony; but, as I have said, we were neither of us in a condition to judge soberly, and had a thirst for action that drove us to do something, right or wrong, rather than endure the agony of waiting. Moreover, as we were both convinced that the hollows of the links were alive with hidden spies upon our movements, we hoped that our appearance with the box might lead to a parley, and, perhaps, a compromise.

It was nearly three when we issued from the pavilion. The rain had taken off; the sun shone quite cheerfully. I have never seen the gulls fly so close about the house or approach so fearlessly to human beings. On the very doorstep one flapped heavily past our heads, and uttered its wild cry in my very ear.

"There is an omen for you," said Northmour, who like all freethinkers was much under the influence of superstition. "They think we are already dead."

I made some light rejoinder, but it was with half my heart; for the circumstance had impressed me.

A yard or two before the gate, on a patch of smooth turf, we set down the dispatch box; and Northmour waved a white handkerchief over his head. Nothing replied. We raised our voices, and cried aloud in Italian that we were there as ambassadors to arrange the quarrel; but the stillness remained unbroken save by the seagulls and the surf. I had a weight at my heart when we desisted; and I saw that even Northmour was unusually pale. He looked over his shoulder nervously, as though he feared that someone had crept between him and the pavilion door.

"By God," he said in a whisper, "this is too much for me!"

I replied in the same key: "Suppose there should be none, after all!"

"Look there," he returned, nodding with his head, as though he had been afraid to point.

I glanced in the direction indicated; and there, from the northern quarter of the Sea-Wood, beheld a thin column of smoke rising steadily against the now cloudless sky.

"Northmour," I said (we still continued to talk in whispers), "it is not possible to endure this suspense. I prefer death fifty times over. Stay you here to watch the pavilion; I will go forward and make sure, if I have to walk right into their camp."

He looked once again all round him with puckered eyes, and then nodded assentingly to my proposal.

My heart beat like a sledgehammer as I set out walking rapidly in the direction of the smoke; and, though up to that moment I had felt chill and shivering, I was suddenly conscious of a glow of heat over all my body. The ground in this direction was very uneven; a hundred men might have lain hidden in as many square yards about my path. But I had not practised the business in vain, chose such routes as cut at the very root of concealment, and, by keeping along the most convenient ridges, commanded several hollows at a time. It was not long before I was rewarded for my caution. Coming suddenly on to a mound somewhat more elevated than the surrounding hummocks, I saw, not thirty yards away, a man bent almost double, and running as fast as his attitude permitted, along the bottom of a gully. I had dislodged one of the spies from his ambush. As soon as I sighted him, I called loudly both in English and Italian; and he, seeing concealment was no longer possible, straightened himself out, leaped from the gully, and made off as straight as an arrow for the borders of the wood.

It was none of my business to pursue; I had learned what I wanted—that we were beleaguered and watched in the pavilion; and I returned at once, and walking as nearly as possible in my old footsteps, to where Northmour awaited me beside the dispatch box. He was even paler than when I had left him, and his voice shook a little.

"Could you see what he was like?" he asked.

"He kept his back turned," I replied.

"Let us get into the house, Frank. I don't think I'm a coward, but I can stand no more of this," he whispered.

All was still and sunshiny about the pavilion, as we turned to re-enter it; even the gulls had flown in a wider circuit, and were seen flickering along the beach and sandhills; and this loneliness terrified me more than a regiment under arms. It was not until the door was barricaded that I could draw a full inspiration and relieve the weight that lay upon my bosom. Northmour and I exchanged a steady glance; and I suppose each made his own reflections on the white and startled aspect of the other.

"You were right," I said. "All is over. Shake hands, old man, for the last time."

"Yes," replied he, "I will shake hands; for, as sure as I am here, I bear no malice. But, remember, if, by some impossible accident, we should give the slip to these blackguards, I'll take the upper hand of you by fair or foul."

"Oh," said I, "you weary me!"

He seemed hurt, and walked away in silence to the foot of the stairs, where he paused.

"You do not understand," said he. "I am not a swindler, and I guard myself; that is all. It may weary you or not, Mr. Cassilis, I do not care a rush; I speak for my own satisfaction, and not for your amusement. You had better go upstairs and court the girl; for my part, I stay here."

"And I stay with you," I returned. "Do you think I would steal a march, even with your permission?"

"Frank," he said, smiling, "it's a pity you are an ass, for you have the makings of a man. I think I must be *fey* today; you cannot irritate me even when you try. Do you know," he continued softly, "I think we are the two most miserable men in England, you and I? we have got on to thirty without wife or child, or so much as a shop to look after—poor, pitiful, lost devils, both! And now we clash about a girl! As if there were not several millions in the United Kingdom! Ah, Frank, Frank, the one who loses this throw, be it you or me, he has my pity! It were better for him—how does the Bible say?—that a millstone were hanged about his neck and he were cast into the depth of the sea. Let us take a drink," he concluded suddenly, but without any levity of tone.

I was touched by his words, and consented. He sat down on the table in the dining room, and held up the glass of sherry to his eye.

"If you beat me, Frank," he said, "I shall take to drink. What will you do, if it goes the other way?"

"God knows," I returned.

"Well," said he, "here is a toast in the meantime: '*Italia irredenta!*'"

The remainder of the day was passed in the same dreadful tedium and suspense. I laid the table for dinner, while Northmour and Clara prepared the meal together in the kitchen. I could hear their talk as I went to and fro, and was surprised to find it ran all the time upon myself. Northmour again bracketed us together, and rallied Clara on a choice of husbands; but he continued to speak of me with some feeling, and uttered nothing to my prejudice unless he included himself in the condemnation. This awakened a sense of gratitude in my heart, which combined with the immediateness of our peril to fill my eyes with tears. After all, I thought—and perhaps the thought was laughably vain—we were here three very noble human beings to perish in defence of a thieving banker.

Before we sat down to table, I looked forth from an upstairs window. The day was beginning to decline; the links were utterly deserted; the dispatch box still lay untouched where we had left it hours before.

Mr. Huddlestone, in a long yellow dressing gown, took one end of the table, Clara the other; while Northmour and I faced each other from the sides. The lamp was brightly trimmed; the wine was good; the viands, although mostly cold, excellent of their sort. We seemed to have agreed tacitly; all reference to the impending catastrophe was carefully avoided; and, considering our tragic circumstances, we made a merrier party than could have been expected. From time to time, it is true, Northmour or I would rise from table and make a round of the defences; and, on each of these occasions, Mr. Huddlestone was recalled to a sense of his tragic predicament, glanced up with ghastly eyes, and bore for an instant on his countenance the stamp of terror. But he hastened to empty his glass, wiped his forehead with his handkerchief, and joined again in the conversation.

I was astonished at the wit and information he displayed. Mr. Huddlestone's was certainly no ordinary character; he had read and observed for himself; his gifts were sound; and, though I could never have learned to love the man, I began to understand his success in business, and the great respect in which he had been held before his failure. He had, above all, the talent of society; and though I never heard him speak but on this one and most unfavourable occasion, I set him down among the most brilliant conversationalists I ever met.

He was relating with great gusto, and seemingly no feeling of shame, the manoeuvers of a scoundrelly commission merchant whom he had known and studied in his youth, and we were all listening with an odd mixture of mirth and embarrassment, when our little party was brought abruptly to an end in the most startling manner.

A noise like that of a wet finger on the windowpane interrupted

Mr. Huddlestone's tale; and in an instant we were all four as white as paper, and sat tongue-tied and motionless round the table.

"A snail," I said at last; for I had heard that these animals make a noise somewhat similar in character.

"Snail be d—d!" said Northmour. "Hush!"

The same sound was repeated twice at regular intervals; and then a formidable voice shouted through the shutters the Italian word "*Traditore!*"

Mr. Huddlestone threw his head in the air; his eyelids quivered; next moment he fell insensible below the table. Northmour and I had each run to the armoury and seized a gun. Clara was on her feet with her hand at her throat.

So we stood waiting, for we thought the hour of attack was certainly come; but second passed after second, and all but the surf remained silent in the neighbourhood of the pavilion.

"Quick," said Northmour; "upstairs with him before they come."

Chapter Eight
Tells the last of the tall man

Somehow or other, by hook and crook, and between the three of us, we got Bernard Huddlestone bundled upstairs and laid upon the bed in *My Uncle's Room*. During the whole process, which was rough enough, he gave no sign of consciousness, and he remained, as we had thrown him, without changing the position of a finger. His daughter opened his shirt and began to wet his head and bosom; while Northmour and I ran to the window. The weather continued clear; the moon, which was now about full, had risen and shed a very clear light upon the links; yet, strain our eyes as we might, we could distinguish nothing moving. A few dark spots, more or less, on the uneven expanse were not to be identified; they might be crouching men, they might be shadows; it was impossible to be sure.

"Thank God," said Northmour, "Aggie is not coming tonight."

Aggie was the name of the old nurse; he had not thought of her till now; but that he should think of her at all, was a trait that surprised me in the man.

We were again reduced to waiting. Northmour went to the fireplace and spread his hands before the red embers, as if he were cold. I followed him mechanically with my eyes, and in so doing turned my back upon the window. At that moment a very faint report was audible from without, and a ball shivered a pane of glass, and buried itself in the shutter two inches from my head. I heard Clara scream; and though I whipped instantly out of range and into a corner, she was there, so to speak, before me, beseeching to know if I were hurt. I felt that I could stand to be shot at every day and all day long, with such marks of solicitude for a reward; and I continued to reassure her, with the tenderest caresses and in complete forgetfulness of our situation, till the voice of Northmour recalled me to myself.

"An air gun," he said. "They wish to make no noise."

I put Clara aside, and looked at him. He was standing with his back to the fire and his hands clasped behind him; and I knew by the black look on his face, that passion was boiling within. I had seen just such a look before he attacked me, that March night, in the adjoining chamber; and, though I could make every allowance for his anger, I confess I trembled for the consequences. He gazed straight before him; but he could see us with the tail of his eye, and his temper kept rising like a gale of wind. With regular battle awaiting us outside, this prospect of an internecine strife within the walls began to daunt me.

Suddenly, as I was thus closely watching his expression and prepared against the worst, I saw a change, a flash, a look of relief, upon his face. He took up the lamp which stood beside him on the table, and turned to us with an air of some excitement.

There is one point that we must know," said he. "Are they going to butcher the lot of us, or only Huddlestone? Did they take you for him, or fire at you for your own *beaux yeux?*"

"They took me for him, for certain," I replied. "I am near as tall, and my head is fair."

"I am going to make sure," returned Northmour; and he stepped up to the window, holding the lamp above his head, and stood there, quietly affronting death, for half a minute.

Clara sought to rush forward and pull him from the place of danger; but I had the pardonable selfishness to hold her back by force.

"Yes," said Northmour, turning coolly from the window; "it's only Huddlestone they want."

"Oh, Mr. Northmour!" cried Clara; but found no more to add; the temerity she had just witnessed seeming beyond the reach of words.

He, on his part, looked at me, cocking his head, with a fire of triumph in his eyes; and I understood at once that he had thus hazarded his life, merely to attract Clara's notice, and depose me from my position as the hero of the hour. He snapped his fingers.

"The fire is only beginning," said he. "When they warm up to their work, they won't be so particular."

A voice was now heard hailing us from the entrance. From the window we could see the figure of a man in the moonlight; he stood motionless, his face uplifted to ours, and a rag of something white on his extended arm; and as we looked right down upon him, though he was a good many yards distant on the links, we could see the moonlight glitter on his eyes.

He opened his lips again, and spoke for some minutes on end, in a key so loud that he might have been heard in every corner of the pavilion, and as far away as the borders of the wood. It was the same voice that had already shouted "*Traditore!*" through the shutters of the dining room; this time it made a complete and clear statement. If the traitor "Oddlestone" were given up, all others should be spared; if not, no one should escape to tell the tale.

"Well, Huddlestone, what do you say to that?" asked Northmour, turning to the bed.

Up to that moment the banker had given no sign of life, and I, at least, had supposed him to be still lying in a faint; but he replied at once, and in such tones as I have never heard elsewhere, save from a delirious patient, adjured and besought us not to desert him. It was the most hideous and abject performance that my imagination can conceive.

"Enough," cried Northmour; and then he threw open the window, leaned out into the night, and in a tone of exultation, and with a total forgetfulness of what was due to the presence of a lady, poured out upon the ambassador a string of the most abominable raillery both in English and Italian, and bade him be gone where he had come from. I believe that nothing so delighted Northmour at that moment as the thought that we must all infallibly perish before the night was out.

Meantime the Italian put his flag of truce into his pocket, and disappeared, at a leisurely pace, among the sandhills.

"They make honourable war," said Northmour. "They are all gentlemen and soldiers. For the credit of the thing, I wish we could change sides—you and I, Frank, and you too, Missy my darling—and leave that being on the bed to someone else. Tut! Don't look shocked! We are all going post to what they call eternity, and may as well be aboveboard while there's time. As far as I'm concerned, if I could first strangle Huddlestone and then get Clara in my arms, I could die with some pride and satisfaction. And as it is, by God, I'll have a kiss!"

Before I could do anything to interfere, he had rudely embraced and repeatedly kissed the resisting girl. Next moment I had pulled him away with fury, and flung him heavily against the wall. He laughed loud and long, and I feared his wits had given way under the strain; for even in the best of days he had been a sparing and a quiet laugher.

"Now, Frank," said he, when his mirth was somewhat appeased, "it's your turn. Here's my hand. Good-bye; farewell!" Then, seeing me stand rigid and indignant, and holding Clara to my side—"Man!" he broke out, "are you angry? Did you think we were going to die with all the airs and graces of society? I took a kiss; I'm glad I had it; and now you can take another if you like, and square accounts."

I turned from him with a feeling of contempt which I did not seek to dissemble.

"As you please," said he. "You've been a prig in life; a prig you'll die."

And with that he sat down in a chair, a rifle over his knee, and amused himself with snapping the lock; but I could see that his ebullition of light spirits (the only one I ever knew him to display) had already come to an end, and was succeeded by a sullen, scowling humour.

All this time our assailants might have been entering the house, and we been none the wiser; we had in truth almost forgotten the danger that so imminently overhung our days. But just then Mr. Huddlestone uttered a cry, and leaped from the bed.

I asked him what was wrong.

"Fire!" he cried. "They have set the house on fire!"

Northmour was on his feet in an instant, and he and I ran through the door of communication with the study. The room was illuminated by a red and angry light. Almost at the moment of our entrance, a tower of flame arose in front of the window, and, with a tingling report, a pane fell inwards on the carpet. They had set fire to the lean-to outhouse, where Northmour used to nurse his negatives.

"Hot work," said Northmour. "Let us try in your old room."

We ran thither in a breath, threw up the casement, and looked forth. Along the whole back wall of the pavilion piles of fuel had been arranged and kindled; and it is probable they had been drenched with mineral oil, for, in spite of the morning's rain, they all burned bravely. The fire had taken a firm hold already on the outhouse, which blazed higher and higher every moment; the back door was in the centre of a red-hot bonfire; the eaves we could see, as we looked upward, were already smouldering, for the roof overhung, and was supported by considerable beams of wood. At the same time, hot, pungent, and choking volumes of smoke began to fill the house. There was not a human being to be seen to right or left.

"Ah, well!" said Northmour, "here's the end, thank God."

And we returned to *My Uncle's Room*. Mr. Huddlestone was putting on his boots, still violently trembling, but with an air of determination such as I had not hitherto observed. Clara stood close by him, with her cloak in both hands ready to throw about her shoulders, and a strange look in her eyes, as if she were half hopeful, half doubtful of her father.

"Well, boys and girls," said Northmour, "how about a sally? The oven is heating; it is not good to stay here and be baked; and, for my part, I want to come to my hands with them, and be done."

"There is nothing else left," I replied.

And both Clara and Mr. Huddlestone, though with a very different intonation, added, "Nothing."

As we went downstairs the heat was excessive, and the roaring of the fire filled our ears; and we had scarce reached the passage before the stairs window fell in, a branch of flame shot brandishing through the aperture, and the interior of the pavilion became lit up with that dreadful and fluctuating glare. At the same moment we heard the fall of something heavy and inelastic in the upper story. The whole pavilion, it was plain, had gone alight like a box of matches, and now not only flamed sky-high to land and sea, but threatened with every moment to crumble and fall in about our ears.

Northmour and I cocked our revolvers. Mr. Huddlestone, who had already refused a firearm, put us behind him with a manner of command.

"Let Clara open the door," said he. "So, if they fire a volley, she will be protected. And in the meantime stand behind me. I am the scapegoat; my sins have found me out."

I heard him, as I stood breathless by his shoulder, with my pistol ready, pattering off prayers in a tremulous, rapid whisper; and I confess, horrid as the thought may seem, I despised him for thinking of supplications in a moment so critical and thrilling. In the meantime, Clara, who was dead white but still possessed her faculties, had displaced the barricade from the front door. Another moment, and she had pulled it open. Firelight and moonlight illuminated the links with confused and changeful lustre, and far away against the sky we could see a long trail of glowing smoke.

Mr. Huddlestone, filled for the moment with a strength greater than his own, struck Northmour and myself a backhander in the chest; and while we were thus for the moment incapacitated from action, lifting his arms above his head like one about to dive, he ran straight forward out of the pavilion.

"Here am I!" he cried—"Huddlestone! Kill me, and spare the others!"

His sudden appearance daunted, I suppose, our hidden enemies; for Northmour and I had time to recover, to seize Clara between us, one by each arm, and to rush forth to his assistance, ere anything further had taken place. But scarce had we passed the threshold when there came near a dozen reports and flashes from every direction among the hollows of the links. Mr. Huddlestone staggered, uttered a weird and freezing cry, threw up his arms over his head, and fell backward on the turf.

"*Traditore! Traditore!*" cried the invisible avengers.

And just then, a part of the roof of the pavilion fell in, so rapid was the progress of the fire. A loud, vague, and horrible noise accompanied the collapse, and a vast volume of flame went soaring up to heaven. It must have been visible at that moment from twenty miles out at sea, from the shore at Graden Wester, and far inland from the peak of Graystiel, the most eastern summit of the Caulder Hills. Bernard Huddlestone, although God knows what were his obsequies, had a fine pyre at the moment of his death.

Chapter Nine
Tells how Northmour carried out his threat

I should have the greatest difficulty to tell you what followed next after this tragic circumstance. It is all to me, as I look back upon it, mixed, strenuous, and ineffectual, like the struggles of a sleeper in a nightmare. Clara, I remember, uttered a broken sigh and would have fallen forward to earth, had not Northmour and I supported her insensible body. I do not think we were attacked; I do not remember even to have seen an assailant; and I believe we deserted Mr. Huddlestone without a glance. I only remember running like a man in a panic, now carrying Clara altogether in my own arms, now sharing her weight with Northmour, now scuffling confusedly for the possession of that dear burden. Why we should have made for my camp in the Hemlock Den, or how we reached it, are points lost for ever to my recollection. The first moment at which I became definitely sure, Clara had been suffered to fall against the outside of my little tent, Northmour and I were tumbling together on the ground, and he, with contained ferocity, was striking for my head with the butt of his revolver. He had already twice wounded me on the scalp; and it is to the consequent loss of blood that I am tempted to attribute the sudden clearness of my mind.

I caught him by the wrist.

"Northmour," I remember saying, "you can kill me afterwards. Let us first attend to Clara."

He was at the moment uppermost. Scarcely had the words passed my lips, when he had leaped to his feet and ran towards the tent; and the next moment, he was straining Clara to his heart and covering her unconscious hands and face with his caresses.

"Shame!" I cried. "Shame to you, Northmour!"

And, giddy though I still was, I struck him repeatedly upon the head and shoulders.

He relinquished his grasp, and faced me in the broken moonlight.

"I had you under, and I let you go," said he; "and now you strike me! Coward!"

"You are the coward," I retorted. "Did she wish your kisses while she was still sensible of what she wanted? Not she! And now she may be dying; and you waste this precious time, and abuse her helplessness. Stand aside, and let me help her."

He confronted me for a moment, white and menacing; then suddenly he stepped aside.

"Help her then," said he.

I threw myself on my knees beside her, and loosened, as well as I was able, her dress and corset; but while I was thus engaged, a grasp descended on my shoulder.

"Keep your hands off her," said Northmour fiercely. "Do you think I have no blood in my veins?"

"Northmour," I cried, "if you will neither help her yourself, nor let me do so, do you know that I shall have to kill you?"

"That is better!" he cried. "Let her die also, where's the harm? Step aside from that girl! and stand up to fight."

"You will observe," said I, half rising, "that I have not kissed her yet."

"I dare you to," he cried.

I do not know what possessed me; it was one of the things I am most ashamed of in my life, though, as my wife used to say, I knew that my kisses would be always welcome were she dead or living; down I fell again upon my knees, parted the hair from her forehead, and, with the dearest respect, laid my lips for a moment on that cold brow. It was such a caress as a father might have given; it was such a one as was not unbecoming from a man soon to die to a woman already dead.

"And now," said I, "I am at your service, Mr. Northmour."

But I saw, to my surprise, that he had turned his back upon me.

"Do you hear?" I asked.

"Yes," said he, "I do. If you wish to fight, I am ready. If not, go on and save Clara. All is one to me."

I did not wait to be twice bidden; but, stooping again over Clara, continued my efforts to revive her. She still lay white and lifeless; I began to fear that her sweet spirit had indeed fled beyond recall, and horror and a sense of utter desolation seized upon my heart. I called her by name with the most endearing inflections; I chafed and beat her hands; now I laid her head low, now supported it against my knee; but all seemed to be in vain, and the lids still lay heavy on her eyes.

"Northmour," I said, "there is my hat. For God's sake bring some water from the spring."

Almost in a moment he was by my side with the water.

"I have brought it in my own," he said. "You do not grudge me the privilege?"

"Northmour," I was beginning to say, as I laved her head and breast; but he interrupted me savagely.

"Oh, you hush up!" he said. "The best thing you can do is to say nothing."

I had certainly no desire to talk, my mind being swallowed up in concern for my dear love and her condition; so I continued in silence to do my best towards her recovery, and, when the hat was empty, returned it to him, with one word—"More." He had, perhaps, gone several times upon this errand, when Clara reopened her eyes.

"Now," said he, "since she is better, you can spare me, can you not? I wish you a good night, Mr. Cassilis."

And with that he was gone among the thicket. I made a fire, for I had now no fear of the Italians, who had even spared all the little possessions left in my encampment; and, broken as she was by the excitement and the hideous catastrophe of the evening, I managed, in one way or another—by persuasion, encouragement, warmth, and such simple remedies as I could lay my hand on—to bring her back to some composure of mind and strength of body.

Day had already come, when a sharp "Hist!" sounded from the thicket. I started from the ground; but the voice of Northmour was heard adding, in the most tranquil tones: "Come here, Cassilis, and alone; I want to show you something."

I consulted Clara with my eyes, and, receiving her tacit permission, left her alone, and clambered out of the den. At some distance off I saw Northmour leaning against an elder; and, as soon as he perceived me, he began walking seaward. I had almost overtaken him as he reached the outskirts of the wood.

"Look," said he, pausing.

A couple of steps more brought me out of the foliage. The light of the morning lay cold and clear over that well-known scene. The pavilion was but a blackened wreck; the roof had fallen in, one of the gables had fallen out; and, far and near, the face of the links was cicatrised with little patches of burnt furze. Thick smoke still went straight upwards in the windless air of the morning, and a great pile of ardent cinders filled the bare walls of the house, like coals in an open grate. Close by the islet a schooner yacht lay to, and a well-manned boat was pulling vigorously for the shore.

"The *Red Earl!*" I cried. "The *Red Earl* twelve hours too late!"

"Feel in your pocket, Frank. Are you armed?" asked Northmour.

I obeyed him, and I think I must have become deadly pale. My revolver had been taken from me.

"You see I have you in my power," he continued. "I disarmed you last night while you were nursing Clara; but this morning—

here—take your pistol. No thanks!" he cried, holding up his hand. "I do not like them; that is the only way you can annoy me now."

He began to walk forward across the links to meet the boat, and I followed a step or two behind. In front of the pavilion I paused to see where Mr. Huddlestone had fallen; but there was no sign of him, nor so much as a trace of blood.

"Graden Floe," said Northmour.

He continued to advance till we had come to the head of the beach.

"No farther, please," said he. "Would you like to take her to Graden House?"

"Thank you," replied I; "I shall try to get her to the minister's at Graden Wester."

The prow of the boat here grated on the beach, and a sailor jumped ashore with a line in his hand.

"Wait a minute, lads!" cried Northmour; and then lower and to my private ear: "You had better say nothing of all this to her," he added.

"On the contrary!" I broke out, "she shall know everything that I can tell."

"You do not understand," he returned, with an air of great dignity. "It will be nothing to her; she expects it of me. Good-bye!" he added, with a nod.

I offered him my hand.

"Excuse me," said he. "It's small, I know; but I can't push things quite so far as that. I don't wish any sentimental business, to sit by your hearth a white-haired wanderer, and all that. Quite the contrary: I hope to God I shall never again clap eyes on either one of you."

"Well, God bless you, Northmour!" I said heartily.

"Oh, yes," he returned.

He walked down the beach; and the man who was ashore gave him an arm on board, and then shoved off and leaped into the bows himself. Northmour took the tiller; the boat rose to the waves, and the oars between the tholepins sounded crisp and measured in the morning air.

They were not yet half way to the *Red Earl*, and I was still watching their progress, when the sun rose out of the sea.

One word more, and my story is done. Years after, Northmour was killed fighting under the colours of Garibaldi for the liberation of the Tyrol.

A LODGING FOR THE NIGHT

I t was late in November 1456. The snow fell over Paris with rigorous, relentless persistence; sometimes the wind made a sally and scattered it in flying vortices; sometimes there was a lull, and flake after flake descended out of the black night air, silent, circuitous, interminable. To poor people, looking up under moist eyebrows, it seemed a wonder where it all came from. Master Francis Villon had propounded an alternative that afternoon, at a tavern window: was it only Pagan Jupiter plucking geese upon Olympus? or were the holy angels moulting? He was only a poor Master of Arts, he went on; and as the question somewhat touched upon divinity, he durst not venture to conclude. A silly old priest from Montargis, who was among the company, treated the young rascal to a bottle of wine in honour of the jest and the grimaces with which it was accompanied, and swore on his own white beard that he had been just such another irreverent dog when he was Villon's age.

The air was raw and pointed, but not far below freezing; and the flakes were large, damp, and adhesive. The whole city was sheeted up. An army might have marched from end to end and not a footfall given the alarm. If there were any belated birds in heaven, they saw the island like a large white patch, and the bridges like slim white spars, on the black ground of the river. High up overhead the snow settled among the tracery of the cathedral towers. Many a niche was drifted full; many a statue wore a long white bonnet on its grotesque or sainted head. The gargoyles had been transformed into great false noses, drooping towards the point. The crockets were like upright pillows swollen on one side. In the intervals of the wind, there was a dull sound of dripping about the precincts of the church.

The cemetery of St. John had taken its own share of the snow. All the graves were decently covered; tall white housetops stood around in grave array; worthy burghers were long ago in bed, benightcapped like their domiciles; there was no light in all the neighbourhood but a little peep from a lamp that hung swinging in the church choir, and tossed the shadows to and fro in time to its oscillations. The clock was hard on ten when the patrol went by with halberds and a lantern, beating their hands; and they saw nothing suspicious about the cemetery of St. John.

Yet there was a small house, backed up against the cemetery wall, which was still awake, and awake to evil purpose, in that snoring district. There was not much to betray it from without; only a stream of warm vapour from the chimney top, a patch where the snow melted on the roof, and a few half-obliterated footprints at the door. But within, behind the shuttered windows, Master Francis Villon the poet, and some of the thievish crew with whom he consorted, were keeping the night alive and passing round the bottle.

A great pile of living embers diffused a strong and ruddy glow from the arched chimney. Before this straddled Dom Nicolas, the Picardy monk, with his skirts picked up and his fat legs bared to the comfortable warmth. His dilated shadow cut the room in half; and the firelight only escaped on either side of his broad person, and in a little pool between his outspread feet. His face had the beery, bruised appearance of the continual drinker's; it was covered with a network of congested veins, purple in ordinary circumstances, but now pale violet, for even with his back to the fire the cold pinched him on the other side. His cowl had half fallen back, and made a strange excrescence on either side of his bull neck. So he straddled, grumbling, and cut the room in half with the shadow of his portly frame.

On the right, Villon and Guy Tabary were huddled together over a scrap of parchment; Villon making a ballade which he was to call the "Ballade of Roast Fish," and Tabary spluttering admiration at his shoulder. The poet was a rag of a man, dark, little, and lean, with hollow cheeks and thin black locks. He carried his four-and-twenty years with feverish animation. Greed had made folds about his eyes, evil smiles had puckered his mouth. The wolf and pig struggled together in his face. It was an eloquent, sharp, ugly, earthly countenance. His hands were small and prehensile, with fingers knotted like a cord; and they were continually flickering in front of him in violent and expressive pantomime. As for Tabary, a broad, complacent, admiring imbecility breathed from his squash nose and slobbering lips: he had become a thief, just as he might have become the most decent of burgesses, by the imperious chance that rules the lives of human geese and human donkeys.

At the monk's other hand, Montigny and Thevenin Pensete played a game of chance. About the first there clung some flavour of good birth and training, as about a fallen angel; something long, lithe, and courtly in the person; something aquiline and darkling in the face. Thevenin, poor soul, was in great feather: he had done a good stroke of knavery that afternoon in the Faubourg St. Jacques, and all night he had been gaining from Montigny. A flat smile illuminated his face; his bald head shone rosily in a garland of red curls; his little protuberant stomach shook with silent chucklings as he swept in his gains.

"Doubles or quits?" said Thevenin.

Montigny nodded grimly.

"*Some may prefer to dine in state,*" wrote Villon, "*On bread and cheese on silver plate.* Or—or—help me out, Guido!"

Tabary giggled.

"*Or parsley on a golden dish,*" scribbled the poet.

The wind was freshening without; it drove the snow before it, and sometimes raised its voice in a victorious whoop, and made sepulchral grumblings in the chimney. The cold was growing sharper as the night went on. Villon, protruding his lips, imitated the gust with something between a whistle and a groan. It was an eerie, uncomfortable talent of the poet's, much detested by the Picardy monk.

"Can't you hear it rattle in the gibbet?" said Villon. "They are all dancing the devil's jig on nothing, up there. You may dance, my gallants, you'll be none the warmer! Whew! what a gust! Down went somebody just now! A medlar the fewer on the three-legged medlar tree!—I say, Dom Nicolas, it'll be cold tonight on the St. Denis Road?" he asked.

Dom Nicolas winked both his big eyes, and seemed to choke upon his Adam's apple. Montfaucon, the great grisly Paris gibbet, stood hard by the St. Denis Road, and the pleasantry touched him on the raw. As for Tabary, he laughed immoderately over the medlars; he had never heard anything more lighthearted; and he held his sides and crowed. Villon fetched him a fillip on the nose, which turned his mirth into an attack of coughing.

"Oh, stop that row," said Villon, "and think of rhymes to 'fish.'"

"Doubles or quits," said Montigny doggedly.

"With all my heart," quoth Thevenin.

"Is there any more in that bottle?" asked the monk.

"Open another," said Villon. "How do you ever hope to fill that big hogshead, your body, with little things like bottles? And how do you expect to get to heaven? How many angels, do you fancy, can be spared to carry up a single monk from Picardy? Or do you think yourself another Elias—and they'll send the coach for you?"

"*Hominibus impossibile*," replied the monk, as he filled his glass.

Tabary was in ecstasies.

Villon filliped his nose again

"Laugh at my jokes, if you like," he said.

"It was very good," objected Tabary.

Villon made a face at him. "Think of rhymes to 'fish,'" he said. "What have you to do with Latin? You'll wish you knew none of it at the great assizes, when the devil calls for Guido Tabary, clericus—the devil with the humpback and red-hot fingernails. Talking of the devil," he added in a whisper, "look at Montigny!"

All three peered covertly at the gamester. He did not seem to be enjoying his luck. His mouth was a little to a side; one nostril nearly shut, and the other much inflated. The black dog was on his back, as people say, in terrifying nursery metaphor; and he breathed hard under the gruesome burden.

"He looks as if he could knife him," whispered Tabary, with round eyes.

The monk shuddered, and turned his face and spread his open

hands to the red embers. It was the cold that thus affected Dom Nicolas, and not any excess of moral sensibility.

"Come now," said Villon—"about this ballade. How does it run so far?" And beating time with his hand, he read it aloud to Tabary.

They were interrupted at the fourth rhyme by a brief and fatal movement among the gamesters. The round was completed, and Thevenin was just opening his mouth to claim another victory, when Montigny leaped up, swift as an adder, and stabbed him to the heart. The blow took effect before he had time to utter a cry, before he had time to move. A tremor or two convulsed his frame; his hands opened and shut, his heels rattled on the floor; then his head rolled backward over one shoulder with the eyes wide open; and Thevenin Pensete's spirit had returned to Him who made it.

Everyone sprang to his feet; but the business was over in two twos. The four living fellows looked at each other in rather a ghastly fashion; the dead man contemplating a corner of the roof with a singular and ugly leer.

"My God!" said Tabary; and he began to pray in Latin.

Villon broke out into hysterical laughter. He came a step forward and ducked a ridiculous bow at Thevenin, and laughed still louder. Then he sat down suddenly, all of a heap, upon a stool, and continued laughing bitterly as though he would shake himself to pieces.

Montigny recovered his composure first.

"Let's see what he has about him," he remarked; and he picked the dead man's pockets with a practised hand, and divided the money into four equal portions on the table. "There's for you," he said.

The monk received his share with a deep sigh, and a single stealthy glance at the dead Thevenin, who was beginning to sink into himself and topple sideways off the chair.

"We're all in for it," cried Villon, swallowing his mirth. "It's a hanging job for every man jack of us that's here—not to speak of those who aren't." He made a shocking gesture in the air with his raised right hand, and put out his tongue and threw his head on one side, so as to counterfeit the appearance of one who has been hanged. Then he pocketed his share of the spoil, and executed a shuffle with his feet as if to restore the circulation.

Tabary was the last to help himself; he made a dash at the money, and retired to the other end of the apartment.

Montigny stuck Thevenin upright in the chair, and drew out the dagger, which was followed by a jet of blood.

"You fellows had better be moving," he said, as he wiped the blade on his victim's doublet.

"I think we had," returned Villon with a gulp. "Damn his fat head!" he broke out. "It sticks in my throat like phlegm. What right has a man to have red hair when he is dead?" And he fell all of a heap again upon the stool, and fairly covered his face with his hands.

Montigny and Dom Nicolas laughed aloud, even Tabary feebly chiming in.

"Cry baby," said the monk.

"I always said he was a woman," added Montigny with a sneer. "Sit up, can't you?" he went on, giving another shake to the murdered body. "Tread out that fire, Nick!"

But Nick was better employed; he was quietly taking Villon's purse, as the poet sat, limp and trembling, on the stool where he had been making a ballade not three minutes before. Montigny and Tabary dumbly demanded a share of the booty, which the monk silently promised as he passed the little bag into the bosom of his gown. In many ways an artistic nature unfits a man for practical existence.

No sooner had the theft been accomplished than Villon shook himself, jumped to his feet, and began helping to scatter and extinguish the embers. Meanwhile Montigny opened the door and cautiously peered into the street. The coast was clear; there was no meddlesome patrol in sight. Still it was judged wiser to slip out severally; and as Villon was himself in a hurry to escape from the neighbourhood of the dead Thevenin, and the rest were in a still greater hurry to get rid of him before he should discover the loss of his money, he was the first by general consent to issue forth into the street.

The wind had triumphed and swept all the clouds from heaven.

Only a few vapours, as thin as moonlight, fleeted rapidly across the stars. It was bitter cold; and by a common optical effect, things seemed almost more definite than in the broadest daylight. The sleeping city was absolutely still: a company of white hoods, a field full of little Alps, below the twinkling stars. Villon cursed his fortune. Would it were still snowing! Now, wherever he went, he left an indelible trail behind him on the glittering streets; wherever he went he was still tethered to the house by the cemetery of St. John; wherever he went he must weave, with his own plodding feet, the rope that bound him to the crime and would bind him to the gallows. The leer of the dead man came back to him with a new significance. He snapped his fingers as if to pluck up his own spirits, and choosing a street at random, stepped boldly forward in the snow.

Two things preoccupied him as he went: the aspect of the gallows at Montfaucon in this bright windy phase of the night's existence, for one; and for another, the look of the dead man with his bald head and garland of red curls. Both struck cold upon his heart, and he kept quickening his pace as if he could escape from unpleasant thoughts by mere fleetness of foot. Sometimes, he looked back over his shoulder with a sudden nervous jerk; but he was the only moving thing in the white streets, except when the wind swooped round a corner and threw up the snow, which was beginning to freeze, in spouts of glittering dust.

Suddenly he saw, a long way before him, a black clump and a couple of lanterns. The clump was in motion, and the lanterns swung as though carried by men walking. It was a patrol. And though it was merely crossing his line of march, he judged it wiser to get out of eyeshot as speedily as he could. He was not in the humour to be challenged, and he was conscious of making a very conspicuous mark upon the snow. Just on his left hand there stood a great hotel, with some turrets and a large porch before the door; it was half-ruinous, he remembered, and had long stood empty; and so he made three steps of it and jumped into the shelter of the porch. It was pretty dark inside, after the glimmer of the snowy streets, and he was groping forward with outspread hands, when he stumbled over some substance which offered an indescribable mixture of resistances, hard and soft, firm and loose. His heart gave a leap, and he sprang two steps back and stared dreadfully at the obstacle. Then he gave a little laugh of relief. It was only a woman, and she dead. He knelt beside her to make sure upon this latter point. She was freezing cold, and rigid like a stick. A little ragged finery fluttered in the wind about her hair, and her cheeks had been heavily rouged that same afternoon. Her pockets were quite empty; but in her stocking, underneath the garter, Villon found two of the small coins that went by the name of whites. It was little enough; but it was always something; and the poet was moved with a deep sense of pathos that she should have died before she had spent her money. That seemed to him a dark and pitiable mystery; and he looked from the coins in his hand to the dead woman, and back again to the coins, shaking his head over the riddle of man's life. Henry V. of England, dying at Vincennes just after he had conquered France, and this poor jade cut off by a cold draught in a great man's doorway, before she had time to spend her couple of whites—it seemed a cruel way to carry on the world. Two whites would have taken such a little while to squander; and yet it would have been one more good taste in the mouth, one more smack of the lips, before the devil got the soul, and the body was left to birds and vermin. He would like to use all his tallow before the light was blown out and the lantern broken.

While these thoughts were passing through his mind, he was feeling, half mechanically, for his purse. Suddenly his heart stopped beating; a feeling of cold scales passed up the back of his legs, and a cold blow seemed to fall upon his scalp. He stood petrified for a moment; then he felt again with one feverish movement; and then his loss burst upon him, and he was covered at once with perspiration. To spendthrifts money is so living and actual—it is such a thin veil between them and their pleasures! There is only one limit to their fortune—that of time; and a spendthrift with only a few crowns is the Emperor of Rome until they are spent. For such a person to lose his money is to suffer the most shocking reverse, and fall from heaven to hell, from all to nothing, in a breath. And all the more if he has put his head in the halter for it; if he may be hanged tomorrow for that same purse, so dearly earned, so foolishly departed! Villon stood and cursed; he threw the two whites into the street; he shook his fist at heaven; he stamped, and was not horrified to find himself trampling the poor corpse. Then he began rapidly to retrace his steps towards the house beside the cemetery. He had forgotten all fear of the patrol, which was long gone by at any rate, and had no idea but that of his lost purse. It was in vain that he looked right and left upon the snow: nothing was to be seen. He had not dropped it in the streets. Had it fallen in the house? He would have liked dearly to go in and see; but the idea of the grisly occupant unmanned him. And he saw besides, as he drew near, that their efforts to put out the fire had been unsuccessful; on the contrary, it had broken into a blaze, and a changeful light played in the chinks of door and window, and revived his terror for the authorities and Paris gibbet.

He returned to the hotel with the porch, and groped about upon the snow for the money he had thrown away in his childish passion. But he could only find one white; the other had probably struck sideways and sunk deeply in. With a single white in his pocket, all his projects for a rousing night in some wild tavern vanished utterly away. And it was not only pleasure that fled laughing from his grasp; positive discomfort, positive pain, attacked him as he stood ruefully before the porch. His perspiration had dried upon him; and though the wind had now fallen, a binding frost was setting in stronger with every hour, and he felt benumbed and sick at heart. What was to be done? Late as was the hour, improbable as was success, he would try the house of his adopted father, the chaplain of St. Benoît.

He ran there all the way, and knocked timidly. There was no answer. He knocked again and again, taking heart with every stroke; and at last steps were heard approaching from within. A barred wicket fell open in the iron-studded door, and emitted a gush of yellow light.

"Hold up your face to the wicket," said the chaplain from within.

"It's only me," whimpered Villon.

"Oh, it's only you, is it?" returned the chaplain; and he cursed him with foul unpriestly oaths for disturbing him at such an hour, and bade him be off to hell, where he came from.

"My hands are blue to the wrist," pleaded Villon; "my feet are dead and full of twinges; my nose aches with the sharp air; the cold lies at my heart. I may be dead before morning. Only this once, father, and before God I will never ask again!"

"You should have come earlier," said the ecclesiastic coolly. "Young men require a lesson now and then." He shut the wicket and retired deliberately into the interior of the house.

Villon was beside himself; he beat upon the door with his hands and feet, and shouted hoarsely after the chaplain.

"Wormy old fox!" he cried. "If I had my hand under your twist, I would send you flying headlong into the bottomless pit."

A door shut in the interior, faintly audible to the poet down long passages. He passed his hand over his mouth with an oath. And then the humour of the situation struck him, and he laughed and looked lightly up to heaven, where the stars seemed to be winking over his discomfiture.

What was to be done? It looked very like a night in the frosty streets. The idea of the dead woman popped into his imagination, and gave him a hearty fright; what had happened to her in the early night might very well happen to him before morning. And he so young! and with such immense possibilities of disorderly amusement before him! He felt quite pathetic over the notion of his own fate, as if it had been someone else's, and made a little imaginative vignette of the scene in the morning when they should find his body.

He passed all his chances under review, turning the white between his thumb and forefinger. Unfortunately he was on bad terms with some old friends who would once have taken pity on him in such a plight. He had lampooned them in verses, he had beaten and cheated them; and yet now, when he was in so close a pinch, he thought there was at least one who might perhaps relent. It was a chance. It was worth trying at least, and he would go and see.

On the way, two little accidents happened to him which coloured his musings in a very different manner. For, first, he fell in with the track of a patrol, and walked in it for some hundred yards, although it lay out of his direction. And this spirited him up; at least he had confused his trail; for he was still possessed with the idea of people tracking him all about Paris over the snow, and collaring him next morning before he was awake. The other matter affected him very differently. He passed a street corner, where, not so long before, a woman and her child had been devoured by wolves. This was just the kind of weather, he reflected, when wolves might take it into their heads to enter Paris again; and a lone man in these deserted streets would run the chance of something worse than a mere scare. He stopped and looked upon the place with an unpleasant interest—it was a centre where several lanes intersected each other; and he looked down them all one after another, and held his breath to listen, lest he should detect some galloping black things on the snow or hear the sound of howling between him and the river. He remembered his mother telling him the story and pointing out the spot, while he was yet a child. His mother! If he only knew where she lived, he might make sure at least of shelter. He determined he would inquire upon the morrow; nay, he would go and see her too, poor old girl! So thinking, he arrived at his destination—his last hope for the night.

The house was quite dark, like its neighbours; and yet after a few taps, he heard a movement overhead, a door opening, and a cautious voice asking who was there. The poet named himself in a loud whisper, and waited, not without some trepidation, the result. Nor had he to wait long. A window was suddenly opened, and a pailful of slops splashed down upon the doorstep. Villon had not been unprepared for something of the sort, and had put himself as much in shelter as the nature of the porch admitted; but for all that, he was deplorably drenched below the waist. His hose began to freeze almost at once. Death from cold and exposure stared him in the face; he remembered he was of phthisical tendency, and began coughing tentatively. But the gravity of the danger steadied his nerves. He stopped a few hundred yards from the door where he had been so rudely used, and reflected with his finger to his nose. He could only see one way of getting a lodging, and that was to take it. He had noticed a house not far away, which looked as if it might be easily broken into, and thither he betook himself promptly, entertaining himself on the way with the idea of a room still hot, with a table still loaded with the remains of supper, where he might pass the rest of the black hours, and whence he should issue, on the morrow, with an armful of valuable plate. He even considered on what viands and what wines he should prefer; and as he was calling the roll of his favourite dainties, roast fish presented itself to his mind with an odd mixture of amusement and horror.

"I shall never finish that ballade," he thought to himself; and then, with another shudder at the recollection, "Oh, damn his fat head!" he repeated fervently, and spat upon the snow.

The house in question looked dark at first sight; but as Villon made a preliminary inspection in search of the handiest point of attack, a little twinkle of light caught his eye from behind a curtained window.

"The devil!" he thought. "People awake! Some student or some saint, confound the crew! Can't they get drunk and lie in bed snoring like their neighbours! What's the good of curfew, and poor devils of bell-ringers jumping at a rope's end in bell-towers? What's the use of day, if people sit up all night? The gripes to them!" He grinned as he saw where his logic was leading him. "Every man to his business, after all," added he, "and if they're awake, by the lord, I may come by a supper honestly for this once, and cheat the devil."

He went boldly to the door and knocked with an assured hand. On both previous occasions, he had knocked timidly and with some dread of attracting notice; but now when he had just discarded the thought of a burglarious entry, knocking at a door seemed a mighty simple and innocent proceeding. The sound of his blows echoed through the house with thin, phantasmal reverberations, as though it were quite empty; but these had scarcely died away before a measured tread drew near, a couple of bolts were withdrawn, and one wing was opened broadly, as though no guile or fear of guile were known to those within. A tall figure of a man, muscular and spare, but a little bent, confronted Villon. The head was massive in bulk, but finely sculptured; the nose blunt at the bottom, but refining upward to where it joined a pair of strong and honest eyebrows; the mouth and eyes surrounded with delicate markings, and the whole face based upon a thick white beard, boldly and squarely trimmed. Seen as it was by the light of a flickering handlamp, it looked perhaps nobler than it had a right to do; but it was a fine face, honourable rather than intelligent, strong, simple, and righteous.

"You knock late, sir," said the old man in resonant, courteous tones.

Villon cringed, and brought up many servile words of apology; at a crisis of this sort, the beggar was uppermost in him, and the man of genius hid his head with confusion.

"You are cold," repeated the old man, "and hungry? Well, step in." And he ordered him into the house with a noble enough gesture.

"Some great seigneur," thought Villon, as his host, setting down the lamp on the flagged pavement of the entry, shot the bolts once more into their places.

"You will pardon me if I go in front," he said, when this was done; and he preceded the poet upstairs into a large apartment, warmed with a pan of charcoal and lit by a great lamp hanging from the roof. It was very bare of furniture: only some gold plate on a sideboard; some folios; and a stand of armour between the windows. Some smart tapestry hung upon the walls, representing the crucifixion of our Lord in one piece, and in another a scene of shepherds and shepherdesses by a running stream. Over the chimney was a shield of arms.

"Will you seat yourself," said the old man, "and forgive me if I leave you? I am alone in my house tonight, and if you are to eat I must forage for you myself."

No sooner was his host gone than Villon leaped from the chair on which he had just seated himself, and began examining the room, with the stealth and passion of a cat. He weighed the gold flagons in his hand, opened all the folios, and investigated the arms upon the shield, and the stuff with which the seats were lined. He raised the window curtains, and saw that the windows were set with rich stained glass in figures, so far as he could see, of martial import. Then he stood in the middle of the room, drew a long breath, and retaining it with puffed cheeks, looked round and round him, turning on his heels, as if to impress every feature of the apartment on his memory.

"Seven pieces of plate," he said. "If there had been ten, I would have risked it. A fine house, and a fine old master, so help me all the saints!"

And just then, hearing the old man's tread returning along the corridor, he stole back to his chair, and began humbly toasting his wet legs before the charcoal pan.

His entertainer had a plate of meat in one hand and a jug of wine in the other. He set down the plate upon the table, motioning Villon to draw in his chair, and going to the sideboard, brought back two goblets, which he filled.

"I drink to your better fortune," he said, gravely touching Villon's cup with his own.

"To our better acquaintance," said the poet, growing bold. A mere man of the people would have been awed by the courtesy of the old seigneur, but Villon was hardened in that matter; he had made mirth for great lords before now, and found them as black rascals as himself. And so he devoted himself to the viands with a ravenous gusto, while the old man, leaning backward, watched him with steady, curious eyes.

"You have blood on your shoulder, my man," he said.

Montigny must have laid his wet right hand upon him as he left the house. He cursed Montigny in his heart.

"It was none of my shedding," he stammered.

"I had not supposed so," returned his host quietly. "A brawl?"

"Well, something of that sort," Villon admitted with a quaver.

"Perhaps a fellow murdered?"

"Oh, no, not murdered," said the poet, more and more confused. "It was all fair play—murdered by accident. I had no hand in it, God strike me dead!" he added fervently.

"One rogue the fewer, I dare say," observed the master of the house.

"You may dare to say that," agreed Villon, infinitely relieved. "As big a rogue as there is between here and Jerusalem. He turned up his toes like a lamb. But it was a nasty thing to look at. I dare say you've seen dead men in your time, my lord?" he added, glancing at the armour.

"Many," said the old man. "I have followed the wars, as you imagine."

Villon laid down his knife and fork, which he had just taken up again.

"Were any of them bald?" he asked.

"Oh yes, and with hair as white as mine."

"I don't think I should mind the white so much," said Villon. "His was red." And he had a return of his shuddering and tendency to laughter, which he drowned with a great draught of wine. "I'm a little put out when I think of it," he went on. "I knew him—damn him! And then the cold gives a man fancies—or the fancies give a man cold, I don't know which."

"Have you any money?" asked the old man.

"I have one white," returned the poet, laughing. "I got it out of a dead jade's stocking in a porch. She was as dead as Caesar, poor wench, and as cold as a church, with bits of ribbon sticking in her hair. This is a hard world in winter for wolves and wenches and poor rogues like me."

"I," said the old man, "am Enguerrand de la Feuillée, seigneur de Brisetout, bailly du Patatrac. Who and what may you be?"

Villon rose and made a suitable reverence. "I am called Francis Villon," he said, "a poor Master of Arts of this university. I know some Latin, and a deal of vice. I can make chansons, ballades, lais, virelais, and roundels, and I am very fond of wine. I was born in a garret, and I shall not improbably die upon the gallows. I may add, my lord, that from this night forward I am your lordship's very obsequious servant to command."

"No servant of mine," said the knight; "my guest for this evening, and no more."

"A very grateful guest," said Villon politely; and he drank in dumb show to his entertainer.

"You are shrewd," began the old man, tapping his forehead, "very shrewd; you have learning; you are a clerk; and yet you take a small piece of money off a dead woman in the street. Is it not a kind of theft?"

"It is a kind of theft much practised in the wars, my lord."

"The wars are the field of honour," returned the old man proudly. "There a man plays his life upon the cast; he fights in the name of his lord the king, his Lord God, and all their lordships the holy saints and angels."

"Put it," said Villon, "that I were really a thief, should I not play my life also, and against heavier odds?"

"For gain, but not for honour."

"Gain?" repeated Villon with a shrug. "Gain! The poor fellow wants supper, and takes it. So does the soldier in a campaign. Why, what are all these requisitions we hear so much about? If they are not gain to those who take them, they are loss enough to the others. The men-at-arms drink by a good fire, while the burgher bites his nails to buy them wine and wood. I have seen a good many ploughmen swinging on trees about the country; ay, I have seen thirty on one elm, and a very poor figure they made; and when I asked someone how all these came to be hanged, I was told it was because they could not scrape together enough crowns to satisfy the men-at-arms."

"These things are a necessity of war, which the low-born must endure with constancy. It is true that some captains drive overhard; there are spirits in every rank not easily moved by pity; and indeed many follow arms who are no better than brigands."

"You see," said the poet, "you cannot separate the soldier from the brigand; and what is a thief but an isolated brigand with circumspect manners? I steal a couple of mutton chops, without so much as disturbing people's sleep; the farmer grumbles a bit, but sups none the less wholesomely on what remains. You come up blowing gloriously on a trumpet, take away the whole sheep, and beat the farmer pitifully into the bargain. I have no trumpet; I am only Tom, Dick, or Harry; I am a rogue and a dog, and hanging's too good for me—with all my heart; but just you ask the farmer which of us he prefers, just find out which of us he lies awake to curse on cold nights."

"Look at us two," said his lordship. "I am old, strong, and honoured. If I were turned from my house tomorrow, hundreds would be proud to shelter me. Poor people would go out and pass the night in the streets with their children, if I merely hinted that I wished to be alone. And I find you up, wandering homeless, and picking farthings off dead women by the wayside! I fear no man and nothing; I have seen you tremble and lose countenance at a word. I wait God's summons contentedly in my own house, or, if it please the king to call me out again, upon the field of battle. You look for the gallows; a rough, swift death, without hope or honour. Is there no difference between these two?"

"As far as to the moon," Villon acquiesced. "But if I had been born lord of Brisetout, and you had been the poor scholar Francis, would the difference have been any the less? Should not I have been warming my knees at this charcoal pan, and would not you have been groping for farthings in the snow? Should not I have been the soldier, and you the thief?"

"A thief!" cried the old man. "I a thief! If you understood your words, you would repent them."

Villon turned out his hands with a gesture of inimitable impudence. "If your lordship had done me the honour to follow my argument!" he said.

"I do you too much honour in submitting to your presence," said the knight. "Learn to curb your tongue when you speak with old and honourable men, or some one hastier than I may reprove you in a sharper fashion." And he rose and paced the lower end of the apartment, struggling with anger and antipathy. Villon surreptitiously refilled his cup, and settled himself more comfortably in the chair, crossing his knees and leaning his head upon one hand and the elbow against the back of the chair. He was now replete and warm; and he was in nowise frightened for his host, having gauged him as justly as was possible between two such different characters. The night was far spent, and in a very comfortable fashion after all; and he felt morally certain of a safe departure on the morrow.

"Tell me one thing," said the old man, pausing in his walk. "Are you really a thief?"

"I claim the sacred rights of hospitality," returned the poet. "My lord, I am."

"You are very young," the knight continued.

"I should never have been so old," replied Villon, showing his fingers, "if I had not helped myself with these ten talents. They have been my nursing mothers and my nursing fathers."

"You may still repent and change."

"I repent daily," said the poet. "There are few people more given to repentance than poor Francis. As for change, let somebody change my circumstances. A man must continue to eat, if it were only that he may continue to repent."

"The change must begin in the heart," returned the old man solemnly.

"My dear lord," answered Villon, "do you really fancy that I steal for pleasure? I hate stealing, like any other piece of work or of danger. My teeth chatter when I see a gallows. But I must eat, I must drink, I must mix in society of some sort. What the devil! Man is not a solitary animal—*Cui Deus faeminam tradit.* Make me king's pantler—make me abbot of St. Denis; make me bailly of the Patatrac; and then I shall be changed indeed. But as long as you leave me the poor scholar Francis Villon, without a farthing, why, of course, I remain the same."

"The grace of God is all-powerful."

"I should be a heretic to question it," said Francis. "It has made you lord of Brisetout and bailly of the Patatrac; it has given me nothing but the quick wits under my hat and these ten toes upon my hands. May I help myself to wine? I thank you respectfully. By God's grace, you have a very superior vintage."

The lord of Brisetout walked to and fro with his hands behind his back. Perhaps he was not yet quite settled in his mind about the parallel between thieves and soldiers; perhaps Villon had interested him by some cross-thread of sympathy; perhaps his wits were simply muddled by so much unfamiliar reasoning; but whatever the cause, he somehow yearned to convert the young man to a better way of thinking, and could not make up his mind to drive him forth again into the street.

"There is something more than I can understand in this," he said at length. "Your mouth is full of subtleties, and the devil has led you very far astray; but the devil is only a very weak spirit before God's truth, and all his subtleties vanish at a word of true honour, like darkness at morning. Listen to me once more. I learned long ago that a gentleman should live chivalrously and lovingly to God, and the king, and his lady; and though I have seen many strange things done, I have still striven to command my ways upon that rule. It is not only written in all noble histories, but in every man's heart, if he will take care to read. You speak of food and wine, and I know very well that hunger is a difficult trial to endure; but you do not speak of other wants; you say nothing of honour, of faith to God and other men, of courtesy, of love without reproach. It may be that I am not very wise—and yet I think I am—but you seem to me like one who has lost his way and made a great error in life. You are attending to the little wants, and you have totally forgotten the great and only real ones, like a man who should be doctoring a toothache on the Judgment Day. For such things as honour and love and faith are not only nobler than food and drink, but indeed I think that we desire them more, and suffer more sharply for their absence. I speak to you as I think you will most easily understand me. Are you not, while careful to fill your belly, disregarding another appetite in your heart, which spoils the pleasure of your life and keeps you continually wretched?"

Villon was sensibly nettled under all this sermonising. "You think I have no sense of honour!" he cried. "I'm poor enough, God knows! It's hard to see rich people with their gloves, and you blowing in your hands. An empty belly is a bitter thing, although you speak so lightly of it. If you had had as many as I, perhaps you would change your tune. Anyway I'm a thief—make the most of that— but I'm not a devil from hell, God strike me dead. I would have you to know I've an honour of my own, as good as yours, though I don't prate about it all day long, as if it was a God's miracle to have any. It seems quite natural to me; I keep it in its box till it's wanted. Why now, look you here, how long have I been in this room with you? Did you not tell me you were alone in the house? Look at your gold plate! You're strong, if you like, but you're old and unarmed, and I have my knife. What did I want but a jerk of the elbow and here would have been you with the cold steel in your bowels, and there would have been me, linking in the streets, with an armful of gold cups! Did you suppose I hadn't wit enough to see that? And I scorned the action. There are your damned goblets, as safe as in a church; there are you, with your heart ticking as good as new; and here am I, ready to go out again as poor as I came in, with my one white that you threw in my teeth! And you think I have no sense of honour—God strike me dead!"

The old man stretched out his right arm. "I will tell you what you are," he said. "You are a rogue, my man, an impudent and a black-hearted rogue and vagabond. I have passed an hour with you. Oh! believe me, I feel myself disgraced! And you have eaten and drunk at my table. But now I am sick at your presence; the day has come, and the night bird should be off to his roost. Will you go before, or after?"

"Which you please," returned the poet, rising. "I believe you to be strictly honourable." He thoughtfully emptied his cup. "I wish I could add you were intelligent," he went on, knocking on his head with his knuckles. "Age, age! the brains stiff and rheumatic."

The old man preceded him from a point of self-respect; Villon followed, whistling, with his thumbs in his girdle.

"God pity you," said the lord of Brisetout at the door.

"Good-bye, papa," returned Villon with a yawn. "Many thanks for the cold mutton."

The door closed behind him. The dawn was breaking over the white roofs. A chill, uncomfortable morning ushered in the day. Villon stood and heartily stretched himself in the middle of the road.

"A very dull old gentleman," he thought. "I wonder what his goblets may be worth."

THE MERRY MEN

Chapter One
Eilean Aros

I t was a beautiful morning in the late July when I set forth on
foot for the last time for Aros. A boat had put me ashore the
night before at Grisapol; I had such breakfast as the little inn
afforded, and leaving all my baggage till I had an occasion to
come round for it by sea, struck right across the promontory
with a cheerful heart.

I was far from being a native of these parts, springing, as I did,
from an unmixed lowland stock. But an uncle of mine, Gordon
Darnaway, after a poor, rough youth, and some years at sea, had
married a young wife in the islands; Mary Maclean she was called,
the last of her family; and when she died in giving birth to a
daughter, Aros, the sea-girt farm, had remained in his possession. It
brought him in nothing but the means of life, as I was well aware;
but he was a man whom ill-fortune had pursued; he feared, cum-
bered as he was with the young child, to make a fresh adventure
upon life; and remained in Aros, biting his nails at destiny. Years
passed over his head in that isolation, and brought neither help nor
contentment. Meantime our family was dying out in the lowlands;
there is little luck for any of that race; and perhaps my father was the
luckiest of all, for not only was he one of the last to die, but he left a
son to his name and a little money to support it. I was a student of
Edinburgh University, living well enough at my own charges, but
without kith or kin; when some news of me found its way to Uncle
Gordon on the Ross of Grisapol; and he, as he was a man who held
blood thicker than water, wrote to me the day he heard of my
existence, and taught me to count Aros as my home. Thus it was that

I came to spend my vacations in that part of the country, so far from all society and comfort, between the codfish and the moorcocks; and thus it was that now, when I had done with my classes, I was returning thither with so light a heart that July day.

The Ross, as we call it, is a promontory neither wide nor high, but as rough as God made it to this day; the deep sea on either hand of it, full of rugged isles and reefs most perilous to seamen—all overlooked from the eastward by some very high cliffs and the great peak of Ben Kyaw. *The Mountain of the Mist*, they say the words signify in the Gaelic tongue; and it is well named. For that hilltop, which is more than three thousand feet in height, catches all the clouds that come blowing from the seaward; and indeed, I used often to think that it must make them for itself; since when all heaven was clear to the sea level, there would ever be a streamer on Ben Kyaw. It brought water, too, and was mossy* to the top in consequence. I have seen us sitting in broad sunshine on the Ross, and the rain falling black like crape upon the mountain. But the wetness of it made it often appear more beautiful to my eyes; for when the sun struck upon the hillsides, there were many wet rocks and watercourses that shone like jewels even as far as Aros, fifteen miles away.

The road that I followed was a cattle track. It twisted so as nearly to double the length of my journey; it went over rough boulders so that a man had to leap from one to another, and through soft bottoms where the moss came nearly to the knee. There was no cultivation anywhere, and not one house in the ten miles from Grisapol to Aros. Houses of course there were—three at least; but they lay so far on the one side or the other that no stranger could have found them from the track. A large part of the Ross is covered with big granite rocks, some of them larger than a two-roomed house, one beside another, with fern and deep heather in between them where the vipers breed. Any way the wind was, it was always sea air, as salt as on a ship; the gulls were as free as moorfowl over all the Ross; and whenever the way rose a little, your eye would kindle with the brightness of the sea. From the very midst of the land, on a

*Boggy. [R.L.S.]

day of wind and a high spring, I have heard the Roost roaring like a battle where it runs by Aros, and the great and fearful voices of the breakers that we call the Merry Men.

Aros itself—Aros Jay, I have heard the natives call it, and they say it means *the House of God*—Aros itself was not properly a piece of the Ross, nor was it quite an islet. It formed the southwest corner of the land, fitted close to it, and was in one place only separated from the coast by a little gut of the sea, not forty feet across the narrowest. When the tide was full, this was clear and still, like a pool on a land river; only there was a difference in the weeds and fishes, and the water itself was green instead of brown; but when the tide went out, in the bottom of the ebb, there was a day or two in every month when you could pass dryshod from Aros to the mainland. There was some good pasture, where my uncle fed the sheep he lived on; perhaps the feed was better because the ground rose higher on the islet than the main level of the Ross, but this I am not skilled enough to settle. The house was a good one for that country, two storeys high. It looked westward over a bay, with a pier hard by for a boat, and from the door you could watch the vapours blowing on Ben Kyaw.

On all this part of the coast, and especially near Aros, these great granite rocks that I have spoken of go down together in troops into the sea, like cattle on a summer's day. There they stand, for all the world like their neighbours ashore; only the salt water sobbing between them instead of the quiet earth, and clots of sea pink blooming on their sides instead of heather; and the great sea conger to wreathe about the base of them instead of the poisonous viper of the land. On calm days you can go wandering between them in a boat for hours, echoes following you about the labyrinth; but when the sea is up, Heaven help the man that hears that cauldron boiling.

Off the southwest end of Aros these blocks are very many, and much greater in size. Indeed, they must grow monstrously bigger out to sea, for there must be ten sea miles of open water sown with them as thick as a country place with houses, some standing thirty feet above the tides, some covered, but all perilous to ships; so that on a clear, westerly blowing day, I have counted, from the top of Aros, the great rollers breaking white and heavy over as many as six-and-forty buried reefs. But it is nearer in shore that the danger is worst; for the tide, here running like a mill race, makes a long belt of broken water—a *Roost* we call it—at the tail of the land. I have often been out there in a dead calm at the slack of the tide; and a strange place it is, with the sea swirling and combing up and boiling like the cauldrons of a linn, and now and again a little dancing mutter of sound as though the Roost were talking to itself. But when the tide begins to run again, and above all in heavy weather, there is no man could take a boat within half a mile of it, nor a ship afloat that could either steer or live in such a place. You can hear the roaring of it six miles away. At the seaward end there comes the strongest of the bubble; and it's here that these big breakers dance together—the dance of death, it may be called—that have got the name, in these parts, of the Merry Men. I have heard it said that they run fifty feet high; but that must be the green water only, for the spray runs twice as high as that. Whether they got the name from their movements, which are swift and antic, or from the shouting they make about the turn of the tide, so that all Aros shakes with it, is more than I can tell.

The truth is, that in a southwesterly wind, that part of our archipelago is no better than a trap. If a ship got through the reefs, and weathered the Merry Men, it would be to come ashore on the south coast of Aros, in Sandag Bay, where so many dismal things befell our family, as I propose to tell. The thought of all these dangers, in the place I knew so long, makes me particularly welcome the works now going forward to set lights upon the headlands and buoys along the channels of our ironbound, inhospitable islands.

The country people had many a story about Aros, as I used to hear from my uncle's man, Rorie, an old servant of the Macleans, who had transferred his services without afterthought on the occasion of the marriage. There was some tale of an unlucky creature, a sea-kelpie, that dwelt and did business in some fearful manner of his own among the boiling breakers of the Roost. A mermaid had once met a piper on Sandag beach, and there sang to him a long, bright midsummer's night, so that in the morning he was found stricken crazy, and from thenceforward, till the day he died, said only one form of words; what they were in the original Gaelic I cannot tell, but they were thus translated: "Ah, the sweet singing out of the sea."

Seals that haunted on that coast have been known to speak to man in his own tongue, presaging great disasters. It was here that a certain saint first landed on his voyage out of Ireland to convert the Hebrideans. And, indeed, I think he had some claim to be called saint; for, with the boats of that past age, to make so rough a passage, and land on such a ticklish coast, was surely not far short of the miraculous. It was to him, or to some of his monkish underlings who had a cell there, that the islet owes its holy and beautiful name, the House of God.

Among these old wives' stories there was one which I was inclined to hear with more credulity. As I was told, in that tempest which scattered the ships of the Invincible Armada over all the north and west of Scotland, one great vessel came ashore on Aros, and before the eyes of some solitary people on a hilltop, went down in a moment with all hands, her colours flying even as she sank. There was some likelihood in this tale; for another of that fleet lay sunk on the north side, twenty miles from Grisapol. It was told, I thought, with more detail and gravity than its companion stories, and there was one particularity which went far to convince me of its truth: the name, that is, of the ship was still remembered, and sounded, in my ears, Spanishly. The *Espirito Santo* they called it, a great ship of many decks of guns, laden with treasure and grandees of Spain, and fierce soldadoes, that now lay fathom deep to all eternity, done with her wars and voyages, in Sandag bay, upon the west of Aros. No more salvos of ordinance for that tall ship, the "Holy Spirit," no more fair winds or happy ventures; only to rot there deep in the sea tangle and hear the shoutings of the Merry Men as the tide ran high about the island. It was a strange thought to me first and last, and only grew stranger as I learned the more of Spain, from which she had set sail with so proud a company, and King Philip, the wealthy king, that sent her on that voyage.

And now I must tell you, as I walked from Grisapol that day, the *Espirito Santo* was very much in my reflections. I had been favourably remarked by our then Principal in Edinburgh College, that famous writer, Dr. Robertson, and by him had been set to work on some papers of an ancient date to rearrange and sift of what was worthless; and in one of these, to my great wonder, I found a note of this very ship, the *Espirito Santo*, with her captain's name, and how she carried a great part of the Spaniard's treasure, and had been lost upon the Ross of Grisapol; but in what particular spot, the wild tribes of that place and period would give no information to the king's inquiries. Putting one thing with another, and taking our island tradition together with this note of old King Jamie's perquisitions after wealth, it had come strongly on my mind that the spot for which he sought in vain could be no other than the small bay of Sandag on my uncle's land; and being a fellow of a mechanical turn, I had ever since been plotting how to weigh that good ship up again with all her ingots, ounces, and doubloons, and bring back our house of Darnaway to its long-forgotten dignity and wealth.

This was a design of which I soon had reason to repent. My mind was sharply turned on different reflections; and since I became the witness of a strange judgment of God's, the thought of dead men's treasures has been intolerable to my conscience. But even at that time I must acquit myself of sordid greed; for if I desired riches, it was not for their own sake, but for the sake of a person who was dear to my heart—my uncle's daughter, Mary Ellen. She had been educated well, and had been a time to school upon the mainland; which, poor girl, she would have been happier without. For Aros was no place for her, with old Rorie the servant, and her father, who was one of the unhappiest men in Scotland, plainly bred up in a country place among Cameronians, long a skipper sailing out of the Clyde about the islands, and now, with infinite discontent, managing his sheep and a little 'long shore fishing for the necessary bread. If it was sometimes weariful to me, who was there but a month or two, you may fancy what it was to her who dwelt in that same desert all the year round, with the sheep and flying sea gulls, and the Merry Men singing and dancing in the Roost!

Chapter Two
What the wreck had brought to Aros

It was half-flood when I got the length of Aros; and there was nothing for it but to stand on the far shore and whistle for Rorie with the boat. I had no need to repeat the signal. At the first sound, Mary was at the door flying a handkerchief by way of answer, and the old long-legged servingman was shambling down the gravel to the pier. For all his hurry, it took him a long while to pull across the bay; and I observed him several times to pause, go into the stern, and look over curiously into the wake. As he came nearer, he seemed to me aged and haggard, and I thought he avoided my eye. The coble had been repaired, with two new thwarts and several patches of some rare and beautiful foreign wood, the name of it unknown to me.

"Why, Rorie," said I, as we began the return voyage, "this is fine wood. How came you by that?"

"It will be hard to cheesel," Rorie opined reluctantly; and just then, dropping the oars, he made another of those dives into the stern which I had remarked as he came across to fetch me, and, leaning his hand on my shoulder, stared with an awful look into the waters of the bay.

"What is wrong?" I asked, a good deal startled.

"It will be a great feesh," said the old man, returning to his oars; and nothing more could I get out of him, but strange glances and an ominous nodding of the head. In spite of myself, I was infected with a measure of uneasiness; I turned also, and studied the wake. The water was still and transparent, but, out here in the middle of the bay, exceeding deep. For some time I could see naught; but at last it did seem to me as if something dark—a great fish, or perhaps only a shadow—followed studiously in the track of the moving coble. And then I remembered one of Rorie's superstitions: how in a ferry in Morven, in some great, exterminating feud among the clans, a fish, the like of it unknown in all our waters, followed for some years the passage of the ferryboat, until no man dared to make the crossing.

"He will be waiting for the right man," said Rorie.

Mary met me on the beach, and led me up the brae and into the house of Aros. Outside and inside there were many changes. The garden was fenced with the same wood that I had noted in the boat; there were chairs in the kitchen covered with strange brocade; curtains of brocade hung from the window; a clock stood silent on the dresser; a lamp of brass was swinging from the roof; the table was set for dinner with the finest of linen and silver; and all these new riches were displayed in the plain old kitchen that I knew so well, with the high-backed settle, and the stools, and the closet bed for Rorie; with the wide chimney the sun shone into, and the clear-smouldering peats; with the pipes on the mantelshelf and the three-cornered spittoons, filled with seashells instead of sand, on the floor; with the bare stone walls and the bare wooden floor, and the three patchwork rugs that were of yore its sole adornment—poor man's patchwork, the like of it unknown in cities, woven with homespun, and Sunday black, and sea cloth polished on the bench of rowing. The room, like the house, had been a sort of wonder in that countryside, it was so neat and habitable; and to see it now, shamed by these incongruous additions, filled me with indignation and a kind of anger. In view of the errand I had come upon to Aros, the feeling was baseless and unjust; but it burned high, at the first moment, in my heart.

"Mary, girl," said I, "this is the place I had learned to call my home, and I do not know it."

"It is my home by nature, not by the learning," she replied; "the place I was born and the place I'm like to die in; and I neither like these changes, nor the way they came, nor that which came with them. I would have liked better, under God's pleasure, they had gone down into the sea, and the Merry Men were dancing on them now."

Mary was always serious; it was perhaps the only trait that she shared with her father; but the tone with which she uttered these words was even graver than of custom.

"Ay," said I, "I feared it came by wreck, and that's by death; yet when my father died, I took his goods without remorse."

"Your father died a clean strae death, as the folk say," said Mary.

"True," I returned; "and a wreck is like a judgment. What was she called?"

"They ca'd her the *Christ-Anna,*" said a voice behind me; and, turning round, I saw my uncle standing in the doorway.

He was a sour, small, bilious man, with a long face and very dark eyes; fifty-six years old, sound and active in body, and with an air somewhat between that of a shepherd and that of a man following the sea. He never laughed, that I heard; read long at the Bible; prayed much, like the Cameronians he had been brought up among; and indeed, in many ways, used to remind me of one of the hillpreachers in the killing times before the Revolution. But he never got much comfort, nor even, as I used to think, much guidance, by his piety. He had his black fits when he was afraid of hell; but he had led a rough life, to which he would look back with envy, and was still a rough, cold, gloomy man.

As he came in at the door out of the sunlight, with his bonnet on his head and a pipe hanging in his buttonhole, he seemed, like Rorie, to have grown older and paler, the lines were deeplier ploughed upon his face, and the whites of his eyes were yellow, like old stained ivory, or the bones of the dead.

"Ay," he repeated, dwelling upon the first part of the word, "the *Christ-Anna*. It's an awfu' name."

I made him my salutations, and complimented him upon his look of health; for I feared he had perhaps been ill.

"I'm in the body," he replied, ungraciously enough; "aye in the body and the sins of the body, like yoursel'. Denner," he said abruptly to Mary, and then ran on to me: "They're grand braws, thir that we hae gotten, are they no? Yon's a bonny knock,* but it'll no gang; and the napery's by ordnar. Bonny, bairnly braws; it's for the like o' them folk sells the peace of God that passeth understanding; it's for the like o' them, an' maybe no even sae muckle worth, folk daunton God to His face and burn in muckle hell; and it's for that reason the Scripture ca's them, as I read the passage, the accursed thing. Mary, ye girzie," he interrupted himself to cry with some asperity, "what for hae ye no put out the twa candlesticks?"

"Why should we need them at high noon?" she asked.

But my uncle was not to be turned from his idea. "We'll bruik† them while we may," he said; and so two massive candlesticks of wrought silver were added to the table equipage, already so unsuited to that rough seaside farm.

"She cam' ashore Februar' 10, about ten at nicht," he went on to me. "There was nae wind, and a sair run o' sea; and she was in the sook o' the Roost, as I jaloose. We had seen her a' day, Rorie and me, beating to the wind. She wasnae a handy craft, I'm thinking, that *Christ-Anna*; for she would neither steer nor stey wi' them. A sair day

*Clock. [R.L.S.]
†Enjoy. [R.L.S.]

they had of it; their hands was never aff the sheets, and it perishin' cauld—ower cauld to snaw; and aye they would get a bit nip o' wind, and awa' again, to put the emp'y hope into them. Eh, man! but they had a sair day for the last o't! He would have had a prood, prood heart that won ashore upon the back o' that."

"And were all lost?" I cried. "God help them!"

"Wheesht!" he said sternly. "Nane shall pray for the deid on my hearth-stane."

I disclaimed a Popish sense for my ejaculation; and he seemed to accept my disclaimer with unusual facility, and ran on once more upon what had evidently become a favourite subject.

"We fand her in Sandag Bay, Rorie an' me, and a' thae braws in the inside of her. There's a kittle bit, ye see, about Sandag; whiles the sook rins strong for the Merry Men; an' whiles again, when the tide's makin' hard an' ye can hear the Roost blawin' at the far-end of Aros, there comes a back-spang of current straucht into Sandag Bay. Weel, there's the thing that got the grip on the *Christ-Anna*. She but to have come in ram-stam an' stern forrit; for the bows of her are aften under, and the back-side of her is clear at hie-water o' neaps. But, man! the dunt that she cam doon wi' when she struck! Lord save us a'! but it's an unco life to be a sailor—a cauld, wanchancy life. Mony's the gliff I got mysel' in the great deep; and why the Lord should hae made yon unco water is mair than ever I could win to understand. He made the vales and the pastures, the bonny green yaird, the halesome, canty land—

> And now they shout and sing to Thee,
> For Thou hast made them glad,

as the Psalms say in the metrical version. No that I would preen my faith to that clink neither; but it's bonny, and easier to mind. 'Who go to sea in ships,' they hae't again—

> And in
> Great waters trading be,
> Within the deep these men God's works
> And His great wonders see.

Weel, it's easy sayin' sae. Maybe Dauvit wasnae very weel acquant wi' the sea. But, troth, if it wasnae prentit in the Bible, I wad whiles be temp'it to think it wasnae the Lord, but the muckle, black deil that made the sea. There's naething good comes oot o't but the fish; an' the spentacle o' God riding on the tempest, to be shüre, whilk would be what Dauvit was likely ettling at. But, man, they were sair wonders that God showed to the *Christ-Anna*—wonders, do I ca' them? Judgments, rather: judgments in the mirk nicht among the draygons o' the deep. And their souls—to think o' that—their souls, man, maybe no prepared! The sea—a muckle yett to hell!"

I observed, as my uncle spoke, that his voice was unnaturally moved and his manner unwontedly demonstrative. He leaned forward at these last words, for example, and touched me on the knee with his spread fingers, looking up into my face with a certain pallor, and I could see that his eyes shone with a deep-seated fire, and that the lines about his mouth were drawn and tremulous.

Even the entrance of Rorie, and the beginning of our meal, did not detach him from his train of thought beyond a moment. He condescended, indeed, to ask me some questions as to my success at college, but I thought it was with half his mind; and even in his extempore grace, which was, as usual, long and wandering, I could find the trace of his preoccupation, praying, as he did, that God would "remember in mercy fower puir, feckless, fiddling, sinful creatures here by their lee-lane beside the great and dowie waters."

Soon there came an interchange of speeches between him and Rorie.

"Was it there?" asked my uncle.

"Ou, ay!" said Rorie.

I observed that they both spoke in a manner of aside, and with some show of embarrassment, and that Mary herself appeared to colour, and looked down on her plate. Partly to show my knowledge, and so relieve the party from an awkward strain, partly because I was curious, I pursued the subject.

"You mean the fish?" I asked.

"Whatten fish?" cried my uncle. "Fish, quo' he! Fish! Your een are fu' o' fatness, man; your heid dozened wi' carnal leir. Fish! it's a bogle!"

He spoke with great vehemence, as though angry; and perhaps I was not very willing to be put down so shortly, for young men are disputatious. At least I remember I retorted hotly, crying out upon childish superstitions.

"And ye come frae the College!" sneered Uncle Gordon. "Gude kens what they learn folk there; it's no muckle service onyway. Do ye think, man, that there's naething in a' yon saut wilderness o' a world oot wast there, wi' the sea grasses growin', an' the sea beasts fechtin', an' the sun glintin' down into it, day by day? Na; the sea's like the land, but fearsomer. If there's folk ashore, there's folk in the sea—deid they may be, but they're folk whatever; and as for deils, there's nane that's like the sea deils. There's no sae muckle harm in the land deils, when a's said and done. Lang syne, when I was a callant in the south country, I mind there was an auld, bald bogle in the Peewie Moss. I got a glisk o' him mysel', sittin' on his hunkers in a hag, as gray's a tombstane. An', troth, he was a fearsome-like taed. But he steered naebody. Nae doobt, if ane that was a reprobate, ane the Lord hated, had gane by there wi' his sin still upon his stamach, nae doobt the creature would hae lowped upo' the likes o' him. But there's deils in the deep sea would yoke on a communicant! Eh, sirs, if ye had gane doon wi' the puir lads in the *Christ-Anna*, ye would ken by now the mercy o' the seas. If ye had sailed it for as lang as me, ye would hate the thocht of it as I do. If ye had but used the een God gave ye, ye would hae learned the wickedness o' that fause, saut, cauld, buller-ing creature, and of a' that's in it by the Lord's permission: labsters an' partans, an' sic like, howking in the deid; muckle, gutsy, blawing whales; an' fish—the hale clan o' them—cauld-wamed, blind-eed uncanny ferlies. O, sirs," he cried, "the horror—the horror o' the sea!"

We were all somewhat staggered by this outburst; and the speaker himself, after that last hoarse apostrophe, appeared to sink gloomily into his own thoughts. But Rorie, who was greedy of superstitious lore, recalled him to the subject by a question.

"You will not ever have seen a teevil of the sea?" he asked.

"No clearly," replied the other. "I misdoobt if a mere man could see ane clearly and conteenue in the body. I hae sailed wi' a lad—they ca'd him Sandy Gabart; he saw ane, shüre eneuch, an' shüre eneuch it was the end of him. We were seeven days oot frae the Clyde—a sair wark we had had—gaun north wi' seeds an' braws an' things for the Macleod. We had got in ower near under the Cutchull'ns, an' had just gane about by Soa, an' were off on a lang tack, we thocht would maybe hauld as far's Copnahow. I mind the nicht weel; a mune smoored wi' mist; a fine gaun breeze upon the water, but no steedy; an'—what nane o' us likit to hear—anither wund gurlin' owerheid, amang thae fearsome, auld stane craigs o' the Cutchull'ns. Weel, Sandy was forrit wi' the jib sheet; we couldnae see him for the mains'l, that had just begude to draw, when a' at ance he gied a skirl. I luffed for my life, for I thocht we were ower near Soa; but na, it wasnae that, it was puir Sandy Gabart's deid skreigh, or near hand, for he was deid in half an hour. A't he could tell was that a sea deil, or sea bogle, or sea spenster, or sic-like, had clum up by the bowsprit, an' gi'en him ae cauld, uncanny look. An', or the life was oot o' Sandy's body, we kent weel what the thing betokened, and why the wund gurled in the taps o' the Cutchull'ns; for doon it cam'—a wund do I ca' it! it was the wund o' the Lord's anger—an' a' that nicht we foucht like men dementit, and the niest that we kenned we were ashore in Loch Uskevagh, an' the cocks were crawin' in Benbecula."

"It will have been a merman," Rorie said.

"A merman!" screamed my uncle with immeasurable scorn. "Auld wives' clavers! There's nae sic things as mermen."

"But what was the creature like?" I asked.

"What like was it? Gude forbid that we suld ken what like it was! It had a kind of a heid upon it—man could say nae mair."

Then Rorie, smarting under the affront, told several tales of mermen, mermaids, and sea-horses that had come ashore upon the islands and attacked the crews of boats upon the sea; and my uncle, in spite of his incredulity, listened with uneasy interest.

"Aweel, aweel," he said, "it may be sae; I may be wrang; but I find nae word o' mermen in the Scriptures."

"And you will find nae word of Aros Roost, maybe," objected Rorie, and his argument appeared to carry weight.

When dinner was over, my uncle carried me forth with him to a bank behind the house. It was a very hot and quiet afternoon; scarce a ripple anywhere upon the sea, nor any voice but the familiar voice of sheep and gulls; and perhaps in consequence of this repose in nature, my kinsman showed himself more rational and tranquil than before. He spoke evenly and almost cheerfully of my career, with every now and then a reference to the lost ship or the treasures it had brought to Aros. For my part, I listened to him in a sort of trance, gazing with all my heart on that remembered scene, and drinking gladly the sea air and the smoke of peats that had been lit by Mary.

Perhaps an hour had passed when my uncle, who had all the while been covertly gazing on the surface of the little bay, rose to his feet and bade me follow his example. Now I should say that the great run of tide at the southwest end of Aros exercises a perturbing influence round all the coast. In Sandag Bay, to the south, a strong current runs at certain periods of the flood and ebb respectively; but in this northern bay—Aros Bay, as it is called—where the house stands and on which my uncle was now gazing, the only sign of disturbance is towards the end of the ebb, and even then it is too slight to be remarkable. When there is any swell, nothing can be seen at all; but when it is calm, as it often is, there appear certain strange, undecipherable marks—sea-runes, as we may name them—on the glassy surface of the bay. The like is common in a thousand places on the coast; and many a boy must have amused himself as I did, seeking to read in them some reference to himself or those he loved. It was to these marks that my uncle now directed my attention, struggling, as he did so, with an evident reluctance.

"Do ye see yon scart upo' the water?" he inquired; "yon ane wast the gray stane? Ay? Weel, it'll no be like a letter, wull it?"

"Certainly it is," I replied. "I have often remarked it. It is like a C."

He heaved a sigh as if heavily disappointed with my answer, and then added below his breath: "Ay, for the *Christ-Anna*."

"I used to suppose, sir, it was for myself," said I; "for my name is Charles."

"And so ye saw't afore?" he ran on, not heeding my remark. "Weel, weel, but that's unco strange. Maybe, it's been there waitin', as a man wad say, through a' the weary ages. Man, but that's awfu'." And then, breaking off: "Ye'll no see anither, will ye?" he asked.

"Yes," said I. "I see another very plainly, near the Ross side, where the road comes down—an M."

"An M," he repeated very low; and then, again after another pause: "An' what wad ye make o' that?" he inquired.

"I had always thought it to mean Mary, sir," I answered, growing somewhat red, convinced as I was in my own mind that I was on the threshold of a decisive explanation.

But we were each following his own train of thought to the exclusion of the other's. My uncle once more paid no attention to my words; only hung his head and held his peace; and I might have been led to fancy that he had not heard me, if his next speech had not contained a kind of echo from my own.

"I would say naething o' thae clavers to Mary," he observed, and began to walk forward.

There is a belt of turf along the side of Aros Bay where walking is easy; and it was along this that I silently followed my silent kinsman. I was perhaps a little disappointed at having lost so good an opportunity to declare my love; but I was at the same time far more deeply exercised at the change that had befallen my uncle. He was never an ordinary, never, in the strict sense, an amiable, man; but there was nothing in even the worst that I had known of him before, to prepare me for so strange a transformation. It was impossible to close the eyes against one fact; that he had, as the saying goes, something on his mind; and as I mentally ran over the different words which might be represented by the letter M—misery, mercy, marriage, money, and the like—I was arrested with a sort of start by the word murder. I was still considering the ugly sound and fatal meaning of the word, when the direction of our walk brought us to a point from which a view was to be had to either side, back towards Aros Bay and homestead, and forward on the ocean, dotted to the north with isles, and lying to the southward blue and open to the sky. There my guide came to a halt, and stood staring for awhile on that expanse. Then he turned to me and laid a hand on my arm.

"Ye think there's naething there?" he said, pointing with his pipe; and then cried out aloud, with a kind of exultation: "I'll tell ye, man! The deid are down there—thick like rattons!"

He turned at once, and, without another word, we retraced our steps to the house of Aros.

I was eager to be alone with Mary; yet it was not till after supper, and then but for a short while, that I could have a word with her. I lost no time beating about the bush, but spoke out plainly what was on my mind.

"Mary," I said, "I have not come to Aros without a hope. If that should prove well founded, we may all leave and go somewhere else, secure of daily bread and comfort; secure, perhaps, of something far beyond that, which it would seem extravagant in me to promise. But there's a hope that lies nearer to my heart than money." And at that I paused. "You can guess fine what that is, Mary," I said. She looked away from me in silence, and that was small encouragement, but I was not to be put off. "All my days I have thought the world of you," I continued; "the time goes on and I think always the more of you; I could not think to be happy or hearty in my life without you: you are the apple of my eye." Still she looked away, and said never a word; but I thought I saw that her hands shook. "Mary," I cried in fear, "do ye no like me?"

"O, Charlie man," she said, "is this a time to speak of it? Let me be, a while; let me be the way I am; it'll not be you that loses by the waiting!"

I made out by her voice that she was nearly weeping, and this put me out of any thought but to compose her. "Mary Ellen," I said, "say no more; I did not come to trouble you: your way shall be mine, and your time too; and you have told me all I wanted. Only just this one thing more: what ails you?"

She owned it was her father, but would enter into no particulars, only shook her head, and said he was not well and not like himself, and it was a great pity. She knew nothing of the wreck. "I havenae been near it," said she. "What for would I go near it, Charlie lad? The poor souls are gone to their account long syne; and I would just have wished they had ta'en their gear with them—poor souls!"

This was scarcely any great encouragement for me to tell her of the *Espirito Santo*; yet I did so, and at the very first word she cried out in surprise. "There was a man at Grisapol," she said, "in the month of May—a little, yellow, black-avised body, they tell me, with gold rings upon his fingers, and a beard; and he was speiring high and low for that same ship."

It was towards the end of April that I had been given these papers to sort out by Dr. Robertson: and it came suddenly back upon my mind that they were thus prepared for a Spanish historian, or a man calling himself such, who had come with high recommendations to the Principal, on a mission of inquiry as to the dispersion of the great Armada. Putting one thing with another, I fancied that the visitor "with the gold rings upon his fingers" might be the same with Dr. Robertson's historian from Madrid. If that were so, he would be more likely after treasure for himself than information for a learned society. I made up my mind, I should lose no time over my undertaking; and if the ship lay sunk in Sandag Bay, as perhaps both he and I supposed, it should not be for the advantage of this ringed adventurer, but for Mary and myself, and for the good, old, honest, kindly family of the Darnaways.

Chapter Three
Land and sea in Sandag Bay

I was early afoot next morning; and as soon as I had a bite to eat, set forth upon a tour of exploration. Something in my heart distinctly told me that I should find the ship of the Armada; and although I did not give way entirely to such hopeful thoughts, I was still very light in spirits and walked upon air. Aros is a very rough islet, its surface strewn with great rocks and shaggy with fern and heather; and my way lay almost north and south across the highest knoll; and though the whole distance was inside of two miles, it took more time and exertion than four upon a level road. Upon the summit, I paused. Although not very high—not three hundred feet, as I think—it yet outtops all the neighbouring lowlands of the Ross, and commands a great view of sea and islands. The sun, which had been up some time, was already hot upon my neck; the air was listless and thundery, although purely clear; away over the northwest, where the isles lie thickliest congregated, some half-a-dozen small and ragged clouds hung together in a covey; and the head of Ben Kyaw wore, not merely a few streamers, but a solid hood of vapour. There was a threat in the weather. The sea, it is true, was smooth like glass: even the Roost was but a seam on that wide mirror, and the Merry Men no more than caps of foam; but to my eye and ear, so long familiar with these places, the sea also seemed to lie uneasily; a sound of it, like a long sigh, mounted to me where I stood; and, quiet as it was, the Roost itself appeared to be revolving mischief. For I ought to say that all we dwellers in these parts attributed, if not prescience, at least a quality of warning, to that strange and dangerous creature of the tides.

I hurried on, then, with the greater speed, and had soon descended the slope of Aros to the part that we call Sandag Bay. It is a pretty large piece of water compared with the size of the isle; well sheltered from all but the prevailing wind; sandy and shoal and bounded by low sandhills to the west, but to the eastward lying several fathoms deep along a ledge of rocks. It is upon that side that, at a certain time each flood, the current mentioned by my uncle sets so strong into the bay; a little later, when the Roost begins to work higher, an undertow runs still more strongly in the reverse direction; and it is the action of this last, as I suppose, that has scoured that part so deep. Nothing is to be seen out of Sandag Bay but one small segment of the horizon and, in heavy weather, the breakers flying high over a deep sea reef.

From halfway down the hill, I had perceived the wreck of February last, a brig of considerable tonnage, lying, with her back broken, high and dry on the east corner of the sands; and I was making directly towards it, and already almost on the margin of the turf, when my eyes were suddenly arrested by a spot, cleared of fern and heather, and marked by one of those long, low, and almost human-looking mounds that we see so commonly in graveyards. I stopped like a man shot. Nothing had been said to me of any dead man or interment on the island; Rorie, Mary, and my uncle had all equally held their peace; of her at least, I was certain that she must be ignorant; and yet here, before my eyes, was proof indubitable of the fact. Here was a grave; and I had to ask myself, with a chill, what manner of man lay there in his last sleep, awaiting the signal of the Lord in that solitary, sea-beat resting-place? My mind supplied no answer but what I feared to entertain. Shipwrecked, at least, he must have been; perhaps, like the old Armada mariners, from some far and rich land oversea; or perhaps one of my own race, perishing within eyesight of the smoke of home. I stood awhile uncovered by his side, and I could have desired that it had lain in our religion to put up some prayer for that unhappy stranger, or, in the old classic way, outwardly to honour his misfortune. I knew, although his bones lay there, a part of Aros, till the trumpet sounded, his imperishable soul was forth and far away, among the raptures of the everlasting Sabbath or the pangs of hell; and yet my mind misgave me even with a fear, that perhaps he was near me where I stood, guarding his sepulchre, and lingering on the scene of his unhappy fate.

Certainly it was with a spirit somewhat overshadowed that I turned away from the grave to the hardly less melancholy spectacle of the wreck. Her stem was above the first arc of the flood; she was broken in two a little abaft the foremast—though indeed she had none, both masts having broken short in her disaster; and as the pitch of the beach was very sharp and sudden, and the bows lay many feet below the stern, the fracture gaped widely open, and you could see right through her poor hull upon the farther side. Her name was much defaced, and I could not make out clearly whether she was called *Christiania*, after the Norwegian city, or *Christiana*, after the good woman, Christian's wife, in that old book the "Pilgrim's Progress." By her build she was a foreign ship, but I was not certain of her nationality. She had been painted green, but the colour was faded and weathered, and the paint peeling off in strips. The wreck of the mainmast lay alongside, half-buried in sand. She was a forlorn sight, indeed, and I could not look without emotion at the bits of rope that still hung about her, so often handled of yore by shouting seamen; or the little scuttle where they had passed up and down to their affairs; or that poor noseless angel of a figurehead that had dipped into so many running billows.

I do not know whether it came most from the ship or from the grave, but I fell into some melancholy scruples, as I stood there, leaning with one hand against the battered timbers. The homelessness of men and even of inanimate vessels, cast away upon strange shores, came strongly in upon my mind. To make a profit of such pitiful misadventures seemed an unmanly and a sordid act; and I began to think of my then quest as of something sacrilegious in its nature. But when I remembered Mary, I took heart again. My uncle would never consent to an imprudent marriage, nor would she, as I was persuaded, wed without his full approval. It behoved me, then, to be up and doing for my wife; and I thought with a laugh how long it was since that great sea-castle, the *Espirito Santo*, had left her bones in Sandag Bay, and how weak it would be to consider rights so long extinguished and misfortunes so long forgotten in the process of time.

I had my theory of where to seek for her remains. The set of the current and the soundings both pointed to the east side of the bay under the ledge of rocks. If she had been lost in Sandag Bay, and if, after these centuries, any portion of her held together, it was there that I should find it. The water deepens, as I have said, with great rapidity, and even close alongside the rocks several fathoms may be found. As I walked upon the edge I could see far and wide over the sandy bottom of the bay; the sun shone clear and green and steady in the deeps; the bay seemed rather like a great transparent crystal, as one sees them in a lapidary's shop; there was naught to show that it was water but an internal trembling, a hovering within of sun-glints and netted shadows, and now and then a faint lap and a dying bubble round the edge. The shadows of the rocks lay out for some distance at their feet, so that my own shadow, moving, pausing, and stooping on the top of that, reached sometimes half across the bay. It was above all in this belt of shadows that I hunted for the *Espirito Santo*; since it was there the undertow ran strongest, whether in or out. Cool as the whole water seemed this broiling day, it looked, in that part, yet cooler, and had a mysterious invitation for the eyes. Peer as I pleased, however, I could see nothing but a few fishes or a bush of sea tangle, and here and there a lump of rock that had fallen from above and now lay separate on the sandy floor. Twice did I pass from one end to the other of the rocks, and in the whole distance I could see nothing of the wreck, nor any place but one where it was possible for it to be. This was a large terrace in five fathoms of water, raised off the surface of the sand to a considerable height, and looking from above like a mere outgrowth of the rocks on which I walked. It was one mass of great sea tangles like a grove, which prevented me judging of its nature, but in shape and size it bore some likeness to a vessel's hull. At least it was my best chance. If the *Espirito Santo* lay not there under the tangles, it lay nowhere at all in Sandag Bay; and I prepared to put the question to the proof, once and for all, and either go back to Aros a rich man or cured for ever of my dreams of wealth.

I stripped to the skin, and stood on the extreme margin with my hands clasped, irresolute. The bay at that time was utterly quiet; there was no sound but from a school of porpoises somewhere out of sight behind the point; yet a certain fear withheld me on the threshold of my venture. Sad sea-feelings, scraps of my uncle's superstitions, thoughts of the dead, of the grave, of the old broken ships, drifted through my mind. But the strong sun upon my shoulders warmed me to the heart, and I stooped forward and plunged into the sea.

It was all that I could do to catch a trail of the sea-tangle that grew so thickly on the terrace; but once so far anchored I secured myself by grasping a whole armful of these thick and slimy stalks, and, planting my feet against the edge, I looked around me. On all sides the clear sand stretched forth unbroken; it came to the foot of the rocks, scoured into the likeness of an alley in a garden by the action of the tides; and before me, for as far as I could see, nothing was visible but the same many-folded sand upon the sun-bright bottom of the bay. Yet the terrace to which I was then holding was as thick with strong sea-growths as a tuft of heather, and the cliff from which it bulged hung draped below the waterline with brown lianas. In this complexity of forms, all swaying together in the current, things were hard to be distinguished; and I was still uncertain whether my feet were pressed upon the natural rock or upon the timbers of the Armada treasure ship, when the whole tuft of tangle came away in my hand, and in an instant I was on the surface, and the shores of the bay and the bright water swam before my eyes in a glory of crimson.

I clambered back upon the rocks, and threw the plant of tangle at my feet. Something at the same moment rang sharply, like a falling coin. I stooped, and there, sure enough, crusted with the red rust, there lay an iron shoe-buckle. The sight of this poor human relic thrilled me to the heart, but not with hope nor fear, only with a desolate melancholy. I held it in my hand, and the thought of its owner appeared before me like the presence of an actual man. His weather-beaten face, his sailor's hands, his sea-voice hoarse with singing at the capstan, the very foot that had once worn that buckle and trod so much along the swerving decks—the whole human fact of him, as a creature like myself, with hair and blood and seeing eyes, haunted me in that sunny, solitary place, not like a spectre, but like some friend whom I had basely injured. Was the great treasure ship indeed below there, with her guns and chain and treasure, as she had sailed from Spain; her decks a garden for the seaweed, her cabin a breeding place for fish, soundless but for the dredging water, motionless but for the waving of the tangle upon her battlements—that old, populous, sea-riding castle, now a reef in Sandag Bay? Or, as I thought it likelier, was this a waif from the disaster of the foreign brig—was this shoe-buckle bought but the other day and worn by a man of my own period in the world's history, hearing the same news from day to day, thinking the same thoughts, praying, perhaps, in the same temple with myself? However it was, I was assailed with dreary thoughts; my uncle's words, "the dead are down there," echoed in my ears; and though I determined to dive once more, it was with a strong repugnance that I stepped forward to the margins of the rocks.

A great change passed at that moment over the appearance of the bay. It was no more that clear, visible interior, like a house roofed with glass, where the green, submarine sunshine slept so stilly. A breeze, I suppose, had flawed the surface, and a sort of trouble and blackness filled its bosom, where flashes of light and clouds of shadow tossed confusedly together. Even the terrace below obscurely rocked and quivered. It seemed a graver thing to venture on this place of ambushes; and when I leaped into the sea the second time it was with a quaking in my soul.

I secured myself as at first, and groped among the waving tangle. All that met my touch was cold and soft and gluey. The thicket was alive with crabs and lobsters, trundling to and fro lopsidedly, and I had to harden my heart against the horror of their carrion neighbourhood. On all sides I could feel the grain and the clefts of hard, living stone; no planks, no iron, not a sign of any wreck; the *Espirito Santo* was not there. I remember I had almost a sense of relief in my disappointment, and I was about ready to leave go, when something happened that sent me to the surface with my heart in my mouth. I had already stayed somewhat late over my explorations; the current was freshening with the change of the tide, and Sandag Bay was no longer a safe place for a single swimmer. Well, just at the last moment there came a sudden flush of current, dredging through the tangles like a wave. I lost one hold, was flung sprawling on my side, and, instinctively grasping for a fresh support, my fingers closed on something hard and cold. I think I knew at that moment what it was. At least I instantly left hold of the tangle, leaped for the surface, and clambered out next moment on the friendly rocks with the bone of a man's leg in my grasp.

Mankind is a material creature, slow to think and dull to perceive connections. The grave, the wreck of the brig, and the rusty shoe-buckle were surely plain advertisements. A child might have read their dismal story, and yet it was not until I touched that actual piece of mankind that the full horror of the charnel ocean burst upon my spirit. I laid the bone beside the buckle, picked up my clothes, and ran as I was along the rocks towards the human shore. I could not be far enough from the spot; no fortune was vast enough to tempt me back again. The bones of the drowned dead should henceforth roll undisturbed by me, whether on tangle or minted gold. But as soon as I trod the good earth again, and had covered my nakedness against the sun, I knelt down over against the ruins of the brig, and out of the fulness of my heart prayed long and passionately for all poor souls upon the sea. A generous prayer is never presented in vain; the petition may be refused, but the petitioner is always, I believe, rewarded by some gracious visitation. The horror, at least, was lifted from my mind; I could look with calm of spirit on that great bright creature, God's ocean; and as I set off homeward up the rough sides of Aros, nothing remained of my concern beyond a deep determination to meddle no more with the spoils of wrecked vessels or the treasures of the dead.

I was already some way up the hill before I paused to breathe and look behind me. The sight that met my eyes was doubly strange.

For, first, the storm that I had foreseen was now advancing with almost tropical rapidity. The whole surface of the sea had been dulled from its conspicuous brightness to an ugly hue of corrugated lead; already in the distance the white waves, the "skipper's daughters," had begun to flee before a breeze that was still insensible on Aros; and already along the curve of Sandag Bay there was a splashing run of sea that I could hear from where I stood. The change upon the sky was even more remarkable. There had begun to arise out of the southwest a huge and solid continent of scowling cloud; here and there, through rents in its contexture, the sun still poured a sheaf of spreading rays; and here and there, from all its edges, vast inky streamers lay forth along the yet unclouded sky. The menace was express and imminent. Even as I gazed, the sun was blotted out. At any moment the tempest might fall upon Aros in its might.

The suddenness of this change of weather so fixed my eyes on heaven that it was some seconds before they alighted on the bay, mapped out below my feet, and robbed a moment later of the sun. The knoll which I had just surmounted overflanked a little amphitheatre of lower hillocks sloping towards the sea, and beyond that the yellow arc of beach and the whole extent of Sandag Bay. It was a scene on which I had often looked down, but where I had never before beheld a human figure. I had but just turned my back upon it and left it empty, and my wonder may be fancied when I saw a boat and several men in that deserted spot. The boat was lying by the rocks. A pair of fellows, bareheaded, with their sleeves rolled up, and one with a boathook, kept her with difficulty to her moorings, for the current was growing brisker every moment. A little way off upon the ledge two men in black clothes, whom I judged to be superior in rank, laid their heads together over some task which at first I did not understand, but a second after I had made it out—they were taking bearings with the compass; and just then I saw one of them unroll a sheet of paper and lay his finger down, as though identifying features in a map. Meanwhile a third was walking to and fro, poking among the rocks and peering over the edge into the water. While I was still watching them with the stupefaction of surprise, my mind hardly yet able to work on what my eyes reported, this third person suddenly stooped and summoned his companions with a cry so loud that it reached my ears upon the hill. The others ran to him, even dropping the compass in their hurry, and I could see the bone and the shoe-buckle going from hand to hand, causing the most unusual gesticulations of surprise and interest. Just then I could hear the seamen crying from the boat, and saw them point westward to that cloud continent which was ever the more rapidly unfurling its blackness over heaven. The others seemed to consult; but the danger was too pressing to be braved, and they bundled into the boat carrying my relics with them, and set forth out of the bay with all speed of oars.

I made no more ado about the matter, but turned and ran for the house. Whoever these men were, it was fit my uncle should be instantly informed. It was not then altogether too late in the day for a descent of the Jacobites; and maybe Prince Charlie, whom I knew my uncle to detest, was one of the three superiors whom I had seen upon the rock. Yet as I ran, leaping from rock to rock, and turned the matter loosely in my mind, this theory grew ever the longer the less welcome to my reason. The compass, the map, the interest awakened by the buckle, and the conduct of that one among the strangers who had looked so often below him in the water, all seemed to point to a different explanation of their presence on that outlying, obscure islet of the western sea. The Madrid historian, the search instituted by Dr. Robertson, the bearded stranger with the rings, my own fruitless search that very morning in the deep water of Sandag Bay, ran together, piece by piece, in my memory, and I made sure that these strangers must be Spaniards in quest of ancient treasure and the lost ship of the Armada. But the people living in outlying islands, such as Aros, are answerable for their own security; there is none nearby to protect or even to help them; and the presence in such a spot of a crew of foreign adventurers—poor, greedy, and most likely lawless—filled me with apprehensions for my uncle's money, and even for the safety of his daughter. I was still wondering how we were to get rid of them when I came, all breathless, to the top of Aros. The whole world was shadowed over; only in the extreme east, on a hill of the mainland, one last gleam of sunshine lingered like a jewel; rain had begun to fall, not heavily, but in great drops; the sea was rising with each moment, and already a band of white encircled Aros and the nearer coasts of Grisapol. The boat was still pulling seaward, but I now became aware of what had been hidden from me lower down—a large, heavily sparred, handsome schooner, lying to at the south end of Aros. Since I had not seen her in the morning when I had looked around so closely at the signs of the weather, and upon these lone waters where a sail was rarely visible, it was clear she must have lain last night behind the uninhabited Eilean Gour, and this proved conclusively that she was manned by strangers to our coast, for that anchorage, though good enough to look at, is little better than a trap for ships. With such ignorant sailors upon so wild a coast, the coming gale was not unlikely to bring death upon its wings.

Chapter Four
The gale

I found my uncle at the gable end, watching the signs of the weather, with a pipe in his fingers.

"Uncle," said I, "there were men ashore at Sandag Bay——"

I had no time to go further; indeed, I not only forgot my words, but even my weariness, so strange was the effect on Uncle Gordon. He dropped his pipe and fell back against the end of the house with his jaw fallen, his eyes staring, and his long face as white as paper. We must have looked at one another silently for a quarter of a minute, before he made answer in this extraordinary fashion: "Had he a hair kep on?"

I knew as well as if I had been there that the man who now lay buried at Sandag had worn a hairy cap, and that he had come ashore alive. For the first and only time I lost toleration for the man who was my benefactor and the father of the woman I hoped to call my wife.

"These were living men," said I, "perhaps Jacobites, perhaps the French, perhaps pirates, perhaps adventurers come here to seek the Spanish treasure ship; but, whatever they may be, dangerous at least to your daughter and my cousin. As for your own guilty terrors, man, the dead sleeps well where you have laid him. I stood this morning by his grave; he will not wake before the trump of doom."

My kinsman looked upon me, blinking, while I spoke; then he fixed his eyes for a little on the ground, and pulled his fingers foolishly; but it was plain that he was past the power of speech.

"Come," said I. "You must think for others. You must come up the hill with me, and see this ship."

He obeyed without a word or a look, following slowly after my impatient strides. The spring seemed to have gone out of his body, and he scrambled heavily up and down the rocks, instead of leaping, as he was wont, from one to another. Nor could I, for all my cries, induce him to make better haste. Only once he replied to me complainingly, and like one in bodily pain: "Ay, ay, man, I'm coming." Long before we had reached the top, I had no other thought for him but pity. If the crime had been monstrous, the punishment was in proportion.

At last we emerged above the skyline of the hill, and could see around us. All was black and stormy to the eye; the last gleam of sun had vanished; a wind had sprung up, not yet high, but gusty and unsteady to the point; the rain, on the other hand, had ceased. Short as was the interval, the sea already ran vastly higher than when I had stood there last; already it had begun to break over some of the outward reefs, and already it moaned aloud in the sea-caves of Aros. I looked, at first, in vain for the schooner.

"There she is," I said at last. But her new position, and the course she was now lying, puzzled me. "They cannot mean to beat to sea," I cried.

"That's what they mean," said my uncle, with something like joy; and just then the schooner went about and stood upon another tack, which put the question beyond the reach of doubt. These strangers, seeing a gale on hand, had thought first of sea room. With the wind that threatened, in these reef-sown waters and contending against so violent a stream of tide, their course was certain death.

"Good God!" said I, "they are all lost."

"Ay," returned my uncle, "a'—a' lost. They hadnae a chance but to rin for Kyle Dona. The gate they're gaun the noo, they couldnae win through an the muckle deil were there to pilot them. Eh, man," he continued, touching me on the sleeve, "it's a braw nicht for a shipwreck! Twa in ae twalmonth! Eh, but the Merry Men 'll dance bonny!"

I looked at him, and it was then that I began to fancy him no longer in his right mind. He was peering up to me, as if for sympathy, a timid joy in his eyes. All that had passed between us was already forgotten in the prospect of this fresh disaster.

"If it were not too late," I cried with indignation, "I would take the coble and go out to warn them."

"Na, na," he protested, "ye maunnae interfere; ye maunnae meddle wi' the like o' that. It's His"—doffing his bonnet—"His wull. And, eh, man! but it's a braw nicht for't!"

Something like fear began to creep into my soul; and, reminding him that I had not yet dined, I proposed we should return to the house. But no; nothing would tear him from his place of outlook.

"I maun see the hail thing, man, Cherlie," he explained; and then as the schooner went about a second time, "Eh, but they han'le her bonny!" he cried. "The *Christ-Anna* was naething to this."

Already the men on board the schooner must have begun to realise some part, but not yet the twentieth, of the dangers that environed their doomed ship. At every lull of the capricious wind they must have seen how fast the current swept them back. Each tack was made shorter, as they saw how little it prevailed. Every moment the rising swell began to boom and foam upon another sunken reef; and ever and again a breaker would fall in sounding ruin under the very bows of her, and the brown reef and streaming tangle appear in the hollow of the wave. I tell you, they had to stand to their tackle: there was no idle man aboard that ship, God knows. It was upon the progress of a scene so horrible to any human-hearted man that my misguided uncle now pored and gloated like a connoisseur. As I turned to go down the hill, he was lying on his belly on the summit, with his hands stretched forth and clutching in the heather. He seemed rejuvenated, mind and body.

When I got back to the house already dismally affected, I was still more sadly downcast at the sight of Mary. She had her sleeves rolled up over her strong arms, and was quietly making bread. I got a bannock from the dresser and sat down to eat it in silence.

"Are ye wearied, lad?" she asked after a while.

"I am not so much wearied, Mary," I replied, getting on my feet, "as I am weary of delay, and perhaps of Aros too. You know me well enough to judge me fairly, say what I like. Well, Mary, you may be sure of this: you had better be anywhere but here."

"I'll be sure of one thing," she returned: "I'll be where my duty is."

"You forget, you have a duty to yourself," I said.

"Ay, man?" she replied, pounding at the dough; "will you have found that in the Bible, now?"

"Mary," I said solemnly, "you must not laugh at me just now. God knows I am in no heart for laughing. If we could get your father with us, it would be best; but with him or without him, I want you far away from here, my girl; for your own sake, and for mine, ay, and for your father's too, I want you far—far away from here. I came with other thoughts; I came here as a man comes home; now it is all changed, and I have no desire nor hope but to flee—for that's the word—flee, like a bird out of the fowler's snare, from this accursed island."

She had stopped her work by this time.

"And do you think, now," said she, "do you think, now, I have neither eyes nor ears? Do ye think I havenae broken my heart to have these braws (as he calls them, God forgive him!) thrown into the sea? Do ye think I have lived with him, day in, day out, and not seen what you saw in an hour or two? No," she said, "I know there's wrong in it; what wrong, I neither know nor want to know. There was never an ill thing made better by meddling, that I could hear of. But, my lad, you must never ask me to leave my father. While the breath is in his body, I'll be with him. And he's not long for here, either: that I can tell you, Charlie—he's not long for here. The mark is on his brow; and better so—maybe better so."

I was a while silent, not knowing what to say; and when I roused my head at last to speak, she got before me.

"Charlie," she said, "what's right for me, neednae be right for you. There's sin upon this house and trouble; you are a stranger; take your things upon your back and go your ways to better places and to better folk, and if you were ever minded to come back, though it were twenty years syne, you would find me aye waiting."

"Mary Ellen," I said, "I asked you to be my wife, and you said as good as yes. That's done for good. Wherever you are, I am; as I shall answer to my God."

As I said the words, the wind suddenly burst out raving, and then seemed to stand still and shudder round the house of Aros. It was the first squall, or prologue, of the coming tempest, and as we started and looked about us, we found that a gloom, like the approach of evening, had settled round the house.

"God pity all poor folks at sea!" she said. "We'll see no more of my father till the morrow's morning.

And then she told me, as we sat by the fire and hearkened to the rising gusts, of how this change had fallen upon my uncle. All last winter he had been dark and fitful in his mind. Whenever the Roost ran high, or, as Mary said, whenever the Merry Men were dancing, he would lie out for hours together on the Head, if it were at night, or on the top of Aros by day, watching the tumult of the sea, and sweeping the horizon for a sail. After February the tenth, when the wealth-bringing wreck was cast ashore at Sandag, he had been at first unnaturally gay, and his excitement had never fallen in degree, but only changed in kind from dark to darker. He neglected his work, and kept Rorie idle. The two would speak together by the hour at the gable end, in guarded tones and with an air of secrecy and almost of guilt; and if she questioned either, as at first she sometimes did, her inquiries were put aside with confusion. Since Rorie had first remarked the fish that hung about the ferry, his master had never set foot but once upon the mainland of the Ross. That once—it was in the height of the springs—he had passed dryshod while the tide was out; but, having lingered overlong on the far side, found himself cut off from Aros by the returning waters. It was with a shriek of agony that he had leaped across the gut, and he had reached home thereafter in a fever-fit of fear. A fear of the sea, a constant haunting thought of the sea, appeared in his talk and devotions, and even in his looks when he was silent.

Rorie alone came in to supper; but a little later my uncle appeared, took a bottle under his arm, put some bread in his pocket, and set forth again to his outlook, followed this time by Rorie. I heard that the schooner was losing ground, but the crew were still fighting every inch with hopeless ingenuity and courage; and the news filled my mind with blackness.

A little after sundown the full fury of the gale broke forth, such a gale as I have never seen in summer, nor, seeing how swiftly it had come, even in winter. Mary and I sat in silence, the house quaking overhead, the tempest howling without, the fire between us sputtering with raindrops. Our thoughts were far away with the poor fellows on the schooner, or my not less unhappy uncle, houseless on the promontory; and yet ever and again we were startled back to ourselves, when the wind would rise and strike the gable like a solid body, or suddenly fall and draw away, so that the fire leaped into flame and our hearts bounded in our sides. Now the storm in its might would seize and shake the four corners of the roof, roaring like Leviathan in anger. Anon, in a lull, cold eddies of tempest moved shudderingly in the room, lifting the hair upon our heads and passing between us as we sat. And again the wind would break forth in a chorus of melancholy sounds, hooting low in the chimney, wailing with flutelike softness round the house.

It was perhaps eight o'clock when Rorie came in and pulled me mysteriously to the door. My uncle, it appeared, had frightened even his constant comrade; and Rorie, uneasy at his extravagance, prayed me to come out and share the watch. I hastened to do as I was asked; the more readily as, what with fear and horror, and the electrical tension of the night, I was myself restless and disposed for action. I told Mary to be under no alarm, for I should be a safeguard on her father; and wrapping myself warmly in a plaid, I followed Rorie into the open air.

The night, though we were so little past midsummer, was as dark as January. Intervals of a groping twilight alternated with spells of utter blackness; and it was impossible to trace the reason of these changes in the flying horror of the sky. The wind blew the breath out of a man's nostrils; all heaven seemed to thunder overhead like one huge sail; and when there fell a momentary lull on Aros, we could hear the gusts dismally sweeping in the distance. Over all the low-lands of the Ross, the wind must have blown as fierce as on the open sea; and God only knows the uproar that was raging around the head of Ben Kyaw. Sheets of mingled spray and rain were driven in our faces. All round the isle of Aros the surf, with an incessant, hammering thunder, beat upon the reefs and beaches. Now louder in one place, now lower in another, like the combinations of orchestral music, the constant mass of sound was hardly varied for a moment. And loud above all this hurly-burly I could hear the changeful voices of the Roost and the intermittent roaring of the Merry Men. At that hour, there flashed into my mind the reason of the name that they were called. For the noise of them seemed almost mirthful, as it out-topped the other noises of the night; or if not mirthful, yet instinct with a portentous joviality. Nay, and it seemed even human. As when savage men have drunk away their reason, and, discarding speech, bawl together in their madness by the hour; so, to my ears, these deadly breakers shouted by Aros in the night.

Arm in arm, and staggering against the wind, Rorie and I won every yard of ground with conscious effort. We slipped on the wet sod, we fell together sprawling on the rocks. Bruised, drenched, beaten, and breathless, it must have taken us near half an hour to get from the house down to the Head that overlooks the Roost. There, it seemed, was my uncle's favourite observatory. Right in the face of it, where the cliff is highest and most sheer, a hump of earth, like a parapet, makes a place of shelter from the common winds, where a man may sit in quiet and see the tide and the mad billows contending at his feet. As he might look down from the window of a house upon some street disturbance, so, from this post, he looks down upon the tumbling of the Merry Men. On such a night, of course, he peers upon a world of blackness, where the waters wheel and boil, where the waves joust together with the noise of an explosion, and the foam towers and vanishes in the twinkling of an eye. Never before had I seen the Merry Men thus violent. The fury, height, and transiency of their spoutings was a thing to be seen and not re-counted. High over our heads on the cliff rose their white columns in the darkness; and the same instant, like phantoms, they were gone. Sometimes three at a time would thus aspire and vanish;

sometimes a gust took them, and the spray would fall about us, heavy as a wave. And yet the spectacle was rather maddening in its levity than impressive by its force. Thought was beaten down by the confounding uproar; a gleeful vacancy possessed the brains of men, a state akin to madness; and I found myself at times following the dance of the Merry Men as it were a tune upon a jigging instrument.

I first caught sight of my uncle when we were still some yards away in one of the flying glimpses of twilight that chequered the pitch darkness of the night. He was standing up behind the parapet, his head thrown back and the bottle to his mouth. As he put it down, he saw and recognised us with a toss of one hand fleeringly above his head.

"Has he been drinking?" shouted I to Rorie.

"He will aye be drunk when the wind blaws," returned Rorie in the same high key, and it was all that I could do to hear him.

"Then—was he so—in February?" I inquired.

Rorie's "Ay" was a cause of joy to me. The murder, then, had not sprung in cold blood from calculation; it was an act of madness no more to be condemned than to be pardoned. My uncle was a dangerous madman, if you will, but he was not cruel and base as I had feared. Yet what a scene for a carouse, what an incredible vice, was this that the poor man had chosen! I have always thought drunkenness a wild and almost fearful pleasure, rather demoniacal than human; but drunkenness, out here in the roaring blackness, on the edge of a cliff above that hell of waters, the man's head spinning like the Roost, his foot tottering on the edge of death, his ear watching for the signs of shipwreck, surely that, if it were credible in anyone, was morally impossible in a man like my uncle, whose mind was set upon a damnatory creed and haunted by the darkest superstitions. Yet so it was; and, as we reached the bight of shelter and could breathe again, I saw the man's eyes shining in the night with an unholy glimmer.

"Eh, Charlie, man, it's grand!" he cried. "See to them!" he continued, dragging me to the edge of the abyss from whence arose that deafening clamour and those clouds of spray; "see to them dancin', man! Is that no wicked?"

He pronounced the word with gusto, and I thought it suited with the scene.

"They're yowlin' for thon schooner," he went on, his thin, insane voice clearly audible in the shelter of the bank, "an' she's comin' aye nearer, aye nearer, aye nearer an' nearer an' nearer; an' they ken't, the folk kens it, they ken weel it's by wi' them. Charlie, lad, they're a' drunk in yon schooner, a' dozened wi' drink. They were a' drunk in the *Christ-Anna*, at the hinder end. There's nane could droon at sea wantin' the brandy. Hoot awa, what do you ken?" with a sudden blast of anger. "I tell ye, it cannae be; they daurnae droon withoot it. Ha'e," holding out the bottle, "tak' a sowp."

I was about to refuse, but Rorie touched me as if in warning; and indeed I had already thought better of the movement. I took the bottle, therefore, and not only drank freely myself, but contrived to spill even more as I was doing so. It was pure spirit, and almost strangled me to swallow. My kinsman did not observe the loss, but, once more throwing back his head, drained the remainder to the dregs. Then, with a loud laugh, he cast the bottle forth among the Merry Men, who seemed to leap up, shouting to receive it.

"Ha'e, bairns!" he cried, "there's your han'sel. Ye'll get bonnier nor that, or morning."

Suddenly, out in the black night before us, and not two hundred yards away, we heard, at a moment when the wind was silent, the clear note of a human voice. Instantly the wind swept howling down upon the Head, and the Roost bellowed, and churned, and danced with a new fury. But we had heard the sound, and we knew, with agony, that this was the doomed ship now close on ruin, and that what we had heard was the voice of her master issuing his last command. Crouching together on the edge, we waited, straining every sense, for the inevitable end. It was long, however, and to us it seemed like ages, ere the schooner suddenly appeared for one brief instant, relieved against a tower of glimmering foam. I still see her reefed mainsail flapping loose, as the boom fell heavily across the deck; I still see the black outline of the hull, and still think I can distinguish the figure of a man stretched upon the tiller. Yet the whole sight we had of her passed swifter than lightning; the very wave that disclosed her fell burying her for ever; the mingled cry of many voices at the point of death rose and was quenched in the roaring of the Merry Men. And with that the tragedy was at an end. The strong ship, with all her gear, and the lamp perhaps still burning in the cabin, the lives of so many men, precious surely to others, dear, at least, as heaven to themselves, had all, in that one moment, gone down into the surging waters. They were gone like a dream. And the wind still ran and shouted, and the senseless waters in the Roost still leaped and tumbled as before.

How long we lay there together, we three, speechless and motionless, is more than I can tell, but it must have been for long. At length, one by one, and almost mechanically, we crawled back into the shelter of the bank. As I lay against the parapet, wholly wretched and not entirely master of my mind, I could hear my kinsman maundering to himself in an altered and melancholy mood. Now he would repeat to himself with maudlin iteration, "Sic a fecht as they had—sic a sair fecht as they had, puir lads, puir lads!" and anon he would bewail that "a' the gear was as gude's tint," because the ship had gone down among the Merry Men instead of stranding on the shore; and throughout, the name—the *Christ-Anna*—would come and go in his divagations, pronounced with shuddering awe. The storm all this time was rapidly abating. In half an hour the wind had fallen to a breeze, and the change was accompanied or caused by a heavy, cold, and plumping rain. I must then have fallen asleep, and when I came to myself, drenched, stiff, and unrefreshed, day had already broken, grey, wet, discomfortable day; the wind blew in faint and shifting capfuls, the tide was out, the Roost was at its lowest, and only the strong beating surf round all the coasts of Aros remained to witness of the furies of the night.

Chapter Five
A man out of the sea

Rorie set out for the house in search of warmth and breakfast; but my uncle was bent upon examining the shores of Aros, and I felt it a part of duty to accompany him throughout. He was now docile and quiet, but tremulous and weak in mind and body; and it was with the eagerness of a child that he pursued his exploration. He climbed far down upon the rocks; on the beaches, he pursued the retreating breakers. The merest broken plank or rag of cordage was a treasure in his eyes to be secured at the peril of his life. To see him, with weak and stumbling footsteps, expose himself to the pursuit of the surf, or the snares and pitfalls of the weedy rock, kept me in a perpetual terror. My arm was ready to support him, my hand clutched him by the skirt, I helped him to draw his pitiful discoveries beyond the reach of the returning wave; a nurse accompanying a child of seven would have had no different experience.

Yet, weakened as he was by the reaction from his madness of the night before, the passions that smouldered in his nature were those of a strong man. His terror of the sea, although conquered for the moment, was still undiminished; had the sea been a lake of living flames, he could not have shrunk more panically from its touch; and once, when his foot slipped and he plunged to the midleg into a pool of water, the shriek that came up out of his soul was like the cry of death. He sat still for a while, panting like a dog, after that; but his desire for the spoils of shipwreck triumphed once more over his fears; once more he tottered among the curded foam; once more he crawled upon the rocks among the bursting bubbles; once more his whole heart seemed to be set on driftwood, fit, if it was fit for anything, to throw upon the fire. Pleased as he was with what he found, he still incessantly grumbled at his ill-fortune.

"Aros," he said, "is no a place for wrecks ava'—no ava'. A' the years I've dwalt here, this ane maks the second; and the best o' the gear clean tint!"

"Uncle," said I, for we were now on a stretch of open sand, where there was nothing to divert his mind, "I saw you last night, as I never thought to see you—you were drunk."

"Na, na," he said, "no as bad as that. I had been drinking, though. And to tell ye the God's truth, it's a thing I cannae mend. There's nae soberer man than me in my ordnar; but when I hear the wind blaw in my lug, it's my belief that I gang gyte."

"You are a religious man," I replied, "and this is sin."

"Oh," he returned, "if it wasnae sin, I dinnae ken that I would care for't. Ye see, man, it's defiance. There's a sair spang o' the auld sin o' the warld in yon sea; it's an unchristian business at the best o't; an' whiles when it gets up, an' the wind skreighs—the wind an' her are a kind of sib, I'm thinkin'—an' thae Merry Men, the daft callants, blawin' and lauchin', and puir souls in the deid thraws warstlin' the leelang nicht wi' their bit ships—weel, it comes ower me like a glamour. I'm a deil, I ken't. But I think naething o' the puir sailor lads; I'm wi' the sea, I'm just like ane o' her ain Merry Men."

I thought I should touch him in a joint of his harness. I turned me towards the sea; the surf was running gaily, wave after wave, with their manes blowing behind them, riding one after another up the beach, towering, curving, falling one upon another on the trampled sand. Without, the salt air, the scared gulls, the widespread army of the sea-chargers, neighing to each other, as they gathered together to the assault of Aros; and close before us, that line on the flat sands that, with all their number and their fury, they might never pass.

"Thus far shalt thou go," said I, "and no farther." And then I quoted as solemnly as I was able a verse that I had often before fitted to the chorus of the breakers:

> But yet the Lord that is on high,
> Is more of might by far,
> Than noise of many waters is,
> As great sea billows are.

"Ay," said my kinsman, "at the hinder end, the Lord will triumph; I dinnae misdoobt that. But here on earth, even silly menfolk daur Him to His face. It is nae wise; I am nae sayin' that it's wise; but it's the pride of the eye, and it's the lust o' life, an' it's the wale o' pleesures."

I said no more, for we had now begun to cross a neck of land that lay between us and Sandag; and I withheld my last appeal to the man's better reason till we should stand upon the spot associated with his crime. Nor did he pursue the subject; but he walked beside me with a firmer step. The call that I had made upon his mind acted like a stimulant, and I could see that he had forgotten his search for worthless jetsam, in a profound, gloomy, and yet stirring train of thought. In three or four minutes we had topped the brae and begun to go down upon Sandag. The wreck had been roughly handled by the sea; the stem had been spun round and dragged a little lower down; and perhaps the stern had been forced a little higher, for the two parts now lay entirely separate on the beach. When we came to the grave I stopped, uncovered my head in the thick rain, and, looking my kinsman in the face, addressed him.

"A man," said I, "was in God's providence suffered to escape from mortal dangers; he was poor, he was naked, he was wet, he was weary, he was a stranger; he had every claim upon the bowels of your compassion; it may be that he was the salt of the earth, holy, helpful, and kind; it may be he was a man laden with iniquities to whom death was the beginning of torment. I ask you in the sight of heaven: Gordon Darnaway, where is the man for whom Christ died?"

He started visibly at the last words; but there came no answer, and his face expressed no feeling but a vague alarm.

"You were my father's brother," I continued; "you have taught me to count your house as if it were my father's house; and we are both sinful men walking before the Lord among the sins and dangers of this life. It is by our evil that God leads us into good; we sin, I dare not say by His temptation, but I must say with His consent; and to any but the brutish man his sins are the beginning of wisdom. God has warned you by this crime; He warns you still by the bloody grave between our feet; and if there shall follow no repentance, no improvement, no return to Him, what can we look for but the following of some memorable judgment?"

Even as I spoke the words, the eyes of my uncle wandered from my face. A change fell upon his looks that cannot be described; his features seemed to dwindle in size, the colour faded from his cheeks, one hand rose waveringly and pointed over my shoulder into the distance, and the oft-repeated name fell once more from his lips: "The *Christ-Anna!*"

I turned; and if I was not appalled to the same degree, as I return thanks to Heaven that I had not the cause, I was still startled by the sight that met my eyes. The form of a man stood upright on the cabin-hutch of the wrecked ship; his back was towards us; he appeared to be scanning the offing with shaded eyes, and his figure was relieved to its full height, which was plainly very great, against the sea and sky. I have said a thousand times that I am not superstitious; but at that moment, with my mind running upon death and sin, the unexplained appearance of a stranger on that sea-girt, solitary island filled me with a surprise that bordered close on terror. It seemed scarce possible that any human soul should have come ashore alive in such a sea as had raged last night along the coasts of Aros; and the only vessel within miles had gone down before our eyes among the Merry Men. I was assailed with doubts that made suspense unbearable, and, to put the matter to the touch at once, stepped forward and hailed the figure like a ship.

He turned about, and I thought he started to behold us. At this my courage instantly revived, and I called and signed to him to draw near, and he, on his part, dropped immediately to the sands, and began slowly to approach, with many stops and hesitations. At each repeated mark of the man's uneasiness I grew the more confident myself; and I advanced another step, encouraging him as I did so with my head and hand. It was plain the castaway had heard indifferent accounts of our island hospitality; and indeed, about this time, the people farther north had a sorry reputation.

"Why," I said, "the man is black!"

And just at that moment, in a voice that I could scarce have recognised, my kinsman began swearing and praying in a mingled stream. I looked at him; he had fallen on his knees, his face was agonised; at each step of the castaway's the pitch of his voice rose, the volubility of his utterance and the fervour of his language redoubled. I call it prayer, for it was addressed to God; but surely no such ranting incongruities were ever before addressed to the Creator by a creature: surely if prayer can be a sin, this mad harangue was sinful. I ran to my kinsman, I seized him by the shoulders, I dragged him to his feet.

"Silence, man," said I, "respect your God in words, if not in action. Here, on the very scene of your transgressions, He sends you an occasion of atonement. Forward and embrace it; welcome like a father yon creature who comes trembling to your mercy."

With that, I tried to force him towards the black; but he felled me to the ground, burst from my grasp, leaving the shoulder of his jacket, and fled up the hillside towards the top of Aros like a deer. I staggered to my feet again, bruised and somewhat stunned; the negro had paused in surprise, perhaps in terror, some halfway between me and the wreck; my uncle was already far away, bounding from rock to rock; and I thus found myself torn for a time between two duties. But I judged, and I pray Heaven that I judged rightly, in favour of the poor wretch upon the sands; his misfortune was at least not plainly of his own creation; it was one, besides, that I could certainly relieve; and I had begun by that time to regard my uncle as an incurable and dismal lunatic. I advanced accordingly towards the black, who now awaited my approach with folded arms, like one prepared for either destiny. As I came nearer, he reached forth his hand with a great gesture, such as I had seen from the pulpit, and spoke to me in something of a pulpit voice, but not a word was comprehensible. I tried him first in English, then in Gaelic, both in vain; so that it was clear we must rely upon the tongue of looks and gestures. Thereupon I signed to him to follow me, which he did readily and with a grave obeisance like a fallen king; all the while there had come no shade of alteration in his face, neither of anxiety while he was still waiting, nor of relief now that he was reassured; if he were a slave, as I supposed, I could not but judge he must have fallen from some high place in his own country, and fallen as he was, I could not but admire his bearing. As we passed the grave, I paused and raised my hands and eyes to heaven in token of respect and sorrow for the dead; and he, as if in answer, bowed low and spread his hands abroad; it was a strange motion, but done like a thing of common custom; and I supposed it was ceremonial in the land from which he came. At the same time he pointed to my uncle, whom we could just see perched upon a knoll, and touched his head to indicate that he was mad.

We took the long way round the shore, for I feared to excite my uncle if we struck across the island; and as we walked, I had time enough to mature the little dramatic exhibition by which I hoped to satisfy my doubts. Accordingly, pausing on a rock, I proceeded to imitate before the negro the action of the man whom I had seen the day before taking bearings with the compass at Sandag. He understood me at once, and, taking the imitation out of my hands, showed me where the boat was, pointed out seaward as if to indicate the position of the schooner, and then down along the edge of the rock with the words "Espirito Santo," strangely pronounced, but clear enough for recognition. I had thus been right in my conjecture; the pretended historical inquiry had been but a cloak for treasure hunting; the man who had played on Dr. Robertson was the same as the foreigner who visited Grisapol in spring, and now, with many others, lay dead under the Roost of Aros: there had their greed brought them, there should their bones be tossed for evermore. In the meantime the black continued his imitation of the scene, now looking up skyward as though watching the approach of the storm; now, in the character of a seaman, waving the rest to come aboard; now as an officer, running along the rock and entering the boat; and anon bending over imaginary oars with the air of a hurried boatman; but all with the same solemnity of manner, so that I was never even moved to smile. Lastly, he indicated to me, by a pantomime not to be described in words, how he himself had gone up to examine the stranded wreck, and, to his grief and indignation, had been deserted by his comrades; and thereupon folded his arms once more, and stooped his head, like one accepting fate.

The mystery of his presence being thus solved for me, I explained to him by means of a sketch the fate of the vessel and of all aboard her. He showed no surprise nor sorrow, and, with a sudden lifting of his open hand, seemed to dismiss his former friends or masters (whichever they had been) into God's pleasure. Respect came upon me and grew stronger, the more I observed him; I saw he had a powerful mind and a sober and severe character, such as I loved to commune with; and before we reached the house of Aros I had almost forgotten, and wholly forgiven him, his uncanny colour.

To Mary I told all that had passed without suppression, though I own my heart failed me; but I did wrong to doubt her sense of justice.

"You did the right," she said. "God's will be done." And she set out meat for us at once.

As soon as I was satisfied, I bade Rorie keep an eye upon the castaway, who was still eating, and set forth again myself to find my uncle. I had not gone far before I saw him sitting in the same place, upon the very topmost knoll, and seemingly in the same attitude as when I had last observed him. From that point, as I have said, the most of Aros and the neighbouring Ross would be spread below him like a map; and it was plain that he kept a bright lookout in all directions, for my head had scarcely risen above the summit of the first ascent before he had leaped to his feet and turned as if to face me. I hailed him at once, as well as I was able, in the same tones and words as I had often used before, when I had come to summon him to dinner. He made not so much as a movement in reply. I passed on a little farther, and again tried parley, with the same result. But when I began a second time to advance, his insane fears blazed up again, and still in dead silence, but with incredible speed, he began to flee from before me along the rocky summit of the hill. An hour before, he had been dead weary, and I had been comparatively active. But now his strength was recruited by the fervour of insanity, and it would have been vain for me to dream of pursuit. Nay, the very attempt, I thought, might have inflamed his terrors, and thus increased the miseries of our position. And I had nothing left but to turn homeward and make my sad report to Mary.

She heard it, as she had heard the first, with a concerned composure, and, bidding me lie down and take that rest of which I stood so much in need, set forth herself in quest of her misguided father. At that age it would have been a strange thing that put me from either meat or sleep; I slept long and deep; and it was already long past noon before I awoke and came downstairs into the kitchen. Mary, Rorie, and the black castaway were seated about the fire in silence; and I could see that Mary had been weeping. There was cause enough, as I soon learned, for tears. First she, and then Rorie, had been forth to seek my uncle; each in turn had found him perched upon the hilltop, and from each in turn he had silently and swiftly fled. Rorie had tried to chase him, but in vain; madness lent a new vigour to his bounds; he sprang from rock to rock over the widest gullies; he scoured like the wind along the hilltops; he doubled and twisted like a hare before the dogs; and Rorie at length gave in; and the last that he saw, my uncle was seated as before upon the crest of Aros. Even during the hottest excitement of the chase, even when the fleet-footed servant had come, for a moment, very near to capture him, the poor lunatic had uttered not a sound. He fled, and he was silent, like a beast; and this silence had terrified his pursuer.

There was something heartbreaking in the situation. How to capture the madman, how to feed him in the meanwhile, and what to do with him when he was captured, were the three difficulties that we had to solve.

"The black," said I, "is the cause of this attack. It may even be his presence in the house that keeps my uncle on the hill. We have done the fair thing; he has been fed and warmed under this roof; now I propose that Rorie put him across the bay in the coble, and take him through the Ross as far as Grisapol."

In this proposal Mary heartily concurred; and bidding the black follow us, we all three descended to the pier. Certainly, Heaven's will was declared against Gordon Darnaway; a thing had happened, never paralleled before in Aros; during the storm, the coble had broken loose, and, striking on the rough splinters of the pier, now lay in four feet of water with one side stove in. Three days of work at least would be required to make her float. But I was not to be beaten. I led the whole party round to where the gut was narrowest, swam to the other side, and called to the black to follow me. He signed, with the same clearness and quiet as before, that he knew not the art; and there was truth apparent in his signals, it would have occurred to none of us to doubt his truth; and that hope being over, we must all go back even as we came to the house of Aros, the negro walking in our midst without embarrassment.

All we could do that day was to make one more attempt to communicate with the unhappy madman. Again he was visible on his perch; again he fled in silence. But food and a great cloak were at least left for his comfort; the rain, besides, had cleared away, and the night promised to be even warm. We might compose ourselves, we thought, until the morrow; rest was the chief requisite, that we might be strengthened for unusual exertions; and as none cared to talk, we separated at an early hour.

I lay long awake, planning a campaign for the morrow. I was to place the black on the side of Sandag, whence he should head my uncle towards the house; Rorie in the west, I on the east, were to complete the cordon, as best we might. It seemed to me, the more I recalled the configuration of the island, that it should be possible, though hard, to force him down upon the low ground along Aros Bay; and once there, even with the strength of his madness, ultimate escape was hardly to be feared. It was on his terror of the black that I relied; for I made sure, however he might run, it would not be in the direction of the man whom he supposed to have returned from the dead, and thus one point of the compass at least would be secure.

When at length I fell asleep, it was to be awakened shortly after by a dream of wrecks, black men, and submarine adventure; and I found myself so shaken and fevered that I arose, descended the stair, and stepped out before the house. Within, Rorie and the black were asleep together in the kitchen; outside was a wonderful clear night of stars, with here and there a cloud still hanging, last stragglers of the tempest. It was near the top of the flood, and the Merry Men were roaring in the windless quiet of the night. Never, not even in the height of the tempest, had I heard their song with greater awe. Now, when the winds were gathered home, when the deep was dandling itself back into its summer slumber, and when the stars rained their gentle light over land and sea, the voice of these tide-breakers was still raised for havoc. They seemed, indeed, to be a part of the world's evil and the tragic side of life. Nor were their meaningless vociferations the only sounds that broke the silence of the night. For I could hear, now shrill and thrilling and now almost drowned, the note of a human voice that accompanied the uproar of the Roost. I knew it for my kinsman's; and a great fear fell upon me of God's judgments, and the evil in the world. I went back again into the darkness of the house as into a place of shelter, and lay long upon my bed, pondering these mysteries.

It was late when I again woke, and I leaped into my clothes and hurried to the kitchen. No one was there; Rorie and the black had both stealthily departed long before; and my heart stood still at the discovery. I could rely on Rorie's heart, but I placed no trust in his discretion. If he had thus set out without a word, he was plainly bent upon some service to my uncle. But what service could he hope to render even alone, far less in the company of the man in whom my uncle found his fears incarnated? Even if I were not already too late to prevent some deadly mischief, it was plain I must delay no longer. With the thought I was out of the house; and often as I have run on the rough sides of Aros, I never ran as I did that fatal morning. I do not believe I put twelve minutes to the whole ascent.

My uncle was gone from his perch. The basket had indeed been torn open and the meat scattered on the turf; but, as we found afterwards, no mouthful had been tasted; and there was not another trace of human existence in that wide field of view. Day had already filled the clear heavens; the sun already lighted in a rosy bloom upon the crest of Ben Kyaw; but all below me the rude knolls of Aros and the shield of sea lay steeped in the clear darkling twilight of the dawn.

"Rorie!" I cried; and again "Rorie!" My voice died in the silence, but there came no answer back. If there were indeed an enterprise afoot to catch my uncle, it was plainly not in fleetness of foot, but in dexterity of stalking, that the hunters placed their trust. I ran on farther, keeping the higher spurs, and looking right and left, nor did I pause again till I was on the mount above Sandag. I could see the wreck, the uncovered belt of sand, the waves idly beating, the long ledge of rocks, and on either hand the tumbled knolls, boulders, and gullies of the island. But still no human thing.

At a stride the sunshine fell on Aros, and the shadows and colours leaped into being. Not half a moment later, below me to the west, sheep began to scatter as in a panic. There came a cry. I saw my uncle running. I saw the black jump up in hot pursuit; and before I had time to understand, Rorie also had appeared, calling directions in Gaelic as to a dog herding sheep.

I took to my heels to interfere, and perhaps I had done better to have waited where I was, for I was the means of cutting off the madman's last escape. There was nothing before him from that moment but the grave, the wreck, and the sea in Sandag Bay. And yet Heaven knows that what I did was for the best.

My uncle Gordon saw in what direction, horrible to him, the chase was driving him. He doubled, darting to the right and left; but high as the fever ran in his veins, the black was still the swifter. Turn where he would, he was still forestalled, still driven toward the scene of his crime. Suddenly he began to shriek aloud, so that the coast re-echoed; and now both I and Rorie were calling on the black to stop. But all was vain, for it was written otherwise. The pursuer still ran, the chase still sped before him screaming; they avoided the grave, and skimmed close past the timbers of the wreck; in a breath they had cleared the sand; and still my kinsman did not pause, but dashed straight into the surf; and the black, now almost within reach, still followed swiftly behind him. Rorie and I both stopped, for the thing was now beyond the hands of men, and these were the decrees of God that came to pass before our eyes. There was never a sharper ending. On that steep beach they were beyond their depth at a bound; neither could swim; the black rose once for a moment with a throttling cry; but the current had them, racing seaward; and if ever they came up again, which God alone can tell, it would be ten minutes after, at the far end of Aros Roost, where the seabirds hover fishing.

MARKHEIM

Yes," said the dealer, "our windfalls are of various kinds. Some customers are ignorant, and then I touch a dividend on my superior knowledge. Some are dishonest," and here he held up the candle, so that the light fell strongly on his visitor, "and in that case," he continued, "I profit by my virtue."

Markheim had but just entered from the daylight streets, and his eyes had not yet grown familiar with the mingled shine and darkness in the shop. At these pointed words, and before the near presence of the flame, he blinked painfully and looked aside.

The dealer chuckled. "You come to me on Christmas Day," he resumed, "when you know that I am alone in my house, put up my shutters, and make a point of refusing business. Well, you will have to pay for that; you will have to pay for my derangement, when I should be balancing my books; you will have to pay, besides, for a kind of manner that I remark in you today very strongly. I am the essence of discretion, and ask no awkward question; but when a customer cannot look me in the eye, he has to pay for it." The dealer once more chuckled; and then, changing to his usual business voice though still with a note of irony: "You can give, as usual, a clear account of how you came into the possession of the object?" he continued. "Still your uncle's cabinet? A remarkable collector, sir!"

And the little, pale, round-shouldered dealer, stood almost on tiptoe, looking over the top of his gold spectacles, and nodding his head with every mark of disbelief. Markheim returned his gaze with one of infinite pity, and a touch of horror.

"This time," said he, "you are in error. I have not come to sell, but to buy. I have no curios to dispose of; my uncle's cabinet is bare to the wainscot; even were it still intact, I have done well on the stock exchange, and should more likely add to it than otherwise; and my errand today is simplicity itself. I seek a Christmas present for a lady," he continued waxing more fluent as he struck into the speech he had prepared; "and certainly I owe you every excuse for thus disturbing you upon so small a matter. But the thing was neglected yesterday; I must produce my little compliment at dinner; and as you very well know, a rich marriage is not a thing to be neglected."

There followed a pause during which the dealer seemed to weigh this statement incredulously. The ticking of many clocks among the curious lumber of the shop, and the faint rushing of the cabs in a near thoroughfare, filled up the interval of silence.

"Well, sir," said the dealer, "be it so. You are an old customer after all; and if, as you say you have the chance of a good marriage, far be it from me to be an obstacle. Here is a nice thing for a lady now," he went on, "this hand glass: fifteenth century, warranted; comes from a good collection, too; but I reserve the name in the interests of my customer, who was just like yourself, my dear sir, the nephew and sole heir of a re-markable collector.

The dealer, while he thus ran on in his dry and biting voice, had stooped to take the object from its place; and as he had done so, a shock had passed through Markheim, a start both of hand and foot, a sudden leap of many tumultuous passions to the face. It passed as swiftly as it came, and left no trace beyond a certain tremulousness in the hand that now received the glass.

"A glass?" he said, hoarsely, and then paused, and repeated it more clearly. "A glass? For Christmas? Surely not?"

"And why not?" cried the dealer. "Why not a glass?"

Markheim was looking upon him with an indefinable expression. "You ask me why not?" he said. "Why, look here—look in it—look at yourself! Do you like to see it? No! nor I—nor any man."

The little man had jumped back when Markheim had so suddenly confronted him with the mirror; but now, perceiving there was nothing worse on hand, he chuckled. "Your future lady, sir, must be pretty hard favoured," said he.

"No," said Markheim, with great conviction. "But about you: I ask you for a Christmas present and you give me this—this damned reminder of years and sins and follies, this hand-conscience! Did you mean it? Had you a thought in your mind? Tell me. It will be better for you if you do. Come, tell me about yourself. I hazard a guess now, that you are in secret a very charitable man?"

The dealer looked closely at his companion; it was very odd, Markheim did not appear to be laughing; there was something in his face like an eager sparkle of hope, but nothing of mirth.

"What are you driving at?" the dealer asked.

"Not charitable?" returned the other, gloomily. "Not charitable; not pious; not scrupulous; unloving, unbeloved; a hand to get money, a safe to keep it. Is that all? dear God, man, is that all?"

"I will tell you what it is," began the dealer, with some sharpness, and then broke off again into a chuckle. "But I see this is a love match of yours, and you have been drinking the lady's health."

"Ah!" cried Markheim, with a strange curiosity. "Ah, have you been in love? Tell me about that."

"I?" cried the dealer. "I in love! I never had the time, nor have I the time today for all this nonsense. Will you take the glass?"

"Where is the hurry?" returned Markheim. "It is very pleasant to stand here talking; and life is so short and insecure that I would not hurry away from any pleasure—no, not even from so mild a one as this. We should rather cling, cling to what little we can get, like a man at a cliff's edge. Every second is a cliff, if you think upon it: a cliff a mile high, high enough, if we fall, to dash us out of every feature of humanity. Hence it is best to talk pleasantly. Let us talk of each other; why should we wear this mask? Let us be confidential. Who knows, we might become friends?"

"I have just one word to say to you," said the dealer: "Either make your purchase, or walk out of my shop!"

"True, true," said Markheim. "Enough fooling. To business. Show me something else."

The dealer stooped once more, this time to replace the glass upon the shelf, his thin, blond hair falling over his eyes as he did so. Markheim moved a little nearer, with one hand in the pocket of his greatcoat; he drew himself up and filled his lungs; at the same time many different emotions were depicted together on his face—terror, horror, and resolve, fascination and a physical repulsion; and through a haggard lift of his upper lip his teeth looked out.

"This perhaps may suit," observed the dealer; and then, as he began to re-arise, Markheim bounded from behind upon his victim. The long, skewerlike dagger flashed and fell. The dealer struggled like a hen, striking his temple on the shelf, and then tumbled on the floor in a heap.

Time had some score of small voices in that shop, some stately and slow as was becoming to their great age; others garrulous and hurried. All these told out the seconds in an intricate chorus of tickings. Then the passage of a lad's feet, heavily running on the pavement, broke in upon these smaller noises and startled Markheim into the consciousness of his surroundings. He looked about him awfully. The candle stood on the counter, its flame solemnly wagging in a draught; and by that inconsiderable movement, the whole room was filled with noiseless bustle, and kept heaving like a sea: the tall shadows nodding, the gross blots of darkness swelling and dwindling as with respiration, the faces of the portraits and the China gods changing and wavering like images in water. The inner door stood ajar, and peered into that leaguer of shadows with a long slit of daylight like a pointing finger.

From these fear-stricken rovings, Markheim's eyes returned to the body of his victim, where it lay both humped and sprawling, incredibly small, and strangely meaner than in life. In these poor miserly clothes, in that ungainly attitude, the dealer lay like so much sawdust. Markheim had feared to see it, and lo! it was nothing. And yet as he gazed, this bundle of old clothes and pool of blood began to find eloquent voices. There it must lie; there was none to work the cunning hinges or direct the miracle of locomotion—there it must lie till it was found. Found? ay, and then? Then would this dead flesh lift up a cry that would echo over England, and fill the world with the echoes of pursuit. Ay, dead or not, this was still the enemy. "Time was that when the brains were out," he thought; and the first word struck into his mind. Time, now that the deed was accomplished—time, which had closed for the victim, had become instant and momentous for the slayer.

The thought was yet in his mind, when first one and then another, with every variety of pace and voice, one deep as the bell from a cathedral turret, another ringing on its treble notes the prelude of a waltz, the clocks began to strike the hour of three in the afternoon.

The sudden outbreak of so many tongues in that dumb chamber staggered him. He began to bestir himself, going to and fro with the candle, beleaguered by moving shadows, and startled to the soul by chance reflections. In many rich mirrors, some of home design, some from Venice or Amsterdam, he saw his face repeated and repeated, as it were an army of spies; his own eyes met and detected him; and the sound of his own steps, lightly as they fell, vexed the surrounding quiet. And still as he continued to fill his pockets, his mind accused him with a sickening iteration of the thousand faults of his design. He should have chosen a more quiet hour; he should have prepared an alibi; he should not have used a knife; he should have been more cautious, and only bound and gagged the dealer, and not killed him; he should have been more bold, and killed the servant also; he should have done all things otherwise: poignant regrets, weary, incessant toiling of the mind to change what was unchangeable, to plan what was now useless, to be the architect of the irrevocable past. Meanwhile, and behind all this activity, brute terrors, like the scurrying of rats in a deserted attic, filled the more remote chambers of his brain with riot: the hand of the constable would fall heavy on his shoulder, and his nerves would jerk like a hooked fish; or he beheld, in galloping defile, the dock, the prison, the gallows and the black coffin.

Terror of the people in the street sat down before his mind like a besieging army. It was impossible, he thought, but that some rumour of the struggle must have reached their ears and set on edge their curiosity; and now in all the neighbouring houses, he divined them sitting motionless and with uplifted ear: solitary people, condemned to spend Christmas dwelling alone on memories of the past, and now startingly recalled from that tender exercise; happy, family parties struck into silence round the table, the mother still with raised finger: every degree and age and humour, but all, by their own hearths, prying and hearkening and weaving the rope that was to hang him. Sometimes it seemed to him he could not move too softly; the clink of the tall Bohemian goblets rang out loudly like a bell; and alarmed by the bigness of the ticking, he was tempted to stop the clocks. And then again, with a swift transition of his terrors, the very silence of the house appeared a source of peril, and a thing to strike and freeze the passer-by; and he would step more boldly, and bustle aloud among the contents of the shop, and imitate, with elaborate bravado, the movements of a busy man at ease in his own house.

But he was now so pulled about by different alarms, that while one portion of his mind was still alert and cunning, another trembled on the brink of lunacy. One hallucination, in particular took a strong hold on his credulity. The neighbour hearkening with white face beside his window, the passer-by arrested by a horrible surmise on the pavement—these could at worst suspect, they could not know; through the brick walls and shuttered windows, only sounds could penetrate. But here, within the house, was he alone? He knew he was; he had watched the servant set forth sweethearting, in her poor best, "out for the day" written in every ribbon and smile. Yes, he was alone of course; and yet in the bulk of empty house above him, he could surely hear a stir of delicate footing—he was surely conscious, inexplicably conscious of some presence. Ay, surely: to every room and corner of the house his imagination followed it; and now it was a faceless thing, that yet had eyes to see with; and again it was a shadow of himself; and yet again, and behold the image of the dead dealer reinspired with cunning and hatred.

At times, with a strong effort, he would glance at the open door which still seemed to repel his eyes. The house was tall, the skylight small and dirty, the day blind with fog; and the light that filtered down to the ground story was exceeding faint and showed dimly on the threshold of the shop. And yet, in that strip of doubtful brightness, did there not hang wavering a shadow?

Suddenly from the street outside, a very jovial gentleman began to beat with a staff on the shop door, accompanying his blows with shouts and railleries in which the dealer was continually called upon by name. Markheim, smitten into ice, glanced at the dead man. But no; he lay quite still; he was fled away far beyond earshot of these blows and shoutings; he was sunk beneath seas of silence; and his name, which would once have caught his notice above the howling of a storm, had become an empty sound. And presently the jovial gentleman desisted from his knocking and departed.

Here was a broad hint to hurry what remained to be done, to get forth from this accusing neighbourhood, to plunge into a bath of London multitudes, and to reach, on the other side of day, that haven of safety and apparent innocence—his bed. One visitor had come; at any moment another might follow and be more obstinate. To have done the deed, and yet not to reap the profit, would be too abhorred a failure. The money, that was now Markheim's concern; and as a means to that, the keys.

He glanced over his shoulder at the open door, where the shadow was still lingering and shivering; and with no conscious repugnance of the mind, yet with a tremor of the belly, he drew near the body of his victim. The human character had quite departed; like a suit half-stuffed with bran, the limbs lay scattered, the trunk doubled, on the floor; and yet the thing repelled him. Although so dingy and inconsiderable to the eye, he feared it might have more significance to the touch. He took the body by the shoulders and turned it on its back. It was strangely light and supple, and the limbs, as if they had been broken, fell into the oddest postures. The face was robbed of all expression; but it was as pale as wax and shockingly smeared with blood about one temple. That was, for Markheim, the one displeasing circumstance. It carried him back upon the instant to a certain fair-day in a fishers' village: a gray day, a piping wind, a crowd upon the street, the blare of brasses, the booming of drums, the nasal voice of a ballad singer; and a boy going to and fro, buried over head in the crowd and divided between interest and fear, until, coming out upon the chief place of con-course, he beheld a booth and a great screen with pictures, dismally designed, garishly coloured: Brownrigg with her apprentice, the Mannings with their murdered guest, Weare in the death-grip of Thurtell, and a score besides of famous crimes. The thing was as clear as an illusion; he had shrunk back into that little boy; he was looking once again, and with the same sense of physical revolt, at these vile pictures; he was still stunned by the thumping of the drums. A bar of that day's music returned upon his memory; and at that, for the first time, a qualm came over him, a breath of nausea, a sudden weakness of the joints, which he must instantly resist and conquer.

He judged it more prudent to confront than to flee from these considerations; looking the more hardily in the dead face, bending his mind to realise the nature and greatness of his crime. So little a while ago that face had moved with every change of sentiment, that pale mouth had spoken, that body had been all on fire with governable energies; and now, and by his act, that piece of life had been arrested, as the horologist, with interjected finger, arrests the beating of the clock. So he reasoned in vain; he could rise to no remorseful consciousness; the same heart which had shuddered before these painted effigies of crime, looked on its reality unmoved. At best, he felt a gleam of pity, for one who had been endowed in vain with all those faculties that can make the world a garden of enchantment, one who had never lived and who was now dead. But of penitence, no, not a tremor.

With that, shaking himself clear of these considerations, he found the keys and advanced towards the open door of the shop. Outside, it had begun to rain smartly; and the sound of the shower upon the roof had banished silence. Like some dropping cavern, the chambers of the house were haunted by a faint, incessant echoing, which filled the ear and mingled with the ticking of the clocks. And as Markheim approached the door he seemed to hear, in answer to his own cautious tread, the steps of another foot withdrawing up the stair. The shadow still palpitated loosely on the threshold. He threw a ton's weight of resolve upon his muscles, and drew back the door.

The faint, foggy daylight glimmered dimly on the bare floor and stairs; on the bright suit of armour posted, halbert in hand, upon the landing; and on the dark wood carvings and framed pictures that hung against the yellow panels of the wainscot. So loud was the beating of the rain through all the house that, in Markheim's ears, it began to be distinguished into many different sounds. Footsteps and sighs, the tread of regiments marching in the distance, the chink of money in the counting, and the creaking of doors held stealthily ajar, appeared to mingle with the patter of the drops upon the cupola and the gushing of the water in the pipes. The sense that he was not alone grew upon him to the verge of madness. On every side he was hunted and begirt by presences. He heard them moving stealthily in the upper chambers; from the shop, he heard the dead man getting to his legs; and as he began with a great effort to mount the stairs, feet fled quietly before him and followed guardedly behind. If he were but deaf, he thought, how tranquilly he would possess his soul! And then again, and hearkening with ever fresh attention, he blessed himself for that unresting sense which held the outposts and stood a trusty sentinel upon his life. His head turned continually on his neck; his eyes, which seemed starting from their orbits, scouted on every side, and on every side were half-rewarded as with the tail of something nameless vanishing. The four and twenty steps to the first floor were four and twenty agonies.

On that first story, the doors stood ajar, three of them like three ambushes, shaking his nerves like the throats of cannon. He could never again, he felt, be sufficiently immured and fortified from men's observing eyes; the sole joy for which he longed was to be home, girt in by walls, buried among bed clothes, and invisible to all but God. And at the thought he wondered a little, recollecting tales of other murderers and the fear they were said to entertain of heavenly avengers. It was not so, at least, with him. He feared the laws of nature lest, in their callous and immutable procedure, they should preserve some damning evidence of his crime. He feared tenfold more, with a slavish, superstitious terror, some scission in the continuity of man's experience, some wilful illegality of nature. He played a game of skill, depending on the rules, calculating consequence from cause; and what if nature, as the defeated tyrant overthrew the chessboard, should break the mould of their succession? The like had befallen Napoleon (so writers said) when the winter changed the time of its appearance. The like might befall Markheim: the solid walls might become transparent and reveal his doings like those of bees in a glass hive; the stout planks might yield under his foot like quicksands and detain him in their clutch; ay, and there were soberer accidents that might destroy him, if, for instance, the house should fall and imprison him beside the body of his victim; or the house next door should fly on fire, and the firemen invade him from all sides. These things he feared; and in a sense these things might be called the hands of God reached forth against sin. But about God himself he was at ease; his act was doubtless exceptional, but so were his excuses, which God knew; it was there, and not among men, that he felt sure of justice.

When he had got safe into the drawing room and shut the door behind him, he was aware of a respite from alarms. The room was quite dismantled, uncarpeted besides, and strewn with packing cases and incongruous furniture; several great pier-glasses, in which he beheld himself at various angles, like an actor on a theatre; many pictures, framed and unframed, standing with their faces to the wall; a fine Sheraton sideboard, a cabinet of marquetry, and a great old bed with tapestry hangings. The windows opened to the floor; but by great good fortune the lower part of the shutters had been closed, and this concealed him from the neighbours. Here then Markheim drew in a packing case before the cabinet, and began to search among the keys. It was a long business, for there were many; and it was irksome, besides; for after all there might be nothing in the cabinet, and time was on the wing. But the closeness of the occupation sobered him. With the tail of his eye he saw the door; even glanced at it, from time to time directly, like a besieged commander pleased to verify the good estate of his defences. But in truth he was at peace. The rain falling in the street sounded natural and pleasant. Presently, on the other side, the notes of a piano were wakened to the music of a hymn, and the voices of many children took up the air and words. How stately, how comfortable was the melody! how fresh the youthful voices! Markheim gave ear to it smilingly, as he sorted out the keys; and his mind was thronged with answerable ideas and images; churchgoing children and the pealing of the high organ; children afield, bathers by the brookside, ramblers on the brambly common, kite-flyers in the windy and cloud-navigated sky; and then, at another cadence of the hymn, back again to church, and the somnolence of summer Sundays, and the high genteel voice of the parson (which he smiled a little to recall) and the painted Jacobean tombs, and the dim lettering of the ten commandments in the chancel.

And as he sat thus, at once busy and absent, he was startled to his feet. A flash of ice, a flash of fire, a bursting gush of blood, went over him, and then he stood transfixed and thrilling. A step mounted the stair slowly and steadily; and presently a hand was laid upon the knob, and the lock clicked, and the door opened. Fear held Markheim in a vice; what to expect he knew not, whether the dead man walking, or the official ministers of human justice, or some chance witness blindly stumbling in to consign him to the gallows. But when a face was thrust into the aperture, glanced round the room, looked at him, nodded and smiled as if in friendly recognition, and then withdrew again, and the door closed behind it—his fear broke loose from his control in a hoarse cry. At the sound of this, the visitant returned.

"Did you call me?" he asked pleasantly, and with that he entered the room, and closed the door behind him.

But Markheim stood and gazed at him with all his eyes. Perhaps there was a film upon his sight, but the outlines of the new-comer seemed to change and waver like those of the idols in the wavering candlelight of the shop; and at times, he thought he knew him; and at times he thought he bore a likeness to himself; and always, like a lump of living terror, there lay in his bosom the conviction, that this thing was not of the earth and not of God.

And yet the creature had a strange air of the commonplace, as he stepped in and stood looking on Markheim with a smile; and when he added: "You are looking for the money, I believe?" it was in the tones of everyday politeness.

Markheim made no answer.

"I should warn you," resumed the other, "that the maid has left her sweetheart earlier than usual, and will soon be here. If Mr. Markheim be found in this house, I need not describe to him the consequences."

"You know me?" cried the murderer.

The visitor smiled. "You have long been a favourite of mine," he said; "and I have long observed and often sought to help you."

"What are you?" cried Markheim. "The devil?"

"What I may be," returned the other, "cannot affect the service I propose to render you."

"It can," cried Markheim. "It does! Be helped by you? no, never!

not by you! You do not know me yet—thank God, you do not know me!"

"Know you?" replied the visitant, with a sort of kind severity or rather firmness, "I know you to the soul."

"Know me?" cried Markheim. "Who can do so? My life is but a travesty and slander on myself. I have lived to belie my nature. All men do; all men are better than this disguise that grows about and stifles them. You see each dragged away by life, like one whom bravos have seized and muffled in a cloak; if they had their own control—if you could see their faces, they would be altogether different, they would shine out for heroes and saints! I am worse than most; myself is more overlaid; my excuse is known to me and God. But had I the time, I could disclose myself."

"To me?" inquired the visitor.

"To you before all," returned the murderer. "I supposed you were intelligent; I thought—since you exist—you would prove a reader of the heart. And yet you would propose to judge me by my acts—think of it—my acts! I was born and I have lived in a land of giants; giants have dragged me by the wrists since I was born out of my mother—the giants of circumstance. And you would judge me by my acts! But can you not look within? Can you not understand that evil is hateful to me? Can you not see within me the clear writing of conscience, never blurred by any wilful sophistry, although too often disregarded? Can you not read me for a thing that surely must be common as humanity—the unwilling sinner?"

"All this is very feelingly expressed," was the reply, "but it regards me not. These points of casuistry are beyond my province; and I care not in the least by what compulsion you may have been dragged away, so as you are but carried in the right direction. But time flies; the servant delays, looking in the faces of the crowd and at the pictures on the hoardings; but still she keeps moving nearer; and remember, it is as if the gallows itself was walking towards you through the Christmas streets! Shall I help you—I, who know all? shall I tell you where to find the money?"

"For what price?" asked Markheim.

"I offer you the service for a Christmas gift," returned the other.

Markheim could not refrain from smiling with a kind of bitter triumph. "No," said he, "I will take nothing at your hands; if I were dying of thirst, and it was your hand that put the pitcher to my lips, I should find the courage to refuse it. It may be credulous, but I will do nothing to commit myself to evil."

"I have no objection to a death-bed repentance," observed the visitant.

"Because you disbelieve their efficacy!" Markheim cried.

"I do not say so," returned the other; "but I look on these things from a different side; and when the life is done, my interest falls. The man has lived to serve me, to spread black looks under colour of religion, or to sow tares in the wheatfield, as you do, in a course of weak compliance with desire. Now that he draws so near to his deliverance, he can add but one act of service—to repent, to die smiling, and thus to build up in confidence and hope the more timorous of my surviving followers. I am not so hard a master. Try me. Accept my help; please yourself in life as you have done hitherto; please yourself more amply, spread your elbows at the board; and when the night begins to fall and the curtains to be drawn, I tell you, for your greater comfort, that you will find it even easy to compound your quarrel with your conscience and to make a truckling peace with God. I came but now from such a deathbed; and the room was full of sincere mourners, listening to the man's last words; and when I looked into that face, which had been set as a flint against mercy, I found it smiling with hope."

"And do you then suppose me such a creature?" asked Markheim. "Do you think I have no more generous aspiration than to sin and sin and sin, and, at the last, sneak into heaven? My heart rises at the thought! Is this, then, your experience of mankind? or is it because you find me with red hands that you presume such baseness? and is this crime of murder indeed so impious as to dry up the very springs of good?"

"Murder is to me no special category," replied the other. "All sins are murder, even as all life is war. I behold your race, like starving mariners on a raft, plucking crusts out of the hands of famine and feeding on each other's lives. I follow sins beyond the moment of their acting; I find in all that the last consequence is death; and to my eyes, the pretty maid who thwarts her mother with such taking graces on a question of a ball, drips no less visibly with human gore than such a murderer as yourself. Do I say that I follow sins? I follow virtues also; they differ not by the thickness of a nail; they are both scythes for the reaping angel of death. Evil, for which I live, consists not in action but in character; the bad man is dear to me, not the bad act, whose fruits, if we could follow them far enough down the hurtling cataract of the ages, might yet be found more blessed than those of the rarest virtues; and it is not because you have killed a dealer, but because your name is Markheim, that I offer to forward your escape."

"I will lay my heart open to you," answered Markheim. "This crime on which you find me is my last. On my way to it, I have learned many lessons; itself is a lesson, a momentous lesson. Hitherto I have been driven with revolt to what I would not; I was a bond-slave to poverty, driven and scourged. There are robust virtues that can stand in these temptations; mine was not so, I had a thirst of pleasure. But today, and out of this deed, I pluck both warning and riches—both the power and a fresh resolve to be myself. I become in all things a free actor in the world; and I begin to see myself all changed, these hands the agents of good, this heart at peace. Something comes over me out of the past; something of what I have dreamed on sabbath evenings to the sound of the church-organ, of what I forecast when I shed tears over noble books or talked, an innocent child, with my mother. There lies my life; I have wandered a few years, but now I see once more my city of destination."

"You are to use this money on the stock exchange, I think?" remarked the visitor. "And there, if I mistake not, you have already lost some thousands."

"Ah," said Markheim, "but this time I have a sure thing."

"This time again, you will lose," replied the visitor quietly.

"Ah, but I keep back the half!" cried Markheim.

"That also you will lose," said the other.

The sweat started upon Markheim's brow. "Well, then, what matter?" he exclaimed. "Say it be lost, say I am plunged again in poverty, shall one part of me, and that the worse, continue until the end to override the better? Evil and good run strong in me, haling

me both ways. I do not love the one thing, I love all. I can conceive great deeds, renunciations, martyrdoms; and though I be fallen to such a crime as murder, pity is not stranger to my thoughts. I pity the poor—who knows their trials better than myself? I pity and help them; I prize love, I love honest laughter; there is no good thing nor true thing on earth, but I love it from my heart. And are my vices only to direct my life, and my virtues to lie without effect, like some passive lumber of the mind? Not so; good, also, is a spring of acts."

But the visitant raised his finger. "For six-and-thirty years that you have been in this world," said he, "through many changes of fortune and varieties of humour, I have watched you steadily fall. Fifteen years ago, you would have started at a theft. Three years back, you would have blenched at the name of murder. Is there any crime, is there any cruelty or meanness, from which you still recoil? Five years from now, I shall detect you in the fact! Downward, downward, lies your way; nor can anything but death avail to stop you."

"It is true," he said huskily. "I have in some degree complied with evil. But it is so with all: the very saints, in the mere exercise of living, grow less dainty and take on the tone of their surroundings."

"I will propound to you one simple question," said the other, "and as you answer, I shall read to you your moral horoscope. You have grown in many things more lax; possibly you do right to be so; and at any account, it is the same with all men. But granting that, are you in any one particular, however trifling, more difficult to please with your own conduct? Or do you go in all things with a looser rein?"

"In any one?" repeated Markheim, with an anguish of consideration. "No," he added, with despair, "in none! I have gone down in all."

"Then," said the visitor, "content yourself with what you are, for you will never change; and the words of your part on this stage are irrevocably written down."

Markheim stood for a long while silent, and indeed it was the visitor who first broke the silence. "That being so," he said, "shall I show you the money?"

"And grace?" cried Markheim.

"Have you not tried it?" returned the other. "Two or three years ago, did I not see you on the platform of revival meetings, and was not your voice the loudest in the hymn?"

"It is true," said Markheim, "and I see clearly what remains for me by way of duty. I thank you for these lessons from my soul; my eyes are opened and I behold myself at last for what I am."

At this moment, the sharp note of the door bell rang through the house; and the visitant, as though this were some concerted signal for which he had been waiting, sprang instantly upon his feet.

"The maid!" he cried. "She has returned, as I forewarned you, and there is now before you one more difficult passage. Her master, you must say, is ill; you must let her in, with an assured but rather serious countenance—no smiles, no overacting, and I promise you success! Once the girl within and the door closed, the same dexterity that has already rid you of the dealer will relieve you of this last danger in your path. Thenceforward, you have the whole evening— the whole night, if needful—to ransack the treasures of the house and to make good your safety. This is help that comes to you with the mask of danger. Up!" he cried; "up, friend; your life hangs trembling in the scales; up, and act!"

Markheim steadily regarded his counsellor. "If I be condemned to evil acts," he said, "there is still one door of freedom open: I can cease from action. If my life be an ill thing, I can lay it down. Though I be, as you say truly, at the beck of every small temptation, I can yet, by one decisive gesture, place myself beyond their reach. My love of good is damned to barrenness; it may, and let it be! But I have still my hatred of evil; and from that, to your galling disappointment, you shall see that I can draw both energy and courage."

The features of the visitor began to undergo a wonderful and lovely change: they brightened and softened with a tender triumph, and even as they brightened, faded and dislimned. But Markheim did not pause to watch or understand the transformation. He opened the door and went downstairs very slowly, thinking to himself. His past went soberly before him; he beheld it as it was, ugly and strenuous like a dream, random as chance-medley; a scene of defeat. Life, as he thus reviewed it, tempted him no longer; but on the farther side he perceived a quiet haven for his bark.

He paused in the passage, and looked into the shop where the candle still burned by the dead body. It was strangely silent. Thoughts of the dealer swarmed into his mind, as he stood gazing. And then the bell once more broke out into impatient clamour.

He confronted the maid upon the threshold with something like a smile.

"You had better go for the police," said he: "I have killed your master."

THRAWN JANET

The Reverend Murdoch Soulis was long minister of the moorland parish of Balweary, in the vale of Dule. A severe, bleak-faced old man, dreadful to his hearers, he dwelt in the last years of his life, without relative or servant or any human company, in the small and lonely manse under the Hanging Shaw. In spite of the iron composure of his features, his eye was wild, scared, and uncertain; and when he dwelt, in private admonitions, on the future of the impenitent, it seemed as if his eye pierced through the storms of time to the terrors of eternity. Many young persons, coming to prepare themselves against the season of the Holy Communion, were dreadfully affected by his talk. He had a sermon on 1st Peter, v. and 8th, "The devil as a roaring lion," on the Sunday after every seventeenth of August, and he was accustomed to surpass himself upon that text both by the appalling nature of the matter and the terror of his bearing in the pulpit. The children were frightened into fits, and the old looked more than usually oracular, and were, all that day, full of those hints that Hamlet deprecated. The manse itself, where it stood by the water of Dule among some thick trees, with the Shaw overhanging it on the one side, and on the other many cold, moorish hilltops rising towards the sky, had begun, at a very early period of Mr. Soulis's ministry, to be avoided in the dusk hours by all who valued themselves upon their prudence; and guidmen sitting at the clachan alehouse shook their heads together at the thought of passing late by that uncanny neighbourhood. There was one spot, to be more particular, which was regraded with especial awe. The manse stood between the high road and the water of Dule, with a gable to each; its back was towards the kirktown of Balweary, nearly half a mile away; in front of it, a bare garden, hedged with thorn, occupied the land between the river and the road. The house was two stories high, with two large rooms on each. It opened not directly on the garden, but on a causewayed path, or passage, giving on the road on the one hand, and closed on the other by the tall willows and elders that bordered on the stream. And it was this strip of causeway that enjoyed among the young parishioners of Balweary so infamous a reputation. The minister walked there often after dark, sometimes groaning aloud in the instancy of his unspoken prayers; and when he was from home, and the manse door was locked, the more daring schoolboys ventured, with beating hearts, to "follow my leader" across that legendary spot.

This atmosphere of terror, surrounding, as it did, a man of God of spotless character and orthodoxy, was a common cause of wonder and subject of inquiry among the few strangers who were led by chance or business into that unknown, outlying country. But many even of the people of the parish were ignorant of the strange events which had marked the first year of Mr. Soulis's ministrations; and among those who were better informed, some were naturally reticent, and others shy of that particular topic. Now and again, only, one of the older folk would warm into courage over his third tumbler, and recount the cause of the minister's strange looks and solitary life.

Fifty years syne, when Mr. Soulis cam first into Ba'weary, he was still a young man—a callant, the folk said—fu' o' book learnin' and grand at the exposition, but, as was natural in sae young a man, wi' nae leevin' experience in religion. The younger sort were greatly taken wi' his gifts and his gab; but auld, concerned, serious men and women were moved even to prayer for the young man, whom they took to be a self-deceiver, and the parish that was like to be sae ill-supplied. It was before the days o' the moderates—weary fa' them; but ill things are like guid—they baith come bit by bit, a pickle at a time; and there were folk even then that said the Lord had left the college professors to their ain devices, an' the lads that went to study wi' them wad hae done mair and better sittin' in a peat-bog, like their forbears of the persecution, wi' a Bible under their oxter and a speerit o' prayer in their heart. There was nae doubt, onyway, but that Mr. Soulis had been ower lang at the college. He was careful and troubled for mony things besides the ae thing needful. He had a feck o' books wi' him—mair than had ever been seen before in a' that presbytery; and a sair wark the carrier had wi' them, for they were a' like to have smoored in the Deil's Hag between this and Kilmackerlie. They were books o' divinity, to be sure, or so they ca'd them; but the serious were o' opinion there was little service for sae mony, when the hail o' God's Word would gang in the neuk of a plaid. Then he wad sit half the day and half the nicht forbye, which was scant decent—writin', nae less; and first, they were feared he wad read his sermons; and syne it proved he was writin' a book himsel', which was surely no fittin' for ane of his years an' sma' experience.

Onyway it behoved him to get an auld, decent wife to keep the manse for him an' see to his bit denners; and he was recommended to an auld limmer—Janet M'Clour, they ca'd her—and sae far left to himsel' as to be ower persuaded. There was mony advised him to the contrar, for Janet was mair than suspeckit by the best folk in Ba'weary. Lang or that, she had had a wean to a dragoon; she hadnae come forrit* for maybe thretty year; and bairns had seen her mumblin' to hersel' up on Key's Loan in the gloamin', whilk was an unco time an' place for a God-fearin' woman. Howsoever, it was the laird himsel' that had first tauld the minister o' Janet; and in thae days he wad have gane a far gate to pleesure the laird. When folk tauld him that Janet was sib to the deil, it was a' superstition by his way of it; an' when they cast up the Bible to him an' the witch of Endor, he wad threep it doun their thrapples that thir days were a' gane by, and the deil was mercifully restrained.

Weel, when it got about the clachan that Janet M'Clour was to be servant at the manse, the folk were fair mad wi' her an' him thegether; and some o' the guidwives had nae better to dae than get round her door cheeks and chairge her wi' a' that was ken't again her, frae the sodger's bairn to John Tamson's twa kye. She was nae great speaker; folk usually let her gang her ain gate, an' she let them gang theirs, wi' neither Fair-guid-een nor Fair-guid-day; but when she

---

*To come forrit—to offer oneself as a communicant. [R.L.S.]

buckled to, she had a tongue to deave the miller. Up she got, an' there wasnae an auld story in Ba'weary but she gart somebody lowp for it that day; they couldnae say ae thing but she could say twa to it; till, at the hinder end, the guidwives up and claucht haud of her, and clawed the coats aff her back, and pu'd her doun the clachan to the water o' Dule, to see if she were a witch or no, soum or droun. The carline skirled till ye could hear her at the Hangin' Shaw, and she focht like ten; there was mony a guidwife bure the mark of her neist day an' mony a lang day after; and just in the hettest o' the collieshangie, wha suld come up (for his sins) but the new minister.

"Women," said he (and he had a grand voice), "I charge you in the Lord's name to let her go."

Janet ran to him—she was fair wud wi' terror—an' clang to him, an' prayed him, for Christ's sake, save her frae the cummers; an' they, for their pairt, tauld him a' that was ken't, and maybe mair.

"Woman," says he to Janet, "is this true?"

"As the Lord sees me," says she, "as the Lord made me, no a word o't. Forbye the bairn," says she, "I've been a decent woman a' my days."

"Will you," says Mr. Soulis, "in the name of God, and before me, His unworthy minister, renounce the devil and his works?"

Weel, it wad appear that when he askit that, she gave a girn that fairly frichtit them that saw her, an' they could hear her teeth play dirl thegether in her chafts; but there was naething for it but the ae way or the ither; an' Janet lifted up her hand and renounced the deil before them a'.

"And now," says Mr. Soulis to the guidwives, "home with ye, one and all, and pray to God for His forgiveness."

And he gied Janet his arm, though she had little on her but a sark, and took her up the clachan to her ain door like a leddy of the land; an' her scrieghin' and laughin' as was a scandal to be heard.

There were mony grave folk lang ower their prayers that nicht; but when the morn cam' there was sic a fear fell upon a' Ba'weary that the bairns hid theirsels, and even the men folk stood and keekit frae their doors. For there was Janet comin' doun the clachan—her or her likeness, nane could tell—wi' her neck thrawn, and her heid on ae side, like a body that has been hangit, and a girn on her face like an unstreakit corp. By an' by they got used wi' it, and even speered at her to ken what was wrang; but frae that day forth she couldnae speak like a Christian woman, but slavered and played click wi' her teeth like a pair o' shears; and frae that day forth the name o' God cam never on her lips. Whiles she wad try to say it, but it michtnae be. Them that kenned best said least; but they never gied that Thing the name o' Janet M'Clour; for the auld Janet, by their way o't, was in muckle hell that day. But the minister was neither to haud nor to bind; he preached about naething but the folk's cruelty that had gi'en her a stroke of the palsy; he skelpt the bairns that meddled her; and he had her up to the manse that same nicht, and dwalled there a' his lane wi' her under the Hangin' Shaw.

Weel, time gaed by: and the idler sort commenced to think mair lichtly o' that black business. The minister was weel thocht o'; he was aye late at the writing, folk wad see his can'le doon by the Dule water after twal' at e'en; and he seemed pleased wi' himsel' and upsitten as at first, though a' body could see that he was dwining. As for Janet she cam an' she gaed; if she didnae speak muckle afore, it was reason she should speak less then; she meddled naebody; but she was an eldritch thing to see, an' nane wad hae mistrysted wi' her for Ba'weary glebe.

About the end o' July there cam' a spell o' weather, the like o't never was in that country side; it was lown an' het an' heartless; the herds couldnae win up the Black Hill, the bairns were ower weariet to play; an' yet it was gousty too, wi' claps o' het wund that rumm'led in the glens, and bits o' shouers that slockened naething. We aye thocht it but to thun'er on the morn; but the morn cam, an' the morn's morning, and it was aye the same uncanny weather, sair on folks and bestial. Of a' that were the waur, nane suffered like Mr. Soulis; he could neither sleep nor eat, he tauld his elders; an' when he wasnae writin' at his weary book, he wad be stravaguin' ower a' the countryside like a man possessed, when a' body else was blythe to keep caller ben the house.

Abune Hangin' Shaw, in the bield o' the Black Hill, there's a bit enclosed grund wi' an iron yett; and it seems, in the auld days, that was the kirkyaird o' Ba'weary, and consecrated by the Papists before the blessed licht shone upon the kingdom. It was a great howff o'

Mr. Soulis's, onyway; there he would sit an' consider his sermons; and indeed it's a bieldy bit. Weel, as he cam ower the wast end o' the Black Hill, ae day, he saw first twa, an syne fower, an' syne seeven corbie craws fleein' round an' round abune the auld kirkyaird. They flew laigh and heavy, an' squawked to ither as they gaed; and it was clear to Mr. Soulis that something had put them frae their ordinar. He wasnae easy fleyed, an' gaed straucht up to the wa's; an' what suld he find there but a man, or the appearance of a man, sittin' in the inside upon a grave. He was of a great stature, an' black as hell, and his e'en were singular to see.* Mr. Soulis had heard tell o' black men, mony's the time; but there was something unco about this black man that daunted him. Het as he was, he took a kind o' cauld grue in the marrow o' his banes; but up he spak for a' that; an' says he: "My friend, are you a stranger in this place?" The black man answered never a word; he got upon his feet, an' begude to hirsle to the wa' on the far side; but he aye lookit at the minister; an' the minister stood an' lookit back; till a' in a meenute the black man was ower the wa' an' rinnin' for the bield o' the trees. Mr. Soulis, he hardly keened why, ran after him; but he was sair forjaskit wi' his walk an' the het, unhalesome weather; and rin as he likit, he got nae mair than a glisk o' the black man amang the birks, till he won doun to the foot o' the hillside, an' there he saw him ance mair, gaun, hap, step, an' lowp, ower Dule water to the manse.

Mr. Soulis wasnae weel pleased that this fearsome gangrel suld mak' sae free wi' Ba'weary manse; an' he ran the harder, an', wet shoon, ower the burn, an' up the walk; but the deil a black man was there to see. He stepped out upon the road, but there was naebody there; he gaed a' ower the gairden, but na, nae black man. At the hinder end, and a bit feared as was but natural, he lifted the hasp and into the manse; and there was Janet M'Clour before his een, wi' her thrawn craig, and nane sae pleased to see him. And he aye minded sinsyne, when first he set his een upon her, he had the same cauld and deidly grue.

*It was a common belief in Scotland that the devil appeared as a black man. This appears in several witch trials and I think in Law's *Memorials*, that delightful storehouse of the quaint and grisly. [R.L.S.]

"Janet," says he, "have you seen a black man?"

"A black man?" quo' she. "Save us a'! Ye're no wise, minister. There's nae black man in a' Ba'weary."

But she didnae speak plain, ye maun understand; but yam-yammered, like a powney wi' the bit in its moo.

"Weel," says he, "Janet, if there was nae black man, I have spoken with the Accuser of the Brethren."

And he sat down like ane wi' a fever, an' his teeth chittered in his heid.

"Hoots," says she, "think shame to yoursel', minister;" an' gied him a drap brandy that she keept aye by her.

Syne Mr. Soulis gaed into his study amang a' his books. It's a lang, laigh, mirk chalmer, perishin' cauld in winter, an' no very dry even in the tap o' the simmer, for the manse stands near the burn. Sae doun he sat, and thocht of a' that had come an' gane since he was in Ba'weary, an' his hame, an' the days when he was a bairn an' ran daffin' on the braes; and that black man aye ran in his heid like the owercome of a sang. Aye the mair he thocht, the mair he thocht o' the black man. He tried the prayer, an' the words wouldnae come to him; an' he tried, they say, to write at his book, but he could nae mak' nae mair o' that. There was whiles he thocht the black man was at his oxter, an' the swat stood upon him cauld as well-water; and there was other whiles, when he cam to himsel' like a christened bairn and minded naething.

The upshot was that he gaed to the window an' stood glowrin' at Dule water. The trees are unco thick, an' the water lies deep an' black under the manse; an' there was Janet washin' the cla'es wi' her coats kilted. She had her back to the minister, an' he, for his pairt, hardly kenned what he was lookin' at. Syne she turned round, an' shawed her face; Mr. Soulis had the same cauld grue as twice that day afore, an' it was borne in upon him what folk said, that Janet was deid lang syne, an' this was a bogle in the clay-cauld flesh. He drew back a pickle and he scanned her narrowly. She was tramp-trampin' in the cla'es, croonin' to hersel'; and eh! Gude guide us, but it was a fearsome face. Whiles she sang louder, but there was nae man born o' woman that could tell the words o' her sang; an' whiles she lookit side-lang doun, but there was naething there for her to look at. There gaed a scunner through the flesh upon his banes; and that was Heeven's advertisement. But Mr. Soulis just blamed himsel', he said, to think sae ill of a puir, auld afflicted wife that hadnae a freend forbye himsel'; an' he put up a bit prayer for him and her, an' drank a little caller water—for his heart rose again the meat—an' gaed up to his naked bed in the gloaming.

That was a nicht that has never been forgotten in Ba'weary, the nicht o' the seeventeenth of August, seventeen hun'er' an twal'. It had been het afore, as I hae said, but that nicht it was hetter than ever. The sun gaed doun amang unco-lookin' clouds; it fell as mirk as the pit; no a star, no a breath o' wund; ye couldnae see your han' afore your face, and even the auld folk cuist the covers frae their beds and lay pechin' for their breath. Wi' a' that he had upon his mind, it was gey and unlikely Mr. Soulis wad get muckle sleep. He lay an' he tummled; the gude, caller bed that he got into brunt his very banes; whiles he slept, and whiles he waukened; whiles he heard the time o' nicht, and whiles a tyke yowlin' up the muir, as if somebody was deid; whiles he thocht he heard bogles claverin' in his lug, an' whiles he saw spunkies in the room. He behoved, he judged, to be sick; an' sick he was—little he jaloosed the sickness.

At the hinder end, he got a clearness in his mind, sat up in his sark on the bedside, and fell thinkin' ance mair o' the black man an' Janet. He couldnae weel tell how—maybe it was the cauld to his feet—but it cam' in upon him wi' a spate that there was some connection between thir twa, an' that either or baith o' them were bogles. And just at that moment, in Janet's room, which was neist to his, there cam' a stramp o' feet as if men were wars'lin', an' then a loud bang; an' then a wund gaed reishling round the fower quarters of the house; an' then a' was aince mair as seelent as the grave.

Mr. Soulis was feared for neither man nor deevil. He got his tinderbox, an' lit a can'le, an' made three steps o't ower to Janet's door. It was on the hasp, an' he pushed it open, an' keeked bauldly in. It was a big room, as big as the minister's ain, an' plenished wi' grand, auld, solid gear, for he had naething else. There was a fower-posted bed wi' auld tapestry; and a braw cabinet of aik, that was fu' o' the minister's divinity books, an' put there to be out o' the gate; an' a wheen duds o' Janet's lying here and there about the floor. But nae Janet could Mr. Soulis see; nor ony sign of a contention. In he gaed (an' there's few that wad ha'e followed him) an' lookit a' round, an' listened. But there was naethin' to be heard, neither inside the manse nor in a Ba'weary parish, an' naethin' to be seen but the muckle shadows turnin' round the can'le. An' then a' at aince, the minister's heart played dunt an' stood stock-still; an' a cauld wund blew amang the hairs o' his heid. Whaten a weary sicht was that for the puir man's een! For there was Janet hangin' frae a nail beside the auld aik cabinet: her heid aye lay on her shoother, her een were steeked, the tongue projekit frae her mouth, and her heels were twa feet clear abune the floor.

"God forgive us all!" thocht Mr. Soulis; "poor Janet's dead."

He cam' a step nearer to the corp; an' then his heart fair whammled in his inside. For by what cantrip it wad ill-beseem a man to judge, she was hingin' frae a single nail an' by a single wursted thread for darnin' hose.

It's an awfu' thing to be your lane at nicht wi' siccan prodigies o' darkness; but Mr. Soulis was strong in the Lord. He turned an' gaed his ways oot o' that room, and lockit the door ahint him; and step by step, doon the stairs, as heavy as leed; and set doon the can'le on the table at the stairfoot. He couldnae pray, he couldnae think, he was dreepin' wi' caul' swat, an' naething could he hear but the dunt-dunt-duntin' o' his ain heart. He micht maybe have stood there an hour, or maybe twa, he minded sae little; when a' o' a sudden, he heard a laigh, uncanny steer upstairs; a foot gaed to an' fro in the cha'mer whaur the corp was hingin'; syne the door was opened, though he minded weel that he had lockit it; an' syne there was a step upon the landin', an' it seemed to him as if the corp was lookin' ower the rail and doun upon him whaur he stood.

He took up the can'le again (for he couldnae want the licht), and as saftly as ever he could, gaed straucht oot o' the manse an' to the far end o' the causeway. It was aye pit-mirk; the flame o' the can'le, when he set it on the grund, brunt steedy and clear as in a room; naething moved, but the Dule water seepin' and sabbin' doon the glen, an' yon unhaly footstep that cam' ploddin doun the stairs inside the manse. He kenned the foot over weel, for it was Janet's; and at ilka step that cam' a wee thing nearer, the cauld got deeper in his vitals. He commended his soul to Him that made an' keepit him; "and O Lord," said he, "give me strength this night to war against the powers of evil."

By this time the foot was comin' through the passage for the door; he could hear a hand skirt alang the wa', as if the fearsome thing was feelin' for its way. The saughs tossed an' maned thegether, a lang sigh cam' ower the hills, the flame o' the can'le was blawn aboot; an' there stood the corp of Thrawn Janet, wi' her grogram goun an' her black mutch, wi' the heid aye upon the shouther, an' the girn still upon the face o't—leevin', ye wad hae said—deid, as Mr. Soulis weel kenned—upon the threshold o' the manse.

It's a strange thing that the saul of man should be that thirled into his perishable body; but the minister saw that, an' his heart didnae break.

She didnae stand there lang; she began to move again an' cam' slowly towards Mr. Soulis whaur he stood under the saughs. A' the life o' his body, a' the strength o' his speerit, were glowerin' frae his een. It seemed she was gaun to speak, but wanted words, an' made a sign wi' the left hand. There cam' a clap o' wund, like a cat's fuff; oot gaed the can'le, the saughs skrieghed like folk; an' Mr. Soulis kenned that, live or die, this was the end o't.

"Witch, beldame, devil!" he cried, "I charge you, by the power of God, begone—if you be dead, to the grave—if you be damned, to hell."

An' at that moment the Lord's ain hand out o' the Heevens struck the Horror whaur it stood; the auld, deid, desecrated corp o' the witch-wife, sae lang keepit frae the grave and hirsled round by deils, lowed up like a brunstane spunk and fell in ashes to the grund; the thunder followed, peal on dirling peal, the rairing rain upon the back o' that; and Mr. Soulis lowped through the garden hedge, and ran, wi' skelloch upon skelloch, for the clachan.

That same mornin', John Christie saw the Black Man pass the Muckle Cairn as it was chappin' six; before eicht, he gaed by the change house at Knockdow; an' no lang after, Sandy M'Lellan saw him gaun linkin' doun the braes frae Kilmackerlie. There's little doubt but it was him that dwalled sae lang in Janet's body; but he was awa' at last; and sinsyne the deil has never fashed us in Ba'weary.

But it was a sair dispensation for the minister; lang, lang he lay ravin' in his bed; and frae that hour to this, he was the man ye ken the day.

THE BOTTLE IMP

NOTE—ANY STUDENT OF THAT VERY UNLITERARY PRODUCT, THE ENGLISH DRAMA OF THE EARLY PART OF THE CENTURY, WILL HERE RECOGNISE THE NAME AND THE ROOT IDEA OF A PIECE ONCE RENDERED POPULAR BY THE REDOUBTABLE O. SMITH. THE ROOT IDEA IS THERE AND IDENTICAL, AND YET I HOPE I HAVE MADE IT A NEW THING. AND THE FACT THAT THE TALE HAS BEEN DESIGNED AND WRITTEN FOR A POLYNESIAN AUDIENCE MAY LEND IT SOME EXTRANEOUS INTEREST NEARER HOME.—R. L. S.

There was a man of the Island of Hawaii, whom I shall call Keawe; for the truth is, he still lives, and his name must be kept secret; but the place of his birth was not far from Honaunau, where the bones of Keawe the Great lie hidden in a cave. This man was poor, brave, and active; he could read and write like a schoolmaster; he was a first-rate mariner besides, sailed for some time in the island steamers, and steered a whaleboat on the Hamakua coast. At length it came in Keawe's mind to have a sight of the great world and foreign cities, and he shipped on a vessel bound to San Francisco.

This is a fine town, with a fine harbour, and rich people uncountable; and, in particular, there is one hill which is covered with palaces. Upon this hill Keawe was one day taking a walk with his pocket full of money, viewing the great houses upon either hand with pleasure. "What fine houses these are!" he was thinking, "and how happy must those people be who dwell in them, and take no care for the morrow!" The thought was in his mind when he came abreast of a house that was smaller than some others, but all finished and beautified like a toy; the steps of that house shone like silver, and the borders of the garden bloomed like garlands, and the windows were bright like diamonds; and Keawe stopped and wondered at the excellence of all he saw. So stopping, he was aware of a man that looked forth upon him through a window so clear that Keawe could see him as you see a fish in a pool upon the reef. The man was elderly, with a bald head and a black beard; and his face was heavy with sorrow, and he bitterly sighed. And the truth of it is, that as Keawe looked in upon the man, and the man looked out upon Keawe, each envied the other.

All of a sudden, the man smiled and nodded, and beckoned Keawe to enter, and met him at the door of the house.

"This is a fine house of mine," said the man, and bitterly sighed. "Would you not care to view the chambers?"

So he led Keawe all over it, from the cellar to the roof, and there was nothing there that was not perfect of its kind, and Keawe was astonished.

"Truly," said Keawe, "this is a beautiful house; if I lived in the like of it, I should be laughing all day long. How comes it, then, that you should be sighing?"

"There is no reason," said the man, "why you should not have a house in all points similar to this, and finer, if you wish. You have some money, I suppose?"

"I have fifty dollars," said Keawe; "but a house like this will cost more than fifty dollars."

The man made a computation. "I am sorry you have no more," said he, "for it may raise you trouble in the future; but it shall be yours at fifty dollars."

"The house?" asked Keawe.

"No, not the house," replied the man; "but the bottle. For, I must tell you, although I appear to you so rich and fortunate, all my fortune, and this house itself and its garden, came out of a bottle not much bigger than a pint. This is it."

And he opened a lockfast place, and took out a round-bellied bottle with a long neck; the glass of it was white like milk, with changing rainbow colours in the grain. Withinsides something obscurely moved, like a shadow and a fire.

"This is the bottle," said the man; and, when Keawe laughed, "You do not believe me?" he added. "Try, then, for yourself. See if you can break it."

So Keawe took the bottle up and dashed it on the floor till he was weary; but it jumped on the floor like a child's ball, and was not injured.

"This is a strange thing," said Keawe. "For by the touch of it, as well as by the look, the bottle should be of glass."

"Of glass it is," replied the man, sighing more heavily than ever; "but the glass of it was tempered in the flames of hell. An imp lives in it, and that is the shadow we behold there moving: or so I suppose. If any man buy this bottle the imp is at his command; all that he desires—love, fame, money, houses like this house, ay, or a city like this city—all are his at the word uttered. Napoleon had this bottle, and by it he grew to be the king of the world; but he sold it at the last, and fell. Captain Cook had this bottle, and by it he found his way to so many islands; but he, too, sold it, and was slain upon Hawaii. For, once it is sold, the power goes and the protection; and unless a man remain content with what he has, ill will befall him."

"And yet you talk of selling it yourself?" Keawe said.

"I have all I wish, and I am growing elderly," replied the man. "There is one thing the imp cannot do—he cannot prolong life; and, it would not be fair to conceal from you, there is a drawback to the bottle; for if a man die before he sells it, he must burn in hell forever."

"To be sure, that is a drawback and no mistake," cried Keawe. "I would not meddle with the thing. I can do without a house, thank God; but there is one thing I could not be doing with one particle, and that is to be damned."

"Dear me, you must not run away with things," returned the man. "All you have to do is to use the power of the imp in moderation, and then sell it to someone else, as I do to you, and finish your life in comfort."

"Well, I observe two things," said Keawe. "All the time you keep sighing like a maid in love, that is one; and, for the other, you sell this bottle very cheap."

"I have told you already why I sigh," said the man. "It is because I fear my health is breaking up; and, as you said yourself, to die and go to the devil is a pity for anyone. As for why I sell so cheap, I must explain to you there is a peculiarity about the bottle. Long ago, when the devil brought it first upon earth, it was extremely expensive, and was sold first of all to Prester John for many millions of dollars; but it cannot be sold at all, unless sold at a loss. If you sell it for as much as you paid for it, back it comes to you again like a homing pigeon. It follows that the price has kept falling in these centuries, and the bottle is now remarkably cheap. I bought it myself from one of my great neighbours on this hill, and the price I paid was only ninety dollars. I could sell it for as high as eighty-nine dollars and ninety-nine cents, but not a penny dearer, or back the thing must come to me. Now, about this there are two bothers. First, when you offer a bottle so singular for eighty odd dollars, people suppose you to be jesting. And second—but there is no hurry about that—and I need not go into it. Only remember it must be coined money that you sell it for."

"How am I to know that this is all true?" asked Keawe.

"Some of it you can try at once," replied the man. "Give me your fifty dollars, take the bottle, and wish your fifty dollars back into your pocket. If that does not happen, I pledge you my honour I will cry off the bargain and restore your money."

"You are not deceiving me?" said Keawe.

The man bound himself with a great oath.

"Well, I will risk that much," said Keawe, "for that can do no harm." And he paid over his money to the man, and the man handed him the bottle.

"Imp of the bottle," said Keawe, "I want my fifty dollars back." And sure enough he had scarce said the word before his pocket was as heavy as ever.

"To be sure this is a wonderful bottle," said Keawe.

"And now good-morning to you, my fine fellow, and the devil go with you for me!" said the man.

"Hold on," said Keawe, "I don't want any more of this fun. Here, take your bottle back."

"You have bought it for less than I paid for it," replied the man, rubbing his hands. "It is yours now; and, for my part, I am only concerned to see the back of you." And with that he rang for his Chinese servant, and had Keawe shown out of the house.

Now, when Keawe was in the street, with the bottle under his arm, he began to think. "If all is true about this bottle, I may have made a losing bargain," thinks he. "But perhaps the man was only fooling me." The first thing he did was to count his money; the sum was exact—forty-nine dollars American money, and one Chili piece. "That looks like the truth," said Keawe. "Now I will try another part."

The streets in that part of the city were as clean as a ship's decks, and though it was noon, there were no passengers. Keawe set the bottle in the gutter and walked away. Twice he looked back, and there was the milky, round-bellied bottle where he left it. A third time he looked back, and turned a corner; but he had scarce done so, when something knocked upon his elbow, and behold! it was the long neck sticking up; and as for the round belly, it was jammed into the pocket of his pilot-coat.

"And that looks like the truth," said Keawe.

The next thing he did was to buy a corkscrew in a shop, and go apart into a secret place in the fields. And there he tried to draw the cork, but as often as he put the screw in, out it came again, and the cork as whole as ever.

"This is some new sort of cork," said Keawe, and all at once he began to shake and sweat, for he was afraid of that bottle.

On his way back to the port side, he saw a shop where a man sold shells and clubs from the wild islands, old heathen deities, old coined money, pictures from China and Japan, and all manner of things that sailors bring in their sea chests. And here he had an idea. So he went in and offered the bottle for a hundred dollars. The man of the shop laughed at him at the first, and offered him five; but, indeed, it was a curious bottle—such glass was never blown in any human glassworks, so prettily the colors shone under the milky white, and so strangely the shadow hovered in the midst; so, after he had disputed awhile after the manner of his kind, the shopman gave Keawe sixty silver dollars for the thing, and set it on a shelf in the midst of his window.

"Now," said Keawe, "I have sold that for sixty which I bought for fifty—or, to say truth, a little less, because one of my dollars was from Chili. Now I shall know the truth upon another point."

So he went back on board his ship, and, when he opened his

chest, there was the bottle, and had come more quickly than himself. Now Keawe had a mate on board whose name was Lopaka.

"What ails you?" said Lopaka, "that you stare in your chest?"

They were alone in the ship's forecastle, and Keawe bound him to secrecy, and told all.

"This is a very strange affair," said Lopaka; "and I fear you will be in trouble about this bottle. But there is one point very clear— that you are sure of the trouble, and you had better have the profit in the bargain. Make up your mind what you want with it; give the order, and if it is done as you desire, I will buy the bottle myself; for I have an idea of my own to get a schooner, and go trading through the islands."

"That is not my idea," said Keawe; "but to have a beautiful house and garden on the Kona Coast, where I was born, the sun shining in at the door, flowers in the garden, glass in the windows, pictures on the walls, and toys and fine carpets on the tables, for all the world like the house I was in this day—only a story higher, and with balconies all about like the King's palace; and to live there without care and make merry with my friends and relatives."

"Well," said Lopaka, "let us carry it back with us to Hawaii; and if all comes true, as you suppose, I will buy the bottle, as I said, and ask a schooner."

Upon that they were agreed, and it was not long before the ship returned to Honolulu, carrying Keawe and Lopaka, and the bottle. They were scarce come ashore when they met a friend upon the beach, who began at once to condole with Keawe.

"I do not know what I am to be condoled about," said Keawe.

"Is it possible you have not heard," said the friend, "your uncle—that good old man—is dead, and your cousin—that beautiful boy—was drowned at sea?"

Keawe was filled with sorrow, and, beginning to weep and to lament, he forgot about the bottle. But Lopaka was thinking to himself, and presently, when Keawe's grief was a little abated, "I have been thinking," said Lopaka. "Had not your uncle lands in Hawaii, in the district of Kaü?"

"No," said Keawe, "not in Kaü: they are on the mountain-side—a little way south of Hookena."

"These lands will now be yours?" asked Lopaka.

"And so they will," says Keawe, and began again to lament for his relatives.

"No," said Lopaka, "do not lament at present. I have a thought in my mind. How if this should be the doing of the bottle? For here is the place ready for your house."

"If this be so," cried Keawe, "it is a very ill way to serve me by killing my relatives. But it may be, indeed; for it was in just such a station that I saw the house with my mind's eye."

"The house, however, is not yet built," said Lopaka.

"No, nor like to be!" said Keawe; "for though my uncle has some coffee and ava and bananas, it will not be more than will keep me in comfort; and the rest of that land is the black lava."

"Let us go to the lawyer," said Lopaka; "I have still this idea in my mind."

Now, when they came to the lawyer's, it appeared Keawe's uncle had grown monstrous rich in the last days, and there was a fund of money.

"And here is the money for the house!" cried Lopaka.

"If you are thinking of a new house," said the lawyer, "here is the card of a new architect, of whom they tell me great things."

"Better and better!" cried Lopaka. "Here is all made plain for us. Let us continue to obey orders."

So they went to the architect, and he had drawings of houses on his table.

"You want something out of the way," said the architect. "How do you like this?" and he handed a drawing to Keawe.

Now, when Keawe set eyes on the drawing, he cried out aloud, for it was the picture of his thought exactly drawn.

"I am in for this house," thought he. "Little as I like the way it comes to me, I am in for it now, and I may as well take the good along with the evil."

So he told the architect all that he wished, and how he would have that house furnished, and about the pictures on the wall and the knick-knacks on the tables; and he asked the man plainly for how much he would undertake the whole affair.

The architect put many questions, and took his pen and made a computation; and when he had done he named the very sum that Keawe had inherited.

Lopaka and Keawe looked at one another and nodded.

"It is quite clear," thought Keawe, "that I am to have this house, whether or no. It comes from the devil, and I fear I will get little good by that; and of one thing I am sure, I will make no more wishes as long as I have this bottle. But with the house I am saddled, and I may as well take the good along with the evil."

So he made his terms with the architect, and they signed a paper; and Keawe and Lopaka took ship again and sailed to Australia; for it was concluded between them they should not interfere at all, but leave the architect and the bottle imp to build and to adorn that house at their own pleasure.

The voyage was a good voyage, only all the time Keawe was holding in his breath, for he had sworn he would utter no more wishes, and take no more favours from the devil. The time was up when they got back. The architect told them that the house was ready, and Keawe and Lopaka took a passage in the *Hall*, and went down Kona way to view the house, and see if all had been done fitly according to the thought that was in Keawe's mind.

Now, the house stood on the mountain side, visible to ships. Above, the forest ran up into the clouds of rain; below, the black lava fell in cliffs, where the kings of old lay buried. A garden bloomed about that house with every hue of flowers; and there was an orchard of papaia on the one hand and an orchard of breadfruit on the other, and right in front, toward the sea, a ship's mast had been rigged up and bore a flag. As for the house, it was three stories high, with great chambers and broad balconies on each. The windows were of glass, so excellent that it was as clear as water and as bright as day. All manner of furniture adorned the chambers. Pictures hung upon the wall in golden frames: pictures of ships, and men fighting, and of the most beautiful women, and of singular places; nowhere in the world are there pictures of so bright a colour as those Keawe found hanging in his house. As for the knick-knacks, they were extraordinary fine; chiming clocks and musical boxes, little men with nodding heads, books filled with pictures, weapons of price from all quarters of the world, and the most elegant puzzles to entertain the leisure of a solitary man. And as no one would care to live in such chambers, only to walk through and view them, the balconies were made so broad that a whole town might have lived upon them in delight; and Keawe knew not which to prefer, whether the back porch, where you got the land breeze, and looked upon the orchards and the flowers, or the front balcony, where you could drink the wind of the sea, and look down the steep wall of the mountain and see the *Hall* going by once a week or so between Hookena and the hills of Pele, or the schooners plying up the coast for wood and ava and bananas.

When they had viewed all, Keawe and Lopaka sat on the porch.

"Well," said Lopaka, "is it all as you designed?"

"Words cannot utter it," said Keawe. "It is better than I dreamed, and I am sick with satisfaction."

"There is but one thing to consider," said Lopaka; "all this may be quite natural, and the bottle imp have nothing whatever to say to it. If I were to buy the bottle, and got no schooner after all, I should have put my hand in the fire for nothing. I gave you my word, I know; but yet I think you would not grudge me one more proof."

"I have sworn I would take no more favours," said Keawe. "I have gone already deep enough."

"This is no favour I am thinking of," replied Lopaka. "It is only to see the imp himself. There is nothing to be gained by that, and so nothing to be ashamed of; and yet, if I once saw him, I should be sure of the whole matter. So indulge me so far, and let me see the imp; and, after that, here is the money in my hand, and I will buy it."

"There is only one thing I am afraid of," said Keawe. "The imp may be very ugly to view; and if you once set eyes upon him you might be very undesirous of the bottle."

"I am a man of my word," said Lopaka. "And here is the money betwixt us."

"Very well," replied Keawe. "I have a curiosity myself. So come, let us have one look at you, Mr. Imp."

Now as soon as that was said, the imp looked out of the bottle, and in again, swift as a lizard; and there sat Keawe and Lopaka turned to stone. The night had quite come, before either found a thought to say or voice to say it with; and then Lopaka pushed the money over and took the bottle.

"I am a man of my word," said he, "and had need to be so, or I would not touch this bottle with my foot. Well, I shall get my schooner and a dollar or two for my pocket; and then I will be rid of this devil as fast as I can. For to tell you the plain truth, the look of him has cast me down."

"Lopaka," said Keawe, "do not you think any worse of me than you can help; I know it is night, and the roads bad, and the pass by the tombs an ill place to go by so late, but I declare since I have seen that little face, I cannot eat or sleep or pray till it is gone from me. I will give you a lantern, and a basket to put the bottle in, and any picture or fine thing in all my house that takes your fancy;—and be gone at once, and go sleep at Hookena with Nahinu."

"Keawe," said Lopaka, "many a man would take this ill; above all, when I am doing you a turn so friendly, as to keep my word and buy the bottle; and for that matter, the night and the dark, and the way by the tombs, must be all tenfold more dangerous to a man with such a sin upon his conscience, and such a bottle under his arm. But for my part, I am so extremely terrified myself, I have not the heart to blame you. Here I go then; and I pray God you may be happy in your house, and I fortunate with my schooner, and both get to heaven in the end in spite of the devil and his bottle."

So Lopaka went down the mountain; and Keawe stood in his front balcony, and listened to the clink of the horse's shoes, and watched the lantern go shining down the path, and along the cliff of caves where the old dead are buried; and all the time he trembled and clasped his hands, and prayed for his friend, and gave glory to God that he himself was escaped out of that trouble.

But the next day came very brightly, and that new house of his was so delightful to behold that he forgot his terrors. One day followed another, and Keawe dwelt there in perpetual joy. He had his place on the back porch; it was there he ate and lived, and read the stories in the Honolulu newspapers; but when anyone came by they would go in and view the chambers and the pictures. And the fame of the house went far and wide; it was called *Ka-Hale Nui*—the

Great House—in all Kona; and sometimes the Bright House, for Keawe kept a Chinaman, who was all day dusting and furbishing; and the glass, and the gilt, and the fine stuffs, and the pictures, shone as bright as the morning. As for Keawe himself, he could not walk in the chambers without singing, his heart was so enlarged; and when ships sailed by upon the sea, he would fly his colours on the mast.

So time went by, until one day Keawe went upon a visit as far as Kailua to certain of his friends. There he was well feasted; and left as soon as he could the next morning, and rode hard, for he was impatient to behold his beautiful house; and, besides, the night then coming on was the night in which the dead of old days go abroad in the sides of Kona; and having already meddled with the devil, he was the more chary of meeting with the dead. A little beyond Honaunau, looking far ahead, he was aware of a woman bathing in the edge of the sea; and she seemed a well-grown girl, but he thought no more of it. Then he saw her white shift flutter as she put it on, and then her red holoku; and by the time he came abreast of her she was done with her toilet, and had come up from the sea, and stood by the track side in her red holoku, and she was all freshened with the bath, and her eyes shone and were kind. Now Keawe no sooner beheld her than he drew rein.

"I thought I knew everyone in this country," said he. "How comes it that I do not know you?"

"I am Kokua, daughter of Kiano," said the girl, "and I have just returned from Oahu. Who are you?"

"I will tell you who I am in a little," said Keawe, dismounting from his horse, "but not now. For I have a thought in my mind, and if you knew who I was, you might have heard of me, and would not give me a true answer. But tell me, first of all, one thing: Are you married?"

At this Kokua laughed out aloud. "It is you who ask questions," she said. "Are you married yourself?"

"Indeed, Kokua, I am not," replied Keawe, "and never thought to be until this hour. But here is the plain truth. I have met you here at the roadside, and I saw your eyes, which are like the stars, and my heart went to you as swift as a bird. And so now, if you want none of me, say so, and I will go on to my own place; but if you think me no worse than any other young man, say so, too, and I will turn aside to your father's for the night, and tomorrow I will talk with the good man."

Kokua said never a word, but she looked at the sea and laughed.

"Kokua," said Keawe, "if you say nothing, I will take that for the good answer; so let us be stepping to your father's door."

She went on ahead of him, still without speech; only sometimes she glanced back and glanced away again, and she kept the strings of her hat in her mouth.

Now, when they had come to the door, Kiano came out on his verandah, and cried out and welcomed Keawe by name. At that the girl looked over, for the fame of the great house had come to her ears; and, to be sure, it was a great temptation. All that evening they were very merry together; and the girl was as bold as brass under the eyes of her parents, and made a mock of Keawe, for she had a quick wit. The next day he had a word with Kiano, and found the girl alone.

"Kokua," said he, "you made a mock of me all the evening; and it is still time to bid me go. I would not tell you who I was, because I have so fine a house, and I feared you would think too much of that house and too little of the man that loves you. Now you know all, and if you wish to have seen the last of me, say so at once."

"No," said Kokua; but this time she did not laugh, nor did Keawe ask for more.

This was the wooing of Keawe; things had gone quickly; but so an arrow goes, and the ball of a rifle swifter still, and yet both may strike the target. Things had gone fast, but they had gone far also, and the thought of Keawe rang in the maiden's head; she heard his voice in the breach of the surf upon the lava, and for this young man that she had seen but twice she would have left father and mother and her native islands. As for Keawe himself, his horse flew up the path of the mountain under the cliff of tombs, and the sound of the hoofs, and the sound of Keawe singing to himself for pleasure, echoed in the caverns of the dead. He came to the Bright House, and still he was singing. He sat and ate in the broad balcony, and the Chinaman wondered at his master, to hear how he sang between the mouthfuls. The sun went down into the sea, and the night came;

and Keawe walked the balconies by lamplight, high on the mountains, and the voice of his singing startled men on ships.

"Here am I now upon my high place," he said to himself. "Life may be no better; this is the mountain top; and all shelves about me toward the worse. For the first time I will light up the chambers, and bathe in my fine bath with the hot water and the cold, and sleep alone in the bed of my bridal chamber."

So the Chinaman had word, and he must rise from sleep and light the furnaces; and as he wrought below, beside the boilers, he heard his master singing and rejoicing above him in the lighted chambers. When the water began to be hot the Chinaman cried to his master, and Keawe went into the bathroom; and the Chinaman heard him sing as he filled the marble basin; and heard him sing, and the singing broken, as he undressed; until of a sudden, the song ceased. The Chinaman listened, and listened; he called up the house to Keawe to ask if all were well, and Keawe answered him "Yes," and bade him to go bed; but there was no more singing in the Bright House; and all night long, the Chinaman heard his master's feet go round and round the balconies without repose.

Now the truth of it was this: as Keawe undressed for his bath, he spied upon his flesh a patch like a patch of lichen on a rock, and it was then that he stopped singing. For he knew the likeness of that patch, and knew that he was fallen in the Chinese Evil.

Now, it is a sad thing for any man to fall into this sickness. And it would be a sad thing for anyone to leave a house so beautiful and so commodious, and depart from all his friends to the north coast of Molokai, between the mighty cliff and the sea-breakers. But what was that to the case of the man Keawe, he who had met his love but yesterday, and won her but that morning, and now saw all his hopes break, in a moment, like a piece of glass?

Awhile he sat upon the edge of the bath; then sprang, with a cry, and ran outside; and to and fro, to and fro, along the balcony, like one despairing.

"Very willingly could I leave Hawaii, the home of my fathers," Keawe was thinking. "Very lightly could I leave my house, the high-placed, the many-windowed, here upon the mountains. Very bravely could I go to Molokai, to Kalaupapa by the cliffs, to live with the smitten and to sleep there, far from my fathers. But what wrong have I done, what sin lies upon my soul, that I should have encountered Kokua coming cool from the sea-water in the evening? Kokua, the soul ensnarer! Kokua, the light of my life! Her may I never wed, her may I look upon no longer, her may I no more handle with my loving hand; and it is for this, it is for you, O Kokua! that I pour my lamentations!"

Now you are to observe what sort of a man Keawe was, for he might have dwelt there in the Bright House for years, and no one been the wiser of his sickness; but he reckoned nothing of that, if he must lose Kokua. And again, he might have wed Kokua even as he was; and so many would have done, because they have the souls of pigs; but Keawe loved the maid manfully, and he would do her no hurt and bring her in no danger.

A little beyond the midst of the night, there came in his mind the recollection of that bottle. He went round to the back porch, and called to memory the day when the devil had looked forth; and at the thought ice ran in his veins.

"A dreadful thing is the bottle," thought Keawe, "and dreadful is the imp, and it is a dreadful thing to risk the flames of hell. But what other hope have I to cure my sickness or to wed Kokua? What!" he thought, "would I beard the devil once, only to get me a house, and not face him again to win Kokua?"

Thereupon he called to mind it was the next day the *Hall* went by on her return to Honolulu. "There must I go first," he thought, "and see Lopaka. For the best hope that I have now is to find that same bottle I was so pleased to be rid of."

Never a wink could he sleep; the food stuck in his throat; but he sent a letter to Kiano, and about the time when the steamer would be coming, rode down beside the cliff of the tombs. It rained; his horse went heavily; he looked up at the black mouths of the caves, and he envied the dead that slept there and were done with trouble; and called to mind how he had galloped by the day before, and was astonished. So he came down to Hookena, and there was all the country gathered for the steamer as usual. In the shed before the store they sat and jested and passed the news; but there was no matter of speech in Keawe's bosom, and he sat in their midst and looked without on the rain falling on the houses, and the surf beating among the rocks, and the sighs arose in his throat.

"Keawe of the Bright House is out of spirits," said one to another. Indeed, and so he was, and little wonder.

Then the *Hall* came, and the whaleboat carried him on board. The afterpart of the ship was full of Haoles who had been to visit the volcano, as their custom is; and the midst was crowded with Kanakas, and the forepart with wild bulls from Hilo and horses from Kaü; but Keawe sat apart from all in his sorrow, and watched for the house of Kiano. There it sat, low upon the shore in the black rocks, and shaded by the cocoa palms, and there by the door was a red holoku, no greater than a fly, and going to and fro with a fly's busyness. "Ah, queen of my heart," he cried, "I'll venture my dear soul to win you!"

Soon after, darkness fell, and the cabins were lit up, and the Haoles sat and played at the cards and drank whiskey as their custom is; but Keawe walked the deck all night; and all the next day, as they steamed under the lee of Maui or of Molokai, he was still pacing to and fro like a wild animal in a menagerie.

Towards evening they passed Diamond Head, and came to the pier of Honolulu. Keawe stepped out among the crowd and began to ask for Lopaka. It seemed he had become the owner of a schooner—none better in the islands—and was gone upon an adventure as far as Pola-Pola or Kahiki; so there was no help to be looked for from Lopaka. Keawe called to mind a friend of his, a lawyer in the town (I must not tell his name), and inquired of him. They said he was grown suddenly rich, and had a fine new house upon Waikiki shore; and this put a thought in Keawe's head, and he called a hack and drove to the lawyer's house.

The house was all brand new, and the trees in the garden no greater than walking-sticks, and the lawyer, when he came, had the air of a man well pleased.

"What can I do to serve you?" said the lawyer.

"You are a friend of Lopaka's," replied Keawe, "and Lopaka purchased from me a certain piece of goods that I thought you might enable me to trace."

The lawyer's face became very dark. "I do not profess to misunderstand you, Mr. Keawe," said he, "though this is an ugly business to be stirring in. You may be sure I know nothing, but yet I have a guess, and if you would apply in a certain quarter I think you might have news."

And he named the name of a man, which, again, I had better not repeat. So it was for days, and Keawe went from one to another, finding everywhere new clothes and carriages, and fine new houses and men everywhere in great contentment, although, to be sure, when he hinted at his business their faces would cloud over.

"No doubt I am upon the track," thought Keawe. "These new clothes and carriages are all the gifts of the little imp, and these glad faces are the faces of men who have taken their profit and got rid of the accursed thing in safety. When I see pale cheeks and hear sighing, I shall know that I am near the bottle."

So it befell at last that he was recommended to a Haole in Beritania Street. When he came to the door, about the hour of the evening meal, there were the usual marks of the new house, and the young garden, and the electric light shining in the windows; but when the owner came, a shock of hope and fear ran through Keawe; for here was a young man, white as a corpse, and black about the eyes, the hair shedding from his head, and such a look in his countenance as a man may have when he is waiting for the gallows.

"Here it is, to be sure," thought Keawe, and so with this man he noways veiled his errand. "I am come to buy the bottle," said he.

At the word, the young Haole of Beritania Street reeled against the wall.

"The bottle!" he gasped. "To buy the bottle!" Then he seemed to choke, and seizing Keawe by the arm carried him into a room and poured out wine in two glasses.

"Here is my respects," said Keawe, who had been much about with Haoles in his time. "Yes," he added, "I am come to buy the bottle. What is the price by now?"

At that word the young man let his glass slip through his fingers, and looked upon Keawe like a ghost.

"The price," says he; "the price! You do not know the price?"

"It is for that I am asking you," returned Keawe. "But why are you so much concerned? Is there anything wrong about the price?"

"It has dropped a great deal in value since your time, Mr. Keawe," said the young man, stammering.

"Well, well, I shall have the less to pay for it," says Keawe. "How much did it cost you?"

The young man was as white as a sheet. "Two cents," said he.

"What?" cried Keawe, "two cents? Why, then, you can only sell it for one. And he who buys it——" The words died upon Keawe's tongue; he who bought it could never sell it again, the bottle and the bottle imp must abide with him until he died, and when he died must carry him to the red end of hell.

The young man of Beritania Street fell upon his knees. "For God's sake buy it!" he cried. "You can have all my fortune in the bargain. I was mad when I bought it at that price. I had embezzled money at my store; I was lost else; I must have gone to jail."

"Poor creature," said Keawe, "you would risk your soul upon so desperate an adventure, and to avoid the proper punishment of your own disgrace; and you think I could hesitate with love in front of me. Give me the bottle, and the change which I make sure you have all ready. Here is a five-cent piece."

It was as Keawe supposed; the young man had the change ready in a drawer; the bottle changed hands, and Keawe's fingers were no sooner clasped upon the stalk than he had breathed his wish to be a clean man. And, sure enough, when he got home to his room, and stripped himself before a glass, his flesh was whole like an infant's. And here was the strange thing: he had no sooner seen this miracle, than his mind was changed within him, and he cared naught for the Chinese Evil, and little enough for Kokua; and had but the one thought, that here he was bound to the bottle imp for time and for eternity, and had no better hope but to be a cinder for ever in the flames of hell. Away ahead of him he saw them blaze with his mind's eye, and his soul shrank, and darkness fell upon the light.

When Keawe came to himself a little, he was aware it was the night when the band played at the hotel. Thither he went, because he feared to be alone; and there, among happy faces, walked to and fro, and heard the tunes go up and down, and saw Berger beat the measure, and all the while he heard the flames crackle, and saw the red fire burning in the bottomless pit. Of a sudden the band played

Hiki-ao-ao; that was a song that he had sung with Kokua, and at the strain courage returned to him.

"It is done now," he thought, "and once more let me take the good along with the evil."

So it befell that he returned to Hawaii by the first steamer, and as soon as it could be managed he was wedded to Kokua, and carried her up the mountain side to the Bright House.

Now it was so with these two, that when they were together, Keawe's heart was stilled; but so soon as he was alone he fell into a brooding horror, and heard the flames crackle, and saw the red fire burn in the bottomless pit. The girl, indeed, had come to him wholly; her heart leapt in her side at sight of him, her hand clung to his; and she was so fashioned from the hair upon her head to the nails upon her toes that none could see her without joy. She was pleasant in her nature. She had the good word always. Full of song she was, and went to and fro in the Bright House, the brightest thing in its three stories, carolling like the birds. And Keawe beheld and heard her with delight, and then must shrink upon one side, and weep and groan to think upon the price that he had paid for her; and then he must dry his eyes, and wash his face, and go and sit with her on the broad balconies, joining in her songs, and, with a sick spirit, answering her smiles.

There came a day when her feet began to be heavy and her songs more rare; and now it was not Keawe only that would weep apart, but each would sunder from the other and sit in opposite balconies with the whole width of the Bright House betwixt. Keawe was so sunk in his despair, he scarce observed the change, and was only glad he had more hours to sit alone and brood upon his destiny, and was not so frequently condemned to pull a smiling face on a sick heart. But one day, coming softly through the house, he heard the sound of a child sobbing, and there was Kokua rolling her face upon the balcony floor, and weeping like the lost.

"You do well to weep in this house, Kokua," he said. "And yet I would give the head off my body that you (at least) might have been happy."

"Happy!" she cried. "Keawe, when you lived alone in your Bright House, you were the word of the island for a happy man;

laughter and song were in your mouth, and your face was as bright as the sunrise. Then you wedded poor Kokua; and the good God knows what is amiss in her—but from that day you have not smiled. Oh!" she cried, "what ails me? I thought I was pretty, and I knew I loved him. What ails me that I throw this cloud upon my husband?"

"Poor Kokua," said Keawe. He sat down by her side, and sought to take her hand; but that she plucked away. "Poor Kokua," he said, again. "My poor child—my pretty. And I had thought all this while to spare you! Well, you shall know all. Then, at least, you will pity poor Keawe; then you will understand how much he loved you in the past—that he dared hell for your possession—and how much he loves you still (the poor condemned one), that he can yet call up a smile when he beholds you."

With that, he told her all, even from the beginning.

"You have done this for me?" she cried. "Ah, well, then what do I care!"—and she clasped and wept upon him.

"Ah, child!" said Keawe, "and yet, when I consider of the fire of hell, I care a good deal!"

"Never tell me," said she; "no man can be lost because he loved Kokua, and no other fault. I tell you, Keawe, I shall save you with these hands, or perish in your company. What! you loved me and gave your soul, and you think I will not die to save you in return?"

"Ah, my dear! you might die a hundred times, and what difference would that make?" he cried, "except to leave me lonely till the time comes of my damnation?"

"You know nothing," said she. "I was educated in a school in Honolulu; I am no common girl. And I tell you, I shall save my lover. What is this you say about a cent? But all the world is not American. In England they have a piece they call a farthing, which is about half a cent. Ah! sorrow!" she cried, "that makes it scarcely better, for the buyer must be lost, and we shall find none so brave as my Keawe! But, then, there is France; they have a small coin there which they call a centime, and these go five to the cent or thereabout. We could not do better. Come, Keawe, let us go to the French islands; let us go to Tahiti, as fast as ships can bear us. There we have four centimes, three centimes, two centimes, one centime; four possible sales to come and go on; and two of us to push the bargain. Come, my Keawe! kiss me, and banish care. Kokua will defend you."

"Gift of God!" he cried. "I cannot think that God will punish me for desiring aught so good! Be it as you will, then; take me where you please: I put my life and my salvation in your hands."

Early the next day Kokua was about her preparations. She took Keawe's chest that he went with sailoring; and first she put the bottle in a corner; and then packed it with the richest of their clothes and the bravest of the knick-knacks in the house. "For," said she, "we must seem to be rich folks, or who will believe in the bottle?" All the time of her preparation she was as gay as a bird; only when she looked upon Keawe, the tears would spring in her eye, and she must run and kiss him. As for Keawe, a weight was off his soul; now that he had his secret shared, and some hope in front of him, he seemed like a new man, his feet went lightly on the earth, and his breath was good to him again. Yet was terror still at his elbow; and ever and again, as the wind blows out a taper, hope died in him, and he saw the flames toss and the red fire burn in hell.

It was given out in the country they were gone pleasuring to the States, which was thought a strange thing, and yet not so strange as the truth, if any could have guessed it. So they went to Honolulu in the *Hall*, and thence in the *Umatilla* to San Francisco with a crowd of Haoles, and at San Francisco took their passage by the mail brigantine, the *Tropic Bird*, for Papeete, the chief place of the French in the south islands. Thither they came, after a pleasant voyage, on a fair day of the Trade Wind, and saw the reef with the surf breaking, and Motuiti with its palms, and the schooner riding within-side, and the white houses of the town low down along the shore among green trees, and overhead the mountains and the clouds of Tahiti, the wise island.

It was judged the most wise to hire a house, which they did accordingly, opposite the British Consul's, to make a great parade of money, and themselves conspicuous with carriages and horses. This it was very easy to do, so long as they had the bottle in their possession; for Kokua was more bold than Keawe, and, whenever she had a mind, called on the imp for twenty or a hundred dollars. At this rate they soon grew to be remarked in the town; and the strangers from Hawaii, their riding and their driving, the fine holokus and the rich lace of Kokua, became the matter of much talk.

They got on well after the first with the Tahitian language, which is indeed like to the Hawaiian, with a change of certain letters; and as soon as they had any freedom of speech, began to push the bottle. You are to consider it was not an easy subject to introduce; it was not easy to persuade people you were in earnest, when you offered to sell them for four centimes the spring of health and riches inexhaustible. It was necessary besides to explain the dangers of the bottle; and either people disbelieved the whole thing and laughed, or they thought the more of the darker part, became overcast with gravity, and drew away from Keawe and Kokua, as from persons who had dealings with the devil. So far from gaining ground, these two began to find they were avoided in the town; the children ran away from them screaming, a thing intolerable to Kokua; Catholics crossed themselves as they went by; and all persons began with one accord to disengage themselves from their advances.

Depression fell upon their spirits. They would sit at night in their new house, after a day's weariness, and not exchange one word, or the silence would be broken by Kokua bursting suddenly into sobs. Sometimes they would pray together; sometimes they would have the bottle out upon the floor, and sit all evening watching how the shadow hovered in the midst. At such times they would be afraid to go to rest. It was long ere slumber came to them, and, if either dozed off, it would be to wake and find the other silently weeping in the dark, or, perhaps, to wake alone, the other having fled from the house and the neighbourhood of that bottle, to pace under the bananas in the little garden, or to wander on the beach by moonlight.

One night it was so when Kokua awoke. Keawe was gone. She felt in the bed and his place was cold. Then fear fell upon her, and she sat up in bed. A little moonshine filtered through the shutters. The room was bright, and she could spy the bottle on the floor. Outside it blew high, the great trees of the avenue cried aloud, and the fallen leaves rattled in the verandah. In the midst of this Kokua was aware of another sound; whether of a beast or of a man she could scarce tell, but it was as sad as death, and cut her to the soul. Softly she arose, set the door ajar, and looked forth into the moonlit yard. There, under the bananas, lay Keawe, his mouth in the dust, and as he lay he moaned.

It was Kokua's first thought to run forward and console him; her second potently withheld her. Keawe had borne himself before his wife like a brave man; it became her little in the hour of weakness to intrude upon his shame. With the thought she drew back into the house.

"Heaven!" she thought, "how careless have I been—how weak! It is he, not I, that stands in this eternal peril; it was he, not I, that took the curse upon his soul. It is for my sake, and for the love of a creature of so little worth and such poor help, that he now beholds so close to him the flames of hell—ay, and smells the smoke of it, lying without there in the wind and moonlight. Am I so dull of spirit that never till now I have surmised my duty, or have I seen it before and turned aside? But now, at least, I take up my soul in both the hands of my affection; now I say farewell to the white steps of heaven and the waiting faces of my friends. A love for a love, and let mine be equalled with Keawe's! A soul for a soul, and be it mine to perish!"

She was a deft woman with her hands, and was soon apparelled. She took in her hands the change—the precious centimes they kept ever at their side; for this coin is little used, and they had made provision at a Government office. When she was forth in the avenue clouds came on the wind, and the moon was blackened. The town slept, and she knew not whither to turn till she heard one coughing in the shadow of the trees.

"Old man," said Kokua, "what do you here abroad in the cold night?"

The old man could scarce express himself for coughing, but she made out that he was old and poor, and a stranger in the island.

"Will you do me a service?" said Kokua. "As one stranger to another, and as an old man to a young woman, will you help a daughter of Hawaii?"

"Ah," said the old man. "So you are the witch from the eight islands, and even my old soul you seek to entangle. But I have heard of you, and defy your wickedness."

"Sit down here," said Kokua, "and let me tell you a tale." And she told him the story of Keawe from the beginning to the end.

"And now," said she, "I am his wife, whom he bought with his soul's welfare. And what should I do? If I went to him myself and offered to buy it, he would refuse. But if you go, he will sell it eagerly; I will await you here; you will buy it for four centimes, and I will buy it again for three. And the Lord strengthen a poor girl!"

"If you meant falsely," said the old man, "I think God would strike you dead."

"He would!" cried Kokua. "Be sure he would. I could not be so treacherous—God would not suffer it."

"Give me the four centimes and await me here," said the old man.

Now, when Kokua stood alone in the street, her spirit died. The wind roared in the trees, and it seemed to her the rushing of the flames of hell; the shadows tossed in the light of the street lamp, and they seemed to her the snatching hands of evil ones. If she had had the strength, she must have run away, and if she had had the breath she must have screamed aloud; but, in truth, she could do neither, and stood and trembled in the avenue, like an affrighted child.

Then she saw the old man returning, and he had the bottle in his hand.

"I have done your bidding," said he, "I left your husband weeping like a child; tonight he will sleep easy." And he held the bottle forth.

"Before you give it me," Kokua panted, "take the good with the evil—ask to be delivered from your cough."

"I am an old man," replied the other, "and too near the gate of the grave to take a favour from the devil. But what is this? Why do you not take the bottle? Do you hesitate?"

"Not hesitate!" cried Kokua. "I am only weak. Give me a moment. It is my hand resists, my flesh shrinks back from the accursed thing. One moment only!"

The old man looked upon Kokua kindly. "Poor child!" said he, "you fear; your soul misgives you. Well, let me keep it. I am old, and can never more be happy in this world, and as for the next——"

"Give it me!" gasped Kokua. "There is your money. Do you think I am so base as that? Give me the bottle."

"God bless you, child," said the old man.

Kokua concealed the bottle under her holoku, said farewell to the old man, and walked off along the avenue, she cared not whither. For all roads were now the same to her, and led equally to hell. Sometimes she walked, and sometimes ran; sometimes she screamed out loud in the night, and sometimes lay by the wayside in the dust and wept. All that she had heard of hell came back to her; she saw the flames blaze, and she smelt the smoke, and her flesh withered on the coals.

Near day she came to her mind again, and returned to the house. It was even as the old man said—Keawe slumbered like a child. Kokua stood and gazed upon his face.

"Now, my husband," said she, "it is your turn to sleep. When you wake it will be your turn to sing and laugh. But for poor Kokua, alas! that meant no evil—for poor Kokua no more sleep, no more singing, no more delight, whether in earth or heaven."

With that she lay down in the bed by his side, and her misery was so extreme that she fell in a deep slumber instantly.

Late in the morning her husband woke her and gave her the good news. It seemed he was silly with delight, for he paid no heed to her distress, ill though she dissembled it. The words stuck in her mouth, it mattered not; Keawe did the speaking. She ate not a bite, but who was to observe it? for Keawe cleared the dish. Kokua saw and heard him, like some strange thing in a dream; there were times when she forgot or doubted, and put her hands to her brow; to know herself doomed and hear her husband babble, seemed so monstrous.

All the while Keawe was eating and talking, and planning the time of their return, and thanking her for saving him, and fondling her, and calling her the true helper after all. He laughed at the old man that was fool enough to buy that bottle.

"A worthy old man he seemed," Keawe said. "But no one can judge by appearances. For why did the old reprobate require the bottle?"

"My husband," said Kokua, humbly, "his purpose may have been good."

Keawe laughed like an angry man.

"Fiddle-de-dee!" cried Keawe. "An old rogue, I tell you; and an old ass to boot. For the bottle was hard enough to sell at four centimes; and at three it will be quite impossible. The margin is not broad enough, the thing begins to smell of scorching—brr!" said he, and shuddered. "It is true I bought it myself at a cent, when I knew not there were smaller coins. I was a fool for my pains; there will never be found another: and whoever has that bottle now will carry it to the pit."

"O my husband!" said Kokua. "Is it not a terrible thing to save oneself by the eternal ruin of another? It seems to me that I could not laugh. I would be humbled. I would be filled with melancholy. I would pray for the poor holder."

Then Keawe, because he felt the truth of what she said, grew the more angry. "Heighty-teighty!" cried he. "You may be filled with melancholy if you please. It is not the mind of a good wife. If you thought at all of me, you would sit shamed."

Thereupon he went out, and Kokua was alone.

What chance had she to sell that bottle at two centimes? None, she perceived. And if she had any, here was her husband hurrying her away to a country where there was nothing lower than a cent. And here—on the morrow of her sacrifice—was her husband leaving her and blaming her.

She would not even try to profit by what time she had, but sat in the house, and now had the bottle out and viewed it with unutterable fear, and now, with loathing, hid it out of sight.

By and by, Keawe came back, and would have her take a drive.

"My husband, I am ill," she said. "I am out of heart. Excuse me, I can take no pleasure."

Then was Keawe more wroth than ever. With her, because he thought she was brooding over the case of the old man; and with himself, because he thought she was right, and was ashamed to be so happy.

"This is your truth," cried he, "and this your affection! Your husband is just saved from eternal ruin, which he encountered for the love of you—and you can take no pleasure! Kokua, you have a disloyal heart."

He went forth again furious, and wandered in the town all day. He met friends, and drank with them; they hired a carriage and drove into the country, and there drank again. All the time Keawe was ill at ease, because he was taking this pastime while his wife was sad, and because he knew in his heart that she was more right than he; and the knowledge made him drink the deeper.

Now there was an old brutal Haole drinking with him, one that had been a boatswain of a whaler, a runaway, a digger in gold mines, a convict in prisons. He had a low mind and a foul mouth; he loved to drink and to see others drunken; and he pressed the glass upon Keawe. Soon there was no more money in the company.

"Here, you!" says the boatswain, "you are rich, you have been always saying. You have a bottle or some foolishness."

"Yes," says Keawe, "I am rich; I will go back and get some money from my wife, who keeps it."

"That's a bad idea, mate," said the boatswain. "Never you trust a petticoat with dollars. They're all as false as water; you keep an eye on her."

Now, this word struck in Keawe's mind; for he was muddled with what he had been drinking.

"I should not wonder but she was false, indeed," thought he. "Why else should she be so cast down at my release? But I will show her I am not the man to be fooled. I will catch her in the act."

Accordingly, when they were back in town, Keawe bade the boatswain wait for him at the corner, by the old calaboose, and went forward up the avenue alone to the door of his house. The night had come again; there was a light within, but never a sound; and Keawe crept about the corner, opened the back door softly, and looked in.

There was Kokua on the floor, the lamp at her side; before her was a milk-white bottle, with a round belly and a long neck; and as she viewed it, Kokua wrung her hands.

A long time Keawe stood and looked in the doorway. At first he was struck stupid; and then fear fell upon him that the bargain had been made amiss, and the bottle had come back to him as it came at San Francisco; and at that his knees were loosened, and the fumes of the wine departed from his head like mists off a river in the morning.

And then he had another thought; and it was a strange one, that made his cheeks to burn.

"I must make sure of this," thought he.

So he closed the door, and went softly round the corner again, and then came noisily in, as though he were but now returned. And, lo! by the time he opened the front door no bottle was to be seen; and Kokua sat in a chair and started up like one awakened out of sleep.

"I have been drinking all day and making merry," said Keawe. "I have been with good companions, and now I only come back for money, and return to drink and carouse with them again."

Both his face and voice were as stern as judgment, but Kokua was too troubled to observe.

"You do well to use your own, my husband," said she, and her words trembled.

"O, I do well in all things," said Keawe, and he went straight to the chest and took out money. But he looked besides in the corner where they kept the bottle, and there was no bottle there.

At that the chest heaved upon the floor like a sea-billow, and the house span about him like a wreath of smoke, for he saw he was lost now, and there was no escape. "It is what I feared," he thought. "It is she who has bought it."

And then he came to himself a little and rose up; but the sweat streamed on his face as thick as the rain and as cold as the well-water.

"Kokua," said he, "I said to you today what ill became me. Now I return to carouse with my jolly companions," and at that he laughed a little quietly. "I will take more pleasure in the cup if you forgive me."

She clasped his knees in a moment; she kissed his knees with flowing tears.

"O," she cried, "I asked but a kind word!"

"Let us never one think hardly of the other," said Keawe, and was gone out of the house.

Now, the money that Keawe had taken was only some of that store of centime pieces they had laid in at their arrival. It was very sure he had no mind to be drinking. His wife had given her soul for him, now he must give his for hers; no other thought was in the world with him.

At the corner, by the old calaboose, there was the boatswain waiting.

"My wife has the bottle," said Keawe, "and, unless you help me to recover it, there can be no more money and no more liquor to-night."

"You do not mean to say you are serious about that bottle?" cried the boatswain.

"There is the lamp," said Keawe. "Do I look as if I was jesting?"

"That is so," said the boatswain. "You look as serious as a ghost."

"Well, then," said Keawe, "here are two centimes; you must go to my wife in the house, and offer her these for the bottle, which (if I am not much mistaken) she will give you instantly. Bring it to me here, and I will buy it back from you for one; for that is the law with this bottle, that it still must be sold for a less sum. But whatever you do, never breathe a word to her that you have come from me."

"Mate, I wonder are you making a fool of me?" asked the boatswain.

"It will do you no harm if I am," returned Keawe.

"That is so, mate," said the boatswain.

"And if you doubt me," added Keawe, "you can try. As soon as you are clear of the house, wish to have your pocket full of money, or a bottle of the best rum, or what you please, and you will see the virtue of the thing."

"Very well, Kanaka," says the boatswain. "I will try; but if you are having your fun out of me, I will take my fun out of you with a belaying pin."

So the whaler-man went off up the avenue; and Keawe stood and waited. It was near the same spot where Kokua had waited the night before; but Keawe was more resolved, and never faltered in his purpose; only his soul was bitter with despair.

It seemed a long time he had to wait before he heard a voice singing in the darkness of the avenue. He knew the voice to be the boatswain's; but it was strange how drunken it appeared upon a sudden.

Next, the man himself came stumbling into the light of the lamp. He had the devil's bottle buttoned in his coat; another bottle was in his hand; and even as he came in view he raised it to his mouth and drank.

"You have it," said Keawe. "I see that."

"Hands off!" cried the boatswain, jumping back. "Take a step near me, and I'll smash your mouth. You thought you could make a cat's-paw of me, did you?"

"What do you mean?" cried Keawe.

"Mean?" cried the boatswain. "This is a pretty good bottle, this is; that's what I mean. How I got it for two centimes I can't make out; but I'm sure you shan't have it for one."

"You mean you won't sell?" gasped Keawe.

"No, *sir!*" cried the boatswain. "But I'll give you a drink of the rum, if you like."

"I tell you," said Keawe, "the man who has that bottle goes to hell."

"I reckon I'm going anyway," returned the sailor; "and this bottle's the best thing to go with I've struck yet. No, sir!" he cried again, "this is my bottle now, and you can go and fish for another."

"Can this be true?" Keawe cried. "For your own sake, I beseech you, sell it me!"

"I don't value any of your talk," replied the boatswain. "You thought I was a flat; now you see I'm not; and there's an end. If you won't have a swallow of the rum, I'll have one myself. Here's your health, and good-night to you!"

So off he went down the avenue towards town, and there goes the bottle out of the story.

But Keawe ran to Kokua light as the wind; and great was their joy that night; and great, since then, has been the peace of all their days in the Bright House.

THE ISLE OF VOICES

Keola was married with Lehua, daughter of Kalamake, the wise man of Molokai, and he kept his dwelling with the father of his wife. There was no man more cunning than that prophet; he read the stars, he could divine by the bodies of the dead and by the means of evil creatures; he would go alone into the highest parts of the mountain, into the region of the hobgoblins, and there he would lay snares to entrap the spirits of the ancient. For this reason no man was more consulted in all the Kingdom of Hawaii; prudent people bought and sold and married and laid out their lives by his counsels; and the King had him twice to Kona to seek the treasures of Kamehameha. Neither was any man more feared: of his enemies, some had dwindled in sickness by the virtue of his incantations, and some had been spirited away, the life and the clay both, so that folk looked in vain for so much as a bone of their bodies. It was rumoured that he had the art or the gift of the old heroes; men had seen him at night upon the mountains, stopping from one cliff to the next; they had seen him walking in the high forest, and his head and shoulders were above the trees. This Kalamake was a strange man to see; he was come of the best blood in Molokai and Maui, of a pure descent; and yet he was more white to look upon than any foreigner, his hair the colour of dry grass, and his eyes red and very blind; so that "Blind as Kalamake that can see across tomorrow," was a byword in the islands.

Of all these doings of his father-in-law, Keola knew a little by the common repute; a little more he suspected; and the rest ignored. But there was one thing troubled him. Kalamake was a man that spared for nothing, whether to eat or to drink or to wear; and for all, he paid in bright new dollars. "Bright as Kalamake's dollars," was another saying in the Eight Isles. Yet he neither sold, nor planted, nor took hire—only now and then for his sorceries—and there was no source conceivable for so much silver coin.

It chanced one day Keola's wife was gone upon a visit to Kaunakakai on the lee side of the island, and the men were forth at the sea-fishing. But Keola was an idle dog; and he lay in the verandah, and watched the surf beat on the shore and the birds fly about the cliff. It was a chief thought with him always: the thought of the bright dollars. When he lay down to bed, he would be wondering why they were so many; and when he woke at morn, he would be wondering why they were all new; and the thing was never absent from his mind. But this day of all days, he made sure in his heart of some discovery. For it seems he had observed the place where Kalamake kept his treasure, which was a lockfast desk against the parlour wall, under the print of Kamehameha the fifth and a photograph of Queen Victoria with her crown; and it seems again that, no later than the night before, he found occasion to look in, and behold! the bag lay there empty. And this was the day of the steamer; he could see her smoke off Kalaupapa; and she must soon arrive with a month's goods, tinned salmon and gin and all manner of rare luxuries, for Kalamake.

"Now if he can pay for his goods today" Keola thought, "I shall know for certain that the man is a warlock, and the dollars come out of the devil's pocket."

While he was so thinking, there was his father-in-law behind him, looking vexed.

"Is that the steamer?" he asked.

"Yes," said Keola. "She has but to call at Pelekunu, and then she will be here."

"There is no help for it, then," returned Kalamake, "and I must take you in my confidence, Keola, for the lack of anyone better. Come here within the house."

So they stepped together into the parlour, which was a very fine room, papered and hung with prints, and furnished with a rocking chair and a table and a sofa in the European style; there was a shelf of books besides, and a family bible in the midst of the table, and the lockfast writing-desk against the wall; so that anyone could see it was the house of a man of substance.

Kalamake made Keola close the shutters of the windows, while he himself locked all the doors and set open the lid of the desk. From this he brought forth a pair of necklaces hung with charms and shells, a bundle of dried herbs and the dried leaves of trees, and a green branch of palm.

"What I am about," said he, "is a thing beyond wonder. The men of old were wise; they wrought marvels, and this among the rest; but that was at night, in the dark, under the fit stars and in the desert. The same will I do here in my own house and under the plain eye of day."

So saying, he put the bible under the cushion of the sofa so that it was all covered, brought out from the same place a mat of a wonderful fine texture, and heaped the herbs and leaves on sand in a tin pan. And then he and Keola put on the necklaces, and took their stand upon the opposite corners of the mat.

"The time comes," said the warlock. "Be not afraid."

With that he set flame to the herbs, and began to mutter and wave the branch of palm. At first the light was dim because of the closed shutters; but the herbs caught strongly afire, and the flames beat upon Keola, and the room glowed with the burning; and next the smoke rose and made his head swim and his eyes darken, and the sound of Kalamake muttering ran in his ears. And suddenly, to the mat on which they were standing, came a snatch or twitch, that seemed to be more swift than lightning. In the same wink, the room was gone and the house, the breath all beaten from Keola's body. Volumes of sun rolled upon his eyes and head; and he found himself transported to a beach of the sea, under a strong sun, with a great surf roaring: he and the warlock standing there on the same mat speechless, gasping and grasping at one another, and passing their hands before their eyes.

"What was this?" cried Keola, who came to himself the first, because he was the younger. "The pang of it was like death."

"It matters not," panted Kalamake. "It is now done."

"And, in the name of God, where are we?" cries Keola.

"That is not the question," replied the sorcerer. "Being here, we have matter in our hands, and that we must attend to. Go—while I recover my breath—into the borders of the wood, and bring me the leaves of such and such a herb, and such and such a tree, which you will find to grow there plentifully: three handfuls of each. And be speedy. We must be home again before the steamer comes; it would seem strange if we had disappeared." And he sat on the sand and panted.

Keola went up the beach, which was of shining sand and coral, strewn with singular shells; and he thought in his heart: "How do I not know this beach? I will come here again and gather shells." In front of him was a line of palms against the sky, not like the palms of the Eight Islands, but tall and fresh and beautiful, and hanging out withered fans like gold among the green; and he thought in his heart: "It is strange I should not have found this grove. I will come here again, when it is warm, to sleep." And he thought: "How warm it has grown suddenly!" for it was winter in Hawaii and the day had been chill. And he thought also: "Where are the gray mountains? and where is the high cliff with the hanging forest and the wheeling birds?" And the more he considered, the less he might conceive in what quarter of the islands he was fallen.

In the border of the grove, where it met the beach, the herb was growing, but the tree farther back. Now, as Keola went toward the tree, he was aware of a young woman who had nothing on her body but a belt of leaves. "Well!" thought Keola, "they are not very particular about their dress in this part of the country." And he paused, supposing she would observe him and escape; and seeing that she still looked before her, stood and hummed aloud. Up she leaped at the sound; her face was ashen; she looked this way and that, and her mouth gaped with the terror of her soul. But it was a strange thing that her eyes did not rest upon Keola.

"Good day," said he. "You need not be so frightened, I will not eat you."

And he had scarce opened his mouth before the young woman fled into the bush.

"These are strange manners," thought Keola, and not thinking what he did, ran after her.

As she ran, the girl kept crying in some speech that was not practised in Hawaii; yet some of the words were the same, and he knew she kept calling and warning others. And presently he saw more people running, men, women and children one with another, all running and crying, like people at a fire. And with that, he began to grow afraid himself, and returned to Kalamake, bringing the leaves. Him he told what he had seen.

"You must pay no heed," said Kalamake. "All this is like a dream and shadows: all will disappear and be forgotten."

"It seemed none saw me," said Keola.

"And none did," replied the sorcerer. "We walk here in the broad sun invisible by reason of these charms. Yet they hear us; and therefore it is well to speak softly as I do."

With that he made a circle round the mat with stones, and in the midst he set the leaves. "It will be your part," said he, "to keep the leaves alight, and feed the fire slowly. While they blaze (which is but for a little moment) I must do my errand; and before the ashes blacken, the same power that brought us carries us away. Be ready now with the match; and do you call me in good time lest the flame burn out, and I be left." As soon as the leaves caught, the sorcerer leaped like a deer out of the circle, and began to race along the beach like a hound that has been bathing: as he ran, he kept stooping to snatch shells; and it seemed to Keola that they glittered as he took them. The leaves blazed with a clear flame that consumed them swiftly; and presently Keola had but a handful left, and the sorcerer was far off, running and stooping. "Back!" cried Keola. "Back! the leaves are near done." At that, Kalamake turned, and if he had run before, now he flew. But fast as he ran, the leaves burned faster. The flame was ready to expire, when with a great leap he bounded on the mat; the wind of his leaping blew it out; and with that the beach was gone, and the sun, and the sea; and they stood once more in the dimness of the shuttered parlour, and were once more shaken and blinded; and on the mat betwixt them, lay a pile of shining dollars. Keola ran to the shutters; and there was the steamer tossing in the swell close in.

The same night Kalamake took his son-in-law apart, and gave him five dollars in his hand. "Keola," said he, "if you are a wise man (which I am doubtful of) you will think you slept this afternoon on the verandah, and dreamed as you were sleeping. I am a man of few words, and I have for my helpers people of short memories."

Never a word more said Kalamake, nor referred again to that affair. But it ran all the while in Keola's head; if he were lazy before, he would now do nothing. "Why should I work?" thought he, "when I have a father-in-law who makes dollars of sea-shells?" Presently his share was spent, and he spent it all upon fine clothes. And then he was sorry. "For," thought he, "I had done better to have bought a concertina, with which I might have entertained myself all day long." And then he began to grow vexed with Kalamake. "This man has the soul of a dog," thought he. "He can gather dollars when he pleases on a beach, and he leaves me to pine for a concertina! Let him beware; I am no child, I am as cunning as he, and hold his secret." With that he spoke to his wife, Lehua, and complained of her father's manners.

"I would let my father be," said Lehua. "He is a dangerous man to cross."

"I care that for him!" cried Keola, and snapped his fingers. "I have him by the nose, I can make him do what I please." And he told Lehua the story.

But she shook her head. "You may do what you like," said she. "But as sure as you thwart my father, you will be no more heard of. Think of this person, and that person; think of Hua, who was a noble of the House of Representatives and went to Honolulu every year; and not a bone or a hair of him was found. Remember Kamau, and how he wasted to a thread, so that his wife lifted him with one hand. Keola, you are a baby in my father's hands; he will take you with his thumb and finger, and eat you like a shrimp."

Now Keola was truly very much afraid of Kalamake, but he was vain too; and these words of his wife incensed him. "Very well," said he. "If that is what you think of me, I will show how much you are deceived." And he went straight to where his father-in-law was sitting in the parlour.

"Kalamake," said he, "I want a concertina."

"Do you indeed?" said Kalamake.

"Yes," said he, "and I may as well tell you plainly, I mean to have it. A man who picks up dollars on the beach can certainly afford a concertina."

"I had no idea you had so much spirit," replied the sorcerer. "I thought you were a timid, useless lad, and I cannot describe how much pleased I am to find I was mistaken. Now, I begin to think I may have found an assistant and successor in my difficult business. A concertina? You shall have the best in Honolulu. And tonight, as soon as it is dark, you and I will go and find the money."

"Shall we return to the beach?" asked Keola.

"No, no," replied Kalamake; "you must begin to learn more of my secrets. Last time, I taught you to pick shells; this time I shall teach you to catch fish. Are you strong enough to launch Pili's boat?"

"I think I am," returned Keola. "But why should we not take your own, which is afloat already?"

"I have a reason, which you will understand thoroughly before tomorrow," says Kalamake. "Pili's boat is the better suited for my purpose. So, if you please, let us meet there as soon as it is dark. And in the meanwhile, let us keep our own counsel, for there is no cause to let the family into our business."

Honey is not more sweet than was the voice of Kalamake; and Keola could scarce contain his satisfaction. "I might have had my concertina weeks ago," thought he, "and there is nothing needed in this world but a little courage." Presently after, he spied Lehua weeping, and was half in a mind to tell her all was well. "But no," thinks he. "I shall wait till I can show her the concertina; we shall see what the chit will do then. Perhaps she will understand in the future that her husband is a man of some intelligence."

As soon as it was dark, father- and son-in-law launched Pili's boat and set the sail. There was a great sea, and it blew strong from the leeward; but the boat was swift and light and dry, and skimmed the waves. The wizard had a lantern, which he lit and held with his finger through the ring; and the two sat in the stern, and smoked cigars, of which Kalamake had always a provision, and spoke like friends of magic, and the great sums of money which they could make by its exercise, and what they should buy first, and what second. And Kalamake talked like a father.

Presently he looked all about, and above him at the stars, and back at the island, which was already three parts sunk under the sea; and he seemed to consider ripely his position.

"Look!" says he. "There is Molokai already far behind us, and Maui like a cloud; and by the bearing of these three stars I know I am come where I desire. This part of the sea is called the Sea of the Dead. It is in this place extraordinary deep, and the floor is all covered with the bones of men, and in the holes of this part gods and goblins keep their habitation. The flow of the sea is to the north, stronger than a shark can swim; and any man, who shall here be thrown out of a ship, it bears away like a wild horse into the uttermost ocean. Presently he is spent and goes down, and his bones are scattered with the rest, and the gods devour his spirit."

Fear came on Keola at the words; and he looked, and by the light of the stars and the lantern, the warlock seemed to change.

"What ails you?" cried Keola, quick and sharp.

"It is not I who am ailing," said the wizard; "but there is one here very sick."

With that he changed his grasp upon the lantern; and behold, as he drew his finger from the ring, the finger stuck and the ring was burst; and his hand was grown to be of the bigness of three.

At that sight Keola screamed and covered his face.

But Kalamake held up the lantern. "Look rather at my face!" said he. And his head was huge as a barrel; and still he grew and grew as a cloud grows on a mountain, and Keola sat before him screaming, and the boat raced on the great seas.

"And now," said the wizard, "what do you think about that concertina? and are you sure you would not rather have a flute? No?" says he. "That is well, for I do not like my family to be changeable of purpose. But I begin to think I had better get out of this paltry boat; for my bulk swells to a very unusual degree, and if we are not the more careful, she will presently be swamped."

With that, he threw his legs over the side. Even as he did so, the greatness of the man grew thirty fold and forty fold as swift as sight or thinking; so that he stood in the deep seas to the armpits, and his head and shoulders rose like a high isle, and the swell beat and burst upon his bosom as it beats and breaks against a cliff. The boat ran still to the north, but he reached out his hand, and took the gunwale by the finger and thumb, and broke the side like a biscuit, and Keola was spilled into the sea. And the pieces of the boat, the sorcerer crushed in the hollow of his hand and flung miles away into the night.

"Excuse me taking the lantern," said he; "for I have a long wade before me, and the land is far, and the bottom of the sea uneven, and I feel the bones under my toes."

And he turned and went off walking with great strides; and as often as Keola sank in the trough, he could see him no longer; but as often as he was heaved upon the crest, there he was striding and dwindling, and he held the lamp high over his head, and the waves broke white about him as he went.

Since first the islands were fished out of the sea, there was never a man so terrified as this Keola. He swam indeed, but he swam as puppies swim when they are cast in to drown, and knew not wherefore. He could but think of the hugeness of the swelling of the warlock, of that face which was great as a mountain, of those shoulders that were broad as an isle, and of the seas that beat on them in vain. He thought too of the concertina, and shame took hold upon him; and of the dead men's bones, and fear shook him.

Of a sudden he was aware of something dark against the stars that tossed, and a light below, and a brightness of the cloven sea; and he heard speech of men. He cried out aloud and a voice answered; and in a twinkling the bows of a ship hung above him on a wave like a thing balanced, and swooped down. He caught with his two hands in the chains of her, and the next moment was buried in the rushing seas, and the next hauled on board by seamen.

They gave him gin and biscuit and dry clothes; and asked him how he came where they found him, and whether the light which they had seen was the lighthouse, Lae o Ka Laau. But Keola knew white men are like children and only believe their own stories; so about himself, he told them what he pleased, and as for the light (which was Kalamake's lantern) he vowed he had seen none.

This ship was a schooner bound for Honolulu, and then to trade in the low islands; and by a very good chance for Keola, she had lost a man off the bowsprit in a squall. It was no use talking, Keola durst not stay in the Eight Islands. Word goes so quickly, and all men are so fond to talk and carry news, that if he hid on the north end of Kauai or in the south end of Kaü, the wizard would have wind of it before a month, and he must perish. So he did what seemed the most prudent, and shipped sailor in the place of the man who had been drowned.

In some ways the ship was a good place. The food was extraordinary rich and plenty, with bis-cuits and salt beef every day, and pea soup and puddings made of flour and suet twice a week, so that Keola grew fat. The captain also was a good man, and the crew no worse than other whites. The trouble was the mate, who was the most difficult man to please Keola ever met with, and beat and cursed him daily both for what he did and what he did not. The blows that he dealt were very sore, for he was strong; and the words he used were very unpalatable, for Keola was come of a good family and accustomed to respect. And what was the worst of all, whenever Keola found a chance to sleep, there was the mate awake and stirring him up with a rope's end. Keola saw it would never do; and he made up his mind to run away.

They were about a month out from Honolulu when they made the land. It was a fine starry night, the sea was smooth as well as the sky fair, it blew a steady trade; and there was the island on their weather bow, a ribbon of palm trees lying flat along the sea. The captain and the mate looked at it with the night glass, and named the name of it, and talked of it, beside the wheel where Keola was steering. It seemed it was an isle where no traders came. By the captain's way, it was an isle besides where no man dwelt; but the mate thought otherwise.

"I don't give a cent for the directory," said he. "I've been past here one night in the schooner *Eugénie;* it was just such a night as this; they were fishing with torches, and the beach was thick with lights like a town."

"Well, well," says the captain, "its steep-to, that's the great point; and there ain't any outlying dangers by the chart; so we'll just hug the lee side of it. Keep her ramping full, don't I tell you!" he cried to Keola, who was listening so hard that he forgot to steer.

And the mate cursed him, and swore that Kanaka was for no use in the world, and if he got started after him with a belaying pin, it would be a cold day for Keola.

And so the captain and mate lay down on the house together, and Keola was left to himself. "This island will do very well for me," he thought. "If no traders deal there, the mate will never come. And as for Kalamake, it is not possible he can ever get as far as this." With that he kept edging the schooner nearer in. He had to do this quietly; for it was the trouble with these white men, and above all with the mate, that you could never be sure of them; they would all be sleeping sound or else pretending, and if a sail shook, they would jump to their feet and fall on you with a rope's end. So Keola edged her up little by little, and kept all drawing. And presently the land was close on board, and the sound of the sea on the sides of it grew loud.

With that, the mate sat up suddenly upon the house. "What are you doing?" he roars. "You'll have the ship ashore!"

And he made one bound for Keola, and Keola made another clean over the rail and plump into the starry sea. When he came up again, the schooner had payed off on her true course, and the mate stood by the wheel himself, and Keola heard him cursing. The sea was smooth under the lee of the island; it was warm besides; and Keola had his sailor's knife, so he had no fear of sharks. A little way before him, the trees stopped; there was a break in the line of the land, like the mouth of a harbour; and the tide, which was then flowing, took him up and carried him through. One minute he was without: and the next within, and floated there in a wide shallow water bright with ten thousand stars, and all about him was the ring of the land with its string of palm trees. And he was amazed, because this was a kind of island he had never heard of.

The time of Keola in that place was in two periods: the period when he was alone; and the period when he was there with the tribe. At first he sought everywhere, and found no man; only some houses standing in a hamlet and the marks of fires. But the ashes of the fires were cold and the rains had washed them away; and the winds had blown, and some of the huts were overthrown. It was here he took his dwelling; and he made a fire drill, and a shell hook, and fished and cooked his fish, and climbed after green cocoanuts, the juice of which he drank, for in all the isle there was no water. The days were long to him, and the nights terrifying. He made a lamp of cocoa shell, and drew the oil of the ripe nuts, and made a wick of fibre; and when evening came, he closed up his hut, and lit his lamp, and lay and trembled till morning. Many a time he thought in his heart he would have been better in the bottom of the sea, his bones rolling there with the others.

All this while he kept by the inside of the island, for the huts were on the shore of the lagoon, and it was there the palms grew best, and the lagoon itself abounded with good fish. And to the other side, he went once only, and looked but the once at the beach of the ocean, and came away shaking. For the look of it, with its bright sand, and strewn shells, and strong sun and surf, went sore against his inclination. "It cannot be," he thought, "and yet it is very like. And how do I know? These white men, although they pretend to know where they are sailing, must take their chance like other people. So that after all we may have sailed in a circle, and I may be quite near to Molokai, and this may be the very beach where my father-in-law gathers his dollars." So after that he was prudent, and kept to the landside.

It was perhaps a month later, when the people of the place arrived, the fill of six great boats. They were a fine race of men, and spoke a tongue that sounded very different from the tongue of Hawaii, but so many of the words were the same that it was not difficult to understand. The men besides were very courteous, and the women very towardly: and they made Keola welcome, and built him a house, and gave him a wife; and what surprised him the most, he was never sent to work with the young men.

And now Keola had three periods. First he had a period of being very sad, and then he had a period when he was pretty merry. Last of all came the third, when he was the most terrified man in the four oceans.

The cause of the first period was the girl he had to wife. He was in doubt about the island; and he might have been in doubt about the speech, of which he had heard so little when he came there with the wizard on the mat. But about his wife there was no mistake conceivable, for she was the same girl that ran from him crying in the wood. So he had sailed all this way, and might as well have stayed in Molokai; and had left home and wife and all his friends, for no other cause but to escape his enemy; and the place he had come to was that wizard's haunting ground, and the place where he walked invisible. It was at this period when he kept the most close to the lagoon side, and as far as he dared, abode in the cover of his hut.

The cause of the second period was talk he heard from his wife and the chief islanders. Keola himself said little; he was never so sure of his new friends, for he judged they were too civil to be wholesome; and since he had grown better acquainted with his father-in-law, the man was grown more cautious. So he told them nothing of himself; but only his name and descent, and that he came from the Eight Islands, and what fine islands these were, and about the King's palace in Honolulu, and how he was a chief friend of the King and the missionaries. But he put many questions, and learned much. The island where he was was called the Isle of Voices; it belonged to the tribe, but they made their home upon another three hours' sail to the southward. There they lived and had their permanent houses, and it was a rich island, where were eggs and chickens and pigs, and ships came trading with rum and tobacco. It was there the schooner had gone after Keola deserted; there, too, the mate had died, like a fool of a white man as he was. It seems, when the ship came, it was the beginning of the sickly season in that isle, when the fish of the lagoon are poisonous, and all who eat of them swell up and die. The mate was told of it; he saw the boats preparing, because in that season the people leave that island and sail to the Isle of Voices. But he was a fool of a white man, who would believe no stories but his own; and he caught one of these fish, cooked it and ate it, and swelled up and died: which was good news to Keola. As for the Isle of Voices, it lay solitary the more part of the year; only now and then a boat's crew came for copra; and in the bad season, when the fish at the main isle were poisonous, the tribe dwelt there in a body. It had its name from a marvel. For it seemed the seaside of it was all beset with invisible devils; day and night, you heard them talking one with another in strange tongues; day and night little fires blazed up and were extinguished on the beach; and what was the cause of these doings no man might conceive. Keola asked them, if it were the same in their own island where they stayed? and they told him no, not there; nor yet in any other of some hundred isles that lay all about them in that sea; but it was a thing peculiar to the Isle of Voices. They told him also that these fires and voices were ever on the seaside and in the seaward fringes of the wood; and a man might dwell by the lagoon two thousand years (if he could live so long) and never be anyway troubled. And even on the seaside the devils did no harm, if let alone. Only once a chief had cast a spear at one of the voices, and the same night he fell out of a cocoanut palm and was killed.

Keola thought a good bit with himself. He saw he would be all right when the tribe returned to the main island; and right enough where he was, if he kept by the lagoon; yet he had a mind to make things righter, if he could. So he told the high chief he had once been in an isle that was pestered the same way, and the folk had found a means to cure that trouble. "There was a tree growing in the bush there," says he, "and it seems these devils came to get the leaves of it. So the people of the isle cut down the tree wherever it was found, and the devils came no more." They asked what kind of tree this was, and he showed them the tree of which Kalamake burned the leaves. They found it hard to believe, yet the idea tickled them. Night after night the old men debated it in their councils; but the high chief (though he was a brave man) was afraid of the matter, and reminded them daily of the chief who cast a spear against the voices and was killed; and the thought of that brought all to a stand again.

Though he could not yet bring about the destruction of the trees, Keola was well enough pleased, and began to look about him, and take pleasure in his days. And among other things he was the kinder to his wife, so that the girl began to love him greatly. One day he came to the hut, and she lay on the ground lamenting.

"Why," said Keola, "what is wrong with you now?"

She declared it was nothing.

The same night she woke him. The lamp burned very low but he saw by her face she was in sorrow.

"Keola," she said, "put your ear to my mouth that I may whisper, for none must hear us. Two days before the boats begin to be got ready, go you to the seaside of the isle and lie in a thicket. We shall choose that place beforehand, you and I, and hide food, and every night I shall come near by there singing. So when a night comes, and you do not hear me, you shall know we are clean gone out of the island, and you may come forth again in safety."

The soul of Keola died within him. "What is this?" he cried. "I cannot live among devils. I will not be left behind upon this isle. I am dying to leave it."

"You will never leave it alive, my poor Keola," said the girl. "For to tell you the truth, my people are eaters of men; but this they keep secret. And the reason they will kill you before we leave is because, in our island, ships come, and Donat-Kimaran comes and talks for the French, and there is a white trader there in a house with a verandah, and a catechist. O, that is a fine place indeed! The trader has barrels filled with flour; and a French warship once came in the lagoon and gave everybody wine and biscuit. Ah, my poor Keola, I wish I could take you there, for great is my love to you, and it is the finest place in the seas except Papeete."

So now Keola was the most terrified man in the four oceans. He had heard tell of eaters of men in the south islands, and the thing had always been a fear to him; and here it was knocking at his door. He had heard besides, by travellers, of their practices, and how when they are in a mind to eat a man, they cherish and fondle him like a mother with a favourite baby. And he saw this must be his own case; and that was why he had been housed, and fed, and wived, and liberated from all work, and why the old men and the chiefs discoursed with him like a person of weight. So he lay on his bed and railed upon his destiny, and the flesh curdled on his bones.

The next day the people of the tribe were very civil as their way was. They were elegant speakers, and they made beautiful poetry, and jested at meals so that a missionary must have died laughing. It was little enough Keola cared for their fine ways; all he saw was the white teeth shining in their mouths, and his gorge rose at the sight; and when they were done eating, he went and lay in the bush like a dead man. The next day it was the same, and then his wife followed him.

"Keola," she said, "if you do not eat, I tell you plainly you will be killed and cooked tomorrow. Some of the old chiefs are murmuring already. They think you are fallen sick and must lose flesh."

With that Keola got to his feet, and anger burned in him.

"It is little I care one way or the other," said he. "I am between the devil and the deep sea. Since die I must, let me die the quickest way; and since I must be eaten at the best of it, let me rather be eaten by hobgoblins than by men. Farewell," said he, and he left her standing, and walked to the seaside of that island.

It was all bare in the strong sun; there was no sign of man, only the beach was trodden; and all about him as he went, the voices talked and whispered, and the little fires sprang up and burned down. All tongues of the earth were spoken there, the French, the Dutch, the Russian, the Tamil, the Chinese. Whatever land knew sorcery, there were some of its people whispering in Keola's ear. That beach was thick as a cried fair, yet no man seen; and as he walked he saw the shells vanish before him, and no man to pick them up. I think the devil would have been afraid to be alone in such a company; but Keola was past fear and courted death. When the fires sprang up, he charged for them like a bull; bodiless voices called to and fro, unseen hands poured sand upon the flames; and they were gone from the beach before he reached them. "It is plain Kalamake is not here," he thought, "or I must have been killed long since." With that he sat him down in the margin of the wood, for he was tired, and put his chin upon his hands. The business before his eyes continued; the beach babbled with voices, and the fires sprang up and sank, and the shells vanished and were renewed again even while he looked. "It was a by-day when I was here before," he thought. "For it was nothing to this." And his head was dizzy with the thought of these millions and millions of dollars, and all these hundreds and hundreds of persons culling them upon the beach and flying in the air higher and swifter than eagles. "And to think how they have fooled me with their talk of mints," says he, "and that money was made there! when it is clear that all the new coin in the world is gathered on these sands! But I will know better the next time," said he. And at last, he knew not very well how or when, sleep fell on Keola and he forgot the island and all his sorrows.

Early the next day, before the sun was yet up, a bustle woke him. He awoke in fear, for he thought the tribe had caught him napping; but it was no such matter. Only, on the beach in front of him, the bodiless voices called and shouted one upon another, and it seemed they all passed, and swept beside him, up the coast of the island.

"What is afoot now?" thinks Keola; and it was plain to him it was something beyond ordinary. For the fires were not lighted nor the shells taken, but the bodiless voices kept posting up the beach and hailing, dying away, and others following, and by the sound of them these wizards should be angry. "It is not me they are angry at," thought Keola, "for they pass me close." As when hounds go by, or horses in a race, or city folk coursing to a fire, and all men join and follow after: so it was now with Keola; and he knew not what he did, nor why he did it, but there, lo and behold! he was running with the voices!

So he turned one point of the island, and this brought him in view of a second; and there he remembered the wizard trees to have been growing by the score together in a wood. From this point there went up a hubbub of men crying not to be described; and by the sound of them, those that he ran with shaped their course for the same quarter. A little nearer, and there began to mingle with the outcry the crash of many axes. And at this a thought came at last into his mind, that the high chief had consented, that the men of the tribe had set to cutting down these trees, that word had gone about the isle from sorcerer to sorcerer, and these were all now assembling to defend their trees. Desire of strange things swept him on. He posted with the voices, crossed the beach, and came into the borders of the wood, and stood astonished. One tree had fallen; others were part hewed away. There was the tribe clustered. They were back to back, and bodies lay and blood flowed among their feet. The hue of fear was on all their faces; their voices went up to heaven shrill as a weasel's cry. Have you seen a child, when he is all alone and has a wooden sword, and fights, leaping and hewing, with the empty air? Even so the man-eaters huddled back to back, and heaved up their axes, and laid on, and screamed as they laid on, and behold! no man to contend with them! Only here and there, Keola saw an axe swinging over against them without hands; and time and again a man of the tribe would fall before it, clove in twain or burst asunder, and his soul sped howling.

For awhile Keola looked upon this prodigy like one that dreams, and then fear took him by the midst as sharp as death, that he should behold such doings. Even in that same flash, the high chief of the clan espied him standing, and pointed and called out his name; thereat the whole tribe saw him also, and their eyes flashed and their teeth clashed. "I am too long here," thought Keola; and ran forth out of the wood and down the beach, not caring whither.

"Keola!" said a voice close by upon the empty sand.

"Lehua! is that you?" he cried, and gasped, and looked in vain for her; but by the eyesight, he was stark alone.

"I saw you pass before," the voice answered. "But you would not hear me. Quick, get the leaves and herbs, and let us flee."

"You are there with the mat?" he asked.

"Here, at your side," said she, and he felt her arms about him. "Quick! the leaves and the herbs, before my father can get back!"

So Keola ran for his life, and fetched the wizard fuel; and Lehua guided him back, and set his feet upon the mat, and made the fire. All the time of its burning, the sound of the battle towered out of the wood; the wizards and the man-eaters hard at fight; the wizards, the viewless ones, roaring out aloud like bulls upon a mountain, and the men of the tribe replying shrill and savage out of the terror of their souls. And all the time of the burning Keola stood there, and listened, and shook, and watched how the unseen hands of Lehua poured the leaves. She poured them fast, and the flame burned high, and scorched Keola's hams; and she speeded and blew the burning with her breath. The last leaf was eaten, the flame fell, and the shock followed, and there were Keola and Lehua in the room at home.

Now when Keola could see his wife at last, he was mighty pleased. And he was mighty pleased to be home again in Molokai, and sit down beside a bowl of *poi*—for they make no poi on board ships and there was none in the Isle of Voices—and he was out of the body with pleasure to be clean escaped out of the hands of the eaters of men. But there was another matter not so clear, and Lehua and Keola talked of it all night, and were troubled. There was Kalamake left upon the isle; if, by the blessing of God, he could but stick there, all were well; but should he escape and return to Molokai, it would be an ill day for his daughter and her husband. They spoke of his gift of swelling, and whether he could wade that distance in the seas. But Keola knew by this time where that island was, and that is to say, in the Low or Dangerous Archipelago; so they fetched the atlas, and looked upon the distance in the map, and by what they could make of it, it seemed a far way for an old gentleman to walk. Still it would not do to make too sure of a warlock like Kalamake, and they determined at last to take counsel of a white missionary.

So the first one that came by, Keola told him everything. And the missionary was very sharp on him for taking the second wife in the low island, but for all the rest, he vowed he could make neither head nor tail of it. "However," says he, "if you think this money of your father's ill gotten, my advice to you would be to give some of it to the lepers and some to the missionary fund; and as for this extraordinary rigmarole, you cannot do better than keep it to yourselves." But he warned the police at Honolulu that, by all he could make out, Kalamake and Keola had been coining false money, and it would not be amiss to watch them.

Keola and Lehua took his advice, and gave many dollars to the lepers and the fund. And no doubt the advice must have been good, for from that day to this, Kalamake has never more been heard of. But whether he was slain in the battle by the trees, or whether he is still kicking his heels upon the Isle of Voices, who shall say?

Glossary

abune	above, overhead
aik	oak
ava'	at all
back-spang	a legal flaw or loophole; a trick or legal quirk
bairnly	childlike
bannock	a round, flat cake
begude	begun
behoved	be under an obligation or necessity
ben	inside, within
bield	shelter, protection (**bieldy**: sheltered or cosy)
birks	a small wood mainly of birches
bogle	a supernatural being, ugly and terrifying
brae, braes	the (steep or sloping) bank of a river or shore of the sea; a hillside
braw, braws	fine, splendid
bruik	enjoy; enjoy the use or possession of
brunstane	brimstone
brunt	burnt
buckled to	joined to, got going
bullering	roaring, bellowing
by	done, over (of past things)
by ordnar	extraordinary, unusual
cairn	a pyramid of loose stones built as a memorial to the dead; frequently used in place names
callant	youth, young man
caller	cool; refreshing
cantrip	spell or charm; trick
canty	lively, cheerful; pleasant

carline	old woman, often disparaging; witch
cauld-wamed	cold-blooded
chafts	cheeks
chalmer	chamber, private room
chappin'	stroking
chittered	chattered
clachan	village
claught	caught, seized
claverin'	gossiping
clavers	idle tales; nonsense
clink	of words, to jingle together, rhyme
coats	petticoat; skirt
collieshangie	noisy dispute, uproar
corbie craws	carrion crows, ravens
craig	neck
cuist	threw off
cummers	gossips, scandalmongers; witches
daffin'	playfully
daunton	taunt
daurnae	dare not
deave	weary with talk
deid thraws	death throes
deil	devil
dirl	rattle, reverberate (**play dirl thegether:** chatter or clash together)
dirling	piercing
door cheeks	lit. the doorpost, by synecdoche the door itself
dowie	melancholy, dismal
dozened	dazed, dulled, stupefied
duds	clothes
dunt	heavy, dull-sounding blow, knock (**played dunt:** throbbed, quickened)
dwining	wasting away
eldritch	weird, ghostly, unearthly
ettling (at)	aiming at

fashed	troubled, bothered
fause	false
fecht, fechtin'	fight, struggle
feck	quantity
ferlies	marvels, curiosities
fleyed	frightened
forbye	besides, in addition to; except for
forjaskit	exhausted
fuff	hiss
gane	gone
gang	see **gate** and **gyte**
gangrel	toad; tramp, vagrant
gart	made, forced
gate	way, path (**gang her ain gate**: go her own way)
gaun	gone; brisk
gear	possessions; movable property, household goods
gey (and)	rather, very
gied	gave
girn	snarl, grimace
girzie	servant maid
glamour	enchantment, magic
glebe	a parish minister's allotted land
gliff	a sudden fright, a scare
glisk	glimpse
gloamin'	twilight, dusk
glowrin'	staring, gazing intently
gousty	dreary, desolate
grogram	a coarse, often stiffened fabric of silk, mohair, or wool, or a blend of these
grue	terror; a shudder of horror or repulsion
gurled, gurlin'	roared; howling
gyte	mad, insane (**gang gyte**: went mad)
ha'e, hae	have

hag	a hollow of marshy ground in a moor
han'sel	gift for luck or celebration
hap	hop
hasp	clasp
haud	hold (**neither to haud nor to bind**: beyond control, unable to be restrained)
hinder	**at the hinder end**: finally, ultimately
hirsle	slither
hoot awa	nonsense
howff	a refuge or shelter
howking	rooting, burrowing
hunkers	**sittin' on his hunkers**: squatting down
ilka	each
jaloose, jaloosed	suspect, guessed
keeked	peered, looked sharply
keekit	peeped, watched surreptitiously
ken	know (**ken't**: know it)
kilted	tucked up
kittle	tricky, somewhat difficult
knock	clock
kye	cows
laigh	low
lee-lane	solitary, all by oneself
leelang	livelong, whole
leevin'	living
limmer	loose woman; contemptuous term for a woman
linkin'	moving fast, walking briskly
linn	pool below a waterfall
lown	calm, still
lowp, lowped	leap, leaped
lug	ear

mad	infuriated; angry, annoyed
maned	moaned
maun; maunnae	must; must not
meddled	interfered with, bothered
mirk	dark, black, gloomy (**mirk nicht**: the dead of night; **mirk as the pit**: dark as a pit or the pit [of hell])
mistrysted	failed to meet, broken faith (with)
muckle	much; large, great (**muckle hell**: the depths of hell)
mutch	a close-fitting cap
napery	table linen
neaps	for **neap tides**, the smallest tides
neuk	corner
niest	next
noo (the)	just now, at present
ordnar	one's regular portion of (chiefly) food or drink
owercome	refrain
oxter	armpit
partans	edible crabs
pechin'	gasping
pickle	a little, a few
plenished	furnished
preen	fasten
ram-stam	headstrong, heedless
rattons	rats
reishling	whistling
rumm'ld	rumbled
sabbin'	soaking
sair	sore; involving hardship, difficulty; severe, stormy (of the weather)

sark	shift or chemise; shirt
saughs	willows
saut	salt; bitter, painful; the sea
scart	a mark or scrape of a pen
scunner	a feeling of disgust or nausea; a repugnant shudder
seepin'	dripping, soaking (**seep-sabbin**: the noise of running water)
shaw	a small, natural wood, a thicket
shoother	shoulder
sib	relative, related by blood
siccan	such
sinsyne	from that time
skelpt	struck, hit
skirled	screamed, shrieked with fear
skriegh	shriek, screech (also **skreighs, scrieghin'**)
slavered	talked nonsense, chattered
slockened	quenched
smoored	smothered; drowned in a bog
sook	flow, current
soum	swim
sowp	sip (used ironically for a draught, a swig)
spang	amount
spate	a flood, a rush
speered	asked, questioned (**speiring**: inquiring)
spenster	sea specter
spentacle	spectacle
spunk	spark
spunkies	spirits, will-o'-the-wisps
steeked	shut tight
steer	stir, commotion
stramp	stamping or trampling
stravaguin'	roaming, wandering
syne	since, thereafter, thereupon, next
taed	toad
thae	those

thirled	bound in servitude
thrapples	windpipes
thrawn	twisted, crooked, misshapen; perverse; cross
threep	assert vehemently (**threep it doun their thrapples**: force the point down their throats)
tint	lost, destroyed, or disappeared
tramp-trampin'	washing clothes by treading in soapsuds
uncanny	dangerous, threatening; unlucky, inauspicious; ominous, eerie
unco	strange, unfamiliar; extraordinary, awful; very, exceedingly
unstreakit	not prepared or laid out for burial
upsitten	indifferent
wa'	wall
wale	the choice, the pick, the best
wanchancy	unlucky, inauspicious; dangerous, unreliable
warstlin'	struggling, wrestling
wast	west
waur	worst
wearied	sad; bored, listless
weary fa'	damn!, the devil take
whammled	turned round
wheen	few
whiles	sometimes, (at) times
win	surmount, proceed
win through	get through
won	reached, arrived at
wud	mad, insane
yam-yammered	clamored, chattered incoherently
yett	gate
yoke on	set on, attack
yowlin'	wailing

Notes

Robert Louis Stevenson was an inveterate reader gifted with a retentive memory and a fluency in languages. Scottish, English, and French history, classical and popular fiction, memoirs and correspondence, legal trials, political tracts, biographies—in short, anything that passed his field of vision was legitimate material for fiction. Stevenson once suggested to his American publisher that they bring out new editions of selected major works with extensive notes by the author, in the manner of Sir Walter Scott's elaborate supplement to the Waverley novels. Fortunately or not, it was a proposal only half-serious, provoked more by Stevenson's momentary desire to affirm the extensive research he commonly conducted and introduced into his texts.

The notes to this edition are designed to aid comprehension: the translation of a Scots vocabulary, the identification of technical and rare words or phrases, and the citation of slang, colloquial, or dialectal expressions. Stevenson had an irregular habit of defining Scots terms in the margins, and these are noted here with the initials "RLS" in brackets following the gloss. Since his general lexicon was both studied and broad, many other terms may seem exotic to the reader but are readily defined in a standard reference, such as the *OED, Webster's Third New International Dictionary,* or *The Random House Dictionary of the English Language.* I have also cited allusions that may not be immediately apparent or available in a standard encyclopaedia, as well as place names that are accessible only in obscure gazetteers. But as Henry James would have said, the main job of interpretation is the reader's: these notes are simply the provisions for a clear reading of the stories.

At the beginning of his career Stevenson published his short stories in established English magazines like the *Cornhill* and *Temple*

Bar, or, in the case of *The Suicide Club* and *The Rajah's Diamond*, in a short-lived polemical journal called *London*, edited by his good friend William Ernest Henley and featuring as one of its contributors George Saintsbury. In a letter written to Saintsbury years later from Samoa, Stevenson recalled those early *London* days: "As the first person who encouraged me to publish my fiction in book form, you may be called the father of my fortunes" ([September 1890], British Library, MS. Add. 45680, ff. 122–23). Stevenson published three collections of his stories during his lifetime: *New Arabian Nights* (London, 1882), *The Merry Men and Other Tales and Fables* (London, 1887), and *Island Nights' Entertainments* (London, 1893). The texts in this volume, with the exception of "Markheim" and "The Isle of Voices," are drawn from these first English editions. For those two stories, the texts are the holographs at the Houghton Library and the Rosenbach Museum and Library. There are numerous differences between the holograph and printed versions of both stories, particularly in the matter of punctuation, but also in details of vocabulary and expression. In "The Isle of Voices," an extraordinary number of alterations were made to Stevenson's paragraphs. He liked to work with large units of prose, both for aesthetic as well as narrative reasons; these were reduced in the printed version to smaller units, breaking up the visual effect and altering the way the narrative is received and processed by the reader. In order to reproduce the manuscripts faithfully, Stevenson's unorthodox use of capitals and lower-case letters has been retained. Emendations have been made in a small number of cases: supplying an absent quotation mark, period, or hyphen, adding or removing an apostrophe, or altering Stevenson's spelling in less than a dozen instances (e.g., *wiegh, niether, nieghbour, siezed, dwellt, Christmass, hasard*). In all cases the emendations conform with the printed versions.

The Suicide Club
Story of the Young Man with the Cream Tarts

p.   38   **temerarious** unreasonably adventurous; rash, reckless.

p.	42	**penny gaff** a cheap, low music hall or theater (J. S. Farmer and W. E. Henley, *Slang and Its Analogues*, 7 vols. [London, 1890–1904], hereafter cited as F&H).
p.	46	**for all who desire to be out of the coil** "For in that sleep of death what dreams may come, / When we have shuffled off this mortal coil, / Must give us pause" (*Hamlet*, 3.1.65–67).
p.	47	**four-wheeler** a four-wheeled hackney carriage.
p.	50	**All Fools'-Day** April Fools' Day.
p.	56	**vogue la galère** "come what may" (proverbial).
p.	58	**pasteboard** playing card.
p.	61	**devil's dozen** thirteen, the original baker's dozen, from the number of witches supposed to gather on a sabbath (F&H).

Story of the Physician and the Saratoga Trunk

p.	66	**Saratoga trunk** a very large trunk used for traveling, named after the upstate New York resort (J. S. Farmer, *Americanisms* [London, 1889]).
p.	69	**counterjumpers** a contemptuous term for junior clerks in dry goods stores.
p.	78	**bistery** scalpel.
p.	83	**dickey** a seat at the back of a carriage, usually for servants.
p.	85	**boots** a hotel servant who cleans boots and offers minor assistance to guests.
p.	86	**consumptive marker** a *marker* keeps score in competitive games; *consumption* was the common term for tuberculosis.

The Adventure of the Hansom Cabs

p.	90	**nine days' vitality** something that causes a sensation for a few days and then passes into oblivion (a nine days' wonder).
p.	93	**paletot** a loose outer coat, or cloak.

p. 94   **Manillas** a cigar (or cheroot) made of tobacco grown in the Philippines.

p. 99   **Joshua in the Bible** "and Joshua chose out thirty thousand mighty men of valour" (Josh. 8:3).

p. 101   *parc aux cerfs* deer park.

        postern a back or side door separate from the main entrance.

p. 107   **"God defend the right!"** *Richard II*, 1.3.101.

p. 107   **hound of hell** Cerberus, the watchdog guarding the entrance to the infernal regions.

The Rajah's Diamond
Story of the Bandbox

p. 112   **Tame Cat** a woman's "fetch-and-carry" (F&H), or gofer.

p. 113   **Mechlin** delicate lace used for dresses and millinery, produced at Mechlin (Belgium).

p. 123   *Gloire de Dijons* a variety of tea rose.

p. 124   **Rag-fair** an old clothes market in Houndsditch, an area surrounding the original wall of the City of London.

p. 131   **oakum** loose fiber obtained by untwisting and picking old rope, used in caulking ships' seams and stopping leaks; picking it was an employment of convicts and workhouse inmates.

        Bendigo a city in central Australia, northwest of Melbourne, founded in 1851 with a rush for gold.

        Trincomalee a town in Sri Lanka (formerly Ceylon) overlooking a fine natural harbor, contested by the Portuguese, Dutch, French, and English and finally ceded to England in the early nineteenth century.

Story of the Young Man in Holy Orders

p. 132   **St. Ambrose** Ambrose (c. 340–97), early father of the

Roman church, noted for oratory, magnanimity, and stainless character.

St. Chrysostom Chrysostom (c. 347–407), one of the fathers of the Greek church, patriarch of Constantinople, noted for wide learning and ascetic discipline.

p. 136   **Gaboriau** Emile Gaboriau (1832–73), French originator of the *roman policier* or police novel (*L'affaire Lerouge*, 1866).

Paley's Evidences William Paley (1743–1805), English theologian and clergyman (*Evidences of Christianity*, 1794).

p. 140   **old gentleman** the devil (John Camden Hotten, *The Slang Dictionary: A New Edition* [London, 1874]).

Story of the House with the Green Blinds

p. 152   ***chevaux-de-frise*** a line of sharp points (as of spikes or nails) set firmly into the top of a fence or wall.

p. 158   **Trichinopoli** a district and city in southern India.

p. 167   **wideawake** a soft felt hat with a broad brim and low crown.

p. 178   **as Jacob served Laban** (Gen. 29:15–20).

The Pavilion on the Links

p. 181   **Fidra** a rocky islet near North Berwick (Francis Groome, *Ordnance Gazetteer of Scotland*, vol. 3 [Edinburgh, 1883]).

Easter eastern, lying toward the east; common in place names and in names of farms (William Grant, ed., *The Scottish National Dictionary*, 10 vols. [Edinburgh, 1931–76], hereafter cited as *SND*).

German Ocean North Sea.

p. 183   **Sea-Wood** situated in or by the sea.

p. 184   **Ness** a promontory, headland; in general use as a place name.

Bullers a loud gurgling noise, the boiling of an eddy or torrent.

p. 187 **Floe** a pool, a marsh or bay, especially in place names (*SND*).

sea quags marshy or boggy spots, especially ones covered with a layer of turf which yields when walked on.

p. 192 **policies** the enclosed grounds of a large country house; the park of an estate (*SND*).

p. 193 **accidented** of uneven surface (Stevenson's use was cited in the *OED*, 2d ed.).

p. 199 **the rose-leaf . . . the Princess** supersensitivity was considered characteristic of nobility, and tales like Andersen's princess and the pea are common, including a Persian story where the princess was in constant pain because a rose leaf "had pressed against her side and had rubbed her skin till the bones showed" (N. M. Penzer, ed., *The Ocean of Story*, vol. 6 [Delhi: Motilal Banarsidass, 1968], 293–94).

p. 202 **Wester** western, lying toward the west, usually in place names (*SND*).

p. 204 **black-avised** dark complexioned (Joseph Wright, *The English Dialect Dictionary*, 6 vols. [Oxford, 1898–1905], hereafter cited as *EDD*).

p. 210 **"She's a trump!"** first-rate, good-natured person (Hotten, *Slang Dictionary*); in the original *Cornhill* magazine version the text reads: "She's a perfect cock-sparrow, Frank."

p. 210 ***carbonaro*** *carbonari* were members of a secret political society that originated in Naples during the French occupation (1808–15); their major aim was the establishment of a republican government.

Tridentino the city of Trent in the Tyrolean Alps. In the nineteenth century it was part of Austria, but because it had always been Italian in language and culture, a strong movement developed for union with Italy, which was achieved in 1919.

Parma capital of the province of Parma in northern Italy.

p. 214	**Kalmuck** a member of a Mongolian people living on the northwest slopes of the Caspian Sea (Stevenson's use is cited in the *OED*, 2d ed.).
p. 215	**tan your liver** "white-livered" = cowardly, mean (F&H).
	precisian one who is rigidly precise in the observance of rules or forms.
p. 220	*fey* fated to die, doomed; also, behaving oddly as if bewitched or crazy (*SND*).
	millstone "It were better for him that a millstone were hanged about his neck, and he cast into the sea, than that he should offend one of these little ones" (Luke 17:2; also, Matt. 18:6; Mark 9:42).
p. 223	**tail of his eye** the outer corner of the eye (F&H).
	beaux yeux beautiful eyes.
p. 231	**cicatrised** marked with scars (Stevenson cited in the *OED*).

A Lodging for the Night

p. 235	**ballade** Stevenson's spelling distinguishes between two different poetic forms: "*Ballade* was by precedent the allotted name of certain verses written after old French models [which] had no kinship whatever with the ordinary ballad" (Gleeson White, "Of the Ballade," *Atalanta* 4 [1890-91]: 303).
p. 237	**Elias** "And it came to pass, as they still went on, and talked, that, behold, there appeared a chariot of fire, and horses of fire, and parted them both asunder; and Elijah went up by a whirlwind into heaven" (2 Kings 2:11).
	Hominibus impossibile impossible for men.
	The black dog was on his back melancholy, depression of spirits (F&H).
p. 238	**two twos** a moment, in a twinkling (F&H).

p. 241	**whites** silver money (Stevenson cited in *OED*).
	Henry V. of England Henry (1388–1422) was proclaimed king in 1413, fought at Agincourt two years later, and died just before consolidating his victories in France.
p. 243	**twist** coarse cloth made from heavy doubled thread (*Funk & Wagnalls* [1928]).
p. 245	**gripes** colic or stomach pains (F&H).
p. 251	**Man is not a solitary animal** "And the Lord God said, *It is* not good that the man should be alone; I will make him an helpmeet for him" (Gen. 2:18).
	Cui Deus faeminam tradit To whom God gives woman.
	pantler a servant or officer in charge of the bread and the pantry in a great family.
p. 252	**linking** walking smartly and vigorously, passing by quickly (*EDD*).

The Merry Men

p. 258	**a certain saint** St. Columba (521–97), the "Apostle of Caledonia," established a monastery on the island of Iona in 563.
	King Philip Philip II of Spain (r. 1556–98), whose naval Armada was defeated in war with England (1588).
	Dr. Robertson William Robertson (1721–93), a distinguished historian of Scotland, England, and America.
p. 259	**King Jamie's** James I (1566–1625), who as James VI was king of Scotland (r. 1567–1603) at the time of the Armada's defeat.
	Cameronians militant sect of Presbyterians founded by Richard Cameron, a young schoolteacher and field preacher who in 1680 renounced allegiance to Charles II.
p. 262	**the killing times** period in Scottish history (c. 1683–85) when Presbyterians (or Covenanters) opposed to Charles II were put to death.
	the peace of God "And the peace of God, which

passeth all understanding, shall keep your hearts and minds through Christ Jesus" (Phil. 4:7).

p. 263   **And now . . . glad** Metrical Psalm 65 (Kenneth Gelder, ed., *Robert Louis Stevenson: The Scottish Stories and Essays* [Edinburgh: Edinburgh University Press, 1989], 286).

And in . . . wonders see Metrical Psalm 107 (Gelder, 286).

p. 266   **Cutchull'ns** Cuchullins or Cuillin Hills, group of rugged and serrated mountain ranges, among the wildest scenery in Scotland, situated on the island of Skye.

Soa Soay, an isle separated from Skye by a channel of the same name.

Loch Uskevagh . . . Benbecula Benbecula is a low island in the Outer Hebrides, indented with bays, including Uskekvagh on its eastern side.

p. 272   **Norwegian city** Christiana was the name of the capital of Norway, which changed back to its original name, Oslo, in 1925.

p. 279   **Eilean Gour** "Not far from the north-eastern extremity of Coll [an island west of Mull, where David Balfour began his highland adventures] is the island Eilean-Mhor, uninhabited" (Samuel Lewis, *A Topographical Dictionary of Scotland*, vol. 2 [London, 1846], 544).

p. 282   **The mark is on his brow** a sign or token of imminent death (God's marks).

Markheim

p. 303   **as he began to re-arise** Stevenson wrote "rëarise" in the manuscript, which was altered to "re-arise" in all the printed texts.

p. 304   **Bohemian goblets** by the end of the seventeenth century Bohemian crystal was the most fashionable in Europe.

p. 305   **the image of the dead dealer reinspired** Stevenson again used the diaeresis in "rëinspired," which was dropped in the printed editions. (He is cited for this word in the *OED*.)

p. 306 **Brownrigg ... Thurtell** Elizabeth Brownrigg, employed by a London parish to look after its poor pregnant women, was executed in 1767 after savagely abusing a young female apprentice to death; Frederick and Maria Manning murdered a dinner guest and buried him under the kitchen floor (they were executed in 1849); John Thurtell, gambler and son of a prosperous merchant, lured William Weare to a rural cottage and slit his throat when he refused to die after a brutal beating (executed in 1823).

p. 307 **Like some dropping cavern** The printed texts substituted "dripping" for Stevenson's less common word.

p. 308 **the defeated tyrant** Napoleon would fly into fits of rage at small irritations such as losses at chess (George Henry Nettleton, ed., *Specimens of the Short Story* [New York: Henry Holt, 1907], 229).

Napoleon The winter of 1812 came unseasonably early and was responsible for much of the disastrous Russian campaign (Nettleton, 229).

p. 309 **Sheraton sideboard** Thomas Sheraton (1751–1806), English furniture maker whose designs were artistically simple and utilitarian.

p. 315 **chance-medley** legal term, unpremeditated wounding or killing in a casual encounter.

Thrawn Janet

p. 312 **those hints that Hamlet deprecated** "To be or not to be" (3.1.55–87)

p. 318 **the moderates** a group of professional clergymen in the late seventeenth century opposed to the traditional Calvinism of the Presbyterians who upheld the Westminster Confession; they controlled the Church of Scotland after 1712.

p. 323 **Accuser of the Brethren** "for the accuser of our brethren is cast down, which accused them before our God day and night" (Rev. 12:10).

The Bottle Imp

p. 331 **Prester John** a legendary Christian king and priest of the Middle Ages whose kingdom (believed to be in either Asia or Africa) was associated with marvelous tales.

p. 340 **Chinese Evil** Hawaiian has no word for leprosy; *ma'i Pake* literally means "Chinese disease."

p. 341 **the smitten** Kalaupapa, on the island of Molokai, was the site of Hawaii's leper colony.

p. 344 **Berger** Henry Berger (1844–1929), composer, arranger, and bandmaster of the Royal Hawaiian Military Band.

p. 351 **the true helper after all** *Kōkua* means help or helper in Hawaiian.

p. 355 **"Very well, Kanaka"** Although "kanaka" means "man" in Hawaiian, it was often used pejoratively by low *haoles* (or whites) to signify "a Hawaiian, a native" (Lorrin Andrews, *A Dictionary of the Hawaiian Language* [Honolulu, 1865]).

p. 356 **a flat** a fool; a dim-witted person.

The Isle of Voices

p. 357 **Lehua** The flower of the *ōhia* tree as well as the tree itself, the *lehua* is now the official flower of the island of Hawaii.

Kamehameha Kamehameha I (1758-1819) united the

Hawaiian islands in 1809. "Kamehameha the First, founder of the realm of the Eight Islands, was a man properly entitled to the style of Great" (Robert Louis Stevenson, *The South Seas*, in *The Works of Robert Louis Stevenson*, vol. 9 [New York: P. F. Collier, 1912], 171).

p. 366   **the directory** Alexander Findlay, *A Directory for the Navigation of the South Pacific Ocean*, 5th ed. (London, 1884).

it was just such a night as this "The moon shines bright. In such a night as this . . . " (*The Merchant of Venice*, 5.1.1).

steep-to said of a coast or shore that rises abrupt from the water.

ramping to sail swiftly.

p. 367   **payed off** the movement by which a ship's head falls off from the wind and drops to leeward.

p. 371   **Donat-Kimaran** a minor government official whom Stevenson met in the Paumotu islands, or the Dangerous Archipelago: "my friend Mr. Donat—Donat-Rimarau, 'Donat the much handed'—acting Vice-Resident, present ruler of the archipelago, by far the man of chief importance on the scene, but known besides for one of an unshakable good temper" (Stevenson, *South Seas*, 128).

p. 372   **cried fair** a fair proclaimed in advance by public announcement.

by-day a day out of the ordinary course, incidental, apart from major events.